KANSAS DREAMER

Fury
in
Sumner
County

Other titles-in-print by Kae Cheatham

HISTORICAL FICTION
The Adventures of Elizabeth Fortune
Spotted Flower and the Ponokomita
Hammer Come Down: Memoirs of a Freedman
On Promised Land

SPECULATIVE FICTION
Child of the Mist
Daughter of the Stone
Dead Heroes

CONTEMPORARY FICTION
Blood and Bond

All titles are available as e-books. See your local online dealer.

Enjoy the mystery.

KANSAS DREAMER

Fury in Sumner County

Kae Cheatham

Kae Cheatham

11/09/17

KAIOS Books

Helena, Montana

KANSAS DREAMER:
Fury in Sumner County

The author developed this story from history, research, and her imagination.
Any similarity to persons living or dead is coincidental.

ISBN
978-097-14287-2-0

2nd printing, September 2013
Printed in the United States of America

KAIOS Books
Helena, Montana

Acknowledgements

Thanks to all the members of Writers in the Sky (Sandy Barker, Diana Boom, Betsy Clark, Stevie Drown, Dorothy Flynn, Carol Rae Lane, Lenore McKelvey Puhek, and Eva Spaulding) for continued enthusiasm and helpful critiques.

Special gratitude goes to Lenore and Carol Rae for their many extra readings of this manuscript and insightful suggestions.

And although they will not read this, my appreciation goes to my good dog Taz, and trusty steeds Dona and CeeJay, who I was often late in feeding while I worked, worked, worked. Their fidelity strengthened me.

1

Southern Kansas—May, 1868

Ellen Hargrove drove the farm wagon on a trail that ran parallel to the rugged banks of the Bluff River. She headed the two sturdy draft horses west-by-north into broad prairie lands. Her youngest brother Pitt sat beside her in a rare moment of silence. The sun glared directly on her straw hat, hotter than usual for late May. Around the burning disc, the sky spread in a pale blue of robins' eggs. No clouds. She wished her mood matched the bright day, but an undefined feeling attended her—gloomy, like the squat, dark patches made by the horses.

"Hup, Phineas. Geedap, Grams!" Ellen urged the two animals down a draw into a swale, muddy from the spring rains. Warm earthy smells teased her nose. A frog lurched from the wagon's approach.

Pitt clung to the seat and stared back at the cargo of homestead supplies in the wagon bed: two bags of seed under canvas cover, two oxen yokes, a butter churn and a gleaming prow-shaped turning blade. Ellen slapped the leather reins on the horses' flanks, and the large bays pulled the laden wagon out of the wash onto drier land.

"I don't know what it takes around here for anyone to think you're grown up," Pitt declared, turning back toward the meager trail before them. His freckled face held a frown. He carried a Trapdoor Springfield rifle across his lap. A shotgun was in a scabbard between them. "And you're as bad as Ma and Pop, dragging me out here," he went on. The family lived six miles east in a small settlement along the

Bluff River. "Why, this is just another way to keep your eye on me since the folks are off to Emporia."

"I can't move that turning blade or those yokes alone," Ellen said, wondering why she even bothered to respond to Pitt's complaint. Pitt grumbled a lot recently. The onset of manhood, their father said. To Ellen, Pitt was still a boy, not a young man, and his unreasonable expectations aggravated her.

"You coulda put a canvas under them. Would've slid right out the back with a good tug," Pitt said. "Besides, Riding Boy and his people will be there to unload."

"Perhaps." Ellen nodded slightly, thinking it would be nice if Riding Boy brought his family to meet them. She hadn't seen any of them since they visited her parents' trading post during a December thaw. Although several years older than Ellen, she thought of Riding Boy's wife, Pretty Willow, as a friend. They shared recipes and the woman had showed her how to plait horsehair. The couple's son, Waits-no-more, was just a year younger than Pitt.

"Don't know why you had to come out here, anyway," Pitt muttered.

"The missionaries made an order and paid for it to be delivered," Ellen said. "We must keep our word to them and the Indians."

She said this to convince herself as well. Perhaps she could have waited until her parents returned from their trip for store supplies, or could have let the Osage come into the store to get the merchandise. But the letter, brought with the order by the Cherokee freighter, included ten dollars with directions to deliver these items to Sycamore Spring.

Sycamore. The big tree that shrouded her dream, clear as a drawn picture. Four weeks ago she had first seen it, but successfully put the dream out of her memory—forced it to be of no consequence—until yesterday and the arrival of this order and delivery request.

Hot air. Cool shade from a big-limbed tree. I am patting my horse, walking on a carpet of spring flowers. They're lovely! But there! A man's feet and legs laying in the

*shade of the tree. I lean on the huge trunk, afraid even
as I look. See: open waist coat, bloody shirt, ants follow
the dark line. Shadows hover. It's the tree. It's huge. I
lean, see gray hair fade to darkness. Darkness crowds
in, surrounds me and the dead man. Face dark with
black glinting eyes. That noise—!*

When that dream happened four weeks ago, she had awakened
moaning loudly enough to rouse her brothers who slept in the
same room—a canvas wall between their double bed and her cot.
"A body," she had cried. "Oh, that poor man."

Now she had been directed to Sycamore Spring—had been
beckoned, perhaps. Her compulsion to see if her dream were correct
set her on this trail. It will be false, she thought. It *has* to be.

"I thought this year would be different, but nothing at all
interesting happens around here," Pitt went on.

"Pretend you're riding shotgun with a gold shipment," Ellen
suggested, squinting into the hazy distance. She always disliked the
way objects seemed to waver in the heat. Today, Osage orange and
hackberry trees quivered in dark bunches along the sloughs as though
they wanted to up and run.

"Riding shotgun. Uh," Pitt snorted. "I want to be going places!
Spencer got to go off mustanging," he said of their brother.

"Spencer's seventeen, Pitt. When you get that age—"

"Yeah, yeah."

Pitt seemed strange to Ellen, even though she knew him
better than anyone. She had taken charge of him when he was a
toddler, being out of his life only the last year and a half, first
when she was teaching in Ottawa County, and then when she
married Johnny Hargrove. After Johnny's sudden death in
November, she found herself back in her parents' household,
still trying to reconcile what had happened, and trying to decide
how to proceed with her life.

Sadness welled in her from the reality that Johnny was gone.
She put her left hand to her throat, fingering the blue wool scarf
she wore like a shawl. It was damp with perspiration.

Two years ago when Spencer traveled to Emporia to escort her home from her teacher's testing, a young man he had met on the trail was with him. Her pleased excitement over her certificate had been ignored by Spencer, but the young man, Johnny Hargrove, doted on her every word and praised her accomplishment. Johnny had traveled to Emporia to buy supplies for his family's farm. He accompanied Ellen and Spencer to Sumner County, although his family lived east in Cowley County. Through the summer he rode often to the store from his family's homestead. When she was teaching, Johnny wrote her letters every month. He proposed marriage when she was home for Christmas.

The wagon wheels creaked, jolting over earth bold with knots of clay. Ellen shifted on the hard seat, her maroon calico skirt falling between her legs. Not too much farther, she thought. Prairie dogs barked warning of the wagon's approach before they dove into burrows. Farther afield, long-legged owls sat like fluffy stumps on some of the holes.

"I oughta take off gold hunting or work a while on the railroad," Pitt said.

"That's immigrant work," Ellen responded, repeating what her in-laws often said. She frowned, displeased with herself. Her parents, Matthew and Belinda Jarvis, had raised her differently.

"Well, ain't nothing left but for me to join a cattle drive," Pitt declared. Ellen trembled at the thought. "Heck! I'm nearly thirteen. There're other boys riding that are only twelve years old."

"And lots older and better than you have died on those drives, Pitt Jarvis. Now just you hush!" She sniffed against the sudden stinging of her eyes. Johnny had died on a cattle drive. Not actually a drive, but moving cattle—helping… The sadness of it continually harried her thoughts, rasping away to expose the shock and her guilt.

Pitt slumped forward, apparently realizing the memory his words had unlocked. After a few moments, he took a harmonica from his possibles sack and started playing, single notes at first, then adding chords. The song was from *The Arkansas Traveler* stage play their mother, Belinda, had seen nearly twenty years ago.

She taught the song to her children. Ellen forced away the dismal memories. She had to stop dwelling on what happened. And Pitt was trying to make amends, she was certain. In a shaky alto voice, she began to sing along.

"'It was raining hard, but the fiddler didn't care. He sawed away at the popular air. Though his roof tree leaked like a waterfall, that didn't seem to bother the man at all.'"

The lively tune quickened the horses' pace and abated Ellen's inner quailing. Pitt kept the beat with a loud pat of his foot while she sang the second verse, went on to the third:

"So the stranger said, 'Now the way it seems to me. You'd better mend your roof,' said he. But the old man said as he played away; 'I couldn't mend my roof on a—'"

Ellen jammed at the foot rail as darkness consumed her mind then produced an explosion of bright colors. She wrenched the horses to a stop. Her very bones felt icy as she stood.

Pitt lurched forward. "What?" he asked in a whisper. He pocketed the mouth harp and cocked the side-mounted hammer of his .58. The horses snorted and backed a bit.

Still standing, Ellen shook her head to clear it. Her heart pounded and she felt the blood rushing through her veins. She stared across the prairie, expecting things to look different, but not so. The dark clump of trees was no closer. Midday brightness dragged color from everything until pale distant land blended into pale sky. She sat back down; the flood of unexpected exhilaration turned to dismay.

"Something's not right," she muttered.

Pitt scanned their surroundings. "You got us lost, I'll bet. Riding Boy's gonna have to find us and lead us home."

"No, we're not lost." Less than an eighth of a mile ahead, she could see the thick stand of greenery and even at this distance could make out the huge signature tree for which the spring was named.

She shook her head before urging the team back to work. The wagon groaned and jerked forward. Pitt gave her a petulant look and nervously fingered the rifle. Soon, the grove stopped quivering through the heat, took on definition and beckoned with shade. The horses began a shambling trot. Ellen gripped the lines until the knuckles of her tanned hands whitened. The certainty that her dream would be true clawed at her like an angry cat.

"I don't see sign of Riding Boy," Pitt said. "Maybe we oughta stop here." He wiped his sweaty hands on his twill trousers.

"Somebody's dead, Pitt. That's all we'll find," Ellen said.

"Dead! How come you say that?"

Ellen pinched her lips together.

Pitt's eyes widened. "Is that what happened back there? You had that dream again where you saw that man's body—"

"No," was her quiet response. "What happened back there was different."

The sudden shadows of the thick grove made it hard to see and Ellen reined the animals to a halt. Crows flushed from the trees, their *scraw! scraw!* echoing. Rodents scurried in the underbrush. The sycamore, its brown flocked trunk massive with centennial age, extended heavy white limbs over the all-season spring that grooved a deep trough down the slope to the Bluff River, half a mile away.

Ellen tied the lines on the brake lever. She clambered down from the wagon.

"Ellen, wait," Pitt protested.

She patted the lead horse on the neck as she passed and headed toward the base of the sycamore. A thick blanket of cowslips and periwinkles softened her path, the blue and white blooms lacing the bed of dark green leaves. Let this not be true, she thought; but already she smelled the cloying scent of blood and saw stockinged feet sticking out from brown corduroy pants. Another step. She tripped and fell against the tree trunk. Looking down, she saw a black riding boot, the leather of the tall side slit from its top to the heel. She leaned forward, bracing herself on the broad trunk of the tree. There: a pallid round face with lips bleached to the color of the skin, thinning gray hair. Watery blue eyes stared up to where the huge tree shrouded the corpse with wavy shadows. A bevy of flies swarmed around the victim's chest creating a black, worrisome cloud.

Mild surprise washed through Ellen. She had expected a different face—darker—with glinting brown eyes, the way her dream image had conveyed. Yet, except for the features, everything else was the same: the stocky body, the open black waistcoat and blue gingham shirt steeped in blood that trailed like dark red syrup over the torso, ants.

The mass of flies moved away in a group, as though to let Ellen see more. The man's throat had been cut.

Ellen pressed her hand to her mouth. The flies returned to their feast, sounding as loud as hornets. Saliva pooled around her tongue and she looked away, willing herself not to be sick. She peered beyond the trees and wondered if Riding Boy and his people had arrived here and seen this. Where would they be now? She swallowed hard. Her head throbbed. And where was the killer?

Foliage crunched and she whirled to face the sound, heart pounding. It was Pitt coming from the wagon. "Great Scot!" he declared when he rounded the sycamore. "It's Mr. Stone!"

The wagon rattled loudly behind her, lighter now with just the body of Mr. Stone. With Pitt's help, Ellen had unloaded the farm equipment at the spring, assuming Riding Boy would come for it. Pitt had followed her directions without comment while they wrapped the body in canvas. Blood still seeped from the wounds in his chest and at his throat, and his left hand had been mutilated—two fingers hacked off behind the second knuckle. Fighting nausea, they had hauled him into the wagon bed, nearly dropping him when thick blood bubbled and air whistled out of his severed neck. Then Ellen hurriedly collected Mr. Stone's belongings: a felt hat propped on a rock at the base of the tree; an open pocket knife near the man's remnant lunch; and saddle bags Pitt found near some horse droppings when he drove the team to the seep for water. No horse, however. They worked quickly, had the wagon turned and started home in less than twenty minutes.

Pitt became suspicious of every flush of grouse or crackle of brush. An inner insistence told Ellen that she and Pitt were in no danger. The drive toward home produced a different concern for her. *It's happened again. A disaster. And I knew in advance.* Since receiving the missionary's instructions, she had known to the core of her bones that Sycamore Spring was the site of her dream vision. Now, a wretched feeling returned with the same strength it had after Johnny's death.

Over the years, Ellen often experienced vivid and unique thoughts—many as dreams. Her mother, Belinda, always gave logical reasons for the odd sleep disturbances: what Ellen had eaten, what she last read, some tale she had heard and remembered. A lot Ellen herself put off to coincidence. Yet when she was fifteen, events in Douglas County made her stop mentioning the obviously prescient thoughts. That summer of 1863, her father had just left with other volunteers to fight for the Union. The family stayed with the small Douglas County store they had set up late in '62. Newspapers were full of battle details from the East. Ellen's nightmares became filled with flames and screaming; she saw terrified faces, some she recognized as neighbors. She babbled out the horrors to her mother, sobbing on hot June nights. "Everyone's talking of war," Belinda had said. "We're all troubled." The dreams continued, waking Ellen with nightly terror and panic. "Fourth of July fireworks," Belinda dismissed. "You aren't used to the busyness of a city." But when the daydreams began—images of dark riders charging out of morning mist—her mother industriously packed the Jarvis conveyances, abandoned the store and took Ellen and the boys away from Lawrence, Kansas.

A week later came news that William Quantrill and over 100 Missourians had attacked and burned Lawrence. Shocked hysteria spread through eastern Kansas as the war tumbled to their doorstep. Ellen was numb with her private horror—stricken by her foreknowledge. She became cautious with every thought and spent hours contemplating Fate and just how her abilities fit into the real world. Her mother refused to talk about it, and insisted they had moved because city life was too hard on her children. When Ellen attempted to articulate her worries, Belinda cut her off by saying, "Hush with that talk!" and ordered her to menial jobs—usually something that kept Ellen away from her mother for a while. Resentment of her mother had ensued and festered to guilt, both for her feelings about her parent and for the unnatural presentiment she exhibited. Slowly her mother softened. "It was nothing, really," Belinda said. "A bizarre coincidence, that's all." She had tried to comfort Ellen with hugs, favorite foods and a new dress.

Truly, that pre-witnessing of the Quantrill raid seemed to stymie Ellen to only vague sensings about peoples' character or household matters (and lots of people could do that, she reasoned). Tension between her and her mother eased; Ellen relaxed, until last year when she experienced two events of foreknowledge—the worst being her dream-witnessing of her own Johnny's death.

He smiles at her from the midst of bobbing heads and shoulders of cattle. The animals melt and become brown froth. Johnny is surrounded—consumed.

The realness of that dream had awakened her trembling in sweat. It was September; she had been married only two months, and that night she huddled against Johnny trying to convince herself the dream was just a nightmare. She grasped her mother's logic— an upsetting diet, a news article she had turned personal. Even when the dream came again, exactly as before, she put it off and refused to believe. The Hargroves were farmers, after all; they owned no cattle. But three weeks later Johnny announced he was going to help his uncle's friend move some cattle. *No!* had been her silent scream. During the weeks after his departure, Ellen experienced a chill flash and rapid heartbeat with even the slightest reference to his trip. Her occasional weakness and sudden change of complexion encouraged her mother-in-law to discreetly ask (with a hopeful smile) if Ellen were "in a family way." "No." *If only it were that simple!* And the dream plagued her, wake and sleep. *No, no, no!* She told no one about it, building a logic of her own: if she didn't speak what she had seen—kept it locked inside—then it wouldn't come true.

Johnny drowned in a river crossing in The Nations. And now, after her advance knowledge, Mr. Stone was dead.

2

*E*llen watched Orioles glitter yellow when they launched up from stems of bulrush along the edge of the trace that followed the north side of the Bluff River. Their flight sent the warning, just as with the barking prairie dogs: Here she comes! The harbinger of death! Late afternoon clouds hung dark gray. Ellen had kept the horses to a brisk pace, even when they passed through brief sprinkles and soft breezes, once with the sun still shining on them. She knew how quickly a heat-relieving shower could turn into a gully washer that would leave the road thick and gummy, or the clouds could broil low on fast winds with thunder and slash lightning. She was glad to finally see the Claytons' cornfield with hand-high green plants sprouting from the tan soil, and turned the wagon north onto the beaten path that led through the middle of the settlement where her family lived.

The north-south trail out of the red flats of The Nations—Beautiful Indian Territory (BIT)—just a mile south, sloped to the Bluff River and then forged to the Fall Creek ford and north toward Camp Wichitaw. The quarter-mile stretch between the river and Fall Creek contained the settlement with her family's sturdy trading post, barn, paddocks, and small house under the trees on the east side of the road; on the west lived Luke and Reba Clayton and their four children in a two-room dugout shored up with wood. Directly across the road from the Jarvis trading post, Luke had set up a canvas-walled structure he called a hotel. Luke insisted he was going to build a *real* hotel to accommodate the cattle-drive men. So far only six small herds had come through on the way to the railhead in Abilene; but the season wasn't very old and expectations were high, especially now that a two-room, high-walled tent had been erected on the rise near Fall Creek. Stone Cattle Company—set up two days ago.

I guess that's where I have to take this body, Ellen thought.

A black and white dog with flop ears and no bigger than a jackrabbit, barked at the team and rushed, growling, at the wagon wheels. Ellen flinched and the youngest Clayton children looked up from where they played in the small grove between the dugout and the hotel. Pitt dropped to the dirt road, his brogans scuffing dust as he ran to them shouting, "Mr. Stone's been killed!"

"That cattle company man? What happened?" Luke Clayton asked as he hurried around the side of the dugout hill. His body was angular with long limbs—awkward, and his thin face looked tighter on hearing the news. His oldest son, Rob, strode with him.

"Well, I declare!" Reba Clayton hurried her winter-thin form to the children, light brown hair wisping from her bonnet. She grabbed up her two-year-old boy and followed the wagon. Her only daughter, Olive, skipped to keep up with her ten-year-old brother Hestor.

Pitt started telling what happened. Ellen kept the team and wagon moving, even though she wanted to just jump off and get away before all the questions started.

"Was it Indians?" Luke's voice quavered a bit with fear.

Pitt kept talking, his voice rising and falling with a dramatic interpretation. Ellen hoped Pitt's recounting wouldn't include news that she had pre-witnessed the event. She clucked the team to a faster walk. The quickened pace left the others behind, and the footfall of Ellen's wagon team almost matched the rhythmic clank of hammer on iron that came from where Tim Fykes lived in a thrown-together barn.

Tim had moved his family to the settlement in spring of last year, and was on contract with the army to supply horses. Tim broke horses for a living, until one of them broke his leg. That was why Ellen's brother, Spencer, had ridden west with Tim's son Hubert to round up the army's next order.

Tim quit work on seeing the wagon; two people with him looked around, and Ellen felt a bit more fortitude on recognizing the Mercys. She drew the wagon up near cattle company sign. The Claytons caught up and crowded around the wagon bed.

"Was it Indians?" Luke asked again.

"Wasn't you out deliverin' to the Injuns, Miz Ellen?" Rob Clayton asked. He was fifteen and felt himself an adult.

"Indians didn't do this," Ellen said.

"There was Indians here earlier," Olive said, a touch of mystery in her voice.

"Really? Riding Boy and Pretty Willow?" Ellen turned to the girl, tension clotting in her stomach.

"Oh, no. These were strangers," Reba said. "In wagons and all, coming from up north."

"Pa made us all stay in the house," Olive said, her disappointment obvious. Ellen could imagine Luke peering from a crack in the shuttered window of the dugout, his family behind him trickling sweat in the hot dark room while he contemplated a possible attack.

"Ellen, where have you been?" came a question. Ellen recognized Lutecia Mercy's voice and turned. "You put us to a worry." The late afternoon light gave the woman's light brown face a reddish glow. If it weren't for the crinkly hair which puffed thick and dark around her head from two braids, she could have been mistaken for an Indian with her prominent cheekbones, almond-shaped eyes, and thin-lipped stoic expression.

Lutecia's husband, Charles, dark skinned and with features as broad as Lutecia's were sharp, stepped up. "With your folks gone, you shouldn't have left the settlement!" he scolded. Beside him, Tim Fykes nodded with a stern look.

"She and Pitt done found a body!" Hestor Clayton chirped.

"A body!"

"That Mr. Stone from the cattle company," Luke put in.

"You found him?" Tim asked. "Where?"

"Out at Sycamore Spring," Pitt said.

"Oh, Lord," Lutecia said. "You all right?" She reached up and took Ellen's hand. Ellen nodded.

"What do you suppose Mr. Stone was doing out there?" Reba asked.

Ellen had wondered that, too. Wondered why she hadn't seen evidence of another traveler headed toward the spring—not that she really looked. And once there, had she checked for hoof prints? What happened to his horse? No. She merely lamented the man's death and her own foreknowledge, dumped the farm equipment and hurried away from the place as if she could escape from the dream-image-turned-real. Even now, pieces of the scene swooped around her thoughts like swallows over a freshly plowed field.

"His horse was stolen," Pitt told. "And he was all cut up—even one of his hands."

"Sounds like Injuns to me," Luke muttered.

"But I can't imagine Riding Boy and his people to do such," Reba declared. "They've been workin' so hard at settlin' down."

"He still had on his waistcoat," Pitt went on. "If 'twas Osage, they'd have taken that, too."

"Blankenship! Blankenship, get down here. You need to deal with this!" Tim started up to the corporate tent.

Ellen wondered what to say to Doyle Blankenship. *I'm sorry about Mr. Stone. I knew about it ahead of time, but I don't think I could have saved him.* Blankenship was the only person from the cattle company Ellen had met. He had come into the store the previous day to buy candles.

"What's going on?" came a baritone voice.

Ellen looked up at Reed Carter who sat a tall bay horse. The man's smooth-shaven face appeared boyish, and if he smiled a dimple showed in his left cheek. But he wasn't smiling. His tent and small wagon set back near the trees not far from the cattle company tent.

"That cattle company man's been killed," Charles said, sounding mystified.

"Good Lord, how awful," Reed said. He stepped from his horse. Sweat rimed the animal's leather martingale. "Thrown from his horse?"

"No. He was murdered!" Pitt declared.

"I'm sure there's some mistake," Ellen heard Blankenship's voice. His striped weskit was open over a blue shirt; tailored tan trousers, quite the opposite of Tim who, in his buckskin pants and calico shirt, still carried the look and raw-edged attitude of a trapper. Blankenship walked with a slight limp, and leaned on the silver-topped cane he always carried. "Stone rode out this morning to scout a herd."

When Blankenship got to the wagon, Pitt climbed into the wagon box and pulled back the canvas, displaying the body.

"Lord A'mighty!" Reba said, turning away.

Ellen gripped the edge of the seat, unable to clear the blank death stare, the flies, the cut throat from her subconscious.

Blankenship tucked his cane under his left armpit and leaned on the wagon wall. He peered into the bed. His right hand shook when he smoothed his thin mustache and then his slick graying hair. "Damn! I don't believe this." He pounded a fist on the side of the wagon.

Tim Fykes had climbed into the wagon bed. "He's been cut real good," Tim said. "Somebody really knows how to use a knife."

"I wanna see!" said a young voice. Ellen heard Hestor start to climb the wagon side.

"Git down from there!" Luke ordered.

Rain began to drizzle down and even with the afternoon sunlight, it chilled Ellen's already damp clothes. She leaned forward, head throbbing, and pressed her palms on her forehead.

"I guess this means we got to bury him," Tim drawled.

"This is too much," Lutecia muttered.

"Indeed. Why don't you step down, now." Reed Carter held out his hand to Ellen. She nodded and he caught her at the waist, lifting her easily to the ground.

"Thank you, Mr. Carter," Ellen said.

"Let's get you home." Lutecia said as Reed escorted Ellen around the front of the team. "There're enough folks here to take care of things, and Charles and Pitt can see to the team and wagon." Lutecia patted her hand.

Ellen barely managed to keep her composure, so grateful she
was for her friend's empathy and assertive manner. She wanted to
curl up someplace and cry. Lutecia put an arm around her shoulder.

"I'll walk with you," Reed Carter said, leading his horse. "I've
seen enough of dead bodies."

Ellen frowned at the comment, then assumed Reed Carter
was another war participant. They started back down the road
and her mind recalled the random sprawl of dead Mr. Stone under
the tree—mouth slightly open, eyes staring nowhere, blood, flies,
stench. *Make that twenty bodies, or eighty, one hundred and eighty!
That's what my father witnessed and contributed to. And Charles
Mercy, and probably Reed Carter.* She pulled from Lutecia's
warm hold and straightened her posture, steeling her resolve to
take this in stride. *Even Lutecia has experienced the horror of
war.* Lutecia had been a nurse with the Kansas Negro regiment
of the Union Army.

For a moment, the rain intensified and they all bent their
heads against a wet breeze. Then the drizzle resumed. Lutecia
took Ellen's hand and asked, "Now tell me, Ellen. Was it like you
dreamed?"

Ellen drew a quick breath and cut her eyes to Reed Carter
before frowning at Lutecia.

"This Mr. Stone," Lutecia went on. "This be the same face
you conjured in that dream?"

Ellen walked a bit faster, passing the north side of the store
her father had inherited from a soldier colleague killed in battle.
"No. It wasn't."

The face which hovered over her dream had been of a younger
man with dark wavy hair and a long mustache on his lean face.
Perhaps a handsome face, if it hadn't seemed so imbued with anger.

"Well, what—"

"I just want to go home," Ellen interrupted. "I'm tired." Her
voice cracked with distress. She wished she hadn't confided her
dream to Lutecia when she asked for herbs to ease her troubled
sleep. No, that wasn't true. The friendship that developed since
then was too good to lose.

"Oh, now, Honey, you'll be all right." Lutecia gave her hand a squeeze. "I be bringing you a brew to help you relax." The woman strode off toward the one-room cabin where she and Charles lived only a stone's throw from where Fall Creek merged with the Bluff River. "And Reed! You just forget what you heard," she called back to him.

"Surely," he said.

Ellen gritted her teeth and didn't look at him, uncertain if he knew the gossip about her. She decided that if she said nothing more, maybe he'd just leave and forget about it.

They passed the barn's dirt paddocks; a sow nursed her litter, grunting from the nearby sty. Ellen stepped quickly along in the steady rain, Reed at her side, trailing his horse. *Kee-ef! Kee-ef!* cried blue jays from the thick-limbed alder by the cistern. The rock structure was next to the sweet-water well which served the whole community. Beyond that by forty or so strides, set her family's quarters.

"I must say it was a decent thing you did, hauling that body back," Reed Carter finally said. He didn't wear a hat and his white shirt looked crisp in the cloudy afternoon shadows. The drizzle lightened to a mist, barely audible as it fell through the tree leaves.

"No more than anyone would do."

"I suppose. Although it bothers me mightily to think of the danger you could have stepped into."

"I did have a few moments of unrest," she said, feeling residual fear race through her.

They had reached the house, originally a two-room cabin onto which Ellen's father had added the extra bedroom for her and her brothers. The room was supposed to be temporary quarters for her. It was assumed she would get a teaching job and move away after finishing her course work—and she did, for one school year. Then she got married and quickly became widowed. *And I knew about that, too*, came her unbidden thought. A narrow dogtrot connected the sections and sheltered the doors.

Reed looped his horse's reins over the hitching rail and joined Ellen in the dogtrot where she took the lantern from the nail by the door. She pulled a match from the oilcloth bag behind it.

"Another thing. I learned of your talents within two days of arriving here, and it wasn't Mrs. Mercy who told me," Reed said, taking the match from her and striking it on a nail head in the wall. The match flared yellow and he held it to the lantern wick. Sulfur tinged the air.

She reset the lantern door, wondering how much he knew about this current situation.

Reed sighed and smoothed back his dark hair, damp and curling along his neck. "Now, you let Mrs. Mercy see to you with no complaints." His mellow voice held a slight drawl.

From Missouri? Kentucky? A Southerner, for certain, Ellen decided. "Of course." She tried to smile.

Ellen had talked to Reed very little, not wanting him to think she was available to be courted. In this land where eligible women were scarce, no one expected her to stay unmarried for long. At least, no one outside of her family. Her mother had suggested other plans—go to college, get a four-year degree. That had always been her mother's hope. In fact, when Ellen began her correspondence course for teachers, she had sensed disappointment from her mother. It wasn't something Belinda said, for neither of her parents interfered with Ellen's decisions—at least not since she was grown. However, her acceptance of Johnny Hargrove's marriage proposal had provoked some words from Belinda. Warnings, perhaps. "You're too young to get married," her mother argued. "There's so much more to life than being a wife and mother!" Ellen knew Belinda had been nearly twenty-four when Ellen was born. "Go to college. Learn all the options that are out there!" her mother had stressed. That's what Belinda had done—college, a bit of travel. Ellen had heard her parents reminisce on it. Belinda's life seemed happy, but, Ellen thought, that was her mother's way, not hers.

Now that Ellen was again living at home, the college idea had resurfaced. Her mother even planned to call on her own family to help pay for it—something Ellen couldn't allow, knowing the strained relationship that existed between her parents and her grandparents. Ellen had never even met them. She knew her mother wrote a letter to them every Christmas time. Belinda received a brief note from Pennsylvania each January. *We are still living, and glad the same for you.*

"When you see Pitt, tell him to come home, if you would," she said to Reed as she opened the door to the house.

"Surely." He hesitated, then started, "About all this. Did you really—" He didn't continue as they heard Lutecia's footsteps in the yard. "Never mind. Good evening, ma'am." He nodded to her and turned away.

"Good evening." She watched him retrieve his horse and walk back toward the main road. *What had he planned to ask?* She wondered if he would tell others about her dream.

"Reed Carter's a good fellow and a gentleman," Lutecia said as she followed Ellen inside.

"He's a stranger. A gambler." Ellen replied, setting the lantern on the table. She pulled off her wet scarf and bonnet.

"He'll keep his peace."

"I hope so." She went to the stove to stoke up the fire. "I hope so."

3

*E*llen wrapped her hand in her apron and grabbed the handle on the iron skillet, lifting it from the black stove with ornate silver-plated fixtures that occupied the northeast corner; a round black pipe climbed to a caulked hole in the wall. The stove was her mother's main concession to modern living, with its three burners and deep water well. The tart scent of crisp ham filled the room. Pitt came in from the dogtrot as Ellen spooned most of the hominy she had fried onto Pitt's plate next to the thick-cut meat. The rest went on her plate, although she didn't feel very hungry.

"Mr. Clayton already sent Rob for the cavalry," Pitt announced. The chair legs scraped the packed earthen floor when he pulled up to the table for breakfast.

"I know. I saw him leave at dawn," Ellen said. As usual, she had been up early.

"He's riding all the way to Fort Harker!" Pitt went on. Pitt had awakened not long after her. He dressed and charged off to glean gossip. Ellen hoped he also did his morning chores. "I wanted to go, but Mr. Fykes said I was needed here, since Pop ain't back yet."

Bless him for that. "It would go hard on you if Pop came back and found you gone," she said. The thumb of her left hand flicked to her third finger to adjust the wedding band that was no longer there. She clenched her teeth, wondering how long it would take for that habit to die. The band had always been a bit large for her slender fingers and, after losing weight over the winter, she now wore the gold band on a chain around her neck, sheltered by the dark blue scarf Johnny had given her. She stroked the edge of it for comfort.

"Pop and Ma mightn't be back for another week. I could ride to Fort Harker and back in that time, sure. It don't take no week."

Ellen set the skillet on a flat rock to cool near the little-used cabin hearth, and wiped perspiration from her forehead with the back of her hand. "Ma will have a fit if she hears you talking like that—ain't, don't," she said, taking her seat. Beyond the gingham curtains at the kitchen window, morning light flickered through the big alder's leaves onto the yard.

"I know. She wants me to talk like some citified Easterner. Men don't talk like that out here. They don't go to college, neither. I bet Spencer doesn't go to college, no matter how much Ma and Pop fuss."

Ellen laughed a bit, unable to imagine her brother Spencer spending most of the day in classrooms. She wasn't too fond of the idea herself. The only appeal from her mother's logic of attending college was the regularity—day in and day out, knowing exactly what you were supposed to do—a time of few decisions.

"Mr. Fykes is starting the coffin. I guess Mrs. Clayton and Mrs. Mercy have already tended the body." Pitt forked hominy into his mouth and chewed.

Ellen was grateful the women hadn't called on her to help. She had already closed the dead man's eyes, her fingers shaking when they touched the cool, soft lids and felt the lifeless orbs beneath. She and Pitt had both gone pale, her stomach tight, when they maneuvered the body onto the canvas. Stone's blood stained her dress. I've already done my part, she thought.

"The burying will be out on Grave Hill at noon," Pitt said.

"Noon. That's just about the time we found him." Ellen sipped her hot coffee, then noticed Pitt's curious stare. "What?" She asked.

"How d'you always know, Ellen?" he asked. "It was nearly a month ago when you dreamed some man was dead. How do you do that?"

Ellen frowned, not wanting to think about it. "It just happens. Rather like stubbing my toe. Mostly I walk along fine, and then on occasion—" She drew a deep breath and got up to pour more coffee in her cup.

"Mostly when something bad's gonna happen," Pitt stated.

"That's not true!" She set the pot down hard on the burner. "I didn't know ahead when our dog got killed by coyotes, or—or when Mrs. Fykes died of pneumonia. There are lots of things I don't know!" How awful, she thought, if people start believing I know everything—can tell anything before it happens.

"Mrs. Mercy talked once about people having the talent," Pitt said after a while. "Talent—like it was something really special."

"Uh." Ellen stirred a sprig of dried mint in her coffee, bruising the leaves against the cup wall with the back of the spoon. Lutecia had asked her about *talent* four weeks ago, had wondered if it were a family trait.

"She said it happens a lot in East Louisiana where she comes from, folks having visions and all. But it's mostly Injuns—"

"Indians," Ellen corrected.

"Yeah, and Negroes," Pitt went on. "She calls it hoo doo and geechie happenings."

"Geechie?" Ellen returned to her chair. "That's an odd word."

"I guess. Can Ma or Pop dream what's ahead?"

"If they can, they surely haven't told me about it." That's what she had told Lutecia four weeks ago, too. She pushed hominy around her plate with her fork, her appetite gone.

"I think Ma can. Pop always calls her his luck. Hardly ever goes against her wishes and it always seems to work out. She didn't mind at all our settlin' here, and, with the cattle movin' up the trail, this is gonna be an important town one day!"

"It'll have some booming years, I'm sure," Ellen said, recalling her mother's ambivalence to the family's move from northeast Kansas to this remote location. That was Belinda's style.

"Well, I gotta go." Pitt said, bounding up. "I'm helping Mr. Clayton dig the hole to plant ol' man Stone."

"Pitt, show more respect!"

"I didn't know him none, and he's gone now."

"You knew him enough to identify the body," Ellen accused.

She herself hadn't seen the man before. Pitt ran out the door.

"Did you milk the cow?" Ellen called after him.

"Yeah!"

"Clean the paddock?"

"I'll do it later!" He was halfway to the store.

Ellen heaved a long sigh, concerned by how hard her brother was working to find adventure. She would have thought the various oddities of their life would be more than enough to keep him content. Their mobile freight-wagon store; the moving about like gypsies.

Years ago Ellen had noticed a common thread in all the places they briefly settled—the odd assortment of people they lived among. This place was no different. Along with them in this wedge between two southernmost waterways in Kansas was a black couple, trying to raise cattle, an ex-mountain man (his wife had been Kiowa) and his son, and a self-confessed Rebel deserter (Ellen was certain Luke Clayton broke from the Confederate ranks because of cowardice and not his political leanings).

Such a mishmash of humanity! She set the last of the dried apples to soak so she could stew them with honey. *The place seems to attract misfits like pipestem flowers draw bees.*

Every place they lived had been like that. A Chinese family settled next to them in Shawnee County—opened a laundry and couldn't convince strangers that they didn't read tea leaves.

And now we've got gamblers and cow people and bawdy girls. She frowned, wondering why she hadn't seen either of those women or the scrawny man, Dillard Winslow, when she returned to the settlement with Mr. Stone's body. The trio had arrived just six days ago and set up tents on the slope behind the Claytons' "hotel."

They were probably entertaining customers, she thought. But who?

She dippered several scoops of hot water from the stove well into a large kettle and carried it from the stove to the table. Hot steam covered her face. The image of Mr. Stone's body flashed to her and her stomach tightened with the gruesome visage. She cleaned the utensils and forced the dead man from her mind, concentrating on each dish she washed as if it were made of gold. By the time she scrubbed out the coffeepot she didn't feel so tense. The cast iron skillet was still too warm to whisk clean with a rough cloth, so she rinsed her big apron in the cooled water, wringing it with quick twists. After hanging the apron from a line tacked along the ceiling, she put on a fresh apron, retied her blue scarf loosely around her neck, and hauled the kettle outside to the garden.

The bright day was already warm. She carefully poured the tepid water along the rows of beans. The flowers her mother had planted below the beans thrived on runoff. From their frilly leaves they bobbed red and yellow buds at her. The hint of gay colors made her smile and triggered awareness of the blue sky with large cottony clouds moving easily along; a light breeze made it not as muggy as the previous day; meadowlarks called.

She set the kettle in the dogtrot and studied the neat yard and tidy buildings. She felt more permanency here than any place they had ever lived. Would it last? she wondered. And what is my place in all this? The irony that she didn't know soured her stomach. *I can know about dead bodies in advance, but I can't even fathom the possibilities for my own family!* Tears of frustration burned her eyes. She smoothed them away and walked to the store, her daily routine. The ritual seemed to settle her—unlock the store's back door, proceed through the narrow hallway, take up the feather duster before climbing three shallow steps to the main room. She drew a deep breath, already calmed.

The building was made of logs over a foot thick, and the one room was nearly twice the size of the family cabin. Morning remained murky obscurity as it would be late afternoon before the west-facing windows allowed in light. The windows had originally been covered with rubbed, oiled canvas. Her father had replaced that with glass last summer before her wedding. A large hearth and several chairs occupied the south end of the room. During the winter, the area had served more as a schoolroom than a store, with Ellen as teacher. Her mother had arranged that—to take her mind off her loss. Her students were the Clayton children, her brother Pitt, Hubert and grown Tim Fykes who had decided it was about time he learned to read. The Pierces, who lived eight miles northeast, had sent their oldest son and daughter down when the weather wasn't too bad and the children had free time—which wouldn't be now, during planting season.

Ellen had officially closed school three weeks ago. *Just as well.* For all her high marks on the qualifying test, Ellen doubted that she was cut out to be a teacher.

She dusted the service counter and the top of the glass-fronted display case along the north wall. The heavy humid weather of the past few days seemed to have settled in the store. She felt a sheen of perspiration on her forehead just from this minimal work. At the front of the store, she lifted the throw bar on the wide door and propped it open with a six-pound iron. A slight breeze wafted in from the porch front where a large brass cow bell hung against the wall. Ellen turned to the shelves on the back wall across from the door. They extended from waist high to the ceiling with only a few items on them, giving way to the narrow hallway that led to the back door. She dusted the bare wood between cans, and passed over the deep shelves that held traps and chain and a few ingots of lead. Behind the service counter set bags of beans, flour, millet, tin barrels for the sugar and oats. Two pull down lanterns hung from the high ceiling beams.

After returning the feather duster to its hook in the hall, she went into the small room off the back entrance where a wall cupboard held most of her parents' books. She opened it, a faint waft of mothballs coming to her, and inspected the four shelves, looking for mouse droppings or beetles. They had over thirty books, and kept them in this cupboard for protection from moisture. Ellen read titles imprinted on the spines, her hand trailing along the leather bindings. She had feasted on these books many times—had consumed them when she was younger, reading Franklin and Mitford, Shakespeare and Goethe. It seemed so long ago, her childhood. *I am twenty, but I feel like an old lady.* Pamphlets and old newspapers filled three leather folders: articles and treatises by and about Fredrick Douglass, Elizabeth Caddy Stanton, Frances Wright. Ellen was fascinated by the political theories presented in these papers, a fact her mother had pointed out to her when Ellen accepted Johnny's marriage proposal. "You've read so many modern principles, why are you turning to this trite station in life!" "I love Johnny," Ellen had simply responded. "You were in love with Pop, and you got married. How is this different?" Belinda had drawn a long weary sigh and turned away, saying nothing.

Ellen closed the cupboard door. Gloom began to penetrate her. *Keep busy, don't think.* Solitude always prompted thoughts of Johnny's death—her loss. That October evening of his announcement to help move cattle buzzed through her mind—the argument with his parents insistent, droning loud; and her captured on a twisting, vine hearing it all again and again: "This is a fool's errand!" Nettie Hargrove's sharp voice whipping at her. "We're here to avoid all that!"

"Think of your wife, Johnny!" exclaimed Johnny's father. "Don't do this!"

"Leave Ellen out of it!" Johnny had raged.

As much as Ellen hadn't wanted Johnny to go, she still couldn't understand the reason for his parents' tirade. Maybe if she had spoken up then—with his parents against the plan, maybe if she had told him what she foresaw, he wouldn't have gone—he wouldn't have died.

Forcing herself up, she insisted, *Not today!* Her hands shook, fingers cold. She clenched them together. *I will not go through that again!*

In the main room, she unlocked the large drawer under the counter and withdrew writing tools and the leather-bound ledger. Carrying them to the table near the north-side window, her attention was drawn up the rise to the cattle company tent where people flanked Doyle Blankenship who was seated in his buggy. It seemed everyone from the settlement was gathered at the buggy except her, including Winslow and the two prostitutes. The stocky gray horse in harness tossed its head. Luke's long arms waved out as he gestured about something; Reba pulled at his shirt. Suddenly the horse lurched to action, bringing the buggy down the slope and along the road at a moderate jog. Ellen watched the others glance after it before continuing their animated discussion. Blankenship stopped the buggy in front of the store and with practiced ease, lowered himself to the ground. Ellen smoothed her hands along her fresh apron and went to the door as Blankenship used his cane to negotiate the steps.

"Thank goodness you're open," the man said as he came in and took off a low-crowned top hat. His round face was sallow and drawn; bluish bags under his eyes looked like bruises. "Those blasted idiots are talking about delaying Francis's burial until after the law has gotten here."

"That would be several days!" Ellen said. She walked to the service counter.

"Indeed. And in this heat." He shook his head. "That Clayton fellow seems to think some unique information can be obtained from the body. That's balderdash! I told him you would be able to give authorities any information necessary."

"I?" Ellen leaned into the counter, wondering what he meant.

"Of course. You and the boy—your brother? After all, you were the ones who found him." Blankenship mopped beads of perspiration from his face with a large white handkerchief. His hand shook. "And then Mrs. Clayton is worried about relatives who would want to be here."

"Does he have family nearby?" Ellen asked, feeling less tense.

"Only a nephew up in Ohio. I have the address somewhere. I'll wire him from— Where would the nearest telegraph be?"

"Emporia," Ellen said.

"That far? Damn. I must say when I hired to Stone's employ, I certainly never expected to be camped on the prairie and then have to deal with *this*."

"Oh, you aren't his partner?"

"Goodness no. I'm his assistant—his secretary. All I know about cattle is that I like my steaks well done."

Ellen had glanced through the side window up the slope while he was talking. The meeting was breaking up. Luke still seemed upset, so she assumed he lost his argument and the funeral would proceed as planned. When she looked back, Blankenship was scowling around the store.

"Do you have some laudanum?" he asked. "I need something to get me through this."

"We don't carry that. If you need something to aid—"

"It's my injury, you see." Not a war wound as Ellen had assumed two days ago when she met the man; he had been injured in a streetcar accident—according to Pitt. "It aches so at times. The travel just to get to this place was horrendous; I seem to have exhausted my supply."

"I'm sure Mrs. Mercy has some herbs that could help."

"Madam, when one is accustomed to laudanum—" He broke off and pivoted for the door. "Perhaps one of those soiled doves would let me purchase a dose. They usually keep a plentiful supply."

Ellen followed him to the door. They stepped onto the porch as Tim Fykes trotted his horse to the back of Blankenship's buggy.

"Mornin', Miz Ellen," he said with a nod of his head.

Blankenship settled his hat and looked at Tim expectantly. "You get some sense talked into them?" he asked.

"It's decided. Burial today as planned."

"Thank the Lord," Blankenship muttered.

"We'd like to borrow your family's wagon, Miz Ellen, to carry the coffin."

"Certainly."

"Thought we could use Winslow's buckboard, since it's settin' right over there, but he wanted to charge us."

"Outrageous!" Blankenship maneuvered himself back to his buggy. "Ma'am." He tipped his shiny hat before he turned the horse to follow Tim back up the slope.

Ellen stepped back into the store and moved slowly to the table where the ledger lay. She recalled how she had mentally flinched when Blankenship said she could tell the authorities all they needed to know. Flinched, assuming he referred to her prescient talents. But he was speaking with practicality. She had found the body, after all. She and Pitt. That was not a dream. She sat down, trying to pull the reality from the pre-knowledge. The reality is what she would have to tell the authorities Rob Clayton brought back, whoever they might be. The military. A federal marshal. What did she know?

What had she really seen?

She pulled a clean sheet of paper from the back of the ledger, opened the ink jar and set the nib of her pen. She forced herself to concentrate on what at the scene had *not* been in her dream—what her reality had observed.

I walked from the wagon, around the horses, went to the tree. I stumbled on something—

The boot. *A boot, cut along the shaft.* That was reality. She jotted down *boot.*

The body, the ants, the bloody torso. *And his throat was slit.* That hadn't been in her dream, but she wouldn't forget it. Would never forget that gruesome wound.

What else? she prompted her thoughts, the chill of memories setting goose bumps along her arms. She wrote: *mutilated hand,* then *open pocketknife; remnants of his lunch; no horse.*

She hadn't turned out the pockets of the man's clothes and she recalled, it didn't appear anyone else had either. The only irregular appearance, withstanding the gore, was Mr. Stone's stockinged feet. Next to the word boot she wrote; *only found one.*

What else would be necessary information? she wondered. She thought of questions someone might ask her. Did she know how long he had been dead?

Not long, she thought. The blood had not gone black and hard. The body wasn't stiff when they wrapped it in canvas.

Body warm, not stiff, she wrote.

Even Pitt had noticed that—had made comment, worry, about how close they had been to witnessing the murder.

And getting murdered ourselves, she now thought. She was certain anyone who would commit such a brutal act would have no hesitation in eliminating observers.

With a shaky hand, she corked the ink jar while glancing through the window and up the road. She wondered what kind of horse Mr. Stone rode. One from Tim Fykes's small string? And the saddlebags. She hadn't looked in them. Where were they now?

The assembly of residents had begun to disperse, and as Luke and Reba started down the road to their dugout, Ellen decided not to stay any longer at the store. She didn't want the Claytons stopping by to tell the details of the argument. She went quickly to the store front and pulled the door shut, lowering the bar. If someone really needed something, they would clang the cow bell. She walked briskly out the back.

Pitt ran through the yard toward the barn as she made her way to the house. "Gonna use our wagon as a hearse!" he called to her.

"Yes. Mr. Fykes asked permission." She went over to help him ready the rig.

"Too bad we ever took Mr. Stone out of it. Would've saved some work," Pitt said.

Ellen gritted her teeth. "Just use Grams," she told him. Grams was the most sedate of the draft horses. While Pitt went to get the horse, Ellen took up an oiled rag and did an extra cleaning job on the harness. They worked in silence.

"You're not going to the funeral?" Pitt asked when they finished fastening the traces on the horse.

"I think not," Ellen said. "I'll work in the cornfield a while."

"Mrs. Clayton said I could wear Rob's dark suit coat since he isn't here."

"Make certain you show proper appreciation," Ellen coached.

"I will," he whined. "Pretty neat, though. Me able to fit into Rob's clothes and him already fifteen."

"Pretty neat," Ellen said, hoping this wouldn't lead to his asking to do some adult task she would have to say no to.

She watched him drive away, the oppressive humid air locking her into inactivity. The rattling of the wagon grew distant. Remembrance of Mr. Stone's body lurked in Ellen's mind, and she wondered if she should go to the funeral. Perhaps it would rid her of the image.

Her horse, Phineas, ambled to the fence, his big head topping hers by more than a foot. Born five years ago; her parents had given him to her when she went north to teach, but Phineas had really been hers since he was an ungainly foal. The attachment between them was immediate when she went to the meadow and found him spraddled beside his mother. She trained him to harness when he was two and to saddle when he was three. He pulled her buggy around Ottawa County and brought her home. He and the buggy went with her when she married—and brought her home.

"Dear Phineas." She scratched his jaw, appreciating the earthy scent of him and the smoothness of his brunette hairs. "You're a help," she said, working her fingers up toward his ear. "Always willing to listen." He dropped his head lower and pressed against her hand so she could reach his ear. "Writing things down helped, too. Real events, and not just what has been in my head these past weeks." She stood on the lower rail of the paddock and combed her fingers through his fetlock. "But, you know, Phineas, I'm worried. I think that other face I envisioned belongs to the murderer. If I could identify him—" She shook her head and stepped down from the rail. "I don't know. I guess I want that dream to be worth more than just a nightmare come true."

Ellen bent into her hoeing, trying not to think about anything. Her work carried her along one corn row and back down another, the knee-high green fronds barely trembling in the still air. She had already withstood the warm kitchen and prepared a kettle of venison stew to simmer, and stirred up sourdough bread. The sun climbed higher. Grave Hill loomed in her mind with its patches marking the dead. Two markers. One for Tim Fykes's wife, and another for a freight driver consumed with gangrene after water moccasins swarmed him when he was crossing the Salt Fork (one of his horses died, too). Grief caught in her throat and she hacked the hoe into the stubborn ground, striking hard. Johnny wasn't buried on Grave Hill. Johnny wasn't buried anywhere, his body lost to the river—the cattle. Or so she assumed. Certainly the Hargroves would have notified her if a proper burial had been possible. They would, wouldn't they? How quickly she was gone from there.

That morning, so unlike today: November gray with frost still whitening the edges of the outbuildings, rider galloping in, hurrying to the main house; Ellen had rushed there, too, the hollow insistence of disaster carrying her to the senior Hargroves' door. "No!" Nettie Hargrove had cried. "Not Johnny. No!" And then it was all a blur, with Ellen dashing in, wanting to hear—yet not. Mr. Hargrove trying to comfort his wife, between fits of anger at the messenger of bitter news. Then he was rushing Ellen to her cabin. "Pack. You'll go home now. This is all too awful and you need to be with your family."

"But *you're* family!" Ellen had declared. "Mother Hargrove needs me." I need her, had been her thought. Someone to hold on to. Then it had struck her: they must have known about her premonition—blamed her—wanted her gone from their house...

Heat wafted against her from the cornfield, and she realized she was standing, hunched against the hoe handle, transfixed with the guilt and the Hargroves' denial of her. *How much time to end this pain?* She swiped away a tear with the back of her hand.

Drawing a long breath, she swung back to her work. Up one row, back down another. The birds didn't flush in panic now, and the squeaky call of blackbirds filled her head. Heat simmered inside her bonnet, and even the five inch brim, tied loosely at her chin, didn't hold back the glare of sunshine. Her shadow began stretching east. It was past noon, but she kept to the work, wielding the hoe along the base of the plants, dislodging burdock and tufted grasses that seemed to take hold overnight. *A thankless job, this farming,* she thought. There had been fields and gardens to tend ever since she could remember. Her parents enjoyed the work. Ellen and brother Spencer had performed tasks because of direct order; and now Ellen was doing it just to get her shoulders aching, her back tired, so she could exhaust herself enough to sleep long and hard without the fitful worry that had been with her for the past eight months.

Dust coated her lips. Her dry throat reminded her that she hadn't brought along a water jug. Standing the hoe blade on the ground, she leaned against the handle. Weakness spread through her like a chill. She closed her eyes against the brightness. Behind her eyelids, a tiny horseman suddenly appeared—sorrel horse trotting and the rider wearing a fringed leather shirt.

"No," Ellen murmured.

The man smiled at her, then lurched and fell sideways while angry brown eyes glinted from darkness that rolled over the scene.

Ellen jerked open her eyes. The hoe fell to the earth as she pressed her palms to her cheeks. "No," she said, startled by the vision. "The sun is really getting to me." Her heart raced and coldness trilled along her back and arms. The memory of the horse and rider clung to her thoughts like sweat on an old bridle. If the vision could speak, it would shout, *Look at me! See me!* And the face, the roiling darkness was just as it had been in her Sycamore Spring dream.

"No!" Ellen said. Frustration replaced the shock she had felt. "This is nothing." She studied at the half acre she had weeded as if the cultivated soil had produced the mental disturbance. "I came out here to get some peace." She grabbed up the hoe from the ground. "And now this!" She stifled the need to sob, or scream, or faint and marched back toward the house.

By the time she reached the yard, she had convinced herself she had been on the edge of heat exhaustion. "Sun. That's all. Too much sun." Once in the shade of the tall alders, she dropped the hoe, pulled off her bonnet and headed toward the well that set beside the cistern her father had built. Improving this place had been a slow-working tonic for him: expand the cabin, build the cistern, clear the fields. The visible progress he made on their surroundings paralleled his brightened spirits. Ellen wished she could discover an interest that would release her from the grim state of mind that had been with her since Johnny's death. Her emotions seemed to be enveloped in a blizzard. She thought her grief from Johnny's death would have dissipated with the cold weather and melted off like the snows. But the chill was still with her, becoming more intense as the days passed.

The pump squeaked mercilessly as she moved the arm up and down. *That man wore a fringed shirt like a trapper or a cavalry scout. Maybe it was an omen that Rob Clayton won't make it to Fort Harker.* Water came out in a trickle, then grew stronger. Leaning to it, she put her hands into the flow and splashed cool water over her face. She started to dunk her whole head under the stream. *If only this would numb my brain!*

"Mrs. Hargrove?"

Ellen whirled to the girlish voice; her heart pounded.

"Oh, dear. I'm sorry." The woman she faced backed up, eyes wide. "I guess I shouldn't have come. I'm Nancy Kincaid—ah. Well. I live up from the hotel?"

Ellen smoothed water from her face and focused on the young woman dressed in a dark blue striped dress with high bodice overlaid in beige lace. A bright red petticoat showed under the ruffled hem and over her ankle-high black shoes. When Nancy and her associates set up small tents up the hill from the Claytons' "hotel," Reba had clucked her tongue in dismay. Pitt had been curious and was ordered to extra work by their father. Ellen was mystified that this little community would suddenly sprout a brothel. She had previously spoken with Rose Schaffner when the skinny woman with bad teeth came to the store. Now here was the other woman—Nancy. "Do you need something from the store? I'm sorry. I didn't hear the bell."

"Well, no." The woman's brown eyes showed worry as she frowned at Ellen. "I know it ain't right my callin' on you, but I was concerned when you wasn't at the funeral." Nancy hunched her shoulders and stepped under the shade of the tree. "It must've been terrible, you findin' that body and all. Well, I just wanted to see how you was doin'." Her attractive face reddened with embarrassment.

"Oh. Thank you. Have a seat." Ellen pointed to the bench near the largest tree. She hoped Nancy's company would keep her thoughts from returning to the vision that had beset her in the cornfield.

"With your ma not here, I thought I'd see if there was something— Well—" Nancy walked to the bench but didn't sit.

"That's nice of you Miss Kincaid."

"Call me Nancy, please, ma'am." Nancy nearly curtsied.

The woman feeling so obviously out of place surprised Ellen. "Only if you'll call me Ellen."

"That's mighty white of you, but I know it ain't proper for my sort to be familiar with regular folk. And you from such a fine family."

"Well, this isn't really a proper town, Nancy. We've got no church, no real school." *And there's not a female soul within forty miles as close to my age as you.* "I'd feel just fine your calling me by name. Sort of like I had a friend. Can I get you a dipper of water?" She turned to the well and felt a moment's dizziness. She braced herself on the cistern wall.

"Miz Ellen, are you most certain you're all right?" Nancy peered at her.

"What? Oh, yes! I—" Ellen smoothed back her hair.

"Ellen!" came a shout. Both women looked toward the store where Pitt charged full speed across the yard. "Ellen! Guess what?"

Ellen put her free hand to her mouth. "What's happened?" *Please don't let Rob be hurt.*

Pitt gawked at Nancy Kincaid but went on. "I just saw the freight wagon! Ma and Pop, they're back early!"

Ellen looked toward the eastern trail, easily making out the three sturdy draft horses splashing the Jarvis freight wagon through the shallows of Fall Creek in the meadow where the horses foraged.

"Well, your family's back. I'll be going," Nancy said, backing away.

"Oh, thank you, Nancy, for stopping by. That was very thoughtful."

Nancy gave a slight smile and waved as she headed back toward the road.

Ellen picked up her bonnet and retrieved the hoe while the freight wagon passed the rocky plot her father wanted to turn for potatoes. The other Jarvis horses sent out whinnies of welcome. Pitt ran toward the wagon, holding his felt hat in place on his head. He would be full of the news about Stone Cattle Company and the order from the missionary. He would tell about Mr. Stone getting killed and how Ellen had known they would find the body. Already she could hear Pitt's excited voice. She sucked in a deep breath before stashing the hoe and bonnet in the tool shed.

Before long, the team snorted past the paddock and into the yard. Ellen forced a smile and waved. Her mother, thin and neat, sitting at her husband's right side, waved back.

"Whoa up there, Bob," Ellen's father called. "Whoa, Clio, Champion!" Her father maneuvered the wagon around the well and parked it at the back entrance of the store.

In a checked shirt and blue corduroy trousers, Matthew Jarvis appeared younger than his forty-six years. His broad-brimmed hat hung from storm straps along his back allowing his steel-gray hair to catch the afternoon light. Matthew set the brake and tied the reins. His hands were long and slender, although the left hand was missing the middle two fingers. An artillery accident in the war. A flash of powder had left a burn scar along his left cheek. When he came home from the war, he had been moody and often depressed. They had come here because he didn't want to be around people. ("We treat our fellow man abominably," he had declared. "I want no part of society as it stands today.") He didn't feel the war had really remedied anything.

"Run get Luke Clayton," Matthew said to Pitt. "Tell him we got that special item he wanted."

Pitt dashed away. Matthew got off the wagon and went around to help Belinda. Her mother's wide-brimmed straw hat was tied onto her head with a filmy pink scarf. Beneath that, her blond hair was short to her chin line—totally out of custom. But then, Belinda had always been unconventional. Once down, she came to Ellen, solemn faced. "We passed the Mercy cow camp on the way in," she said. "They told us about Mr. Stone."

Ellen nodded, wondering if Belinda remembered that Ellen had dreamed about finding the body. Belinda's next words told her she did.

"I'm sorry, dear." Belinda smoothed Ellen's hair and kissed her forehead. "You seem to be taking it in stride this time."

"I'm trying," Ellen said. Would this be the most her mother spoke of it? Take it in stride. Don't bother me. That's all that was usually said.

"At least no one's making hex signs behind her back," Matthew said, as he started unhitching the horses. "Or asking her to bless the grain like they did in Shawnee County." Her father didn't seem to think her abilities were odd and always talked easily of them until Belinda asked him to stop. "You've been telling women when their babies would come since you were a little thing," her father went on. "Predicted Pitt's birth to the time of day, even." Matthew frowned then. "Of course, the women you said nothing to usually never went to term, or—"

"Matthew, stop," Belinda insisted. But Ellen knew the rest. The babies had been stillborn. Her own little sister was the one—the baby girl who would have been two years older than Pitt. Her mother had known how the birth would go because Ellen had known. Only in the last few years had Ellen stopped blaming herself for the baby's death.

"Well, maybe this will be the end of it," Belinda said, turning away. She always said that.

Ellen frowned and thought about her little horse and rider. *Keep it to yourself.*

"I've got a supper ready," Ellen said.

"How wonderful. I'm really famished," Belinda said from where she was releasing Champion from the wagon traces.

Ellen turned toward the house, unnerved as she realized what a large supper she had prepared—more than she and Pitt would have eaten alone. She had known her parents would be home today.

By the time Ellen reached the dogtrot, Luke Clayton came around the corner of the store, Reba close behind with the children skipping along at her side. "You got to Emporia and back already?" Luke asked.

"Only had to go to Eldorado. That's getting to be quite a town!" her mother responded.

Eldorado, she thought. That had shortened their trip short by three days. *When will this stop!*

She set the table for five, knowing what would come next; knowing not by any unreasonable kenning, but because of how things normally went. By the time her parents finished chatting with the Claytons, Tim had ridden down from his barn, as Ellen expected, and helped put up the horses. The three then made their way to the house; her mother had invited Tim to supper—which he didn't refuse. Ellen busied herself serving plates and pouring water (Tim had brought his own tin cup). Her father wanted coffee, and she set the pot to boil. While the others talked of the murder, with Pitt giving details of the Sycamore Spring scene, Ellen kept busy at the stove. No questions for her. No comment about her pre-knowledge—not even from Pitt. Probably warned not to mention it by Ma, Ellen thought. Ellen picked at her food, while they talked about border outlaws and broadsides her parents had brought back with drawings of suspicious characters. After the meal they moved outside where it was cooler. The Claytons ambled over, with Reba excited about the new Dutch oven Luke had purchased for her. Pitt wandered off with Hestor. A Town and Land company had been started up at Camp Wichitaw, her father told, and Luke wanted to know all about that.

From the edge of the dogtrot, Ellen viewed the gathering, feeling as distant as if she were in another county. She went into the kitchen, but had no desire to clean the supper dishes. Feeling dejected, she went to the bedroom she shared with her brothers. From the east wall where a wide window was centered, her father had fashioned a canvas partition that stretched west for most of the room width between her section and that of the boys. Part of the window was on either side of the partition. The hinged wooden awning was opened, letting in a breeze. The hearth, centered on the west wall, warmed both sections in the winter. A curtain stretched from edge of the partition to the outer dogtrot wall, completely secluding her cot, her two-drawer dresser, trunk and wall hooks of clothing.

Ellen entered her small bit of privacy and slumped onto the bed. Laughter came from outside, and Ellen gritted her teeth, wishing she had someone to laugh with. The Claytons, Tim Fykes—they were her parents' friends, her parents' age, more or less. Her only friend was Lutecia—something she had realized only recently. Ellen had always thought of Lutecia as Belinda's friend—assumed they were close in age. Charles was in his late thirties, she knew, and had

smatterings of gray in his hair. But when she really talked to Lutecia—
first confessing her dream and then her worries about it—she learned
Lutecia was only twenty-nine; much closer to Ellen's age than
Belinda's forty-four. Visiting the Mercy cabin Ellen had noticed
several books, and not any borrowed from her parents' library. She
and Lutecia talked about what they had read and she learned a bit
of Lutecia's background: born in bayou Louisiana, sold to a Cajun
tinker's family when she was ten ("That's when I started learning
about herbs and all," Lutecia told her); sold again at thirteen to an
Arkansas Cherokee ("Fate kept workin' me north," she chuckled)
where she worked in the house and learned to read and write—
before she was stolen from them by a slave dealer and sold to a
Missourian when she was twenty. Ellen had difficulty imagining it
all—imagining Lutecia going from a house-oriented life to field
work at age twenty, to be bent over cotton crops, not allowed a
book or even a newspaper, living in a hut. *No wonder she ran away
as soon as the war started!*

With Lutecia, Ellen had shared her experiences in Ottawa
County—little events she found significant, and Lutecia had laughed
or commiserated with her where Ellen's mother had merely made
disparaging comments like, "Oh, the horrors of teaching. I don't
know how you stood it." Or, "I guess it was a good experience for
you." But this evening, Lutecia was out at the cow camp with her
husband. Ellen thought about her earlier conversation with Nancy,
allowing how they could be friends. She wondered what they would
talk about. Could she boldly just walk over to those little tents and
say, "Hi Nancy, how are you?" She shook her head, and without
further thought, changed from her day dress to her night clothes
and went to bed. A busy day tomorrow, she thought, the lilt of
voices coming to her through the open window. Thinking about the
new merchandise gave her a bit of pleasure—doing inventory,
arranging displays. That would keep her occupied.

4

The sun was just shooting morning rays across the yard when Ellen awakened to her brother's grumbling. "It's too early," he was saying.

"Come on, Pitt," came her father's near whisper. "We have to get started early and your mother has breakfast waiting. Shhh. Don't wake your sister."

Most mornings Ellen would have spoken up, let them know she was already awake, roused herself quickly to join the morning activities. Today she lay quietly while her brother dressed and left the divided bedroom, closing the dogtrot door with a gentle tug. After a few moments silence, she got up and dressed, carefully attending to her hair and tying a fresh apron over her maroon work dress. She arranged her dark blue scarf around her neck. It was nearly as large as a shawl, the finely-spun wool soft between her fingers. Johnny had given her the loosely-woven item at Christmas when he proposed. Then when Johnny died, she needed something— something dark—something to represent her loss. She kissed the ends after she tied it and hurried toward the activity in the dogtrot. She needed to get to the store and be ready to do inventory as they unloaded the freight wagon. But when she left the bedroom, she was surprised to see her mother leaving the kitchen in the canvas pants she wore to work in the fields.

"Oh, Ellen! Did you sleep well?" Belinda asked with a bright smile. "I warmed up the bread, and the crock of molasses is still on the table. Coffee's hot." She pulled on thick cotton gloves. "We're going to get started on that potato field."

"But the store goods haven't been unpacked," Ellen said, surprised by this turn of events. She followed her mother through the dogtrot and into the yard.

"Soon enough," Belinda responded. "We need to get started on this field. Right now the soil is soft enough to pry out those rocks. But the next rain will make it an awful mess to do." Belinda smiled at her. "We'll be back around noon. There was plenty of stew left from last night. That will be dinner. Ring the bell if you need something." Belinda strode off to join Pitt and Matthew where they waited near the tool shed.

Ellen sat on one of the chairs that had been left in the yard from the previous evening's socializing. In front of her, beyond the alders at the well, sat the wagon. JARVIS scrolled in blue on the wagon side caught the morning light and showed dull patches from flaked paint.

A half hour later, Ellen was in the store, mug of coffee in hand and a few bread crumbs clinging to the edge of her scarf. After opening the front door, she situated the ledger on one end of the service counter, took a long swallow of coffee, and went to the wagon to start unloading. For any store, the standard staples of flour, sugar, coffee, and beans were always needed, but this store insisted on different items from the other places her family had set up shop. Although the steel and chains and baits bought by trappers were occasionally asked for, the main sellers were items that travelers could use: canvas, sewing kits, accessories for firearms and hunting, whetstones, clothing. The cattle drives brought in drovers with needs for britches and shirts, scarves and socks. People moving to new locations, like Texas and Colorado Territory, wanted brake shoes for their wagons, trace chains, leather strapping, rain capes. Canned goods, especially fruit, gave people a feeling of luxury. The fresh vegetables always offered at any Jarvis store, were welcome by everyone—especially at the reasonable cost her mother charged. Ellen felt Belinda nearly gave away the produce.

Now, as she stood in the high-walled freight wagon with its own sets of shelves and cubicles and filled with the merchandise her parents had brought back from Eldorado, Ellen sighed, amazed at the assortment of nonessentials: a rose-patterned tea set carefully packaged with MADE IN ENGLAND stamped on the box; several cartons of pencils; two dozen chamber pots; six hand-tooled coffee mills. Feeling weary, Ellen carried items into the store, logged them into the ledger and placed them on shelves. One wagon shelf held a heap of clothing. She shook out the items and refolded them, placing the ten canvas pants, and fifteen plaid shirts on the table near the door. Back in the wagon, she could see boxes of items that needed to be put up, but most were secure behind heavy bags. She wrestled with a barrel of sugar and managed to reach a large carton of canned peaches wedged firmly between bags of coffee and cornmeal. Hands on hips, she considered carrying the peaches, can by can, to the store, and shook her head. Frustrated, she secured the door on the freight wagon and locked the store.

At mid-morning, the settlement was quiet. Ellen had seen Reba and the children leaving the dugout to go to their fields to the west. Tim, she assumed, was ensconced in his barn whittling fish hooks or carving elaborate handles for the knives he made. He placed the items at the store for sale, and had been surprised when knives sold at Ellen's prices—much higher than he had stipulated. Rose and Nancy—she didn't want to consider how they might spend their days, or nights.

She supposed she could join her family at their work clearing the new field. She went to the house and retrieved her straw hat, then glanced toward the meadow where the horses grazed. Phineas walked toward the paddock, his steps hampered by the flimsy leather hobbles on his front ankles. She smiled and headed across the yard to the big draft while tying her hat in place. Phineas waited patiently while she unfastened the hobbles, then walked eagerly behind her to the barn. Within moments, Ellen had fastened her sidesaddle onto the gelding and was on the trail headed northeast.

"Going nowhere in particular," she said to the horse. He bobbed his head against the reins that were clipped to the either side of a large bridle. She adjusted her skirt over her right knee that was crooked around the upper saddle support, and tucked the dark material along her left leg so it wouldn't blow in the warm, steady breeze. She had adopted riding sidesaddle when she was thirteen. It had seemed so elegant in the books she read—the Arthurian legends, Jane Austin. Her mother had scoffed, saying the insistence that women only ride sidesaddle was another way for male society to exercise control. Belinda rode astride, often bareback. Ellen always had, too, but the books, and a need to not agree with her mother, increased her desire for the riding style. She had endured the jostling change to the used saddle her father found for her, and feigned complete comfort. Then Phineas came along, with his back too broad to comfortably sit astride and gentle gaits that made riding sidesaddle a joy. Belinda had muttered once that Phineas was a draft horse, not a pleasure horse, but no more was ever said about it.

As Phineas splashed through the shallow part of Fall Creek where it ran across the meadow, a flush of embarrassment stirred through Ellen as she recognized how much subtle obstinacy formed her insistence. A need to be different from her self-assured, outspoken mother. She had seen the same struggle occurring with two of her students in Ottawa County. The similarity between the girls' attitudes and that of her own just a few years before had been alarming.

One of the four Indian ponies they owned looked up from where it dozed. Grams also dozed while standing. Champion and Clio were stretched out on their sides on the warm ground in what Pitt called "the dead horse position." Clio lifted her head a bit, but stayed put. If Ellen had been on Bob, all the horses might have reacted differently. Bob held a position of authority in the meadow. But Phineas was Ellen's.

When they drew close to where her family worked, Ellen kept her eyes straight ahead. Nonetheless, she was aware of Pitt thumping down the wheelbarrow. She could almost feel his glare. Then she heard his petulant voice in complaint that she was out riding while he was sweating and hauling rocks. Ellen lifted the reins a bit and touched her left heel to Phineas's flank. He trotted a few steps and then went into a rolling canter. Ellen drew deeply of the muggy air and smiled, surprised by how such a small thing as riding her horse could help her mood. They loped a quarter mile along the trail and she reined him back to a walk.

"How long has it been?" she said to the horse. "Too long." She leaned forward and patted his strong neck. "I've neglected you. Look at the burs in your mane."

At a lone cottonwood tree, a faint trail branched to the east. Ellen glanced that way and circled Phineas. That was the trail toward Cowley County. The Hargrove place was in that direction— along that trail eight miles—over two small streams, and three washes that would be pure mud this time of year. The Hargrove place. And no one would be there.

She continued Phineas on the northeast trail, still amazed by how quickly the senior Hargroves had left the farm after Johnny's death. Two days, and her father had ridden over there, Matthew angry by the abrupt way they had sent Ellen home—an anger that couldn't be quelled by Belinda's patient attempt to defer it. Two days, and they were gone (just as she had suddenly been gone, just as Johnny—); no sign of furniture, chickens, tools, mules. No explanatory notes tacked to the door. Just gone.

They had blamed her, she was certain, for their son's death. They knew he aspired to a life greater than their little hardscrabble farm, where extra money was made in the winter by running traps in the Ozarks. Had they resented that Johnny had kept his trapping money from the previous year? Set it aside to buy some land of his own, used part of it to give Ellen a store-bought Christmas gift. She fingered the soft blue wool, remorse dragging down the slightly uplifted spirits she had attained during her ride.

"Phineas, it's not right, you know. They shouldn't have left like that, hating me. I didn't want him to do any of that!"

Phineas's right ear flicked back, listening to her. "They haven't even answered the letters I sent them. They must have gotten them. I sent them to Missouri—where Mr. Hargrove's brothers and parents live. Three letters. Seven months. Wouldn't you think they would at least let me know they were alive! A short note, like my grandparents send: *We are still living, glad the same for you.*"

Ellen bit her lip, worried that they wouldn't be glad the same for her. That they would resent that she was alive while their only son, their only child, was dead.

"It doesn't seem to matter what I do, I can't stop thinking about it. But I have to!" She urged Phineas into another canter. They left the main trail, dashing through a huge meadow of tall grasses which swished by Phineas's sturdy legs. Her hat blew from her head and was held in place by the draw strings at her neck. Straight ahead Ellen could make out mottled brown lumps of cattle and she knew she was near the Mercys' cow camp. Although their friendship kept growing stronger, right now she didn't want to talk with Lutecia who seemed to read her moods and was so earnestly sympathetic. She put Phineas into a swooping curve that took them back toward the main trail. They plunged down a slight draw. A rabbit zigzagged across the trail and swerved into a bramble patch as they swept up the other side. She eased back, slowing her steed. She felt a bit better, although she knew she couldn't outrun her thoughts.

"Good boy," she crooned to her horse as he settled into a sedate walk. She patted his neck, enjoying the rich smell of the day—warm horse, fresh growing grass. Clouds drifted above her on a sky so bright it hurt her eyes.

A small freshet ran along the side of the main trail and she stopped her horse for a drink. Adjusting herself on the saddle, she straightened her windblown skirt, resettled her hat and closed her eyes while Phineas thrust his nose to the water. Thrush songs warbled steadily from the wood to the north. A persistent bird answered from the tree by the rivulet. The *scree* of a hawk for a moment silenced them all. The peaceful chorus began again. Then she heard a new sound. Opening her eyes, she looked southeast along the trail. Phineas's head came up, ears pricked forward as the rattling sound grew closer. She backed Phineas so she could turn him quickly, suddenly conscious of being alone.

A trotting gray horse came into view, pulling a buggy. Doyle Blankenship, in shirt sleeves, his cane and jacket wedged along the backboard, held the reins. He pulled up on seeing Ellen.

"My goodness, you gave me a start," the man said. He seemed out of breath.

"I'm sorry," Ellen replied. She walked Phineas onto the trail, curious about seeing the man. A portmanteau, duffel and a wooden crate were in the back of the vehicle. "Are you just out enjoying the day, too?" she asked, although it was obvious the man was permanently leaving the settlement. She noticed the letters S C C painted onto the crate.

"What? Oh no." Blankenship seemed distracted. A profusion of perspiration had dampened the underarms of his shirt so the dark stain was nearly to his waist. "Have to get to a town. Telegraph, you know."

And laudanum, Ellen thought. Either Rose and Nancy had none, or they wouldn't part with any of their supply.

"To contact his partner?" she asked.

"Hum. His partner." He pulled a large handkerchief from his waistband and mopped his face. "I must get going."

"But Mr. Blankenship." There was something she had planned to ask him. "The authorities," she stammered. "Don't you need to be here? To answer questions?"

Blankenship looked at her as if she had two heads. "Joseph and Mary, you sound like that Clayton fellow." He shook his head. "What's to tell? Stone came out to this wilderness to buy cattle; he got himself killed; the end."

"But we'll need information to find the—the person who did this," Ellen persisted.

"Find the murderer." He gave a choked, grim laugh. "Find the murderer in this uncivilized state?" He whisked the reins along the gray's flanks and the horse started up the trail. "I'm back to Missouri and on to St. Joe as fast as possible."

Ellen kept Phineas at a walk beside the vehicle. "What about the other men? The two who set up the tent when you arrived?"

"Hired, is all. Temporary. Did their jobs, got paid and left."

"But who were they? Maybe one of them—"

"Balderdash! They were just earning some funds to see them along the Texas trail."

"His horse," she blurted. "His horse was missing. What horse did he ride?"

"Madam." He seemed to clench his teeth. "A horse. A regular horse." He urged his buggy horse to a faster gait. Ellen put Phineas to a trot to keep up. "Sort of a roan, I think. With a bad eye," he said, his voice raised over the buggy noise.

"The horse was one-eye blind?" Ellen asked incredulous.

"No, no, girl. Had a mean eye; you could see white all around it. Pure trouble, that horse. Now, if you don't mind." Blankenship snapped the buggy whip over the gray's ears and the animal bolted into a long-gaited trot. Thick tan dust spewed up from the wagon tires, shimmering a plume onto Ellen and Phineas. She turned aside, shielding her eyes from the particles. The buggy rattled off, and when she next looked along the trail, Blankenship was headed around the curve near the woods.

"Well, that wasn't worth much," she said, turning Phineas. "Although I would have really fretted if I'd returned home and found Mr. Blankenship gone without my speaking to him." She headed Phineas toward the settlement.

The late morning had warmed even more. Muggy, with gusting breezes. Perspiration itched along her jaw line. She loosened the wool scarf at her neck and noticed her shadow tightening up on her right side. "It's close to dinner time."

She urged Phineas to a slow ground-covering trot, herself perched on his back with her dark skirt catching the breeze. For the first time in weeks her thoughts weren't harried with nebulous concerns and self doubt. At the paddock, she slipped deftly from the saddle and undid the horse's tack. She didn't bother to hobble him, and smiled as he sauntered into the meadow, lay down and rolled in the grass, his dark legs waggling in the air as he heaved himself one side to the other.

She rinsed the bit in the trough and left it with the saddle on the hitching rail. Pulling off the scarf, she went to her room and retrieved the lacquered wash bowl that sat on the low dresser by her cot. In the kitchen, she added wood to the stove and set the leftover stew to simmer. She dippered warm water from the stove well into the bowl and returned to her room. After shaking the dust from her blue scarf, she rinsed if in the water, and carefully stretched it along a small frame she had fashioned in the dogtrot, knowing it would dry quickly. Back inside, she opened her bodice to the waist. How luxurious! to remove her chemise and wipe off with the fresh water. The bedroom, sheltered as it was by generous branches of a sugar maple tree, was relatively cool. She closed her eyes, relishing the trickle of water along her arms. She smiled a bit, recalling how after a long day at harvesting the garden, Johnny would trail a cool cloth along her back, lift her hair, wash her neck and shoulders. And then... and then...

She opened her eyes and blew a long stream of air through her lips. So much for cooling off, she thought. But what a good memory. So good.

When her family came in for dinner, Ellen hid her surprise that no one made comment about her horseback ride. Not even Pitt, who avoided her eyes and spoke very little. Relieved, she watched them return to the field, wondering if she should go help them. She decided against that and proceeded with cleanup from dinner, pleased that she hadn't been reprimanded for her leisure. Her very thought stopped her short. Why was she thinking of herself as a youngster still? Or worse, a servant. These thoughts had commanded her when she was fifteen, and again when she was in Ottawa County when she wondered if she had done enough to earn her board. She shook her head, perturbed. Her board was part of her pay. She earned it with her teaching. But the many times she had corrected her thoughts during that school year had done little good, and she had worried about her performance, about her obligations. At the Hargroves the same feeling had plagued her— was she doing enough? Not for Johnny. She was certain she met his needs, but the senior Hargroves. What could she have done so they wouldn't have turned on her—sent her away so abruptly?

"Hey Pitt!" The call from outside drew her attention. "Pitt! Guess what!?" came Hestor's excited voice.

Ellen hurried to the yard. "Pitt's out in the field, Hestor. What is it?"

The huge grin and wide eyes of the ragamuffin dispelled Ellen's worry.

"Cattle coming! There's a big herd in The Nations seven miles south of the prairie dog town. The trail boss just came in. Said they'd be here by evening!" Hestor could barely stand still. "Gonna bed the herd right up the trail and everything!" He jumped in place a few times and then started toward the eastern field. "I'm gonna tell Pitt and your folks! My ma said!" He sprinted out the work trail before she could respond.

Biting her lip, Ellen looked across the yard at the freight wagon, still full of merchandise. While wondering if Hestor's announcement would bring her father in from the field to get the wagon unloaded, she paced along the side yard, glancing first toward the field and then at the wagon. South of the prairie dog town, she thought. That put the herd west of Old Pond Creek and the trading post there; it could have been two or three weeks since they had anything store-bought. The coffee beans were important; only a handful of the previous batch remained in the store. Canned peaches and tomatoes; the drovers might appreciate a special taste after a long haul. Gunpowder, so the men could hunt. Ellen knew those items were more important than the clothes her mother had bought. The men would purchase those luxuries in Abilene after they sold the cattle. Her parents had the wheelbarrow with them, so she couldn't use that to get the heavy items inside. Again she stared east, hoping to see her family returning. The sun glared brightly on the cornfield and no one came along the work trail.

Finally Ellen went to the tool shed and after a moment of rummaging, came up with a large burlap sack. She retrieved the keys from the kitchen and strode to the wagon. "Where there's a will, there's a way," she muttered to herself. She maneuvered a bag of Java beans onto the gunnysack, slid the makeshift conveyance down the wagon's loading ramp, and, taking firm hold of two corners, began pulling it to the back door of the store. She knew it would be several hours before the herd reached the Bluff River. By then she was certain she could get the store better appointed and inviting to the trail-weary men.

"Mrs. Hargrove, wait a minute. Let me do that!"

Ellen stopped tugging on her burlap sledge and looked up as Reed Carter set Hestor down from the saddle and dismounted his horse. She swiped perspiration from her brow with the back of her hand. "Mr. Carter. Good afternoon. And Hestor. There you are!" She could feel tendrils of hair escaping from the coil in wisps along her neck. She had been working for nearly two hours.

"Hey, Miz Ellen. Your paw said they'd be in pretty soon," Hestor said. "They done sent Pitt and me out to tell the Mercys about the cattle herd—we got to ride Bob bareback—and Mr. Carter rode me back on his horse!"

"Hestor, do go home," Ellen said. "Your mother's been worried for you. You were only supposed to go to my parents' field, not to the cow camp." Reba had come into the store asking after him when she saw Ellen working there, the woman's concern for her son mixed with the excitement about the approaching cattle drive. Reba had already made a list of foods she would cook and was writing the menu with charcoal on a plank of wood. She asked Ellen what she should charge.

"Okay." Hestor's smile had faded. He started around the south end of the freight wagon. "Bye, Mr. Carter. Thanks for the ride."

"I'd say mention of his mother's worry has dampered his exuberance," Reed said. "Where do you want this?" he asked, tapping the bag with his boot.

"Oh, really, that's not necessary," Ellen said to be polite. She was in fact relieved not to have to drag the bag into the hallway and up the three steps to the main room.

He stooped down and with a single move lifted the large bag of grain onto his shoulder. "Where to?" he asked with a smile that dimpled his right cheek.

She could tell he wouldn't be deterred, and led the way into the hallway and up into the store. "Against the wall there," she directed, pointing to the neat row of similar sacks propped against the east wall.

After he set down the bag, Reed looked around. "Have you unloaded all this by yourself? I assumed your father—"

"My parents are clearing a field for fall potatoes," Ellen said, feeling proud of her work that was so obvious to him. "Usually Spencer and Hubert do the unloading. I think my father forgot, actually. And the store has to look productive with this big cattle herd coming through."

"Well, productive is a good word." Reed surveyed the display of canned goods on the service counter, the clothing hanging and laid out. She had made all of the shelves appear full by setting items near the front edge. "But moving full-weight bags of grain on a burlap sack—" He chuckled. "Is there anything else I can do?"

"I don't think so." She suddenly worried that he might he continue his questions from two days ago. Curiosity often drew people to her—or repelled them. "That was a big help, Mr. Carter," Ellen said, walking to the back door. "It was the last item I'd planned to move in, and I admit, my arms were getting rather tired." She had moved three other grain sacks on her own, as well as four kegs of gunpowder, several rods of iron, and shelf goods she took out of the crates and put in her apron twelve at a time. With Reed following, she went to the wagon and closed up the back.

"I was helping the Mercys with their cows," Reed said. "Went out with them first thing this morning, or I would have come to your aid sooner." He took up the reins of his horse, which was browsing the thick grass along the edge of the building. "They'll be in here before long. Charles wants to talk to the trail boss."

"Lutecia told me they want to buy springers any chance they get," Ellen replied as she locked the wagon.

"They're going to have a fine herd of their own by next year this time."

"I expect so." Ellen stood at the open door of the store hall. She had inventory work to do inside, yet she didn't want to seem rude or too abrupt. She was also wishing Reed Carter had come around earlier to lend his strong arm to her tasks. The wagon would be empty if he had been here. And she would have had someone to talk to. A person, not her horse. Someone pleasant. Her need surprised her, and she smoothed her chapped hands along her dusty apron.

"Well, I've got to see to a few things," Reed said. "If you're sure you don't need me here."

"No. No. And thank you again." The day's heat all seemed to be on her face, and she thought of what a mess she must look.

"Think nothing of it." He swung into the saddle and nodded his head to her.

While Ellen marked the inventory in the ledger, she wondered about Reed Carter. He had driven his small ambulance-style wagon into the settlement from the northwest right before the last, surprise snowstorm four weeks past. At first, it seemed he was just waiting for the eastern trail to dry up. But two days later when a cattle herd came through, he unfurled a large striped awning on the side of his green wagon and invited the drovers up for card games. She had expected he would leave with the next freight wagons, but he stayed, even though the traffic along the route was slow. She wondered if he were responsible for the arrival of Winslow and the prostitutes, although she had never seen him talking to them.

Her thoughts then drifted to the Mercys, with whom Reed spent much of his free time. Lutecia and Charles worked so well together, building their cow herd with castoffs from the cattle drives, enjoying each other's company—sharing the work, the worries, the triumphs. Very much the same as her parents. Would it have been like that for her and Johnny? She thought of his laugh and how eager he was for everything. Would that have dulled over the years? Turned sour if things didn't develop the way he wanted?

When the advance wagon from the cattle herd stopped in front of the store, she looked up with surprise, not having heard it splashing through the river ford, nor paid attention to the excited shouts from Olive Clayton.

"Miss," the weary driver said as he stepped through the door and took off his hat. "I'm with that cattle drive a-comin'. In need of some grain. These mules," he tossed his arm toward the door and the wagon outside. "And most of the horses is plumb tuckered. We lost a lot of supplies fording the Red." Seeing the big sacks on the far wall cracked his weather-creased face to a smile, and just this one purchase rewarded Ellen's hard work.

"This'll be all I get now. The trail boss will likely stock up before we move on. Gonna stay a day or two, I guess." He paid for the grain.

"How many men are with the herd?" Ellen asked.

"Seventeen drovers. Pushin' twenty-two hundurt head of beef, we are. Covered put near a thousand miles already."

The size of the herd and the distance they had come stunned Ellen. Had any herd come through here from so far away? Most were in from northern Texas, wanting to avoid tariffs in Missouri and Louisiana and get better prices at the western markets. But 1,000 miles!

"And this place is a godsend, I tell you," the man went on. He shook his head. "We've been through some times."

"Yes, I'm sure you have," Ellen said, realizing they had probably left home in March. That would be springtime 1,000 miles to the south, but still a dusty, winter-cursed trail, with only hopes for decent grass to keep the herd fat.

"I know a lot of the boys will be checking out that home cooking sign across the road."

"Mrs. Clayton has a good menu of fresh food, and reasonable prices, too," Ellen said.

"That'll be real welcome. Our cook is one of the passel of men has been struck with ague. We ain't eaten decent in near a week. And has me drivin' for him. He's laid out in the back of the wagon there."

"Does he need medical assistance?" Ellen asked.

"Don't tell me you got a doc here, too?" His eyes widened.

"Sort of. A woman who has nursed some." Ellen didn't want to mention Lutecia's position in the war, or for which side she had plied her trade. This man was from Texas, after all. Ellen wondered how Charles would fare negotiating with these men for calves.

"I'll mention that to Baxter." He hoisted the bag of grain to his shoulder. "Thank you, Miss. Thank you."

Ellen watched him to his wagon, before returning to the service counter to place the money in the cash drawer built in the underside of the countertop. She stretched against tired aches in her neck and shoulders, then took a chair and her bookkeeping tools onto the porch to sit in the scant breeze the porch provided. After penning in the most recent sale, she looked north, where the driver had stopped the wagon and was talking to Tim. She saw the driver's arm point to the left. Toward the large white tent, Ellen assumed. The out-of-business cattle company.

She pulled the loose paper from the back of the ledger and studied what she had written the previous day, yet much had happened since then, with the funeral she didn't attend, the hoeing, her parents' return. She added: *Doyle Blankenship left the morning after the funeral. Had a small crate with SCC marked on it. Stone Cattle Company?*

She wondered what that could have contained. A cash box with all the company funds? How much would that be? Enough to buy cattle—so at even fifteen dollars a head that would be several thousand dollars. Maybe they were paying in scrip or bank notes. Whatever, a cash box would have valuable contents. What else could have been in the crate? Pen tips and ink, letterhead and stamps. He was the secretary, after all, she thought.

For a few moments she watched George Clayton chase around after the two puppies in the shade of the trees that marked the space between the dugout and the hotel tent. Sometimes Ellen thought the Claytons would be better off living in the large tent. It was brighter, that was for certain, and had better ventilation. Ellen looked back to the paper. Write something else or put it away, she thought. Her pen nib was crusty on one side, the ink quickly drying on the steel point. She capped the ink jar. Twice Olive dashed across the road to the store saying she could hear the cows, but another half hour passed before a wide spume of brown fogged the southern sky.

Ellen carried her writing tools inside, setting the ledger on the table. She loosed her hair and smoothed it back, fastening it more neatly into a coil on the back of her head, and went out the back and to the barn. Twenty-two hundred cows coming through were certain to get the Jarvis animals excited. She brought the horses in from the meadow and secured them in the paddock, checked the latch on the pig sty and put the cow in the barn stall. By the time she returned to the store, the brown smear on the horizon had become a large dust cloud with the lead animals and two riders appearing as silhouettes on the rise, still in Indian Territory.

Ellen took strips of canvas from the back room of the store and went outside on the store porch. After setting the chair inside, she twisted the strips and stuffed them around the cracks at the door frame to keep out dust, then turned her attention to the wooden shutters flanking each of the two front windows. It took several jerks to get one set closed. The hinges squeaked on rusty parts as she pushed them into place. The wooden slats were three inches thick, marked with diamond-shaped holes at shoulder height. Rifle ports, she knew, for times past when previous occupants had defended the place against aggressive Indians. Her family had never utilized these barricades. She went to the north side of the door and began working with the near shutter. It wouldn't budge. She pulled the corner of the frame, then stopped when she heard footsteps on the porch.

"Here, let me help with that," Reed Carter said as he came to her side.

"Mr. Carter!" She laughed a bit. "Just in time."

"That's me. Johnny on the spot."

Ellen drew a quick breath, his colloquial phrase stabbing at her. She moved to the porch railing and fingered the wedding ring on her necklace.

Reed, oblivious to the his comment's effect, examined the hinges and tugged each shutter. Soon he turned and shook his head. "It would take a mule team to pull those loose, and that might bring down the whole wall."

"Thank you for trying," she managed to say.

"No problem." He stepped to the railing a few strides from her. "It's nearly time for business."

"Yes, I expect most of the drovers will stop in the store at some time," Ellen responded. She couldn't believe her family still hadn't come in from the field.

"You know, I didn't see Blankenship's buggy when I was at my site," Reed said. "I wonder if he's going to bid for these cows?"

"Mr. Blankenship is gone. Left for Missouri this morning," Ellen said.

"Really!" Reed shrugged. "Makes sense, I guess. He's got no one to gather and hold cattle anyway."

"Well, Mrs. Clayton stands to prosper," Ellen said. "She baked thirty rounds of honey cakes in that new Dutch oven." Reba had asked Ellen how many loaves she should prepare. Asked as if Ellen could know to the crumb how much these people were going to eat.

"Let's just hope these drovers didn't lose all their money in The Nations. There're some real shysters down there. The Creeks run 'em out and the Indian agents just let them back in."

"I imagine it's the same in Abilene," Ellen said, wanting to ask him questions. His comment about Indian Territory sounded like he had been run out at sometime himself. She wondered if it were for selling whiskey. Pitt and Luke had seen three cases of it when Reed first settled in. He won it, Reed told Luke when Luke asked. Possibly true, since a whiskey peddler would have had more than three cases.

"That's true. Now that it's a railhead, Abilene's going to be a handful," Reed stated.

"Have you been there?"

"For a few months last year. I left when the gambling tax was raised. Some big money men moved in and started building huge establishments. There isn't much room for—average folks."

He sounded amused. Ellen would have expected bitterness from him perhaps run out of business by well-heeled competitors. So he had left Abilene, gone over to Fort Dodge or out to Ellsworth? Those were areas to the northwest—the direction he had arrived from. She wondered why he stopped here.

"Your store should do well, although the cattle drives will be a real test for it," Reed said. "These trail herd boys can get rowdy at times, and today we've both got some stiff competition for those men's time," Reed said, nodding across the road.

Dillard Winslow, a gaudy weskit partially hiding the same dingy shirt Ellen had always seen him in, drove a buckboard to a level spot between the river and the Clayton dugout. Rose and Nancy sat atop the wagon seat, with painted cheeks, perky hats in place on fancy looping hairdos, their dresses short over white cotton stockings. Winslow pulled a sign out of the wagon bed and propped it by the front wheel: NO BEAR GREASE HERE. WHITE WOMEN AT LAST.

He had just started unhitching the haggard-looking horse from the wagon when Reba stormed from the dugout, her daughter Olive right behind her. "You can't park that there!" Reba shrieked. "They'll think the dugout is the—the—crib house!"

"What's a crib house, Ma?" Olive asked.

"You just stand yourself out there and they'll know this ain't the place," Winslow said with a sneer. He led the horse back to the tents. Rose laughed. Reba stomped back to the dugout, pulling Olive with her.

Ellen frowned, thinking of her conversation with Nancy when she allowed they could be friends. She couldn't imagine what they would talk about. That made her think of what else happened yesterday. Looking toward the approaching herd, she was keenly aware that the outriders were about the size of the vision that had come to her in the cornfield. *Maybe a herder is going to be hurt.*

"Mrs. Hargrove," Reed Carter said, his tone so serious she turned toward him with surprise. "At the funeral yesterday, I learned more about this—incident," he said. "How several weeks ago you had foreknowledge of the murder."

Ellen drew back, pulled into herself and turned away.

"I had heard about your abilities when I first moved here, but I didn't realize how specific—" He stepped a bit closer. "That you went out there, knowing in advance what you would find. You could have waited, let it slip by, there would possibly be little evidence after a week or two."

"That wouldn't have been right," Ellen stated. He was touching the worry that plagued her—how to handle these sensings? To mention them put distance between her and others who were skeptical or regarded her with awe. *Not* to mention them left her with guilt when her dreams proved to be true. Guilt, like she felt about Johnny's death.

"I know it's often hard to follow through with something when you know it's going to bring personal discomfort and even notoriety," Reed said. Ellen bit her lip, amazed by his apparent understanding. "Anyway, I just wanted to say I greatly admire your courage."

She swallowed hard and darted a glance his way. "Thank you, Mr. Carter." She didn't know what else to say.

"They're a-comin'!" Olive exclaimed. Reed straightened and looked across the river. Ellen was relieved to end their conversation.

Luke and Hestor Clayton, hurried in from the field. "They're headin' for the river!" shouted Hestor as he ran to the Clayton dugout.

Reba had already come outside, closed the door and shuttered the one window. She and the children joined Luke along the two-foot high rock wall he had built during the winter at the side of their lot. He had built it at Reba's insistence, after some cattle from a drive charged up the hill and over the top of the dugout, caving in part of the earthen ceiling.

From the side of the store, Ellen's father rode up on Bob. "Looks to be a sizeable herd!" Matthew called to Ellen.

Pitt sprinted across the road to join the Clayton children.

"Where's Ma?" Ellen asked.

"At the house."

Ellen nodded, a bit miffed that her parents hadn't helped her prepare for the potential customers.

The persistent drone of hooves on hard ground that had underscored the last half hour became more distinct. Bawling and snorts accompanied the dark bobbing. Within moments, the moving objects went from flat shapes on a horizon to three dimensional creatures coming closer down the long slope. The cloud of dust behind them towered to the sky. Alarmed grouse thundered up from their ground nests. The herd surged toward the river; they trampled low trees, smashed through bushes.

Ellen clutched the porch rail, preparing herself. When the first two herds came through the settlement this spring, she had fled to her room and cried. Now she forced herself to watch the cows. *Not the cows' fault Johnny is gone.* She couldn't see the river because of the high banks. She fought away images of churning brown liquid.

The drive hit the river, spewing water high around bovine bodies. In the shallow ford the leaders milled to stop and drink. Herders yelled and waved their hats, urging on their charges. The push of the coming herd forced the first wet beeves to lunge up the opposite bank. Some stopped to shake off water, but others butted them from behind, and the riders kept yelling "Hiaahhh," their braided rawhide whips snapping like gun shot. Long legged, with bony shoulders and haunches, the beeves snorted and shoved at one another. Their hides were dappled and brown spotted, variegated black, white, and red, with no two looking alike. They jostled up the slope from the ford and onto the twenty-foot wide road that led through the settlement, their widespread horns pointed high over keen eyes and large nostrils.

Ellen clung to the porch rail, dumbfounded as the flow of animals continued to loom over the hill from The Nations, growing wider every second. More animals plunged into the river, lurched up the bank and filled the road. The air became pungent with the wet, sweaty smell of the beasts. By the time the herd leaders were half way to the Fall Creek ford, grit had collected on Ellen's lips and hands. Still the beeves roiled down the slope in The Nations, pushing, almost angrily, at each other—a mass of clacking horns, a din of bovine protest and human urging.

A huge animal blossomed on the edge of the stormy confusion. It rubbed against the hitching post as it lumbered past the front of the store. Reed's hands pulled Ellen from the porch rail. "Get inside!" he shouted. Ellen started for the door just as a big red-splotched steer veered out of the dust and leaped over the porch steps. The hitching rail cracked, gave to the pressure and disappeared.

Ellen and Reed darted into the store, slamming the door shut behind them. Dust seeped in; the building trembled. The porch was surrounded by beeves. Hooves clattered on the porch. Afternoon sunlight, which normally brightened the store through the western facing windows, glowed a murky tan. Ellen hurried behind the counter to settle two jars of pickled watermelon that threatened to jiggle from the shelves. She whirled when something scraped the front door.

"Git on there!" came a yell from outside. A horse snorted.

Through the unshuttered window Ellen could see the torso of a rider. She held her breath and rushed to the window. *Is this what I envisioned?* The horse leaped out of sight, its rider still aboard. She barged around the small table and to the north window. Dust obscured the animals and riders so they blended into a thick undulating ribbon of brown. The shuddering force of cattle subdued to the mere thunderous sound of them on the earthen road.

Dust haze hung in the room, tingeing all the merchandise with tannish powder. Ellen turned away from the window. Reed Carter stood at the end of the service counter with a sheet of paper. He looked up from reading it.

"This was on the floor," he said, handing it out to her. "It brushed off the table when you went to the window."

Ellen edged by the table and took the paper, her heart pounding. "Thank you."

What must he think of me? she thought. Ghoulishly writing details of a murder.

She slid the paper into the back of the ledger and carried it and her writing supplies to the shelf behind the service counter.

Reed had started for the back door. "I wonder how the others are faring." Ellen gave a useless swipe to her dusty dress and followed him outside.

Tan fog hung on the air. Cattle continued to trot, thirty or more abreast, up the road. Ellen's father, a yellow bandanna tied around his nose and lower face, was near the Jarvis barn with a blanket to wave off the cattle that swerved toward the yard. The milk cow mooed while the horses snorted and trotted restlessly around the paddock. The piglets squealed and chased at each other.

Ellen hurried to the north side of the store, Reed keeping pace with long strides. From there she could see the Clayton children standing on the grassy roof of their dugout. They jumped excitedly and hollered, although Ellen couldn't hear them over the noise of the herd. Pitt was there, too, and Reba. Behind them, a bedraggled Rose Schaffner was angrily shaking her parasol at Dillard Winslow. Looking north, Tim's barn was barely visible through the dust, while on the other side of the road—across the moving mesh of high horns and dappled bodies—the cattle company tent and the striped awning of Reed's gambling set up was faint on the rise.

Men walked their mud-streaked horses along the edges of the moving herd; their caps and trousers were dingy remnants of Confederate uniforms. Most wore brogans—a few, cavalry boots. Wool jackets were stained with the red-orange dirt from The Nations; big bandannas protected their noses against the dust.

"After all that fighting," Reed muttered. "Looks like Kansas has finally been invaded by Rebels."

Ellen glanced at him with surprise, having assumed his southern accent identified his loyalties during the war. Although, as she considered that, she remembered that the people in the settlement he seemed most sociable with were the Mercys. That certainly wasn't in keeping with southern temperament. Unmindful of Ellen's perusal, Reed had started toward Tim's, which was parallel to his tent, to wait a chance to cross the continuing stream of Texas beeves and get to what he owned.

Nothing is ever what it seems, Ellen thought, suddenly troubled by the ease with which she had formed her opinions. Not my dreams, not my life. Is there anything that is certain?

5

*E*llen walked across the road between the dugout and the store, taking slow steps to accommodate two-year-old George Clayton. Behind them, came the clank of Reba's cooking utensils and Olive whining about something. A new sound made Ellen look up.

"Lookee, Aunt Ellen!" George said, stopping to stare. Five riders galloped their horses toward them.

Ellen yanked George off the ground and into her arms. She ran for the store front.

"Waaah heee!" came a cry from one of the racing horsemen.

The ground trembled and the wind of the passing animals wafted Ellen's skirt hem. Something plucked at her braid as she leaped to the porch, George clutched in her arms. Looking back, she saw the riders pull up at the steep decline that led to the Bluff River. They turned their horses, laughing, and one rider was grinning at her. He trotted his horse back to the store as she stood George on the porch.

"Almost got you there, purty lady," the young man said from horseback. He looked to be the age of her brother Spencer. His blondish hair was lank and unkempt to his shirt collar, and a hint of beard covered his long jaw. "That's a good lookin' head of hair you got, Missy. Bet the Injuns eye your scalp a plenty, but I'm eyein' more than that." He snuffled a laugh and shifted the suspenders over his sweaty blue shirt.

Ellen turned abruptly and stalked into the store, forcing a reluctant George along with her. "Pop was right," she said to her mother. Belinda sat in the cane-bottom chair near the north-side window mending a pair of Pitt's trousers. "The night herders didn't bother to sleep, just rode on in here."

"I didn't expect them this early," Belinda said. "The sun's barely topped the trees."

"It's a good thing Pop and Pitt repaired the hitching rail and porch support last night."

"Pitt's still complaining about that—how he had wanted to be out at the cow camp talking to the drovers."

"Would Pop have let him go?" Ellen asked as she settled George in a small chair with a slate board and piece of chalk.

"I doubt it." Belinda chuckled. "But your insisting that those rails needed to be fixed kept it from coming up."

Her father came up the stairs from the back, carrying a wide wooden crate filled with canned goods. "This is the end of it," he said, setting it on the floor near the counter.

Pitt came in behind him. "Well, can I, Pop?" Pitt was asking as he set down a keg of nails. Her father and brother had worked steadily since breakfast to get the rest of the merchandise out of the freight wagon. "You haven't answered yet."

Matthew straightened. "I answered this question way last fall, Pitt. You are not riding with any cattle drive."

"But Baxter needs the help," Pitt argued. "And what could happen between here and Abilene?"

"Lots of things," Matthew stated.

"The weather could get ugly and rustlers could attack and steal the herd," Belinda put in.

"Rustlers. Uh!" Pitt shoved at a crate with his foot. "This is gonna be an awful time unless Ellen can dream up some more dead men."

"You hush with that talk!" Belinda's vehemence singed the air.

Ellen bit her lip, there it was again, that hostility—that anger at her because of her dreams. Anger—and some fear, too, Ellen had recently decided.

"Go get the tools together, Pitt," Matthew instructed. Pitt stomped out the back.

Ellen recorded some items in the ledger, gripping the pen, waiting for the tension to recede from the room. George toddled past her father to investigate the crate.

"I can't believe you moved so much in yourself, Ellen," her father said, ignoring the harsh moment. "Why didn't you wait?"

"The store needed to be ready," Ellen said obstinately. She fingered the tie on her dark scarf, wishing she didn't sound so defensive.

"I knew no one would come in here until today," Belinda said, pleasant after her angry tone with Pitt.

"I sold a sack of grain yesterday. And if that man had come in and seen the store sparsely furnished, chances are no one would have come in today." Inside she was tight, hating this charade—this "let's pretend everything is normal"—when her very presence seemed to cause friction and unrest.

"Well, no one's come in yet as it is," Belinda said.

"It looks like they're all headed for Reba's," Matthew said, looking out of the open front door.

"The cook with the trail herd has been sick and hasn't fixed a decent meal in days," Ellen told them. "Several of the drovers are down with it, and last night, Lutecia told me she would go out today with some recipes to ease their symptoms." Ellen had visited the Mercy cabin at dusk, to learn if they had procured any calves from the cattle drive. The trail boss had given Charles three springers (one was a bull) and they purchased two weak yearlings.

"I hope she charges them and doesn't give away her services," Belinda said.

"She thinks of healing as more of a duty than a service," Ellen said. "But I agree, she should charge a bit of something. The time it takes her to collect and store herbs, then to make the tonics has a value beyond duty." She rocked a blotter across her ledger entry.

"Luke told me that the drovers' big horse herd had been forded farther to the west and ran through a part of the their cornfield." Matthew said.

"Rose and Nancy suffered too," Belinda said. She lowered her sewing and laughed. "I wish I could have seen that! The buckboard hit by those cattle. Pitt said Rose was furious. Then Reba was mad when Luke ran to their aid and helped them get behind the stone fence."

Dust had been so heavy, Ellen hadn't witnessed the event.

Matthew chuckled. "That's the last thing Reba wanted, to be standing there with two strumpets."

"They could have really been hurt!" Ellen said. "The best part was that Winslow's sign got trampled into the dust. I doubt any of the herders saw it."

"The back axle on the buckboard was broken, too," Matthew said, heading for the back entrance. He lifted George from behind the counter and sat him back in the chair with the slate. "I'm going on out to the field," Matthew said. "Pitt should have the tools together by now."

"I'll be out soon," Belinda called.

Ellen eyed the stacks of merchandise brought in that morning, then checked items from the receipt before she wrote descriptions in the ledger with a selling price.

"More cloth? Oh, Mother," Ellen complained as she carried a bolt of sky blue moreen to the rack of fabrics on the back wall. Not enough women visited the store to make it worth displaying fabrics, but Belinda always returned from a buying trip with a few more bolts.

"I wonder if Pretty Willow will be by soon," Belinda said. "She was going to have some leather goods to barter."

"She promised me a pair of moccasins since I showed her how to make sourdough starter," Ellen recalled. "Moccasins with beadwork, like that purse I traded her for."

"I don't know how she does that with the beads. Oh, I brought some back; two shades of yellow and blue. I remember you told me blue was hard to come by."

"That's what she told me when she and Riding Boy were last here." Their conversation provoked a sudden disquiet in her. She felt a headache coming on.

Three strangers drifted in, their hard boots clunking heavily on the plank flooring. Dusty shirts, canvas pants, tired eyes. Their expressions brightening when they saw George. "Hey there, little tyke!" one said.

Another stooped before George and ruffled his dark hair. "What's your name?" he asked.

"George," was the boy's timid answer. The men played a bit with the youngster, smiling deeply.

Probably have children at home they miss, Ellen thought, watching them. Families and wives. *I hope they get home safely.*

The men bought essentials (tobacco and wrapping papers, black powder and collodion), and a copy of the *Overland Monthly* and the week-old newspaper from Abilene her parents had brought from Eldorado. They browsed the store, touching their grimy hat brims to Belinda and Ellen. "Thank you, ma'am," they mumbled before they left.

"Bye," George called, waving to them. "Bye-ee!"

Through the window Ellen watched them cross the road to the bench table under the brush arbor by the Clayton dugout. Seven year-old Olive skipped over to get their order, and Ellen returned to her ledger.

"Mama." She studied an invoice. "I noticed this yesterday. You only got half as much of everything as I had written down. Are items being shipped later?"

"Um? Oh, no. I just didn't think we needed all of that."

"But we talked about it before you left. Even Pop agreed that this was the time to lay up goods, with the cattle drives and all. Are we—" Ellen walked over to her mother. "There isn't a problem, is there, with money?" She had maintained the ledger and everything seemed to balance out. She was good with numbers, and had even kept careful records for the postmaster when she taught in Ottawa County. She had boarded at his house, taught three of his five children, helped his wife with laundry; yet he had still considered it part of her duties to do some of his work, too.

"Of course not, dear," Belinda shook her head. "We barely have any expenses, living here self-sufficient as we are."

Ellen sighed.

George had his face pressed on the glass of the side window, making steamy lip marks, his little hands leaving small fingerprints on the pane. As she moved him away, Ellen noticed several men clustered under Reed Carter's striped awning. The gambling had been steady since yesterday evening. The cattle company tent also showed activity.

"That's interesting," Ellen said. "Someone's at the cattle company tent."

"Really? I wonder if it's the fellow on that good looking chestnut with a wide blaze. I noticed him at Tim's when I was coming to the store. Spencer would certainly approve of that animal." Belinda re-threaded the needle. "Spencer should be back from mustanging before long," she said of her son.

Ellen's headache intensified. She refocused George's energies on a family of sock puppets she kept in a basket near the door and went back to the ledger.

"I must say things are fast changing around here this year," Belinda said. "We just left five days ago, and come back to a new business in place, people moving in. It's all so sudden!"

"And gruesome, with these murders so soon after they arrived," Ellen said, penning in a figure.

"What?" Belinda asked.

"They arrive one day. Mr. Stone is killed the next."

Her mother's stare made her feel edgy. Ellen frowned at her. "What?"

"Ellen, you really spend too much time with all this," her mother stated. The abruptness of her words seemed to smack Ellen in the face.

"Too much time with what?" Ellen asked, cautious.

"The store, all this ledger work." Belinda waved her hand as if shooing away a fly. "It will take care of itself. It always has."

"It's something for me to do."

"Well, once Spencer gets back, he can help your father in the fields and I can spend more time here," Belinda said. "That will give you a chance to sew up some nice dresses that you can use at college."

"Is that why you keep buying material?" Ellen asked.

"It's more than that, dear," Belinda went on. "You need to—
to brighten your wardrobe. You've been wearing these same drab
clothes for so long now."

"Mother, I—"

"I know. You're in mourning." Belinda angrily tossed aside
the sewing. "You'd think you were some Philadelphia matron under
scrutiny from protocol-bent neighbors. You've mourned Johnny for
longer than you two were married. Somber clothes, that horrid
blue scarf. Don't you think enough is enough?"

"You never did like him," Ellen stated. She laid her hand flat
on the ledger, pressing her fingers out to keep them from trembling.

"That's not true. Johnny was a very personable young man.
And *my* thoughts weren't what mattered. But Ellen, you can't dwell
on what's lost. You have to go forward and stop grubbing around
like some martyred woman twice your age."

"Martyred," Ellen repeated, the word sounding odd to her.

"Now, I told the Eldorado postmaster to have our mail
forwarded from Emporia," Belinda went on. "College information
should be coming soon, and county offices are going to be getting
their teachers lined up now for the fall. They'll be contacting you,
too."

"I don't want anything to come," Ellen said, her voice flat in
the large room. "I don't want to teach," she said more strongly.

"So go to college; get your four-year degree; that will give
you so many options. You'll feel differently after—"

"You aren't listening, Ma. I don't want to teach, and I'm not
too sure about this college idea. It sounds so lonely!"

Belinda gave her a quizzical look that made Ellen hope for
comment. But her mother closed her eyes and rubbed her fingers
on the smooth skin over her nose. Expectation ebbed from Ellen,
even as Belinda came over and put her arm around Ellen's shoulders.

"Ellen. Dear," Belinda began.

The embrace pulled a chink out of Ellen's protective stoicism.
"Ma, it was so awful." Words crowded in Ellen's head—her fears
and guilt about Johnny's death. "I—I didn't want it to happen!"

"Of course not, dear."

"I kept wanting to say something, but afraid—afraid of what he would think, of the craziness of it all."

Belinda stepped to the porcelain pitcher kept on the low wall shelf and poured a cup of water. Ellen noticed the tight, pinched look on her mother's face. Age lines, usually unnoticed in Belinda's normally cheerful demeanor, were etched between her brows and around her mouth. Ellen took the cup, sipped water. It seemed to knot in her throat; she forced a swallow. Keep talking, she urged herself. Tell her about the confusion that seems to be in my every thought. Maybe then—

Belinda went to the table and pushed the sewing to the center. She was done with it. She was done with the conversation. "I guess the future is like the store. It will take care of itself."

"But what about the past? What I knew and didn't act on?" Ellen's voice had no more substance than a moth's wing.

"I'm going to take some water out to your father and Pitt," Belinda said, lifting her hat from the wall peg.

They're working a stone's throw from Fall Creek. Why would they need water? Ellen set down the cup.

"I'm sure breaking that potato field has them really sweating by now." Belinda continued.

Ellen frowned straight ahead, her throat hurting and a sting of tears behind her eyes.

"Georgie, are you coming with me?" Belinda asked, singsong the way she usually did not talk to children.

"I stay with Aunt Ellen," the child replied. He was building a tower of cans behind the counter, his chubby hands carefully stacking a rounded wall.

"Ring the big bell if you need help," Belinda said, going down the stairs to the back door.

Ellen listened to the solid *whump* of the door closing, and then the gentle *click click* of George stacking cans. She wiped at her eyes with shaky fingers and pinched her lips together. I'm an adult. I don't need her reassurance for something I can't even explain, she silently insisted. I can manage this! She turned her attention back to the ledger. *Keep working.* She inventoried jars of cream of tartar, vinegar, lead dippers, tins of soda crackers. *I will get past this. I just need time.* She rubbed her fingers along the soft blue scarf. ("That horrid blue scarf," her mother had said.)

Ellen shook her head. Just a little more time, she thought. *And some answers,* came a nagging. *If only I could talk with the Hargroves!* She wondered if they would ever answer her letters.

Shaking herself from the distressing thoughts, she studied the ledger, noticing the edge of loose paper. Pulling it free, she recognized her notes on the murder. She frowned, recalling how Reed Carter had picked up this paper—had studied it, or so it seemed. The room had been dim with dust moats swirling. He had handed her the paper and then headed for the back door, barely making mention. With all the questions he'd previously had for her, his lack of comment seemed odd.

She re-read the brief notes she had made, and penned a new line. *People at the settlement. Claytons, Mercys, Misters Fykes and Blankenship.* She paused, wondering again where Nancy and Rose had been, and Mr. Winslow. It was raining, she remembered. They had probably been in their dry tents and felt no need to venture into the damp weather. Then Reed Carter had come down—ridden down on his horse. She recalled the steam rising from the animal. Where had he come from? she wondered. Certainly not just from his camp site.

She twiddled the pen between her fingers, feeling perturbed. She had just started to think nicely of the gambler. Had enjoyed their banter on the porch before the cattle drive arrived. His pleasant, dimpled smile came to mind. And then his haste to leave the store after he handed her this paper. She shook her head. She'd have to ask Lutecia about him. She looked again at the page and wrote, *Reed Carter????*

"Boom!" George exclaimed, pushing over part of the wall of cans he had made.

"Oh, George, you startled me." Ellen put her hand to her throat, amazed by how preoccupied she had become.

"Boom!" George pushed the rest over and held up his hands, laughing. Air tights rolled against Ellen's feet and George scrambled after them.

"Here now, I have to put those up," she told the youngster who crawled around her skirt hem. After scooping him into one arm, she made her way to the far end of the counter, kicking a few cans as she went. "You play with these awhile." She sat him on the floor and handed him a burlap sack filled with smaller bags.

"I wanna see." George declared, instantly mesmerized. He burrowed into the bag, intent on finding something unique.

Once the boy was settled, Ellen capped the ink jar, slid the paper back into the ledger and started picking up disarray of air tights filled with fruits and vegetables. As she placed them on the shelf, she heard someone on the porch and turned. She cocked her head and squinted, because a blur seemed to hide the features of whoever was there. "Yes?" she said. A strange noise came to her and she saw a squirming black and white puppy suspended in front of the darkness.

"It was whining outside the door. I hope you don't mind my bringing it in," said a deep male voice.

He had a smooth southern accent, this man—this blur. She frowned, still unable to make out his features.

"Woofer!" George cried, running around the counter.

"Here you go." The man bent to George, gave him the puppy, and then stood up.

There! He had a face. Ellen drew a sharp breath. She jerked her attention back to the cans she held.

"Fykes up at the livery told me what you did," the man said. "That was quite good of you to bring poor Francis back to civilization."

She had to look at him. It was only polite, but— "Only common decency, sir." Dark brown hair waving over his shirt collar, lean face, eyes deep brown—deep set. Her hand shook as she set down the cans.

He studied her without smiling. "I'm James Montgomery. Stone's partner in the cattle company."

Ellen nodded, refusing to extend her hand to this man—this murderer! She gripped the edge of the counter, swallowing down that incredible thought.

"It was quite a shock when I rode in this morning and learned Francis was gone. And so brutally, too. Damn Indians. Did you actually see them out there?"

George and the puppy scurried behind her, tipping a sack of middling flour. She grabbed the sack, grateful it wasn't open. George kicked at the puppy. It yipped. Ellen picked up the boy, glad to feel his warmth against her. She licked her lips and reprimanded her thoughts. *Just because this man's face was hovering in the death dream doesn't mean he killed Mr. Stone.*

"It was quite a shock," she managed to get out. She dared another glance at James Montgomery while bouncing George in her arms to keep him from wriggling down.

"Did you see any Indians?" Montgomery asked again.

"No. No, Indians. I didn't see any. Not anyone at all," she stammered.

"I've heard your family is on good terms with the locals." Montgomery glanced at the new display of combs, toothbrushes and razors in the glass-fronted cabinet. He bent closer to study the knives Tim had for sale. In a cavalry-style belt, he wore a gun—a thong loop over the hammer. Beside that, strapped tightly along his left hip, was a long, knife sheath. The scrimshaw handle of the weapon touched the edge of his short leather vest.

Ellen stood George on the floor, shocked by the weapon. Mr. Stone's mutilated hand, his slit throat, came unbidden to her mind.

Montgomery straightened. "Well, I just came to thank you again for your decency," Montgomery drawled—a different sound from Luke Clayton's Arkansas twang or Reed Carter's inflections— lazier, Ellen decided; from deeper south. He smiled and touched his fingers to the flat brim of his low crown hat. "And I'm sorry to have disturbed you with unpleasantries." He looked at her a brief moment, or at least Ellen thought he did. She couldn't be sure because his face was again oddly obscured. She heard him say,

"Afternoon, Ma'am." She watched the blur move away from the counter, heard his steps on the porch.

Ellen's breath came shakily after the man left. She wanted to close the door, but the day was already too warm for that. She couldn't rid her thoughts of how that man had at first seemed only a dark blur, then became a face—*the* face. Hard cruel eyes, then a blur again. James Montgomery. She bit her lip as shock and fear filled her. She had seen the actual person from her horrible dream! He was real. He was here! She took up the cup of water her mother had poured for her and sipped the tepid liquid while forcing her trembling to subside.

The room held a strange quiet. Ellen set down the cup. George was missing. "George?" she called. Silence. She scanned the store, then looked outside. Not seeing him, she began a thorough perusal of the store, and after a few minutes found George asleep under the table of overalls, his arm across the fat puppy. She smiled and shook her head at his ease of repose. She put a folded apron under his head for a pillow, wishing she could become as oblivious to her surroundings.

Woofer squirmed loose and started prancing around her feet. Ellen set the puppy outside, forcing herself not to look up the hill. Yet as she finished the inventory, she knew exactly where James Montgomery was. She could look through the window and see that man-sized column of darkness often at the cattle company tent, then once by the livery. The sun climbed near its apex, increasing the heat. She stood in the doorway to get a breeze and noticed the dark blur moving from the little tents behind the hotel toward Reed Carter's place. "James Montgomery," she muttered, correcting her perception. "A man, not a dark blur." Did he already know Rose and Nancy? she wondered. Reed Carter?

She sat down with the sewing her mother had left and finished the britches for Pitt before two other customers came in—both from the cattle drive, both polite. Not long after that, George awakened, bouncy and rambunctious after sleeping nearly two hours. She herded him to the chamber pot in the back room before taking him across to the Claytons' side of the road.

"He getting on your nerves?" Reba asked, her voice weary, although it wasn't much past noon. The long sleeves of her cotton dress were pushed above her elbows while she washed dishes in a galvanized tub. Olive smeared the items dry with a piece of bleached flour sack.

"No. He's fine company," Ellen said. "And he took his morning nap already. How are you doing?"

"I don't know. Luke's planning to find out if Mr. Stone's dying will change plans for a town. That hotel would have been the ticket." She shook suds off a plate and handed it to Olive. "You know, these men et seven whole chickens for breakfast, I tell you! Plus biscuits and hominy. We could make a lot of money if things was set up right."

"You should have a restaurant, not a hotel," Ellen said.

"You think so?" Reba brightened, smiling at her. "A restaurant?"

"You like to cook good enough," Olive piped.

"But you really see us with a restaurant?" Reba asked.

Ellen pinched her lips together, knowing what Reba meant when she said "see."

"I'll just take George on a little walk with me," she said, ignoring Reba's question. "Keep him out of your hair."

"That's right helpful, Ellen. But then he takes to you a heap. That'll keep him from wanting to go with Olive to get more fuel."

"Aw, Ma!" Olive complained. "I hate gettin' cow chips!"

"Nobody likes it, but it's got to be done," Reba said to her daughter.

Ellen pulled George's hand to keep him from eating a beetle when loud voices smacked sharply on the air.

"Great Heavens, what's going on," Reba stared up the road, arms akimbo.

"Looks like a fight!" Olive declared, staring toward the striped awning.

Because of the distance, Ellen couldn't tell who was involved. Tim rode a horse over to investigate; she made out Dillard Winslow standing nearby.

"That Mr. Carter was probably cheatin' at cards," Reba grumbled.

"Reba, why would you say that?" Ellen asked.

"He's a gambler."

"That doesn't mean he's cheating."

"Gamblers are shifty con men. He's probably what got Winslow and those shady ladies down here." Reba sniffed disparagingly. "If I was you, Ellen, I wouldn't keep talking to him like you're doing."

"Oh, Reba!" Ellen looked up the slope, wanting to say more—to defend Reed. But what did she really know about him? Nothing. She picked up George, his closeness a comfort, and noticed something moving toward the striped-awning—a darkness, a moving obscurity. *No, a man. James Montgomery.*

The men's voices came as harsh barks over the distance and then it was over. A red-shirted figure hurried to a horse and rode across Fall Creek toward the cow camp. The others wandered away. All except one other. The blur—Montgomery. He suddenly appeared to her in normal form. He was facing toward where she stood with Reba and the children. Ellen drew a quick breath, because even from that distance she could tell he was staring directly at her.

Why? Who is he?

A killer, came her recurring thought. She flinched.

His very presence provoked the Sycamore Spring scene to her again and again. The persistence tossed her from chills of fear to hot flushes of self-consciousness. I'm imagining it all, she berated herself even as the certainty of this man as a killer wouldn't leave her.

That night:

Horses running. Gunshots. A dark face looms over her—cruel eyes stabbing at her like knife points. Then two men grapple, whirling in bright splotches of color. A blade flashes.

No!

Ellen jolted up in her bed, perspiration sticking her bedclothes to her. The house was silent, while outside came the *oo-oo-whoo* of an owl. A whippoorwill raced its song steadily from the tree outside, answered by another in the woods north of Fall Creek. No moon. She heard Pitt's steady breathing from his bed on the other side of the canvas wall. Carefully she bunched her pillow under her head and right shoulder and stared toward the curtain partition. Sleep was long in returning.

6

*E*llen combed her hair, neatly plaiting two braids and pinning them across the back of her head. She felt good—ready for this day. The fears that mushroomed in her two days ago seemed all for naught. Yesterday, James Montgomery had appeared as a normal person when he came into the store—no blurring, no dark aura. He was courteous and didn't ask a thing about Mr. Stone's murder as he bought cornmeal, liniment and three tins of tomatoes. Ellen held her breath nearly the whole time he was there, certain she would look up and see him distorted, but it didn't happen. As the day progressed, she occasionally recognized the man moving into and out of the cattle company tent. She began to relax, quite willing to dismiss her previous grim assessment of James Montgomery. Her sleep that night was undisturbed by any dreams she could remember.

Now she took up her blue scarf, recalling her mother's words, *You're like some martyred woman…* A martyr to what? What was she giving her life to and was it worth it? Carefully she straightened the scarf and placed it across her neck, around the high collar of her brown blouse, tying it in a loose knot over the bodice. "A little while longer," she muttered.

Outside, her father made a final check on the plow lines attached to workhorse Bob. Wind gusted dust swirls around them. Pitt glowered from where he stood at the side of the plow, a pick ax and shovel propped in the wheelbarrow he held. Meadowlarks whistled melodies through the clearing.

Belinda came from the main cabin, dressed for work. "We'll be back in at noon. Ring the bell if you need us." She put her hand to Ellen's cheek, studying her for a moment, then gave her a quick kiss, before turning to join the others.

Why can't we talk? Ellen wondered. Why can't we communicate?

Back in the cabin, Ellen soaked parched corn for later and turned her energies to housekeeping, sweeping out the main room with vigorous strokes of the broom. She wondered when Spencer would return. It had been two weeks since he left with Hubert Fykes on the mustanging trip. Hubert, nearly twenty-two, knew the ropes from going out with his father. Spencer hoped to catch a string of horses he could have for his own.

After her wedding, Spencer and Johnny talked about owning a ranch. "Got to use the land to feed stock, not plow it up to try and grow back-east vegetables and crops," Johnny often grumbled while he and Ellen helped harvest his parents' fields. "I'll build us a great place, Ellen," he declared. "Spencer will handle the horses, and I'll run the cattle." He had spoken often of this in his letters, too.

Is that why he had gone off to move cattle? she wondered. To earn money, to build a "great place?" She winced from pain of the memories. *Have to stop thinking on it.*

To turn her thoughts, she tried to imagine what her brother and Hubert Fykes were doing. Spencer, where are you? she thought, gripping the broom handle while she concentrated. Conjure, is how Lutecia would put it. Ellen didn't like that term; you needed magic spells to conjure something, or you had to chant odd words. She didn't conjure. In fact, when she tried to get a feeling for any particular situation, like now, she felt almost blank. Then when she least suspected the images would come—dreams, wake and sleep, flashing precise images to her.

Wind buffeted the house. A windowpane rattled and Ellen stepped back with shock on seeing a face at the window. She recognized Dillard Winslow, the panderer with the prostitutes. He peered through the window, a dark cheroot in his thin-lipped mouth. Alarmed, Ellen opened the door and confronted the man who was brazen enough to enter the dogtrot.

"What are you doing back here?" she challenged the scrawny man. Although his suit jacket and plaid pants squeezed his arms and legs, they appeared to be made for someone even smaller than he. He needed a shave and the gray stubble made his face look dirty.

"Are you planning on opening the store today, or are you just gonna stand around starin' off to nothin'?" he asked, fumbling in the pocket of his dingy broadcloth vest. He drew out a sulfur match.

"There's a bell at the store. You should have rung it."

"Now don't get all riled, Mrs. Hargrove," he grinned.

"You can wait on the store porch, Mr. Winslow."

"And how long will I have to wait?" he asked.

"I'll be there in a minute," Ellen replied. She wanted to berate the man for his impertinence of coming to the house, but he was a customer, after all; she would be civil.

Winslow struck the match and cupped his hand around it to light the cheroot before he moved slowly away. Ellen waited until he had cleared the yard and only then did she realize she was holding the broom, handle end forward, as if it were a rifle. She propped it along the wall, worried about how the area had changed. *So many strangers.* She took the store key from the hook on the kitchen wall, pulled on her straw hat and went back out.

Lutecia stood just inside the dogtrot. "What did he want?" she asked. Her hair was tightly plaited and pinned in place under a narrow rose-colored wrap of cloth. The material brought out the red in her tan skin. "I saw him back here, looking things over a good ten minutes ago." A heavy army revolver hung in her hand.

"He wants me to open the store," Ellen said. The wind whipped her skirt around her legs.

"I'll walk with you. I'm on my way to Reba's anyway." They started off. "And how about other things?" Lutecia asked. "You be all right?"

Ellen stuffed her hands into her apron pockets and forced a smile. "Fine," she said. She was grateful she hadn't told Lutecia about James Montgomery's appearance. It had all been a mistake. Part of her martyred perceptions, perhaps. Lutecia studied her a moment. " Really, Lu, I'm fine," Ellen insisted.

"Here." Lutecia handed her the revolver when they reached
the back of the store. Ellen took the odd revolver. The Pettingill
had no hammer; just pulling the trigger made it fire. Lutecia kept
on toward the Claytons.

Ellen unlocked the back door of the store, and while walking
across the broad room, could see through the front windows. Of
the two horses tied at the new hitching rail, one was a chestnut with
a blaze face she knew belonged to Montgomery. She took off her
hat and laid it on the counter. Even with her new decisions about
the man, her hands shook as she went to the door, swung up the
bar latch and opened it. Winslow stood on the porch along with
Mr. Baxter, the trail boss of the cattle drive, and James Montgomery.

"I think we've already survived most of the risks," Baxter was
saying to Montgomery as they entered the store.

"But there are quarantines to consider," Montgomery said.

"He's right about that," Winslow put in. "Don't need none of
your Texas splenic fever in Kansas."

"I drove these cattle through a late blizzard. Couldn't be a
tick left on 'em after that," Baxter said. He took off his slope-
brimmed hat which was soiled with sweat and faded from black to
dark gray. "I'm looking for at least twenty dollars per head." Ellen
walked behind the sales counter and laid the revolver on top, in
easy reach. "No, Montgomery. We'll see the herd on through
ourselves, thank you," Baxter said, pulling at the side of his graying
mustache.

Winslow tossed coins on the counter. "Gimme two pounds of
sowbelly and a half a pound of sugar."

Montgomery and Baxter proceeded with an amiable
conversation about trails and rivers to the south. Ellen got the salt
pork, wrapped it. On the big hanging scale, she weighed the tin
Winslow had with him and then scooped the sugar into it, all the
while very conscious of James Montgomery's presence although
nothing unseemly occurred.

"I wish I'd pulled out this morning, the way the weather feels,"
Baxter was saying. "That's why I came up here, to ask Mrs. Hargrove
about it."

Ellen frowned at the man as she gave Winslow change.

"I understand from Tim Fykes you have a ken for the weather," Baxter continued.

Ellen tried not to show her dismay at being so identified and wondered if the man were mocking her. "Well, anyone who has lived a while in this land can try a guess," she responded.

"It's steamy out there, even with the wind, and looks like a storm down southwest of here. What do you think?" Baxter asked, his gray eyes serious.

"I say probably a cyclone," Winslow said. "They get 'em down this part some time."

Ellen suddenly sensed turbulence and trouble. She looked out of the side window. Don't think about it; don't see anything else! she ordered her mind. "Tornadoes would hit down in The Nations, most likely," she said turning back to the men. "There might be some hard rain, though, going north."

"Is that an educated guess, ma'am? Or more?" Baxter leaned on the counter. "Fykes says you've a history of some way out unusual predictions, like this cattle dealer gettin' killed and all."

"You predicted Stone's death?" Montgomery asked, his eyes wide with amazement.

Ellen's stomach fluttered. "No sir, not predicted. I just—" She darted another look at James Montgomery, seeing instead the image of his face hovered over Sycamore Spring. Dizziness hit her.

Winslow's voice cut in. "I heard that stuff, too, and can't for the life of me see how a little slip of a gal can get everybody all confounded."

Ellen felt out of breath and weightless. The conversation swirled around her like a bad dream.

"You're sure Fykes wasn't talking about that auntie?" Montgomery asked Baxter. "Nigras like to talk themselves up as having pre-knowledge." He wiped at his sweaty neck with a bandanna.

"Lutecia Mercy? Naw," Baxter responded. "That's not a name I'd confuse with Hargrove, especially with her doing so good at relieving the ails of my herd boys."

Francis Stone's slashed body crowded Ellen's mind. She glanced at Montgomery's waist. The knife he wore two days ago was gone.

"That colored woman does know herbs," Winslow said with a nod.

"But *you* knew about Francis's death?" Montgomery leaned on the counter, his brown eyes scanning Ellen with acute interest. Ellen's pulse jumped in her throat. The man's cheek twitched at the corner of his mouth.

Or did she imagine that? She pushed the packages toward Winslow and searched for words.

"What chu a-thinkin', Montgomery," Winslow chuckled. "That this Hargrove gal could tell ya how many beeves you'll take to market by August? I swear, she looks like she's havin' some sort of spell right now."

"Shut up, man," Montgomery snapped.

"Who you think you are, a-givin' me orders!"

"Just get out of here," Montgomery said, glowering at Winslow.

Ellen, her face hot, hoped he *would* leave—that they all would leave. Winslow hesitated a moment and chewed on his cheroot before grabbing up his packages and stalking out.

Montgomery smiled at Ellen, standing straight, his hands lightly on the edge of the counter. "Did you just get an idea someone was dead out there, or did you see the Indians and everything?" he asked.

"Indians didn't kill Mr. Stone," she said, her voice stronger than she expected.

"Oh, really? Do you know who did?"

She didn't look at him. Her hands trembled. "You needed to make a purchase, Mr. Baxter?" Ellen asked.

Baxter seemed embarrassed. "Yes, ma'am. I'd like eight pounds of those Java beans you have."

Ellen was quick to get the coffee. She heard the scuffing of boots on the floor and gritted her teeth, not wanting to deal with another customer. A hard wind rattled the front windows of the store. Before she faced the counter again, Ellen pushed at her hair and worked to overcome renewed revulsion she felt for James Montgomery. But all for naught. The man was gone.

Mr. Baxter lingered after he paid for the coffee. "I'm sorry, ma'am, if I put you in a bad position, bringing up your predictions and all. Unlike those two, I got a fine respect for folks with the sixth sense, and I'm glad you don't feel I'm going to have to deal with a Kansas twister."

Ellen smoothed her hands across the counter top. "Mr. Baxter, no one can predict the workings of nature but the Almighty himself."

"That's true, Mrs. Hargrove. Quite true." Baxter put on his hat and took up the package. "Good day to you, ma'am, and my thanks for allowing us a good rest up here at your place."

She closed the door behind Baxter's departure and glanced through the window, clearly seeing Montgomery trot his handsome horse up the road toward the cattle company tent. A trembling and icy feeling swept her, and she drew several long breaths before taking up the ledger. Just the ritual of inking the pen nib, writing the information about the sales, blotting the ink, helped her regain her composure. She looked at what she had written and noticed the irregular bunching of the figures—she, who had always been complimented for penmanship. But here the five nearly looked like a three. She had put three ƀ in coffee.

She placed Lutecia's revolver into the large pocket of her apron, took up her straw hat, and left through the back door, locking it behind her. Rather than returning to the house, she walked to the paddock where the sow worked its big nose in the food trough. "I think four-leggeds are the only creatures I can talk to anymore." The sow grunted and glanced up at her. Ellen laughed unhappily at the pig's apparent interest in her words. "Here I had just convinced myself I was wrong about Mr. Montgomery, and then—" She shook her head. And then what? rebuked her thoughts. Nothing really happened. Conversation in the store had merely refreshed for her the gruesome murder scene.

And the face hovered over it. Montgomery's face.

She pinched her lips together. Was it Montgomery's face?

The store bell clanged and she turned, her pulse racing, hoping Montgomery hadn't returned with more questions about what she saw at the murder scene.

Olive Clayton came around the corner of the store with George lagging against her hand hold. "Hey, Miz Ellen," she called, walking toward the paddock. "Ma wants some sugar. We even got money to pay ya this time." Olive laughed a bit and hauled George into her skinny arms. The husky boy seemed to dwarf her.

"Was it you rang the bell?" Ellen asked, going to them. She looked toward the street, glanced up the road.

"Yes'm. Wasn't sure you heard it, though."

Ellen took George from Olive and he wrapped his arms around her neck. Warm, soft flesh of his cheek pressed onto hers. Ellen gave him a quick kiss and forced a smile. "Well, let's get that sugar!"

Once in the store, Ellen set George down and began store duties. She had just finished weighing and filling the sugar tin when she heard another customer enter. She took the tin off the scale, bracing for a baritone voice and more troubling questions.

"Hello, Mr. Carter," Olive said in her most proper voice.

"Hi there, Olive. Hi, Georgie," came Reed's friendly response.

The tension that had begun to knot inside her loosened a bit. She turned. "Is that it?" Ellen asked the bright-eyed girl who had taken George up again.

"Yes'm." The several coins she put on the counter summed to greater than the cost of the sugar. "Ma says to put this against our account."

"Certainly, Olive. Can you handle George and the tin, too?"

"Yes'm." She situated George on one small hip and gripped the tin in the circle of her other arm.

"Bye, Aunt Ellen!" George waved as Olive went down the three steps to the street. Ellen waved back, smiling.

"You allow accounts here?" Reed said.

"My mother started one for them last year," Ellen replied. She had been perturbed when she learned her mother never wrote anything down. Luckily, Reba was an honest woman and had kept track of the debits and payments.

Ellen penned figures into the ledger. Reed stood across from her. Ellen took a whisk broom and wiped crumbs of sugar from the counter. She pressed down the lid on the sugar barrel and checked the balance of the scale. "Was there something you needed?" Ellen asked. Something about his presence made her nervous. Perhaps because of the comments Reba expressed the other day.

"You know, when I was a boy I always thought it would be quite grand to have foreknowledge—to know in advance what things would happen and all."

"Mr. Carter, what is this about?" Ellen asked. *Why is Reed Carter so interested in my abilities?*

"Oh, I now know it's not like that. In fact I imagine it can be pretty awful at times." He frowned and then looked away. "When I was in college—"

"College?" Ellen's couldn't conceal her amazement. "I'm sorry. It's just that—"

He looked amused, then went on. "Anyway, I took a course in metaphysical psychology and almost changed my plan of study. But to do so would have meant changing colleges and family plans, and—" He traced his index finger along the grain in the countertop. "If I'd known what was going to happen—" He blew a stream of air through pursed lips. "I'm sorry." He held up his hands.

Ellen was stunned by the touch of sadness she heard. "So what did you study in college, besides metaphysical psychology?" She tried to imagine Reed Carter sitting in a classroom listening to lectures about mesmerism or stimulus reactions. The picture didn't fit.

"I have an engineering degree," he replied.

"Engineering," Ellen intoned.

Reed chuckled at her bafflement. "I know, that's a far cry from being a gambler. But this," He glanced out of the window toward his striped awning. "It's just a way to get by for a while." He seemed melancholy and distracted by personal thoughts.

What to say? Ellen wondered.

Reed straightened. "You have some shaving soap?" he asked.

"Yes. Of course." She got a tan bar from the side shelf.

"Thank you." He paid for it and started for the door. "I'm going to shave and then get a long sleep," he said. "Baxter had quite a lot of risk takers with his herd."

"Isn't gambling taking a risk?" she asked, walking behind him to secure the door after he left.

"Not really. The rules of the games always favor the house. It gives me an edge." He smiled and left the store.

So you see, Reba, he has no reason to cheat, came Ellen's quick thought. She gripped the door and pulled it closed, surprised by her silent defense of Reed Carter.

The day hadn't cooled much, and Ellen's skin felt sticky in the occasional gusts of warm wind. While leading the milk cow from its afternoon tether, she glanced up to where the last rays of the sun flared crimson and lavender on an indigo sky. She wished the light would last forever, to keep away the dark thoughts that hovered in her mind, brooding and heavy, like the clouds that darkened the western horizon. And to the south, a bunker of clouds formed a line as straight as a ruler twenty or so miles distant over BIT.

She put the cow into the fenced area with the horses and latched the gate. She had already tended Phineas, brushing her gelding and combing burs from his abundant mane and tail. Now she started to the house where her parents sat outside the cabin with Charles and Lutecia. Her father and Charles peered at a board spread between them on a nail keg. How they could see a checker board in this dusk was a mystery to Ellen, but they played inside or out until the stars shone, Charles biting down on his pipe that never seemed to be lit and her father going *um hum!* before each move. Whenever the settlement women made candles, her mother and Lutecia each dipped extras and called them the "gaming lights."

Dust swirled on the lane. Ellen gripped material in each fist to keep her skirt from billowing. When she passed the alders by the cistern and stepped into the yard, a coil of rope whizzed from the bushes and hit her right shoulder. She jerked, and another slapped at her left side.

"I almost got her!" came a young voice from the bushes.

Anger replaced Ellen's alarm. "Pitt Jarvis, you scared the waddin' out of me. "

The bushes crackled with movement. She heard giggling as the tossed ropes were dragged away. Ellen grabbed one of the ropes before it disappeared into the bushes, and moved hand-over-hand along the length until she had Pitt by the arm. She pulled him into the lane.

"What were you doing?" she demanded, keeping a grip on his shoulder. Her teacher's voice insisted on a response, but Pitt just stared at her as if she were a stranger.

"It's cattle drive stuff. We're practicing," Hestor said, coming into view.

Pitt shrugged from her grasp. "Yeah. Mr. Montgomery says really good drovers can throw a rope from their galloping horse and catch a bull by the tail."

"I'm going to get you by the tail if you toss things at me anymore!"

"You sound like my maw," Hestor laughed.

Ellen walked toward the house, her good mood souring. Pitt came along behind her, Hestor at his side.

"And Mr. Montgomery can get a big loop going—send it up in the air and sideways," Pitt said. As they neared the house, Pitt tried to twirl a loop but it flopped onto the dusty ground. "It looks real fine!"

"Really?" A chill skittered down Ellen's back.

"I saw him showing you this evening," Belinda said to Pitt from her chair near the dogtrot. The small butter churn set beside her, and she pressed a wooden paddle against the block of butter she held in a wooden mold. "It was fascinating, even at a distance."

"Fancy doings. Like in a circus," Lutecia said.

"I love circuses," Belinda exclaimed as she poured residual milk off of the butter.

Ellen sat on a broad, weathered stump next to Lutecia who bound thatch to a short wooden handle to make a whisk for clothes. Lutecia had completed a dozen of the objects and planned to sell them in the store. Ellen had already worked out the pricing and decided the store's small commission. With her elbows on her knees, chin in her hands, she watched her friend work.

"Hestor!" Reba's voice wafted to them from near the road. "Hestor, get on home!"

Hestor acted like he was deaf and tossed his circle of hemp. It flattened to a straight line.

"Hestor!" Luke's imperative got the boy moving. As he danced around his trailing rope, he yelled good-byes.

Charles gave an amused chuckle after Hestor was out of sight. "You heard how Luke's been badgering people about what businesses are going to come here?" He shook his head. "Luke and his town. He ought to go on off to one, instead of waiting for it to come here." He moved a checker piece.

"We're not too likely to get a town here, with the railroad moving east and west more than a hundred miles to the north of us," Matthew said. "Um hum!" He made a move.

"If there was a town here, what d'ya think they'd name it?" Pitt asked, fiddling with the rope. "Claytonville? Or maybe for you, Pop. Jarvis. Jarvis, Kansas."

"Places don't get named for the people who settle them," Ellen said.

"It's usually the government folks who get the honors," Lutecia added. "Like Atchison and Leavenworth."

"Even this county is named for a politician," Ellen went on. "Charles Sumner."

"A good man," Charles nodded.

"There's Grant County," Belinda put in.

"Grant'll probably be President if Congress impeaches Johnson," Matthew said. "Um hum. There!" Checkers clacked.

"Lincoln County," Belinda went on.

"Seems like all the big names are already given out." Pitt coiled the rope.

"And there still be more congressmen and senators," Lutecia said.

"Sure. Important people like Topeka, Emporia or Manhattan." Pitt's impish grin wasn't hidden by the dim evening light. "Who were they?"

Ellen couldn't keep from laughing at her brother's little joke. The others laughed, too. "All right, all right. You got us," Belinda declared.

"Well, I don't care what they call it, a town would be nice. Things to do!" Pitt started building a loop in the rope. "Mr. Fykes would own the livery. Mr. Mercy the stockyard, and we'd have us a big ol' store. There'd be blacksmiths and a stagecoach."

"And a real school you'd have to go to every day," Ellen reminded him.

"As your father said, Pitt, the times aren't right," Belinda said.

"I'm sure Mr. Montgomery sees that, too," Matthew said. "He seems a sensible man."

"A little scary with that big knife he wears," Ellen said.

"A Bowie?" Matthew asked.

"Nah. I'd remember if he had a fine toad sticker," Pitt declared.

"Stop with that slang," Belinda fussed.

"He doesn't wear a gun or knife or nothing," Pitt went on.

"But, he does!" Ellen insisted. "A knife with a carved ivory handle," Her voice became softer as her certainty drifted away. She hadn't seen a knife today when he was in the store. Had there really been a knife the first time she met him?

Pitt tossed a loop in Ellen's direction, almost encircling her head, but she ducked. "You see that? You see that?" he declared about his near catch.

"Lightning," came Belinda's quiet voice.

Ellen scanned the horizon, dreading lightning and looking for that angry red of a prairie fire. In winter, the gray-white clouds could mean a blizzard and in other seasons—who could tell? Rain? Hail? Maybe just wind that would roll across the flat land for days on end with ceaseless pressure. To the west where Belinda stared, clouds, low and solid, had blotted out the sunset. Even though the evening star jeweled the clear sky directly above them, the dark sky flickered gold and white, and distant thunder sounded like the heavy roll of far off drums.

"It's going to be bad," Belinda said. She took the filled butter mold to hang in a basket in the cool of the cistern. Pitt ran back to the barn to put the cow in its stall while Matthew went to the wagons to check the canvas tie downs. Ellen pulled chairs along the dogtrot and into the kitchen. Charles and Lutecia were already hurrying home. Southeast, a coyote cried its piteous yowl. A few others yipped and then were silent, leaving only a thin chirrup of crickets.

7

*R*ain started in less than an hour, moderate at first, but with increasing intensity during the night. By dawn, the dampness pervaded the bedroom where Ellen lay on her back, staring at the ceiling. Normally the sound of rain was numbing to her, and she could easily sleep out a storm. Today the sound merely reminded her how trapped she was. Her horseback ride of a few days ago seemed an enviable luxury. Amazing, she thought, how much you want to do something when it's an impossibility. But she wanted to be out in sunshine; to walk through a fragrant meadow listening to hawks and robins and tree frogs.

In the gray light, Ellen fumbled with matches and lit the thick candle by her bed. From the top of the trunk she took up the newspaper she had been reading the day before. Opened to the classifieds, she studied the meager listings again, wanting something to lurch forth and compel her interest. Her eyes strayed to the three-inch-square ad requesting homesteaders for Colorado Territory. It was a 5-year prove-up situation. She had a dab of money set aside from her tiny teacher's pay. *If Johnny were here, he'd jump at the chance. With what he'd saved last year, we would have had a good start on homesteading.*

A frown creased her forehead. Johnny had saved money. Where was it? she wondered. He had trapped in the Ozarks the winter before they were married. In his letters he had told about how well his lines were doing. She recalled the long tin box he kept behind a loose wall board at the top of their bed. She hadn't thought of it when Mr. Hargrove hastily packed her possessions into her buggy so he could send her home. The box hadn't occurred to her when she struggled with the appropriate words in the letters she sent to the Hargroves. Again she wished for sunshine rather than the torrent of rain that assaulted the settlement. If it were sunny, she would saddle Phineas, ride to the Hargroves, look for the tin box.

Ellen pulled herself from bed, wrapped a quilt around her shoulders, and went to the window that faced east. She sighed when she heard Pitt stir. No sunny day, and no privacy, either, she thought. Pitt stepped to the window, the canvas partition between them. Stanchions of lightning stabbed from the clouds, and heavy rumbles sounded from the south, as if the clouds had taken hoof and were stampeding.

"The Claytons' dugout is leaking by now," Ellen said to Pitt.

"Yeah, and our horses are probably in mud up to their fetlocks. Bet the river's roaring, too."

Ellen backed from the window, disturbed by all the moisture and thoughts of water rising in the Bluff. It reminded her of the swollen river that swept Johnny away.

If Johnny hadn't gotten married, Ellen often lamented. If he hadn't married me, he may not have felt the need to go on the cattle drive—embark on an attempt to build his own place. "Your family has such a rich life!" he often exclaimed. He had been fascinated by her parents' openness and willingness to seek something new.

Four times she had awakened with the real dream in her head: Johnny riding away into the swamp of cattle and getting sucked down, still smiling, still waving at her while the cattle turned to a rush of water. She had begged him not to go, and maybe if she had gone with him, or ridden down to meet him—to warn him.

Tears welled in her eyes. She lay back on the bed and willed herself to ignore this pain.

Rain.

They gathered in the kitchen and ate a meal of cold biscuits with jelly, and coffee. Ellen attempted sitting on a chair in the dogtrot, but the gusts of wind kept coating her with a fine mist. She went back to her bed—tried to sleep.

Thunder bumped, obscuring her heartbeat. The rain was intense and unending.

"We have to check the animals," came Belinda's sudden call as she knocked on the door.

"Now?" Ellen sat forward, frowning. She wasn't sure how much time had passed. The daylight outside hadn't changed—murky and wet.

Pitt roused from sleep on the bed beyond the partition. "It's pouring out!" he complained. "Why now?"

"Because it's pouring!" Belinda had to raise her voice to be heard over the furious thudding of rain on the roof. "Hurry!"

Their mother's last tone spurred Ellen and Pitt to action. Belinda rarely insisted on anything, and when she did, it was for a just cause. Pitt quickly shrugged into his oiled-canvas poncho and Ellen donned a canvas cape. Within minutes they joined their parents at the barn. Wind-driven rain slashed against them. Rivulets of rainwater sloshed over the brims of their hats. To the south was nothing but gray, moving air as rain fell.

"Grab a shovel, Son," Matthew said to Pitt as he dug a trench to divert a flow of ground water. "Help me get this away from the barn."

"The piglets!" Belinda called to Ellen from the barn door. "I'm making a place for them!"

The sow snorted a protest and stood stubbornly before the pool of water that had formed in the indent of her usual basking place. Six piglets huddled along the fence post near the sow's back legs. Six, where there should be seven. Ellen scanned the narrow sty and bit her lip when she saw the seventh pink creature unmoving, tiny snout covered with mud. Ellen slipped her way to it and stared. *I'm tired of finding dead things.*

"Oh, my God!" Belinda said when she came out of the barn. She hoisted two of the live babies by their back legs. "Get that one out of here before the sow decides to eat it." She whisked a third piglet off the ground.

Ellen's stomach rolled. She glanced at the big sow. It glared at her with no sign of the friendly look it seemed to have the previous day.

"Hurry up, Ellen. Help me move these others." Belinda started back to the barn, three little pigs dangling in her wet grasp.

A sudden shift of wind blew off Ellen's hood and she was instantly drenched and gasping for air in the rain. *Johnny flounders in the surging river of cattle—water—mud, flailing, crying out for help.* "No!" Ellen protested.

Thunder rolled and banged through the darkened sky, trembling the earth. The sow squealed—butted Ellen's legs. She grabbed the fence post for balance, shocked as the sow ran at the remaining babies; they scattered. The large pig turned back to the dead one. Ellen scooped it up while still drowning in the rain and her remembrance. She slogged her way to the barn and swiped at her face, relieved to reach the shelter. Her tears mixed with rain water. Carefully, she lay the piglet on a high shelf and moved staunchly back into the storm. *That's done. Over. Johnny's gone.* She gritted her teeth.

Belinda pointed toward the road and Ellen nodded. The Clayton dugout would be swamped by now. The family would have to move into the store, which was on higher ground. Ellen flinched when a burst of lightning lit the darkness. Nothing could be heard above the torrent and claps of thunder, and her heart pounded as her mother seemed to vanish in the black rain. Ellen made her way to the barn with the remaining piglets. The cow lowed restlessly from its stall.

Back outside, she sheltered herself with the horses along the east wall. They looked like wet statues while thick manes flew sideways from their necks, their tails flailed in the wind. The Kiowa ponies seemed to crouch behind the big bodies of the drafts. Ellen waded through mud to get the store key from the house. Then she had to fight against the wind to reach the store. Once inside, she leaned on the wall, gulping air and resting her muscles. Her cape dripped a puddle around her on the floor. She took it off and went to the main room where she began moving barrels and repositioning merchandise to be out of the reach of George's little hands. This circumstance had occurred before, and Ellen knew the family would help clean the floor, get things righted when the storm was over.

The rain diminished a bit. Visibility improved, but the clouds above broiled with a greenish cast. In the brief respite, Ellen opened the store door while the Claytons hurried cautiously toward the store. Water skidded along the mud-slick road and flowed like a small creek to the dugout door. The air held a tangy scent, like wet iron. Glancing further south, Ellen drew an alarmed breath at seeing river water teeming high along the six-foot bank. It was filled with a flotsam of downed trees and natural debris. A wagon wheel careened by.

Reba carried George into the store wrapped in an armful of blankets; Olive had a lantern and a sack of food. Hestor, with bedding over his shoulder, tugged Ellen's sleeve and pointed southwest. Luke and Belinda stopped on the porch beside Ellen to stare, easily seeing the furious black cone hanging in the clouds less than a mile away. Hanging. Swelling like a snake after feed. It stretched down to the bleak land below and wriggled a moment before plowing away from them. A heavy growl filled the air as the tornado ripped and churned through the orange clay of The Nations. The rain renewed its vigor and slashed down on the settlement as if inflicting punishment for their witness of the dark maw of destruction.

"Cyclones don't cross the creeks," Hestor said with confidence. "Mr. Chisholm hisself told us that last year." Luke pushed the boy inside.

Ellen's pulse thudded in her temples. She swallowed against the lumps of fear and worry that clotted her throat and made her stomach hurt. She looked over her shoulder toward the upper road, unable to see the tents and Tim's barn through the torrent. But it was Mr. Baxter she worried about—him and the cattle drive. She had told him no tornadoes. She hoped her words had been true.

The hours merged one into another with little distinction between daylight and night as the rain continued. The obscure atmosphere reminded Ellen of the gloom in her Sycamore Spring dream and the dark aura that hovered around James Montgomery. She tried not to think of him, but there wasn't much else to do. She paced a lot, did needlework. Once she started to reread the letters Johnny had sent her while she was teaching, but just seeing his careful round handwriting made the damp room seem cold. Instead, she separated the long dark strands of hair she had combed from Phineas's mane and tail, laying them straight on a sheet of paper and wrapping them so they would stay smooth. She planned to collect tail hairs from the sorrel pony, and then she would attempt braiding a small item—perhaps a key chain for her mother—the way Pretty Willow had taught her.

Pretty Willow. I hope she isn't caught in this storm.

They all slept a lot. Meals consisted of cold bread and canned fruits. Belinda lit the stove and fried bacon only once, because wind caught in the stovepipe and flared the fire in the stove. Matthew sharpened axes and shovel blades after repairing harnesses; Pitt, when awake, stood morosely by the window, staring out; Belinda mended blankets and braved the weather twice more to milk the cow.

"I wonder how the others are faring," Matthew commented at their next meager meal.

"I was thinking that, too," Belinda said. "Those little tents surely must be ruined by now."

"Lutecia and Charles are probably out horseback in all this, watching their cows," Ellen said.

"I can't remember a storm lasting this long," Pitt said.

"It's a bad one, all right," Belinda said, her forehead lined with worry.

A leak developed in the dogtrot. Ellen and Pitt took turns emptying the bucket set to catch the water, tossing the contents out into the small swamp that used to be a yard. The sloped mud and rock around the base of the cabin didn't wash away, so the dirt floor remained dry while storms seethed over them, crashing thunder and lightning through the tenebrous sky.

By mid-afternoon on the second day, the heaviest rains had passed; wind made waves across the watery yard. From the bedroom window Ellen could finally see the Mercy's cabin where a steady trail of thin smoke rose from the chimney. Lutecia's buttermilk bay stood forlornly out front, saddle in place, thoroughly drenched.

"The smoke's rising straight," Pitt said, also looking out.

"A sign the weather's clearing."

Soon the rain diminished from its heavy fall to a light shower; the fast-moving clouds were higher, with occasional patches of blue-gray sky visible. Pitt stood on a ladder at the house, inspecting the leaky dogtrot roof, while Belinda and Matthew had ridden horses through the mud to survey the fields. Although the outside air was muggy with damp heat, Ellen enjoyed being out of the stuffy house as she made her way to the barn to clean out the cow stall. To the west, a broad shaft of sunlight poured through a break in the clouds and sparkled the wet plains.

She had just finished spreading dried grass to soak up the dampness in the barn when her mother called, "Ellen, did you see that rainbow!" Ellen went to the door. Her mother seemed engulfed in the long wool cape, a slouch hat pulled down to her ears, gloves, men's work boots.

"No, Ma, I've been in here." She looked to the east and could make out the fading colors against the gray sky.

"It was glorious! Just magnificent!" Belinda sat astride a drab-looking gelding.

"How do the fields look?" Ellen asked, stashing the rake by the door.

Belinda shook her head. "The north section is a bed of quicksand."

"Pitt! Get your hoe, son," Matthew called as he reined up on another runty pony. "We've got to trench out the cornfield."

"The scarecrow's gone. Nearly four inches of water everywhere," Belinda went on. Worry replaced her previous smile. She sighed. "Well, I'm going to check on the Claytons. Would you mind riding up the road to see how the others are doing? If they're able, have them come down here. I'm sure the Claytons can use some strong backs to help dig them out."

Ellen nodded and completed her barn work as sunlight winked and lanced through the thinning clouds.

Shadows had lengthened to the east when she secured the sidesaddle on Phineas, climbed aboard and rode first toward the Mercys. Phineas sank to his fetlocks in mud, but seemed glad to move around. Before she had crossed the yard and started on the field path, she could see that Lutecia's horse was gone. The smoke from the chimney had diminished. Probably taking hot food and dry clothes back out to Charles, Ellen thought. She turned back and started up the road toward Tim's barn.

Phineas's hooves made a sucking sound when they pulled from the mud. To her left, the Claytons' hotel tent had blown in on the west side. The canvas dipped against the toppled poles and held a pool of water. She saw no sign of the tents Nancy and Rose occupied. Tree limbs littered the area; the cattle company tent remained intact. Reed's small wagon, with the striped awning rolled and at the side, appeared unscathed on the knoll.

Several yards from the barn, Ellen heard high giggles and deep laughter from the knock-together structure. Tim had built the place with cottonwood, and already the split logs were warped and shrunken. Drainage from the corrals had cut rivulets down the slope to the road. Tim's voice bellowed, the words of which Ellen couldn't understand. More laughter. She reined Phineas up to the front and dismounted where the doors had been opened to the refreshing sunlight.

"Miz Ellen! What're you doin' up here?" Tim sat up as she stepped in the doorway. He smoothed back his hair. Whenever he was around any of her family he usually straightened his clothes, tried not to swear. Her parents had never said anything to him about his demeanor, and it always surprised Ellen that he didn't scorn them for their store and civilized ways when he had lived so long with the Indians.

Heavy smells of damp leather blended with tobacco smoke and the distinctive scent of whiskey.

"Everything all right at your place?" Tim stood up. He was whip thin and tall, accentuated by his long brown hair which he kept tied back with a thong at this neck; it hung below his shoulders—stringy looking. A permanent tobacco stain etched one corner of his down-turned mouth.

"We're fine, Mr. Fykes. Thank you." She tried to hide a slight smile, knowing they'd probably been drinking since yesterday. *That's one way to wait out a storm.*

"Come join us!" Rose Schaffner giggled and held out the jar of amber liquid. "Have a drink." Then she sniggered, "Her have a drink! Miss prim and proper!"

Ellen outwardly ignored the jibe, although inwardly she wished she didn't always appear so *prim and proper.* "Just checking to see that everyone's all right," she said. Little details snapped out at her, like the missing second button on Rose's dark-brown weskit, and the orderly row of halters on the back wall.

"Oh, yeah. Your family thinks its keepers of this place," Dillard Winslow said, his voice slurred. His hair was combed long over the balding spot atop his head, as if to hide it. "Ya sit down there in your snug lodgings—"

"Shut yer stupid mouth, Dillard!" Tim broke in. He lurched toward the man, the bottle he held clunking on the chair. Rose laughed hysterically.

"Don't break that!" came another voice. Nancy. She wore a light-colored calico dress with puffy sleeves. Her body seemed oddly bent, and Ellen realized Nancy was slouched in the lap of—Ellen's stomach tightened. *James Montgomery!*

The man gave Nancy a squeeze. "That's not the only bottle, darlin'."

"Good." Nancy's head drooped to a black pit.

No! To Montgomery's shoulder. Ellen gritted her teeth, captivated by the distortion that matched the way she had seen him when he first came into the store.

"Oh, Ja-ames," Rose said, singsong. "I think Miz Hargrove just noticed how you fit in them snug Mexican britches." Rose cackled.

"She's always starin' at me," Montgomery drawled in lazy tones. "You got something to say to me, Mrs. Hargrove?"

"No. I—" Ellen's pulse raced. The distortion vanished, and she could see Montgomery clearly. She gripped a fold in her skirt and turned stiffly to Tim. "We're helping dig out the Claytons," she said.

"I'll get myself together," Tim said. He stumbled on the chair and fell down. Rose's shrieking laughter reverberated through the barn.

"James. Get me a drink," Nancy said with a hiccup.

Ellen hurried outside and climbed on a corral rail to get back into the saddle. Phineas seemed as eager to be away from the place as she was. While she turned the horse, she kept recalling Nancy with James Montgomery, his arm like a tentacle around her—pulling her into his darkness.

"No. I didn't see that," she muttered. "Just people drinking their way through the storm."

Phineas picked back to the road and Ellen headed him across to the higher side where the mire didn't look as heavy. Glancing up the slope, she noticed Reed Carter hunched awkwardly beside his bay harness horse. His other horse was under saddle and tied to the side of the boxy wagon that Reed lived out of. Concerned, Ellen headed up the slight hill, passed the cattle company tent, toward Reed. She soon realized he was holding the mare's front leg and examining her foot.

"Has your mare been hurt?" she asked when she got close.

He looked over his shoulder at her and smiled, letting down the animal's leg. "Good afternoon," he said as he straightened.

"Is she injured?" Ellen asked again, aware of her boldness of riding to his campsite uninvited.

"Just a scrape from something blowing around during the storm. It looks much worse than it is." He stepped back to reveal the dark stain of blood along the horse's leg. It started just above the ankle and had dribbled across her hoof. "I was just checking to make sure nothing was embedded."

"We have various remedies at the store if you need."

"Thank you, but I have some here." He wore brown twill pants and a white shirt—always a white shirt—the sleeves rolled up. "Looks like the blow has ended," he said as he rinsed his hands in a pan of water.

"A few people probably haven't realized that yet," she said, cocking her head toward Tim's barn.

Reed chuckled as he wiped his hands. "Probably not. I sold Winslow my last two cases of whiskey the morning before the storm, and I'm glad to have it gone. Your family held up all right, I presume."

"Yes. But the Clayton dugout is swamped."

"Of course. And I'll bet they waited till the middle of the storm to move up to the store."

Ellen ignored his sarcasm and truth. She wondered if his biting tone was because he knew that Reba didn't "approve" of him. "Ma's gone to help, and I was checking to see that everyone else was sound."

"I was about to check on the Mercys. Have you seen them?"

"Lutecia was at their cabin a bit a go, but left already. We'll probably need some help at the Claytons, if you could." Harsh laughter floated from across the road. "They'll be of no use— Nancy Kincaid all snuggled up with that Mr. Montgomery." She shook her head. "That's a mistake, her tying up with him."

"Really? They seem sort of peas in a pod to me." Reed smiled, slightly amused. He bridled his riding horse while he spoke.

"Everyone is so taken with him, and for the life of me I can't see why," Ellen said.

Reed looked up at her, a thoughtful expression on his face. "I suppose he could appear rather—dashing," he said.

"Dashing!" She leaned toward Reed, lowering her voice. "Don't you think it's interesting that he claims to be Mr. Stone's partner; and now he has it all? And I keep wondering what business could a cattle company have down here, anyway, unless they really are going to start a town."

"He'll probably buy from trail herds with tired men, or sick men, or barely any men. There will be a few herders that just won't want to face another hundred and fifty miles to Abilene and will sell here." Reed began tightening the saddle cinch. "Then the cattle company can push the beef on to the railhead—make maybe another five dollars a head. Or sell them at the forts and mining camps out west."

"You seem to know a lot about it." She brushed at a speck of dirt on her skirt, perturbed that her logic was being rent.

"It's another form of gambling."

"Has Mr. Montgomery talked to you about it?" Drawn by the long silence that followed her words, Ellen looked up.

"He asked me about you."

"About me?" Her eyes widened.

"To men with an eye for finer things, you attract a lot of attention, Mrs. Hargrove."

Reed closed up the back of his wagon, securing the door hasp with a large lock.

A lock on his wagon, she thought. Of course; he's a gambler; lots of money. The cattle company tent is right here probably with a strongbox full of money, and then there's the store. This tiny community is ripe for outlaws!

The realization stunned her. They had been an out-of-the-way location for so long, but with the advent of cattle drives the settlement had changed. *Perhaps this is Montgomery's plan; after enough cattle come through where drovers spend money at the store, with Reba's eatery—even with Nancy and Rose—he will kill us all and reap the bounty!*

Reed had pulled into the saddle and reined his horse beside hers. The horse was shorter than Phineas by a hand, yet because of Reed's height, the man could look her in the eye. "You seem deep in thought. What?" he asked.

She looked away. She had to tell someone, yet why this man? She knew not much more about him than she did about Montgomery. But there was something about Reed—his pleasant manner, the way they could talk. She blurted out her belief. "I'm pretty certain he's the one. He—his face." She pivoted to watch Reed's reaction as she spoke the next words. "Montgomery's face is the one I envisioned over the murder scene."

Reed's eyes narrowed, but he didn't break from her stare, as though measuring her along with the words. Ellen flushed under the scrutiny and turned Phineas down the slope. "Forget I said that. I shouldn't have told you."

"Your visions give you that much detail?"

"Sometimes."

"So you knew it was Francis Stone dead, not just a body."

"No. I hadn't met Mr. Stone. Couldn't have identified him."

"And now there's this other part of your vision. A face. That's what Mrs. Mercy alluded to the day you brought back the body."

Was he taking her seriously? She wasn't sure. She was also dismayed that she had divulged her belief. "I'm just letting my imagination get the better of me," she said lightly.

"Amazing. You actually can see physical details; enough to know who you're looking at." Reed's look was intense.

"Please don't mention this to anyone."

"Of course not," Reed smiled at her. "I'm glad you trusted me enough to say something."

Phineas swung his head, gave a low whinny. Ellen heard the approach of a horse and looked up the road. The rider emerged from the woods north of Fall Creek, recklessly urging the mount to a lope along the mushy trail. Ellen started forward. "It's Sarah Pierce," she said, waving to the girl. Sarah's brown calico dress and black stockings were soaked to the knees. "I wonder what's happened."

"Oh, Miss Ellen." Sarah reined up. "Is Lutecia Mercy around?" Her tired animal heaved noisily.

"She's with her husband, checking their cows. What's happened?"

"One wall of our soddy got bashed, but that's not the worst. We found a man—I think he's from a cattle drive. And he's been shot!"

The girl's voice carried to Tim who was starting down to help the Claytons. "What's going on?" he asked.

"An emergency at the Pierces! Tell my family where I've gone," Ellen called to him.

"I'll ride with you," Reed said.

"Sarah, do you know the way to the Mercy cow camp?" Ellen asked the girl.

"Yes ma'am."

"Good. I'll go to your place while you get Mrs. Mercy."

"Thank you. Oh, thank you!" Sarah called while Ellen headed Phineas north. Reed rode beside her.

Fall Creek had overrun its lower north bank, spilling off through the woods and turning every depression into a marsh. The freight road, which cattle drives followed, was thick with mud. Ellen kept Phineas to a quick trot, worried about who might be injured. A drover. From Baxter's herd? A mile north of the settlement, buzzards circled the swamped hackberry grove, gliding dark and silently against the blue sky. Ellen looked away, knowing the birds signaled something dead. Reed said nothing as they rode, sometimes dropping behind her so they could avoid major puddles. Ellen recalled her thoughts just before Sarah arrived; all about outlaws stalking the settlement— waiting for the right moment to attack. She was glad for Reed's company, suddenly distrusting the countryside that had before seemed innocent of treachery. She wondered if she should warn the Pierces of the possible outlaw threat, but shook that thought away, knowing she would sound as irrational as Luke Clayton with his fear of Indians. Her perception had no proof, not even a dream warning. She drew a long breath and concentrated on the task at hand—getting to the Pierces and helping them and the injured man however she could.

After two miles, Ellen angled off the main road and led the way onto a narrow trace. "A short cut, but go single file," she said to Reed. "There's quicksand out here—probably more since the rain."

The twisting route wound past a long strand of haw, their flowers white and clustered, and around large cottonwoods and thick sand patches that oozed water. At the Chikaskia, river water nearly covered the sand bars; the islands of loam had become beaches for downed timber. Water lapped against Phineas's belly when they crossed. Ellen gripped the horse's mane and refused to look into the rushing brown water. Here be dragons, she thought. Dragons of the mind.

Another half mile and they were back on the plains at the place a prairie fire had scorched. *Dragons of the mind.* The prairie fire. Another of her secrets. So real, that dream had been last May! Images of orange flames licking along the winter-dry grass, flaring brush and trees, roaring across the land. Two, three times her dream had awakened her. And one morning, she had felt so certain of her sensing, she had sent her students home only an hour after their arrival at school. She had driven two of them to their family's soddy in her buggy, staying there to aid the family, certain the property would be threatened. Nothing happened. Ellen's relief at being wrong was soon quashed by news that a prairie fire had swept across northern Sumner County. She had wanted the absence of fire in Ottawa County to indicate that her premonitory dreams were no longer valid, that she only suffered nightmares with no forewarning involved.

Her peace of mind was compromised even more when, as Ottawa County stayed calm and green, curious gossip sparked—its own kind of fire—as people constructed details of her past comments that had seemed providential. She learned a few of them, and with most, couldn't even place the circumstances described. But the idle tales flared to doubts about Ellen's ability to handle her position. No matter that she had proceeded through the year without major incident; kept the school a healthy environment through the raw winter, dealt with truculent fourteen-year-old boys who were taller than she was. "My mother says she's getting married this summer," she overheard one girl say. "We won't have to deal with her no more!"

When she came home for the summer, she learned it had been the Pierces' soddy that was threatened during the fire, saved only by a sudden shift of wind. Now Ellen could see patches of wet ash where saplings had been consumed, although buffalo grass was already forming its thick mat, regenerating from the deep roots that held the land together. The land looked flat, but the trail led through several flooded washes and over swells before the Pierces' sod buildings made small lumps on the horizon nearly a mile away. The grain barn was the biggest structure. Ellen led the way along the plow road. In the fields, pooled water glistened in the sunlight and reflected the blue sky around the small green plants.

"They've planted a lot," Reed remarked.

"They were hoping to get sixteen acres in corn this year."

"I think they've done it."

When they reached the yard, Ellen was shocked by the condition of the house. "Look at the north roof!"

"That corner has nearly collapsed," Reed said. A huge limb lay to the side.

Ellen quickly kicked out of the stirrups and slid from Phineas's high back. Reed dismounted and rushed to help Will Pierce and his two boys pull ropes attached to a brick of sod that threatened to fall into the house. Ellen secured Phineas and Reed's horse to a stout hitching rail and hurried inside. "It's Ellen Hargrove, Mrs. Pierce," she announced.

"Good of you to come," was the strained reply.

The one-room structure was dank, the floor turned to mud. Ellen made out stout Lillian Pierce putting good muscle to a forked branch and pushing up on the birch strut that framed the roof where something had crashed down and set the roof askew. Ellen saw no way in which she could help that effort and looked around for the injured man.

"Did you have a tornado up here?" she asked, amazed by the damage.

"We might have; the wind was fierce," Lillian said in a husky, strong voice. She stood taller than most men, and her light brown hair straggled from a massive coiled braid pinned on the back of her head. When loose, the braid reached well below her waist. Her calico work dress was muddy and wet nearly to her knees. "That limb out there must have traveled miles; we've got no trees in the area that big. Mighty fierce."

Baby Eugene, seven months old, began crying from a cot. Ellen slopped across the mud floor and took up the boy, calming him. On the other cot, a man lay so quietly Ellen almost didn't notice him. A canopy had been erected to protect him from the leaky roof.

"That fellow's bad hurt. Shot in the back, I tell you," came Lillian's strident voice. "Is Lutecia Mercy here?"

"Not yet, but I'm sure she's not far behind us." Ellen patted the baby who still whimpered, fingers at his mouth.

Lillian gave a loud groan, pushing the branch. The blocks of sod moved outward, and now the roof support rested properly on it. "Who else with you?" she asked, getting her breath.

"Mr. Carter. Reed Carter," Ellen said, studying the man on the cot.

"Don't know him." Lillian wiped her forehead with the back of her hand streaking mud across her plain-featured face. She rinsed her hands in a bucket of water and then wiped them on her apron.

"He moved to the settlement about a week after your last visit." Ellen touched the injured man's brow, concerned by its dry hotness. "I've seen this boy before," she said as Lillian took the baby from her.

"From some cow herd, Will managed to get from him. His name's Tommy Atherton." She sat on a keg and unbuttoned her calico dress. Baby Eugene quieted when he started nursing.

Ellen wrung out a cloth from the pan near the cot. "He teased me on the street one morning." Her thoughts flashed wonderment about him: did he have family—maybe a wife wondering if he were safe?

She laid the cloth on the cowboy's brow. His eyelids fluttered. "Too many," he muttered. "Can't fight."

"Shhh, now."

His eyes opened and he stared at Ellen. "Ma'am? I—I hurt bad."

"Lutecia Mercy's coming. From the settlement," Ellen said. "Were you with the herd when this happened?"

"They shot me. Great God, it hurts." He writhed on the cot. "Rustlers, right in amongst us. Rus—" His breathing was labored and he seemed to sink more into the cot as though the brush-ticking mattress were absorbing him.

Ellen imagined the driving rain, riders bearing down on the sleeping cattlemen. Lots of riders, shooting. They never had a chance. She went to the big hearth on the far side of the room and pushed at the wood under the hanging eight gallon kettle of water. *Lu will need hot water, especially with all the mud around.* The fire blazed. She went back to the young drover.

"I asked him if 'twere Injuns," Lillian said. "But t'weren't, thank the Lord."

The boy roused again. "Mama?" He blinked, focused on Ellen and almost smiled. "You're that purty one—with the hair." He winced, Ellen tensed with him, wishing she could do something to comfort him. "They shot Baxter, ma'am. And two others. That Lewis was the one. Seemed okay at first. I never thought— I never—"

Ellen frowned. "One of your own drovers?" she asked him. The sound of horses came in through the open door.

"I thought I was gonna get away. I thought—" He gasped. "Judd— Damn him."

Judd. Ellen shook her head, her previous thoughts of outlaws flooding to her again. *Judd.*

"He looked to be in a bad way," Sarah said as she led Lutecia inside.

"I heated some water," Ellen said.

Lutecia hurried over to the cot. "Good. Let's see what we can do for this boy."

"Mama?" the cowboy asked through his confusion.

8

*H*e died before the next dawn, after enduring an afternoon of delirium and pain. Lutecia examined the festering black hole in his back and muttered that the bullet was too deep to probe for in his weakened condition. Ellen had been sadly relieved when he lapsed into unconsciousness. Reed and Will Pierce finished straightening the top of the soddy that evening. They took a brief rest and began making a crude coffin. Ellen hoped the boy couldn't hear the sawing and hammering and know what it was for. She and Lutecia alternated sitting with him and helping Lillian clean the soddy.

Now, with dawn only an hour past and steamy heat still rising from the drying ground, Ellen stood with the clutch of people gathered to pass the boy on to the other world. Wraiths of fog rose. Mist puddled and obscured the base of thickets and short trees, and where the sunlight fell on pooled water, it reflected back as bright as sparks.

"If I could have got to him sooner," Lutecia murmured as Reed and Will climbed out of the hole they had dug on a rise not far from the house.

"You did everything you could, Lu," Ellen said. She watched Reed brush at the mud on his pants. His white shirt was stained with dirt and sweat. He and Will took up ropes and lowered the rough-hewn coffin into the grave. Ellen shook her head, remorse tightening her throat and burning her eyes.

"Here, oh Lord," Will began. "We commend this Tommy Atherton to your eternal care, that he may be free of pain and wants, and forever protected by your grace and infinite love."

"Dear God. They go so quickly," was Lillian's hoarse whisper. She shook her head and pulled her ten-year-old boy against her leg while holding Sarah's hand. Sarah held Eugene in one arm. Ellen didn't looked at the little grave nearby for the Pierces' two-year-old daughter, lost that winter to lung fever. The older boy, thirteen, stood solemnly beside his father.

"He was a stalwart lad," Will added before muttering several disclaimers about what they didn't know.

Ellen had checked his belongings, hoping for a clue as to where he was from, but found nothing. She stared at the narrow yellow, fresh-wood box, almost seeing through it to the canvas-wrapped body. He was buried in his own bedroll. *And this is how it was for Johnny?* Tears welled to her eyes. *Or had he been laid under a stone heap, the coyotes and wolves quickly digging through to scatter his bones.*

"Dust to dust," Lutecia said softly.

Ellen turned away, her chest aching. Lutecia patted her shoulder and they gripped hands.

"Are you all right, Miss Ellen?" Sarah asked, a worry to her voice.

Ellen nodded and tried to compose herself.

"Shhh, Sarah. She's probably thinking about her husband gone," Lillian said.

The shovels Reed and Will wielded were silent when pushed into the mud. Earth fell in sodden clods on the coffin. The baby fretted. Lillian sat on a nearby outcropping to nurse him. Ellen took deep breaths and squared her shoulders. Lutecia gave her an understanding smile. What's done is done, Ellen thought.

They all stood dutifully until the ground was heaped into a damp brown mound over the coffin. Sarah settled a handful of flowers onto the grave; she had plucked them from around the hackberry trees. Then they filed back to the soddy, wordless in the day's increasing heat.

Ellen, Lutecia and Reed declined the meal Lillian offered, knowing the family had more important things to do than care for visitors. Within an hour of burying the drover, they started back to the settlement. The warm day belied the storms that had passed. Sunshine washed them in brightness and warmth, while a steady wind whipped Ellen's and Lutecia's skirts, and tossed the horses' manes and tails into wisps of brown and black against the air.

Ellen looked forward to the ride home, wanting time to contemplate her place in all this. Deep down, she was certain she had known something was going to happen to Mr. Baxter and his herd. When he asked her advice about the weather, she sensed something and turned away from it, had busied herself with a practical answer and didn't take time to study the turmoil that sprang on her thoughts. Now a disaster had occurred, with at least one person dead. Ignoring and trying to turn away from what she sensed seemed the wrong approach. She hid her vision of Johnny. He was dead. She refused to examine the turmoil with Baxter; Tommy Atherton was dead. If events kept unfolding in this way, Ellen knew she would go mad with grief and guilt, and fear of her own thoughts.

She wanted so much to be free of these flickering sensations about the future. How often in the past five years she had wished that, prayed it, all to no avail. Rather than diminishing, as she assumed would happen as she grew older, her encounters with premonitions had become stronger. And to whom could she go for advice? Her mother patently refused to speak about the anomaly of Ellen's visions. An abnormality, Ellen thought of her dreams.

"This water and sun has sprung up all kinds of new growth," Lutecia said loudly. She glanced back to where Ellen lagged behind them. "Just look at that Shepherd's Purse." Lutecia reined to a stop, examining the verdant foliage.

"Which one is that?" Reed asked, scanning the prairie. Tommy Atherton's roan was in tow behind Reed's mount. They brought it with them on the chance that someone from the cattle drive would claim it. The saddle had been left with the Pierces as a payment, of sorts.

"That pale green with all the little leaves." She swung from the saddle. "Help me here, Ellen. Having some fresh edibles will be so nice."

Ellen frowned, not wanting to be roused from her introspection.

"Come on, now. I see some Veronica over there. You gather that. And there's bound to be pennycress in the marshes. Come on, now," Lutecia urged again.

Ellen slid off Phineas who immediately put his head down to tear at the greenery. She forced a smile, knowing her friend hoped to soften her mood.

"I'm afraid I can't help much. I don't know plants very well," Reed said.

"That's okay, Mr. Carter. You can stand guard while we ladies gather," Lutecia said.

"Rather like the Indians do, right?" he said after a chuckle.

Ellen glanced at him, hearing his amusement, but he was scanning their surroundings—examining the horizon. She, too, looked around, again thinking how the region had changed. What types of people were suddenly lurking in the area? In her family's three years here, she had never heard of a murder—not even when the Indians were upset.

She shook her head and added some mallow to her harvest, recalling when that first herd of Texas beeves had passed through the settlement. "I been told this here's a good route to Abilene," the trail boss said two years ago. To Abilene and the new railway line. And the drives had been coming up that trail ever since. Now there was a cattle company. To prey on the drovers' misfortunes, from what Reed had told her. And perhaps to cause them? Montgomery had tried to buy Baxter's herd, and now it had been rustled—men shot and killed. With deliberation, she tried to remember any strangers around the settlement, especially who had frequented the cattle company tent. No one came to mind.

"Well, now I see why women wear big aprons," Reed said as Ellen and Lutecia returned to the horses.

"Indeed," Lutecia laughed. They each had filled the skirts of their aprons. "If we used our dresses this way, we'd give you quite a view of our cotton undies."

Ellen couldn't keep from flushing. The apron seemed cumbersome, and she looked for a fallen tree trunk or protrusion that would help her remount to the sidesaddle.

"Here, Ellen. I've a couple of pokes we can use." Lutecia pulled bleached muslin sacks with draw string openings from the carpetbag of herbs and doctoring tools tied behind the cantle. "Don't know why I didn't think of these at the start." She handed one to Ellen. Reed dismounted and helped them, and soon their bounty was contained.

"Let's be going before the sun wilts our salad," Lutecia said. She pulled easily onto her mare.

Reed laced his fingers and cupped his hands to form a step for Ellen. Once seated, she thanked him while tying the poke to the saddle skirt.

"It's the least I can do, Mrs. Hargrove," he said. His gaze and slight smile gave her a warm feeling, but the moment passed quickly as Reed went to his horse.

"Lutecia did everything she could, but it was too late," Ellen told the group of people who met them as soon as they crossed the Fall Creek ford. Rose was washing clothes and saw them first. Winslow was with her holding a clothes basket. Their call got Pitt's attention. He ran to the road from Tim's barn, a rope coiled over his shoulder, followed by Tim.

"He took a bullet in the back," Reed said. "Leaked out all his energy before Mrs. Mercy got there."

"At least I managed to keep him comfortable," Lutecia put in.

Pitt pointed to the roan horse Reed was trailing. "Isn't that one of the horses you sold Baxter?" he asked Tim. Reed turned the extra horse over to Tim, who mounted it bareback to keep up with the procession.

"That's probably how the cowboy got down to the Pierces. That horse headin' for familiar territory," Tim said, riding along beside them.

"If it weren't for that, he could still be layin' on a trail someplace," Rose said. "Sad thing, I tell you."

"I just can't believe we've had three people murdered in Sumner County in less than two weeks," Ellen said.

"Three?" Tim asked.

Ellen's heart pounded and she frowned. "I mean, two." Pitt frowned up at her as he marched along beside Phineas.

"You said, three, Mrs. Hargrove."

Ellen tensed on hearing James Montgomery's voice and darted a look toward where his chestnut horse walked behind Reed's horse. He appeared normal—James Montgomery—not a blur, no dark aura.

"Why did you say that? What three are you talking about?" the man continued.

"I—" Her palms became sweaty.

"It's assumed Mr. Baxter was killed," Reed said. "Although we don't know for sure."

Thank you, Ellen thought, her breathing coming more easily. That must be what I was thinking.

"Maybe 'twas some of those Wichitaws heading south," Dillard Winslow said, stroking his thick mutton-chop sideburns. "I think they figured they could settle here in Kansas and now they're mad 'cause they're being chased back to The Nations."

"No," Reed began. "The poor fellow surely would have mentioned—"

"He was still conscious when you got there? Conscious and talking?" Montgomery asked.

Ellen glowered at the road that was visible between Phineas's ears, wishing she could prove the man's complicity.

"Oh, yes." Reed let his words gain mystery by his inflection, as if to lure Montgomery—force him to say or ask something that would reveal his knowledge of what happened. Or maybe Ellen imagined that.

No comment from Montgomery.

"I'm going up to my camp," Reed said.

"Thank you for your help," Ellen said. And for not laughing at my suspicion, she thought.

"Come join us for fresh greens, Mr. Carter," Lutecia called.

"I'll plan on that."

"My pleasure, Mrs. Mercy."

Ellen glanced back as Montgomery turned his horse to follow Reed. To ask more about the young drover? Ellen wished she could hear that conversation.

Pitt twirled a little loop of rope as he walked beside Ellen's horse, followed still by Dillard Winslow and Rose. Tim rode beside Lutecia. Although the road had dried considerably, soggy patches showed dark and gooey along the beaten track.

"So 'ol Baxter got hit by rustlers, huh?" Winslow said after a few strides. The laundry basket he carried dripped water around his feet. "Here he was worried about the weather. Probably felt pretty good since Miz Hargrove told him he wouldn't ride into no cyclones. Then, wham! Rustlers."

His words seemed to hit Ellen in the chest and punch the wind out of her.

"How come you didn't warn him, lady gal?" Winslow went on. "He was asking for your predictions about the trail, and you said nothin' at all about rustlers!"

"You got no call to talk like that!" Pitt yelled at Winslow, his freckled cheeks growing red.

"Pitt, don't," Ellen said.

Pitt's fists were knotted. "But he—"

"It's best to just ignore the ignorant," Lutecia said to Pitt.

"Ignorant! Is that what I am, Miz Know-it-all Hargrove?"

"Dillard!" Rose slapped the man's arm. "I've heard you grumbling about how she don't really know anything—can't see what's coming, and now you're faulting her for this?"

"Well, this just proves my point," Winslow declared. "She don't know nothin'. Either that, or she only says what she wants to.

Luring that Baxter into false comfort."

Lutecia glared over at the man. He chewed the end of his cheroot.

"Come on, Dillard, ol' sot," Rose said, hauling at the man's arm. "You get outta here before you get somebody mad." They crossed the road and started through the meadow beside the Clayton hotel.

Luke struggled up from the Bluff River wearing a wooden yoke—the water buckets dangling. He quickly set the yoke aside when he saw the small procession. Reba hurried over from the dugout, trailing Olive, her dog and George trying to catch one of the puppies.

"We got your store cleaned," Reba called. "And almost got things back to normal over there." The chicken yard behind the Clayton dugout was matted with white feathers and pigs were filthy with mud. In the field atop the slight rise, only a few scraggly plants had straightened to the sunshine.

Ellen reined Phineas up by the store, frowning as she dismounted onto the porch step. She gripped the reins in her right hand, while with her left she pressed at a cramp in her lower back. Her head ached from her feeling of culpability. No matter how much she rebuked herself, the sense that she should have known—should have warned Baxter—persisted.

"What happened at the Pierces?" Luke called, eyes wide as he clomped up to them. He was still slightly bent, as though the weight of the buckets remained on his shoulders. "Who got shot?"

"A drover. A strapping young man," Lutecia said, shaking her head. She headed her horse around the side of the store, Pitt following.

"Rustlers shot him when they raided Mr. Baxter's cow herd," Tim reported what had been reported to him. "He didn't make it."

"Oh." Reba murmured. She pulled Olive close and took George's hand, reminding Ellen of Lillian Pierce at the funeral.

"Rustlers? Red ones, I'll bet. I'll be for sure glad when the cavalry gets here," Luke declared. "Those redskins could attack at any time."

"They would have hit us before now, if they'd a mind to," Tim said.

"I know you was married to one of 'em," Luke said. "But that don't mean you know it all." Not a quarrelsome statement, just doubting.

By rights, Ellen thought, they should be spitting at each other most of the time. Luke was a former Confederate (a deserter by his own admission) and Tim a "squaw man" who put a lot of stock in honor and bravery.

Ellen hunched her shoulders as Tim and Luke moved away, still fussing.

"I was dreadful worried when you rode off with that Carter fellow," Reba said, frowning at Ellen. "And gone all night! My land."

"Reba, we were at the Pierces helping in an emergency." Ellen let her exasperation show.

"I know, I know." She turned her children back toward the dugout. "I just don't trust sporting men."

Ellen shook her head and led Phineas around the store and toward the well yard where Lutecia was washing greens at the water pump. Pitt and Belinda stood nearby, the ground and yard still muddy; puddles rippled in the breeze. Clothes and bedding, spread on the low shrubbery, dried in the warm sunshine. Ellen frowned at the rope Pitt flipped around, certain it used to be their clothesline.

"I really wanted to whack him one," Pitt was saying when Ellen reached the watering trough. "That dumb Mr. Winslow faulting Ellen for not telling Mr. Baxter about the rustling."

"He's all mouth," Belinda said. She hitched her skirt above the ankles of her boots and started toward the house with a bucket of water.

"Ellen didn't know nothin' about it. But Mama knew, didn't you?" Pitt continued, looking at his mother's back. " *You* knew they were going to be rustled. Remember, Ellen? Ma said it. When I was askin' to go with the cattle drive, she said they'd be rustled."

Ellen blinked her surprise and thought back to that morning.

Belinda drew up straight and turned to her son. "Why, Pitt, I never—"

"Sure you did."

Pitt's right, Ellen realized.

"I was just helping your Pa dissuade you from wanting to ride with them. Goodness, child!" Belinda waved him off and continued to the house.

"She did say it," Pitt said. He slashed the rope onto the ground.

"Yep. And I say the sun's gonna shine this week. Why, lookee. I'm right!" Lutecia said, holding out her hand to the hot light that filtered along the edge of the trees.

"You're makin' fun of me!" Pitt stalked away.

But Lutecia didn't smile as she lowered her upturned palm. Ellen met her brown-eyed gaze resolutely.

"She's like me, isn't she. Always knowing the weather. She tells it much better than I do." The revelation was aggravating, yet a comfort. "But she tried to deny it just now. Why?"

Lutecia frowned and hunched her shoulders. "Maybe she doesn't want to take responsibility."

"Responsibility for what happens? You mean I'm really responsible for Tommy's and Mr. Stone's deaths, or the killings in Lawrence, or—or—?" *Johnny.*

"No, Ellen. You don't got control over what occurs."

"I can't even control my own thoughts! I surely wouldn't dream any of this if I could help it."

"Of course not. And everything you see ain't necessary to be true, neither. Your ma probably knows that. Has learned to live with those few times she is seeing."

Ellen rubbed the reins with her thumb. "Sometimes there *is* a real certainty." *Like Johnny. If I'd gone with him—if I had warned him—* Her stomach knotted. And now Montgomery, she thought. He shouldn't get away with this!

"Lu, if I truly sensed something important, I ought to do something with that information, wouldn't you say? I mean, if I didn't, then I *would* be responsible for the consequences."

Lutecia cocked her head. "I'm not understanding you, Ellen."

"Nothing. Just thinking out loud, I guess." She couldn't tell

Lutecia what she thought. Not yet. She had to get more proof. It was bad enough she had said something to Reed.

Charles Mercy, mud thick on his heavy work shoes, trotted his big black into the yard. "Well, there you be," he said to Lutecia. "Mornin', Ellen." He tipped his wide-brimmed hat to her.

"Hello, Mr. Mercy."

"I was beginning to worry for you two," Charles said. "What happened?" He took off his hat and wiped his brow with a big bandanna.

Ellen led Phineas to the brimming trough, not wanting to retell about Tommy Atherton. Phineas sucked in water. She loosened the cinch and pulled off the saddle, depressed by Lutecia's sigh and sad voice.

"Aw, now Lu. Don't fret on it. I know you done all you could," Charles said. Charles was off his horse, his arm around Lutecia.

Ellen got a work cloth from the barn and stood up on the edge of the trough, rubbing Phineas's broad back, a pang of envy touching her. She wished for someone to put a strong arm around her—a special man to hold her, just for a bit. Johnny's arms were strong, a comfort; he offered sympathetic comments even about his parents continual work ethic, comments that led to conspiratorial jokes he would toss at her in the field to lift her spirits. Had the senior Hargroves known about that? Understood? Disliked her for turning their son against them?

She led Phineas into the barn to get him a bait of oats.

Lutecia came to the barn door and peered in at her. "You get yourself some rest. And don't start looking to the negative."

Ellen forced a smile, touched by Lutecia's concern. "I'll be all right," she said, not certain that was true.

9

Although Ellen had slept very little, the mysteries of the past days filled her head and thwarted her attempt to nap. "*You got no control over what occurs,*" came Lutecia's voice. "*How come you didn't warn him, lady gal?*" Winslow's face glared accusingly and then darkened into that of James Montgomery. "*Did you see any Indians? Indians, I'll bet.*" Montgomery's face loomed over Sycamore Spring. There, Mr. Baxter tipped his hat to her. Then, "*How come you didn't warn him, lady gal?*"

Ellen pushed up from her bed, aggravated and weary, and left her room for the kitchen. That room was warm and quiet. Belinda's hat was on the wall peg and her work shoes stood outside the open door. "Ma?" Ellen called at the leather door of the room her parents shared. No answer, but Ellen peeked in and saw her mother on the bed. Although Belinda was breathing deeply, Ellen was certain her mother wasn't asleep.

She doesn't want to talk about the circumstances Pitt brought up, she thought while walking into the dogtrot. "But I can't deny it like Ma does," she muttered. *I wonder if she ever felt like this?*

Ellen brought in the dry laundry, folded it and put hers and Pitt's away. Then, steeped in melancholy, Ellen walked to the Mercys where Lutecia was taking a blanket from her clothesline. Ellen grabbed one end and helped fold.

"I couldn't sleep and Ma's lying down," she said. They had the blanket in a neat square, which Ellen held on to while Lutecia collected a basket of clothes. "Did she say anything to you? Is she sick?"

"Monthly complaint," Lutecia responded casually as they walked to the little cabin. "She told me she was 'bout due."

"Oh," Ellen said, not convinced. Rarely had Belinda taken to her bed because of that.

"Come on in for some tea," Lutecia invited.

"Thanks, but Pop will be in from the field pretty soon. I need to fix a dinner."

Lutecia studied her without smiling. "If you want to talk, you know I'll be here," she said.

"Thanks, Lu."

Matthew Jarvis came in from the field at noon. He and Pitt ate. Ellen picked at the food, only enjoying the sweet taste of strawberry jam on a cracker. Her mother was still abed. *She's avoiding me,* Ellen felt certain.

Her father and brother headed to the barn to work and Ellen went to the store. Once inside, she propped open the front door to air out the room. True to her word, Reba had thoroughly wiped down the counter and floor. By habit, Ellen went behind the service counter and drew her hand along the cash drawer. The wood of the drawer was over two inches thick and totally lined with metal. The edge tucked neatly under the counter and was noticeable only to careful scrutiny. It was securely locked; but she recalled her thoughts from yesterday, about how ripe this settlement was becoming for robbers. At night, the cash drawer was usually emptied, the money taken to the house; where her father put it—she wasn't sure. Perhaps it would be safer to leave the money in the store. If robbers wanted to break in and steal the store profits, so be it. But there was less chance of someone being hurt if they robbed the store after hours, than if they came to the house looking for money. *Unless they came during the day, when someone was here, and then—*

Ellen shook her head to drive away the frightening thoughts, and studied the room. None of the tables were in the proper place, and Ellen gladly set to work arranging and rearranging the merchandise displays. It seemed she had worked for hours, but when she closed up the store and returned to the house, the windup clock on the only kitchen shelf read 2:30. She went to her bedroom and finally managed a nap, devoid of any faces or accusing voices, yet she woke with a start. She brushed her hair, redid the long plait and coiled it, fastening it on the back of her head with wooden pins. Beyond the dogtrot, the sun glared brassy on the western sky. Myriad bird songs greeted her. Ellen still saw no sign of her mother. She went back to the store, surprised and relieved that no one had rung the bell. She had just lifted the bar on the front door when the sound of galloping hooves came from the north. Alarmed, she hurried onto the porch. Now what? she thought.

"Hey, Ma!" Rob Clayton loped his horse in the afternoon shadows along the road. He pulled the animal to a fast stop in front of his family's dugout. "Ma!" he called. The animal snorted and tossed clods of earth from its hooves. "I done it! I got the cavalry!"

The cavalry! Ellen felt a moment of despair. She imagined a whole regiment of blue-coated men riding in with their sabers shining and with firm orders to reduce any Indians in the area to nubs. She hurried to the rail and looked up the road. There, leaving the ford at Fall Creek, came eight riders. She let out a relieved sigh. Not a regiment. In fact, only seven wore cavalry uniforms.

Hestor sprinted for the Jarvis barn to tell Pitt. Tim stood at his barn door while the soldiers rode their matching brown horses at a sedate pace. The animals were in excellent condition—better condition than the riders, some of whom slouched in the heavily-laden saddles, caps pushed back. Except for one or two, they seemed as scruffy as some of the cattle drovers who rode through the settlement. Scraggly mustaches, blue wool jackets unbuttoned, they scanned the settlement with tired, amused looks. Two pack horses brought up the rear of the procession.

But as the riders drew parallel to the store, Ellen's stunned observation fastened on the eighth figure in this group. No military dress. He wore frontier clothes, his fringed shirt stained from sweat. "Oh, no!" She hurried down the porch steps, staring at the sorrel horse. The horse's rider, bedecked with longish auburn hair and a short beard, smiled at Ellen, showing straight white teeth. Ellen didn't notice as the image of the horse and rider from her cornfield vision trotted through her mind. Clear and exact, here in the flesh was that sorrel horse and the man in a fringed shirt. Ellen rushed forward.

The man reined up. "Ah, Mam'selle," he began. He beamed at Ellen, who was now right beside his horse. "I must say, I'm as delighted to see you as you are to see me."

Ellen put her hand to her mouth, stunned that she had run out to him. She backed up. The rider swung his right leg over the high pommel and jumped to the ground. "Burton Stamford, U.S. Marshal, at your service, Miss." With a flourish, he took off his hat and bowed to her.

Ellen couldn't suppress her smile. U.S. Marshal, she thought with surprise. His hat was cavalry issue—for an officer. Expensive riding boots; by speech, obviously a Northerner. She had assumed he was commanding this group of troopers. "I—I thought you were going to fall off your horse," she said lamely.

Burton Stamford guffawed—a huge laugh that got the Claytons and the troopers looking their way. "Such concern! I wish I had fallen. It would have been true ecstasy to receive your comforting." His speech was cultured and precise. "I'll try it again, if you wish." He started to mount his horse.

"No! No." Ellen shook her head. *If he stays on the ground, the image couldn't be true.* "Meeting you once is quite enough."

"See, Pitt! Rob got the cavalry and a real U.S. Marshal!" Hestor was declaring as he and Pitt came around the store on the run.

Ellen, suddenly conscious of the marshal's perusal of her, looked past him as if he weren't there and followed the boys to where the troopers clustered in the shaded meadow near the Clayton hotel. Tim joined them, sliding from the back of a brown pony.

"Indians, I tell you," Luke was declaring to the compactly-built sergeant with heavy eyebrows and a dark mustache highlighting his angular face. "There was even a wagon load of them come through right after that."

"Them was Wichitaws," Tim scoffed at Luke. "Tame as can be, headed back to The Nations."

"I've barely slept for worryin' about my family," Luke declared.

"Your own scalp, you mean," Tim shot back.

"Sergeant," Ellen said, hoping to quash the usual Fykes-Clayton fuss. "It's really quite good of you to come all this way, but if your trip was to rectify an Indian problem, I'm afraid it was all for nothing," she said.

"Nothing, my eye!" Luke Clayton said.

"We've never had hostilities with the Indians," Ellen stated.

"They aren't going to come out and announce when they plan to kill someone," the sergeant said, a definite Irish brogue to his speech.

"Well, I'm the one who found the body," Ellen said. "And— and Indians didn't kill Mr. Stone."

"Ah. Then you'd be Mrs. Hargrove." The Rs rang impressively. "The boy has told us about you."

Ellen's heart thumped and she wondered what Rob had said. (*"And we've got this queer woman. She sees the future. Knew all about the murder ahead of time!"*) Rob grinned, proud of himself.

"Sorry that a fair young woman like yerself should have to look on such," the sergeant continued.

"But don't make light of what she says, Sergeant." Her father's voice heartened Ellen. "My daughter hasn't lived a sheltered life, and she has a keen eye for how things are."

Hestor pushed forward. "Why she even saw Mr. Stone de—"

"Hush, Hestor!" Reba grabbed the boy by the ear.

"And you would be?" the sergeant asked Matthew.

"Matthew Jarvis, sir."

"You own the trading post. I'm First Sergeant Malone, Sixth Cavalry, B Company Special Scouts under Major Forsythe." While he identified his troopers, Dillard Winslow and Rose wandered down. Malone introduced the man in the fringed shirt—Burton Stamford.

He nodded to Ellen, green eyes alight with interest, although subdued from his initial cockiness.

"Reliable reports at Fort Harker indicate the Osage have moved down into Indian Territory—closer to Fort Cobb," Malone said. "There's a major treaty meeting going on, you know. Of course, there're always young bucks who think to prove themselves with some bloody heroics, and Kiowas still come this far east. So we can't ignore the request of any Kansas settlers." Malone frowned and stared beyond the group of people. "I must say, Major Forsythe did think there was an actual town here. The boy spoke of a hotel and school." He eyed Tim's ramshackle barn and corrals. "I take it that's the livery?"

Ellen sighed. "Well, just so long as you aren't going to charge around and harass the Indians of the area. We've had little trouble with them ever, and—"

"And how long is ever?"

"My family has lived here for nearly three years," Matthew said, his voice stern as if daring anyone to question the fact.

Malone's eyes widened with surprise. "There's not record one of any long-term settlers down here. Did ya file a homestead claim?"

"Of course not! This is still disputed land—part of the Osage diminished reserve," Matthew blustered.

The sergeant chuckled. "Yer one of them hoping Congress will allow squatters rights, huh. Like those dreamers up at Wichitaw. Bloody Town and Land Company is asking for a garrison to protect 'em."

Matthew sighed. "That's not what I had in mind."

"Did they tell you?" Luke cut in. "Indians attacked a cow herd not but a day north of here."

"Rustling?" The marshal, in his fringed shirt, stepped forward, intent on Luke's words.

"That wasn't done by Indians either," Ellen said with disgust.

"They just buried one of them drovers this morning," Luke went on. "I'm surprised you didn't meet up with the culprits."

"If the herd was headed to Abilene, they were a hard-day's ride east of our path," Sergeant Malone said.

Heavy laughter and Rose's high cackle interrupted their conversation, and Sergeant Malone turned to where his men were joking with the woman. "Well, goodness. Rose Schaffner. This is where ya got to when ya left Ellsworth."

"Since the trail-herd boys weren't comin' to me, I thought I'd just go meet 'em. How you doin', Jabber?" she responded to the sergeant.

Winslow moved beside her possessively, frowning and scratching his bushy sideburns.

Malone nodded to Winslow, but he spoke to Rose. "You still earning his bread and butter?"

"Oh, my." Reba backed away from the bold conversation, dragging Olive with her. Ellen studied her shoes.

"I thought ya would have dumped that old rascal by now," Malone went on.

"He's good with a team and can drop a deer at a hundert'n twenty paces. A girl does what she has to ta get by." Rose's voice was teasing and the troopers laughed. Winslow shuffled aside, his face reddening.

Ellen put her fist to her mouth and coughed to hide her smile over Winslow's discomfort.

"So are you going off after those renegades?" Pitt asked, stepping in front of the sergeant. "You need a guide? I know the area real good!" Matthew tugged him back.

"They need to stay right here, in case we're attacked," Luke declared.

"Can't see what good eight men are going to do," Tim muttered. "And we never had trouble with the Indians."

Malone ordered the troopers to make camp in the woods west of the cattle company tent as the marshal said, "I'd like to see the site where Mr. Stone was killed. That might indicate if Indians were involved."

"Why, that's nearly seven miles from here!" Pitt exclaimed. "I can show you, though!"

"Not tonight, son," Matthew said. "It would be dark by the time they got there."

"True," the marshal said. "I'll just have to content myself with gathering information here." He turned to Ellen. "You found the body, I believe?"

"Yes." Ellen suddenly felt nervous.

"Then perhaps—" He glanced around. "If there's a place we can talk."

"You might wanna palaver with Lutecia Mercy, too," Tim suggested. "She and Miz Clayton prepared the body for burial, and Lutecia knows medicine—could probably tell you just how it happened."

"Mrs. Mercy?" Stamford glanced around.

"Her cabin's back there," Reba said, pointing.

"She might be out at their cow camp with her husband," Pitt said. "I can get her for you!"

The marshal chuckled and glanced at Matthew. "It seems he's anxious to help. Would you mind if he did an errand?"

Matthew smiled. "I don't think so."

"Well, then, sir." He looked directly at Pitt. "Would you tell this Mrs. Mercy that I am here and I would like to speak with her later."

"Sure! I'll tell her!" Pitt rocked up on his toes, anxious to be off, his face in a broad grin.

"Ask her if it's convenient for me to call at her cabin—oh, around eight or so."

"Yes sir!"

"Go on, then Pitt. But don't run your pony ragged," Matthew called as Pitt sprinted off.

"And now. Mrs. Hargrove." To Ellen, the marshal's tone changed—sounded menacing.

"Come up to the store," Matthew suggested. "There are chairs and a table."

Ellen headed in that direction even before the lawman agreed. On entering the store, she perused the large room, wondering if it would appear as dingy and unimportant as the newcomers obviously considered the rest of the settlement. No. The shelves were full, the counters dusted, the arrangement of display tables and racks looked neat and orderly. The pleasant store environs, which she considered her responsibility, boosted her confidence.

She carried another chair to the table near the north window and looked out, surprised to see her father heading back into the yard. She had expected he would come in, too. The light in the room dimmed. Ellen straightened, tense, as the darkness which often surrounded James Montgomery came to mind. She turned toward the door.

"Very nice," Marshal Stamford said, taking in the store interior. The bright rectangles from the sunlit windows and door, were stark contrast to the black shadows of the rest of the room.

Ellen, her apron skirt grasped in clenched hands, swallowed and took a shaky breath. "The store has been here longer than we have," she said. "It belonged to a partner of—"

"Yes. Dutch Bill. Your father informed me of that just a moment ago." He strode to the table and hung his hat on the peg near the window. "He also said he and your mother weren't in the settlement the day you found the body." He sat down, crossed his legs, folded his hands on his top knee and stared at her.

"No." Ellen stood behind the other chair, leaning on the back. She couldn't tell what he was thinking, could barely make out his features. She wasn't sure if she should sit, or wait until he instructed her to do so. Then, upset with her self-degradation, she pulled down a lantern, tweaked a match on the metal frame of the glass-fronted display case and brightened her surroundings. The marshal's aquiline features sprang into view. Above his tufted beard and neat mustache, his green eyes were in high contrast to the tan of his skin, and they studied her shrewdly. She wanted to fidget under his inspection.

"So you are Mrs. Hargrove," he finally said. "Mrs. John Hargrove."

"Mrs. Johnny Hargrove," she replied. Her right hand strayed to the neckline of her dress, caressing the blue scarf Johnny had a given her. "John is—was—his father." Her voice trailed off.

"Of course. They live not far from here, isn't that so?"

"Lived." Ellen said. "They're gone. Moved away after— They moved away last autumn."

"I see. Where do they live now, your in-laws?"

"What? Oh, I imagine they went back to Missouri. That's where Mr. Hargrove's family was from." And to where I sent the letters they have never answered, she thought.

She drew a deep breath and refocused her attention. "I began listing information you might want to know," she said as she walked to the service counter.

"Did you, now? And what things might I want to know?"

"About what we found." With the key, she unlocked the wide cash drawer and took out the ledger. From the back she retrieved the paper she had begun.

"Who was with you?"

"My brother Pitt. The one you just sent to find Mrs. Mercy."

"Just the two of you?"

"Yes. We were delivering farm equipment to an Osage family."

"I thought you hadn't any dealings with the natives."

"No *hostile* dealings. The order had been placed by a church group and they asked that it be delivered to—"

"Do you still have their request? It was written, I presume."

"Yes." She turned back to the counter.

"Don't get it now. I just might want to take a look at it later."

"All right." He's so imperious, she thought as she sat in the chair across from him. The lantern heated that corner of the room, and she wished the side window could be opened. Maybe the store had been more comfortable with oilcloth—before her father put in the glass windows. "My list." She slid the paper across the table toward him.

Stamford studied the paper.

"I listed the people who were in the settlement that day." Her words faltered as she could see her own writing—*Reed Carter* with several question marks after his name. She wanted to snatch back the paper. Reading that, the marshal might surmise that Reed hadn't been here—was a suspect in all this. She certainly didn't want that, not after Reed's helpfulness when they went to the Pierces; not after his supportive attitude when she mentioned her suspicions about James Montgomery.

"Who is this Mr. Blankenship who left after the funeral?"

"He is—was—the secretary or accountant for the cattle company. He worked for Mr. Stone. He left two—no, three days ago. Right before the storm."

"Did he also know your husband?"

"Johnny?" Her hand involuntarily fluttered to her neckline and then away. "Goodness no. Mr. Blankenship only arrived here when Mr. Stone arrived—just a week ago. They set up their tent the day before the murder."

"Have any of your family been around?"

"My family? Well, you met my father and my brother Pitt. My mother is at the house, and my other brother is out on the western plains, rounding up horses."

Stamford leaned his forearms on the table, his head tilted a bit to the side. "So you found a boot—just one, saddle bags and no horse."

"Yes. It appeared Mr. Stone had stopped to eat. Mr. Blankenship told me the horse was fairly fractious, so it may have run off."

"You arrived a bit after midday and the body hadn't yet stiffened. Yet you saw no one else; and besides finding a body, nothing out of the ordinary happened."

"That's right." Ellen suddenly recalled the vivid brightness and shock that had struck her while she and Pitt were singing. What had that been? She had forgotten about it until just now. She pushed up from her chair, her cheeks flushing.

"And the Osage you were taking the farm equipment to. They never showed up?"

"We didn't stay long. Just unloaded the items and—and—" She paced along the front of the counter.

"You seem nervous, Mrs. Hargrove," the marshal said without looking up from his reading. "Are you?"

Ellen tried to smile. "A bit. I've never talked to a law enforcement official before."

"Really?" He gave her a surprised glance before returning his attention to what she had written.

"It seems so warm in here from the lantern. Perhaps we could go onto the porch," Ellen suggested. She was put off by the marshal's intimidating manner, and worried about this suddenly-recalled aspect of that day. But maybe it wasn't anything to worry about, she reprimanded herself. Just a result of tension from taking the trip to Sycamore Spring, anticipation of what she was so certain she would find—what she did find.

Nothing to worry about, she silently reiterated as she stepped onto the porch. *Just like the little horse and rider were nothing. The sorrel horse is here, but the rider didn't fall from his horse. Nothing happened!*

Being on the porch offered a slight breeze that seemed as refreshing to Ellen as a cool damp cloth placed on her forehead. The marshal's horse stood at the hitching rail, a back foot cocked as it dozed. No one was about, and above the Clayton cornfield, clouds to the west were suffused with pink and deep coral. The sun burned fiery bronze two man-heights above the horizon. A flock of dark birds winged southward. With a shift in the clouds, light radiated shafts into the high blue sky, some streaky and hazy yellow, others as stark as hot iron. Ellen placed her hands on the porch rail and took it in, never tiring of the varied beauty the land offered.

"That's magnificent," Marshal Stamford said stepping beside where she stood. "Part of the charm of this country, the way something usually taken as granted becomes suddenly special."

She looked over at him, appreciative of his perspective. "Yes. It's quite marvelous." She returned her attention to the sunset just as Pitt trotted his dun around the corner of the building.

"Hello there, Pitt. Did you find Mrs. Mercy?" the marshal asked as Pitt reined up.

"Yep. She and Mr. Mercy are back at their cabin and says any time is okay with her for you to stop by."

"Well, thank you! I think I'll head that way." The marshal put on his hat and started down the stairs to his horse. "Before I go, Mrs. Hargrove. Would you know who is in charge of the cattle company now that Stone is dead and Blankenship has left?"

"Oh—, yes." Ellen's voice stalled. She wanted to blurt out her suspicion that James Montgomery was the killer. But how to explain her knowledge? And did she really know that was true?

"That'd be James Montgomery," Pitt offered with a grin. "He's teaching me how to rope!"

"James Montgomery," Stamford turned toward Ellen. "His name wasn't in the notes you made."

"I began those notes on the day of the burial," she managed to reply. "He arrived two days later."

"You want me to take a message to him, too?" Pitt's exuberance seemed to crowd the area.

"No, that's not necessary. Thank you, though," the marshal replied. "And thank you, Mrs. Hargrove. You've been very helpful." He inclined his head to her, face expressionless, then got on his horse.

"I'll ride you back to the Mercy place," Pitt said. "Oh, Ellen, Ma said to bring one of those cans of peaches when you come to the house."

"Ma's up?"

"Yeah, and she's got supper just about fixed."

"Then let us get on our way so you won't miss a meal," the marshal said to Pitt. Pitt grinned and rode off with the man.

Ellen wished she could feel enthused about the marshal's presence, but something in his manner disturbed her. She went inside where the lantern flame still burned and got the tin of peaches her mother wanted. Her mother up and cooking as if nothing were wrong. Ellen wondered what conversation would be like at supper. She closed and barred the front door, unhooked the lantern from its chain to carry and see by, and left by the back door.

10

*B*right morning. Peach colors just burning out of the sky. Dew still dampened the prairie grasses. Ellen was glad to be out, riding Phineas again, although her companions and their destination dulled the occasion.

"Hey, look, Pop!" Pitt, riding his pony beside Matthew's big draft, pointed southwest.

Three miles from the settlement, they were on the way to Sycamore Spring to show Marshal Stamford the murder site. From Phineas's back, Ellen looked to where her brother pointed. Beyond the slope of hill and far onto the plains, small brown lumps dotted the green landscape. Only by staring carefully could movement be discerned.

"Bison," Stamford said from where he sat his sorrel. "Must be nearly two miles off."

"Your boy's got a keen eye," Sergeant Malone said to Matthew.

"That he does," Matthew responded.

Ellen adjusted the strings on her brown bonnet and scanned the area. They were going over a knoll that gave them a good view of the region. Stamford at her side, they rode nose to tail with Matthew's and Sergeant Malone's horses. Pitt, on the other side of Matthew, tossed his looped rope at various bushes. She looked back at the loose column of troopers, not appreciating the way Malone was leading this expedition. "You'd think for all that posting of guard they did last night," she muttered, "these soldiers would have sense enough not to skyline themselves."

"The Indians have moved further south," the marshal said.

Except for the young bucks who like to prove themselves, Ellen thought. They might be a worry.

Although morning sunshine fell steadily where they were, huge white clouds billowed from the horizon to high above them, turning the western sky fleecy. Phineas flicked an ear toward a prairie hen that lurched from behind a thatch of grass.

"These animals of yours seem tireless, to keep up with cavalry horses," Malone was saying to Matthew. "As large as they are, I'd have thought they couldn't do a long trip."

"Eight miles is barely long in this country, Sergeant Malone. And endurance is one of the Burgundians' major qualities."

"Burgundian?"

"Yes. Bob and Clio were yearlings in my wife's dowry. Bred for farming back in Pennsylvania, but they've adapted well to the West. These two are offspring."

"Phineas, that's the horse my sister rides, was once stolen by Indians!" Pitt said, coiling the rope around his saddle horn. "Were they Cheyenne or Pawnee, Pop?"

"Cheyenne. That was three years ago come fall, right after we moved here. Certainly had Ellen upset."

Ellen smiled, liking this story.

"And how, by the saints, did you get him back?" Malone asked.

"They brought him back," her father said.

"It was three mornings later," Pitt chimed in, getting his pony to prance sideways so he could see his audience. "There was Phineas tied up at our door. We didn't know what to make of it until Mr. Chisholm came through. He asked us if we got something returned to us recently. Pop told him about Phineas."

"He laughed," Matthew went on. "Said some Cheyenne came into his place teasing one of their young men for his poor choice of horse flesh. It seems he had stolen this big, heavy horse. Fit only for a squaw, they said. The others ridiculed him into taking it back where he found it."

"Mr. Chisholm knew it had to have been one of ours, and hoped we got it back," Pitt exclaimed.

All the horses' ears flicked to attention when Stamford let out with his big laugh. "Well, he certainly isn't a buffalo pony!" Stamford said, laughing more.

"Lucky it wasn't Comanch that got him," Malone said, glancing doubtfully at Matthew. "They'd have at least eaten him for dinner."

"Oooo!" Ellen hunched her shoulders and patted Phineas's neck. "Phineas steak doesn't sound good to me. It'd be like eating one of the family."

Stamford laughed again, but this time Ellen wasn't amused.

Pitt got permission to ride ahead with the point men. The bushy tail of his pony kinked and flipped as Pitt cantered up to the cavalry browns.

"And you've been in these parts for three years?" Sergeant Malone asked Matthew.

"Just about. Moved here when I came home from the war. It's lovely country."

No questions about where he served. Ellen knew most people didn't say much about that. Bad memories, as well as never being certain if the fellow you spoke to might not have served on the other side. Where these troopers fought four and five years ago was anyone's guess. The western forts were manned with whomever they could get. Complicated thing, a civil war, Ellen thought. And yet Tim had driven horses in from the west two summers ago, barely aware there had been a conflict.

"Where did you live before that?" Stamford asked her father. "Southwestern Missouri?"

"No. Up in Shawnee County, near Topeka," Matthew said. "Why do you ask?"

"Just curious."

Ellen frowned, finding the marshal's questions troublesome. His curiosity had a certain direction to it. She wished she knew what it was.

After a moment of quiet riding Stamford asked, "Ever hear of Kyle Montrose?"

"Can't say that I have," Matthew responded, easing around in the saddle to look back at the man.

"No! Don't tell me you've been put on that run around!"
Malone hooted, his Rs rolling. "I'm beginning to wonder if the man
truly exists."

"Oh, he's quite real. A rebel officer quartered in Cassville for
a while. Led a lot of attacks on gold shipments and then went
renegade when the southern war effort slowed. Made off with
Rebel funds, too. Since then I've heard he moved to Mexico
and bought land, although someone else told me he had taken
to gambling on the river boats."

"The latest report I heard had him riding with the Hendricks
gang," Malone said.

Ellen frowned, trying to sort through the marshal's
conversation for some threads of continuity.

"Voss Hendricks?" Matthew asked. "I read that group was all
either jailed or dead."

"Yes. Caught a lot of them last month over in the Ozarks."

Ellen's free hand strayed to her neckline, and then back to the
reins. The weather had become too hot for a wool scarf and she
hadn't worn Johnny's gift today. But that doesn't mean I'm forgetting
him, she reasoned. Just mentioning a place he had been made me
yearn for some connection to him. Her left thumb flicked to her naked
ring finger. She concentrated on the conversation to keep melancholy
at bay.

"But Montrose wasn't one of them, I'll bet," Malone put in.

"Definitely not. That gang wasn't his style, anyway. So there's
still a Grand Jury warrant out on him both here in Kansas and in
Missouri. It would be quite a coup if I could nail him."

"I hear there's a big reward, too," Malone added with a grin
toward Stamford.

"I'm a U.S. Marshal, Sergeant, not a bounty hunter. Accepting
reward money is not part of my job."

"Aye." The sergeant scratched at his chin.

The saddles creaked as the horses jogged through a shallow
wash. Water glinted a narrow stripe of light along the middle.

"So what's this Montrose like?" Matthew asked after they were
on the flat. "We brought some broadsides back from Eldorado.

Maybe he's using a different name."

"I'm sure of that. His general description: tall, good build, dark hair, clean cut."

"Mustache? Beard?" Matthew asked.

"Not usually, but nothing's for certain with him."

Ellen allowed herself a glance in Stamford's direction. She wondered if Montrose had a dimple when he smiled, and then she chastised the sudden thought.

"Do you suspect anyone in particular?" Malone asked.

"I suspect everyone and no one," Stamford said.

Ellen shifted on her sidesaddle, staring over Phineas's ears. "It seems that Mr. Montgomery rather fits that description."

"Montgomery. With the cattle company?" Stamford said. "Haven't met him yet."

"That Stone company is a reputable firm," Malone put in. "That's the reason we were sent down here. Can't have upstanding citizens struck down and ignore it." Malone straightened in the saddle, staring ahead to where a point rider galloped toward the column. "Something's afoot," the sergeant said.

The rider reined up with a hasty salute. "Sergeant Malone, sir. I've cut the sign of a large herd of cattle," the trooper reported. "The boy suggested it might be part of the herd that was rustled."

"What direction was it headed, trooper?"

"South, sir. Into The Nations."

Relieved to be done with the talk of outlaws, Ellen joined the men in a brisk lope. It didn't take them long to reach where Pitt walked his pony along the wide mark the cattle had trod.

"I've been careful up one side and down the other," Pitt announced, frowning. "Can't find a single horse track."

"Just a herd stampeding on its own?" the youngest trooper asked.

"But whose herd? No one at all lives out here," Matthew said.

"The tracks look to be over three days old," Ellen said. "It could be part of Mr. Baxter's herd."

"Tracks that old would have been rained out," a trooper drawled, obviously doubting Ellen's observation.

"No. She's right." Stamford was off his horse, testing moisture in the soil with his fingers, measuring the depth of the marks. "The rain must have quit here before it did further east."

"Injuns," a surly trooper said. "They probably wrapped their horses feet up in burlap so they wouldn't leave a mark."

"Anyone could do that." Ellen leaned over Phineas's shoulder, peering into the dried mud. "Whoever it was probably just kept the horses in with the cattle while they crossed the main trail."

"Murray! Pendleton! Check out the back trail of this herd," Malone called. "Ride up a mile or more. Shod horses could be a good indication that Indians weren't involved." The two men sighed and moved off in a lackadaisical manner.

"Heck, the Indians in The Nations shoe their horses, too," Pitt said eagerly. "They got good blacksmiths down there."

"Pitt, would you hush!" Matthew said. Ellen exchanged a perplexed look with her father, tired of blaming the Indians.

"Most renegade white men shoe their horses, too," she muttered.

"Widow Hargrove." That was Stamford, his voice smooth and guileless. She pinched her lips together and blinked several times, trying not to react to the title *Widow*. She had never before been referred to that way. "I'm curious as to why you're so certain Indians weren't involved in this."

"They just weren't, that's all." Frowning, Ellen again noted the stern look in the marshal's eyes, but he didn't pursue his question.

Two miles more and the scouts had returned, finding nothing. Ahead, the grove at Sycamore Spring stood dark and brushy, the white limbs of its colossal designator shrouding the smaller trees. The verdant shade looked black at all but the perimeter. Pitt was still with the point man and Malone sent two others to scout the area before they rode in.

"Oh, no." Ellen staread wide-eyed at the place. "Oh, Pop. I'm sorry."

"Now girl, don't tell me, that you've brought us to the wrong place!" Malone said.

"No. Not that. It's just that everything's still here."

"What do you mean, Ellen?" her father asked.

"I was sure Riding Boy would come to pick up the equipment, but he didn't."

"You seem quite certain," Stamford said, giving her a puzzled glance.

"I—" She rubbed her forehead. I shouldn't have said anything, she realized, suddenly embarrassed. Maybe it won't be the way I think.

But before long, Pitt was charging back on his pony, holding his hat in place, his possibles sack flopping along his side. "Hey Pop! Guess what! It's still there! We shoulda brought a wagon. Riding Boy never picked up his stuff!"

They dismounted at the edge of the grove. Shaded from the sun's heat, the ground was still mushy from the storms earlier in the week. The farm equipment looked untouched and set where she and Pitt had left it. The breeze wafted a vague fetid odor as Ellen pointed out where she had found the body. The rain had washed clean the cowslips and burdock where Francis Stone had lain.

"There's something over here," a trooper called to Malone. He held up a riding boot, slit down the side.

"That's Mr. Stone's" Ellen said. "We only found one with the body."

"Was it also cut?" her father asked.

"Yes. Cut and pulled apart a bit."

"As if someone were looking for something," Stamford said.

Ellen nodded. She hadn't thought of that at the time, but now it seemed to fit. A robber, looking for hidden money or important papers.

"Marshal!" Sergeant Malone called, his voice urgent and harsh.

Ellen followed Matthew and the marshal to the southwest corner of the glade, but Ellen stopped when she saw a reddish-brown skeleton hand protruding from the lupine. Her stomach rolled.

"Gollee!" Pitt exclaimed while backing up.

"Here's more," a trooper said. "Strung out along the slope there."

"Probably from scavengers," Malone muttered.

Stamford frowned and knelt beside the grisly find.

"A body over here. Looks to be an Indian," another trooper called. "Here's some clothing."

"And a moccasin here," Stamford said, pulling beaded leather from its cover of twining vines.

Ellen, her arm around Pitt's shoulders, looked at what Stamford showed, noting the intricate curving pattern of line and flower. She knew that design—had seen it before.

"Riding Boy," came her father's shocked voice.

"Gollee," Pitt said, sober this time. Ellen closed her eyes, hand to her mouth.

"The bones are pretty clean," Malone said.

"And rain washed. Must have died over a week ago," put in the marshal.

Ellen pivoted away, not wanting to think about the mangled body. And guilt assaulted her.

"Maybe this is the one who killed the big Whig," one of the troopers suggested. "Stone wounded him enough to drop him here."

"I don't think so. Riding Boy was a peaceful fellow," Matthew defended. "Had a small farm northwest of here. Sent his children to missionary school last year. He'd have no reason to attack a lone white man."

"Unless he was attacked first," Pitt suggested.

Ellen shook her head, recalling the casual pose of Stone's body. He had not been attacking anyone. He'd merely stopped to eat his lunch.

"Porter, Daugherty. Ride around and see what else you can find." The troopers seemed more alert, anticipating action.

"Yes," Matthew said. "There may be others. Riding Boy would have had someone with him when he came for the tools."

"There's not a wagon or anything," Pitt was saying.

"Pull that blanket out of my pack, Pitt," Matthew said.

When Ellen saw her father lift a portion of Riding Boy's body, nausea struck her, and she stumbled toward the spring, studying the ground as if answers would be there. Only purple violets were visible, sharing the leafy groundcover with larkspur and Sweet William. Beyond the spring, the glade opened again into prairie, spilling into a short draw that led all the way to the Bluff River. Behind her, the men grunted and muttered to themselves. She could hear them moving back and forth, but refused to look. Sitting on a fallen elm trunk and staring south, she wondered what had really happened here—who was responsible. Why hadn't she considered that Riding Boy could have been in danger that day? He could have been lying there even as she and Pitt struggled with Mr. Stone's body. She didn't even know Mr. Stone! How could she have left Riding Boy—and acquaintance for several years—to this end? In some ways it seemed she could know so much, and yet was left with total ignorance. It didn't seem right.

"We've finished up there," a gentle voice said. Stamford bent to the rivulet where he rinsed his hands. "Are you all right?" His face was tense.

"As well as can be expected." Ellen stood up. Her heavy black work shoes were muddy, dress hem damp from the wet ground.

Stamford shook water from his hands, removed his hat and smoothed his hair and short beard. "Care to fancy a guess about happened here?" he asked. "You seem to be quite good at it."

She faced where he stood three paces from her, hat in hands, auburn hair glinting red as if he were still in sunlight.

"That's not anything you haven't already heard about, I'm sure." She started back to the others, imagining the information Rob had told about her.

"How's that?"

"Rob Clayton. I'm sure he told you about my dreaming all this."

"He would ride hard to the fort if he thought you made this up? He's an eager lad, but I doubt that."

"Rob said nothing about—?" She straightened her shoulders, more than willing to let the subject drop. "Never mind, then." She adjusted her bonnet. It had been so long since she had that first dream about Sycamore Spring—the one she revealed to her family and that Pitt blurted around the settlement—that Rob might have forgotten. *Thank goodness.*

"Never mind? You've mystified me, now for sure. What were you going to say?"

From the distance came quick popping sounds, which Ellen recognized as distant shots. Stamford loosed the holster thong from his revolver. The crack of a rifle was next. Ellen hurried passed where her father was using Pitt's throwing rope to tie the ends of a blanket-wrapped lump—Riding Boy—reduced to a bundle resting under the sprawling shade of sycamore branches. Ellen drew a shaky breath and kept her eyes on the plains.

Stamford pulled his rifle from the scabbard on his saddle. Sergeant Malone stood at the edge of the grove, staring northwest to where troopers Porter and Daugherty galloped their horses for the trees. Behind them, on stout ponies, rode several bare-chested men.

"Indians, Pop," Pitt said.

Ellen ran to the horses, quickly getting Matthew's heavy Hawken from the saddle sheath. Matthew took it and calmly opened a shoulder pouch. He loaded linen and lead, a frown on his face while Sergeant Malone organized a defense. Pitt was already ensconced behind a hummock, his Trapdoor Springfield tight in his hand.

Another pop sounded. Matthew tamped down the lead, added a measure of black powder.

Ellen moved to her family's horses and checked the cinches before taking hold of all three sets of reins.

"At least we aren't stuck with pilgrims," Stamford said to Malone as he fingered a cartridge into his Henry rifle. "Where did you get experience at this? Your father said you've had no trouble with the Indians."

"We lived along the Republican River a few years before the war," Ellen said. She maneuvered Phineas close to a fallen log so she could mount quickly.

The cavalrymen galloped in, dismounting deep in the trees.

"Kiowas, I think," one of them said, out of breath. "We came on them in a draw about a mile up. Had a wagon with them." They tossed their reins to the young trooper who was flushed with fear as he took charge of the horses.

"And I thought I saw a squaw," the other said, readying his old Remington.

Six Indians reined up along the knoll some two hundred yards away. Three carried carbines. Five more with bows and arrows approached after that. Ellen could barely make them out through the leafy veil, but knew the troopers and her father had a clear view.

"Hold your fire everyone," Malone ordered. "Jarvis, that Hawken of yours has the range to pick off one from here. Be ready."

"Those are Osage, not Kiowa," Matthew said, resting the butt of the long rifle to the ground. "Let me see what they're up to."

"Wait, man! You can't just walk out there!" Malone grabbed Matthew's shoulder, holding him down. "When I've got civilians under my protection, I bloody well plan to see them protected!"

"Hey Pop, look!" Pitt said. "That's Waits-no-more." He pointed.

Ellen stepped away from the calm horses to see the new rider who joined the others—a boy Pitt's age.

"Riding Boy's son. I'll bet he's looking for his father," Matthew said.

Matthew shrugged away from Malone. A rifle sound cracked. Earth kicked up a several feet in front of the tree line. The Indians fanned out, right and left.

"You might think you know them, but they obviously aren't friendly!" Malone declared.

Two of the troopers sent useless shots toward the Indians and began reloading.

"But that *is* Waits-no-more. He's been to our store many times," Matthew insisted.

Ellen squinted, recognizing both the boy and the rider he stopped next to. If they could see who we are, they'd stop shooting, she thought. She eased to the horses and took up Phineas' reins. Arrows thudded into the earth several yards in front of the trees as the Indians determined the range.

"Open up with that Hawken, Jarvis," a trooper said. "Show them they've already come too close."

"That's just asking for trouble," Matthew grumbled.

Ellen pulled onto Phineas's back, reined him around and headed for the edge of the grove beyond the troopers. "They'll know this horse," she called to her father.

"What in tarnation are you doing, woman?" Stamford bolted to catch the horse. Ellen put heel to Phineas and the big mount lurched into sunlight, exposing her to the Indians' scrutiny.

"Waits-no-more! It's Big Horse!" she shouted, using the name regional Indians had for her father. "Big Horse wants to talk!"

From the hill, the boy was pointing at Ellen and conferring with an older man. The warrior Ellen recognized shoved at the rifle barrel of a colleague. A shot discharged toward the sky. Ellen smiled, knowing her plan had worked.

The Indian leader, bare chested with a spiky roach tied in his hair, was listening to the others, his rifle still trained toward the grove.

"Why you here, daughter of Big Horse? And with pony soldiers. Where is Big Horse?" the brave called.

"I'm here!" Matthew walked out of the grove, ignoring Malone's blustery protest. "Why are you attacking us? Let's talk!"

Ellen backed Phineas to her father. "Good job," Matthew said to her. Pitt ran to join them as Matthew asked, "Who is that fellow next to Waits-no-more? We know him."

"It's Beaver Laughing. Riding Boy's brother," Ellen replied.

"Ah, yes."

Beaver Laughing listened to their leader, then said. "Talk only if the soldiers show themselves. We not want to be shot down."

"Stand up," Matthew said to the troopers.

"We can take 'em, Sergeant," one man said. "They only got one decent rifle."

"Move on out. Let them see what they're up against," Malone stated.

"He's right." Stamford stepped forward. "No point in ruining a chance to parley. And we do have the better position if a fight occurs." He holstered his pistol.

The sense of potential battle floated away with the breeze as Beaver Laughing and Waits-no-more trotted their horses down from the knoll. The other Indians stayed back, and one man called harshly to the younger ones, insisting on something. Ellen was gripped by the realization that they would have to tell these people about their dead kin. Matthew walked out to meet them. Ellen, still horse back, Pitt, Sergeant Malone and Stamford followed.

Beaver Laughing, thick set with corded muscles in his arms, neck and chest, stopped his horse three paces away and studied Matthew with dark eyes. Around his tanned, rough-lined face, his hair was shoulder length and he wore feathers and beaded leather tied into it. A copper and stone earring was in one ear lobe, and he sat his horse bareback, stocky legs hanging easily along the beast's sides. "We look for my brother. Why you here?" His voice was a strong and demanding.

"There—there has been a tragedy," Matthew said. "A white man was killed here—seven days ago. These soldiers want to find out what happened."

How to tell them? Ellen looked at Waits-no-more's sad, wide face. Dressed in a calico shirt and leather britches, he wore finely beaded moccasins Ellen knew his mother had made. The pattern was nearly identical to that on the moccasin found in the grove.

"Did you come here seven days ago?" Stamford asked.

Beaver Laughing scowled at Stamford, then at Matthew. "We no kill white man, Big Horse."

"No. I don't think you did, but—" Matthew licked his lips, obviously uncomfortable.

"What about the farm tools you were supposed to pick up?" Malone barked. "Did you see the white man dead in the grove?"

Beaver Laughing shifted his gaze from Matthew to Malone and then back.

"I know you will only speak the truth, Beaver Laughing," Matthew encouraged. "You must tell us what you know so the soldiers won't think you were responsible."

The muscular Indian studied Matthew. "And then you tell what *you* know." A sadness filled Beaver Laughing's eyes, replaced quickly by a flat, unreadable calm.

He knows his brother's dead, Ellen realized. Beaver Laughing scrutinized Ellen. I'm sorry. So sorry, Ellen thought.

Beaver Laughing looked away and began his story: He had ridden with his brother and family to get the farm tools. Beaver Laughing didn't trust the new missionary who was not a black robe. He told how long his people had been Catholic, and how they learned to speak like white men, and how they tried to make other changes the White Father wanted.

Sergeant Malone shifted with impatience, but Ellen recognized a certain bewilderment from Beaver Laughing over all the changes his people were being forced through. Beaver Laughing always straddled the breach between Osage tradition and the new ways Riding Boy embraced. Even now, his words reflected that.

"I never sure," the pensive man said. "My brother rides ahead to this place. Comes back in big hurry. White man chases him."

"How far from here?" Stamford asked.

Beaver Laughing frowned at the interruption, but answered. "Maybe one of your miles. Up there—up from where soldiers found us."

Pitt butted in, "But that's not where we fou—"

Matthew held up his hand, silencing Pitt. Sadness returned to Beaver Laughing's eyes.

"This white man," Malone began. "What did he look like? An older man? Graying hair?"

"No. Is man like so." He pointed to Stamford. "Long face hair here." He pulled his fingers around his top lip and down along this mouth. "Bigger, darker man."

Ellen's pulse slowed, thudded. She could see the man he described—she knew.

"Go on with your story, Beaver Laughing," Matthew

encouraged. "What happened?"

Beaver Laughing spit to the ground then looked at Waits-no-more. "His father takes bullet. Still he rides to warn us. Then the white man throws a rope. Catches his father, pulls him from horse."

Ellen's eyes widened.

"I start to him, but the dark one shoots. I have scar to remember." He lifted his thick arm, showing a wound, still puffy and red, along his ribs. "Man drags my brother with the rope. Puts big knife on his throat. Yells at us to leave and not come back."

"We had to leave my father with this evil one," Waits-no-more said, holding back tears.

"Evil?" Ellen asked.

"You didn't shoot this man? Save Riding Boy?" Stamford asked, disbelieving.

Beaver Laughing held up his muzzle loader. "The other, he has good Henry like yours. I not want to see my brother's wife and her son killed."

"My father was alive when we left and we went to our farm, but no one would help," Waits-no-more said, his voice choked with anger. "They said it was a sign that we shouldn't follow the ways of Whites. We had to get help from Knocks-on-the-wagon."

"Riding Boy's father?" Matthew stared toward the knoll.

"That divil!" Sergeant Malone exclaimed. "I thought he was way out on the South Canadian with the Kioway."

Ellen's heart pumped heavily. Knocks-on-the-wagon had never approved of Riding Boy farming. What would he do when they told him his son was dead?

"But why didn't you come back, the three of you, for Riding Boy?" Stamford persisted.

"My uncle was hurt, could barely ride!" exclaimed Waits-no-more.

And Beaver Laughing said, "Bad dark."

"Bad darkness?" Matthew asked.

"A bad thing here. Evil. I see it in this white man. You not face a bad dark alone."

"And then the twister wind came with rain," Waits-no-more said.

"We have now come back. We know my brother is in the spirit place, but—"

"No!" Waits-no-more protested.

"Waits-no-more," Ellen began, but was unable to tell him. "What—what time was it when the white man chased your father? How did the sun sit?" Weakness washed through her, already knowing what he would say.

"It was on our heads. Your noon time, Missus Ellen."

"That was right when we were coming here!" Pitt declared. "That was when—" He stared at Ellen. She wanted to pull Phineas from the group and ride away. "When you stopped the horses that time—felt funny. It was Riding Boy you sensed dead," Pitt said with awe.

"He's not dead! My father is not dead!" Waits-no-more insisted.

Beaver Laughing began talking to him in Osage, his voice stern. The boy covered his face.

Beaver Laughing glowered. "You tell him, Big Horse. And Pretty Willow is there, with wagon." Beaver Laughing thrust his chin toward the hill. "Pretty Willow thinks he just injured, wants to get him—wants to see—"

Yes, Ellen thought. I understand. It's hard to believe they're dead when you haven't seen the body—haven't witnessed the horror.

"You found him," Beaver Laughing stated.

"Yes," Matthew said. "We have found him. I'm—I'm sorry."

Waits-no-more stared, shaking his head, then broke into a high-pitched lament. He pulled his horse around and galloped north. Ellen slapped the reins on Phineas's neck and the big horse lumbered off behind the boy—to go to the wagon where Pretty Willow was; where the woman was already mourning her husband just as Ellen had done last year.

At least she can see to his remains, she thought.

11

*M*alone didn't like it, but Matthew insisted on staying for the Osage ceremony. Ellen and Pitt agreed.

"The man traded at our store for two years," Matthew said.

"I consider Pretty Willow a friend," Ellen said.

"Well, I can hardly leave you alone out here with the heathens," Malone said indignantly.

Knocks-on-the-wagon never came down from the knoll, although three other warriors did. Pretty Willow, in a calf-length fringed-leather skirt and calico blouse, tended the remains while the others cut saplings and lashed together a tall platform. Matthew, grim-faced and as stoic as the braves, helped arrange the platform over the top of the farm implements. It stood nearly seven feet in the air.

"Beaver Laughing said his father won't let them take Riding Boy home," Ellen told the marshal as they watched with Pitt from east of the grove. The troopers, with their horses fanned in a slight arc, faced Knocks-on-the-wagon. "I'm surprised he even came looking for him," Ellen went on.

"Hmm." Stamford fingered his short beard. He had said little to her since she returned, driving the sobbing Pretty Willow's wagon—Phineas tied to the back. "I'm sure the church won't be happy to learn where their money has gone," he said.

"They bought the equipment for Riding Boy. What is done with it now is not their concern," Ellen said. "Besides, there's nothing else from Riding Boy's life here to leave with him. He worked hard at his farm."

"Hmm."

Pretty Willow cried and wailed, rocking over the gruesome remains of her husband. Before long, Beaver Laughing pulled her away and the warriors lifted a blanket sling containing the body onto the platform. Matthew came to where Ellen stood with her brother and Marshal Stamford.

"Are they just going to leave him up there?" Pitt asked.

"Yes, son. That's their way."

"But the vultures and everything will pick at him." Pitt scrunched with discomfort.

"I think they feel a person's spirit has already left the body. This is just a tribute."

Ellen flinched when Pretty Willow, keening steadily, hacked the calves of her leg with a knife tip. No one stopped her and Ellen turned away, having heard about self-mutilation as a sign of lament.

"Stupid heathens," one of the troopers whispered.

The Osage tied feathers and ornaments to the edge of the platform. They had come prepared, Ellen realized. Waits-no-more was with Beaver Laughing now, bare chested as the rest of his uncles, a yellow clay smeared on his face. An older man, who had directed the work, held a hand drum and began singing something in a high monotone. The others joined in while Pretty Willow, her dark hair hiding her face, beat the ground with her fists. Ellen felt her own hands clenching. Here I am at another funeral, she thought. Another young man dead.

"*Oh. Honga u wa-zah zhe,*" sang the older man. The others sang and chanted a few more lines, then they all were quiet except for Pretty Willow's high wail. Ellen heard her father release a long breath, his hat in hand, eyes downcast. Pitt fidgeted beside him.

Ellen, still transfixed by Pretty Willow's distraught figure, could feel tension building. She heard Knocks-on-the-wagon yell something from the hill, and turned to see the man with his rifle held above his head. The Osage men turned away from the platform.

"I think we got trouble," Sergeant Malone said quietly.

Waits-no-more pulled at his mother's arm and spoke to her while Beaver Laughing rode his horse up to Knocks-on-the-wagon.

"What's going on?" Ellen asked.

"I'm not sure," Matthew said, his hands on Pitt's shoulders. The marshal and the cavalry readied their horses.

Knocks-on-the-wagon urged his horse past Beaver Laughing's and called something else. The warriors leaped to their ponies and Pretty Willow, already in the wagon, turned it. In a rush, the warriors rode over the hill, Waits-no-more with them and the wagon following at top speed. Only Beaver Laughing stayed back. Ellen watched him lope down to where her father legged her onto the sidesaddle. Pitt mounted his pony.

"What is it, Beaver Laughing? What's going on?" her father asked.

"Knocks-on-the-wagon blames white men for death of his son. You go now. He not look on you anymore. He avenges his son on next white man he sees."

"You mean us," Matthew said, glancing to the rise over which the Osage had disappeared.

"But that's not fair!" Ellen blurted. "It was only one person who killed Riding Boy."

"Many turn us from our ways," Beaver Laughing said.

"But you saw the white man who did this!" Ellen persisted. "He was different, wasn't he?" Beaver Laughing shifted and yanked at his horse. His discomfort encouraged Ellen. "You said it. The Bad Dark. Evil, you said."

"This not my war party. I only tell you my father's words," Beaver Laughing declared.

"Knocks-on-the-wagon threatens us because he's afraid of who really killed his son! Don't attack us just because you let the Bad Dark get away! Go find him!" Ellen was as shocked by her vehement tone as was Beaver Laughing. The Osage man stared at her with fiery eyes.

Malone and Stamford rode over. "What's going on?" Stamford murmured.

"You go!" Beaver Laughing said. "I— Pretty Willow not want it be you caught in my father's anger." He whirled his horse and sprinted off.

"Knocks-on-the-wagon threatens to kill the next white he sees,"
Matthew told as he mounted his horse. "But he's given us a chance
to leave."

"We can take 'em, Sergeant," called a burly trooper. "Let's
make a stand!"

"We're not here to engage the hostiles, Trooper. Especially
not with treaty talks still going on. We've been given our chance.
Let's ride," Malone said.

Ellen trembled, gripping Phineas's reins. Her own rash words
echoed in her head. *Did I really accuse Beaver Laughing of
cowardice?*

Pitt, riding in front of Matthew, asked the question they all
wondered. "Are they going to chase us?"

"Most likely, son. They've just given us a head start."

"Get moving!" Malone yelled.

The young trooper's face was blanched with fear, eyes wide.
No more deaths, Ellen thought. What have I done? Please, Lord.
No more deaths.

Malone dropped back and Ellen knew he was ordering a rear
guard, although his actual words were lost in the thudding of their
horses' hooves. Stamford's horse alternately surged ahead of hers
and then pulled back. The snorts of the cavalry browns were close
on Phineas's flanks, and after a mile, Ellen realized what was
happening. Phineas and Champion were too slow. They could keep
a steady pace, but had no speed at all. She glanced at her father,
who seemed to have realized the same thing.

"Pick up the pace!" Malone rode up to them. "The redskins
have started their chase! I'll look for a place to take a stand!" With
ease, his horse pulled away from them. Her father whipped
Champion's flank with his hat.

Ellen's pulse seemed to be double the time of the relentless
rise and fall of Phineas's big hooves. *So slow, dear beast.* "Come
on, Phineas." She leaned closer to the horse's bouncing mane,
urging him on.

Heat and dust converged, gritty; wind hot; airborne horse
sweat; her breathing, raspy from the dry air. Her bonnet blew back,

held by the strings around her neck—chafing. Ellen could see her
favorite mount straining. Froth gathered along his mouth, his red-
brown coat nearly black with sweat. How long? Two, three miles?
She wanted water. Phineas needed rest. On a sudden wind shift,
she heard high-pitched distant cries. Then ahead, she saw Malone
stopped on a steep swell of ground, his horse tossing its head. Not
a place for defense, Ellen was certain.

When Phineas clambered up the slight rise, she understood.
There, plodding north in the broad dale below, were buffalo.

"We're trapped," a trooper said.

"Must be the herd I saw earlier," Pitt said, wiping sweat from
his face with his sleeve. His expression matched that of the others—
dismay and fear.

Ellen pulled loose her bonnet strings and used the cloth hat
to wipe her dusty face while she looked onto the humped, brown
backs; the line stretched out of sight to the south with heavy-
haunched bulls on the outside of cows flanking the yellowish calves.
The animals grazed and moved slowly, with the young ones frolicking
in the open spaces.

"Maybe rifle shots will make them scatter," suggested the young
trooper.

"No, son," Malone said. "Buff aren't like cattle. They'd keep
to their path or turn on us. Either way, we're in trouble."

"Can we breach them?" Stamford asked, alternating his attention
from the buffalo to their rear. Ellen refused to look back.

"They'd gore us for sure," Malone said. He and his troopers
drew their rifles.

"But maybe further up," Matthew said. "Near the front of the
herd, the groupings up there don't look as dense. Hurry!" He
reined Champion north and jogged down the slope to within a
hundred feet of the great beasts. Ellen followed, trusting her father.
She glanced over her left shoulder. No Osage. But the land had
small dips and hills. They could be right behind the rise.

Matthew swerved Champion for an open space in the herd
that seemed to extend all the way through the vast river of them.
He slowed, trying not to alarm the beasts. Ellen followed. A cow

snorted at a yellow calf that ran across their path. The cow gave
pursuit, jogging toward Ellen. Stamford spurred his horse toward
the lumbering cow. The cow veered away, but all the bison increased
their pace, forcing the mounted humans to angle north. Dust, gnats
and flies billowed up from the animals' thick hair. The rank smell
made Ellen squint and hold her breath. Horses snorted. They were
in the middle of the flow, now, the huge animals eighty feet on
either side, grunting and snuffling as they moved.

"Osage, sir!" a trooper cried.

On the swell behind them sat Knocks-on-the-wagon and his
warriors. Two braves aimed their powerful bows. Ellen looked away
and put her concentration into maneuvering through the increasingly-
restless buffalo. Her dress was wet with perspiration. Along her
back and under her legs, the cloth seemed to grab her like the fear
she felt.

"No shooting!" came Malone's anxious call. "Get through
these buff."

"Careful, Pitt," Matthew cautioned.

Tramping and heavy snorting came from Ellen's right, and she
looked onto a bull only four strides away, its hump as high as Phineas's
shoulder. I should be afraid, she thought, staring at the creature.
Her pulse was steady, her concerns more curious than distraught.
The bull bellowed low and the cows near it moved more quickly,
thickening the throng around the humans. The bull swung its head
to the right. The left eye, buried in the curly black mat of hair
beneath the wide forehead, seemed to sight on Ellen—fix her with
intent. Phineas plowed on more quickly. The bull snorted and
grumbled—low, like a growl. Ellen heard the action of a rifle.

"Don't!" she said to Stamford, breaking her stare from the
massive creature. "Look!" The way before them was clear and she
pressured Phineas for a trot. The others were already exiting the
far side of the herd. No arrows had zinged or thudded nearby, no
shots fired. No buffalo charged.

Malone and his men trained their rifles toward the Indians as
Ellen and Stamford came out of the herd. The wagon, with Pretty
Willow, appeared on the rise. Ellen rode up the slope to her father

and Pitt, trembling with belated shock. Looking back, she realized they were well out of the Osage firing range across a moving barrier of buffalo more than an eighth mile wide. Her father gripped her shoulder, his fingers quivering.

"I've never been that close to a live buff," Pitt said quietly, staring at the herd.

"And I've no pleasure to repeat the experience," Stamford put in. Sweat trickled along his dusty jaw, making a muddy line.

"Let's go before them savages find a way to get through," Malone ordered. The others needed no more prompting and turned their horses.

"Mrs. Hargrove?" the marshal said, riding back to her.

"A minute." Ellen's curiosity was for the Osage. The warriors pivoted their horses, clumping together and then pulling back, except for two. Beaver Laughing and Knocks-on-the-wagon sat apart from the others, calm and staring across the stream of buffalo.

"What's got into you?" Stamford demanded. "They'll try to get across soon enough. Let's go!" He rode in front of her and grabbed at Phineas's reins.

She pushed his hands away and turned her mount. "They aren't going to come after us," she said, her certainty borne of something she couldn't name. "We're safe." She kicked heel to Phineas and started after the others.

They followed their shadows to the settlement, dark, rough-edged lines reaching out before them as the afternoon sun gleamed on their shoulders. The same lines were in Ellen's mind: dark and formless, consuming her thoughts. A certain dread hunched around her, more pronounced than the sweat-sticky clothes and the grime, more sickening than Riding Boy's murder and his family in mourning. And worse, she couldn't identify the cause of this morass. Several events should have had her in a better mood—they had escaped the wrath of Knocks-on-the-wagon, and the information given by

Beaver Laughing substantiated Ellen's belief that James Montgomery was the killer. Yet her thoughts skittered about like an injured deer that knew wolves were in pursuit, almost frantic, desperately wanting some peace. No one spoke. Perhaps the others also harbored some inner plague heightened by the murder scene and their perilous flight from the Osage.

In the Clayton cornfield, Luke and both of his boys were hard at work with hoes. On reaching the trail that led into the settlement, the first thing Ellen noticed was her mother standing on the store porch, the shotgun propped nearby. Belinda shaded her eyes to see her family. Pitt waved. Matthew encouraged Champion to his wife while Malone issued orders for a night guard and defense of the town.

Olive sprinted from the dugout toward the returning group.

"Olive, don't pester them!" Reba called.

"But, Ma-aw-ah, I wanna be first this time!" she whined, slowing. "I wanna know something before Hestor does."

"Let it be. You'll get any news soon enough."

Up toward Fall Creek, a row of horses were tied to a picket line. Several men stood around the striped awning that marked Reed's place, and more ambled in the vicinity.

"Looks like things have been busy while we were gone," Stamford said.

Ellen nodded, feeling Phineas pick up his pace as he headed for the familiar shade of the well yard. She didn't deter him. Matthew and Pitt had dismounted and led their horses, Belinda tucked into the curve of Matthew's free arm. I am no longer part of this family, Ellen thought. I have to make my own life.

Pitt's excited voice floated to her. "And then Ellen looked him square and said, 'Don't attack us just because you let the bad dark get away'," he related enthusiastically. "Beaver Laughing really got mad!"

How can he still have any energy? Ellen wondered.

"The bad dark?" Belinda questioned.

"I think he just meant the cyclones that were coming," Matthew suggested.

"But Ellen and me—"

"And I," Belinda corrected.

"We didn't see sign of weather when we were out that day," Pitt argued.

Stamford rode beside Ellen and she wanted to send him away, but that took too much effort. Instead, she angled Phineas along the paddock fence and dismounted with the help of the fence slats.

"You're quite an independent one, aren't you," Stamford said, standing down from his horse.

"This country doesn't allow for much else, Marshal." Ellen loosed the cinches on the saddle.

Stamford pulled loose the equipment. "I just realized you've been through all of this riding sidesaddle."

"It's quite comfortable," she said. "Especially with Phineas's easy gait."

"Where shall I put this?"

She led the way to the barn and pointed to a bench before getting a cloth to wipe down her horse. "Thank you." The warm familiar smells increased her tiredness.

"I've been meaning to ask you about a comment your brother made—about your sensing that Indian dead."

She couldn't respond, had hoped no one remembered with all else that occurred.

"What did he mean by that?"

"Who knows what a youngster means," she said, trying to laugh. Even in the dimly lit barn, she felt exposed and trapped.

"From what he said, you had some strange sensing—you stopped the wagon and everything."

"I swear. His imagination. I felt a moment of disquiet, being all that way from home alone, and he made it into something scary."

I sound just like my mother! she thought, hearing her dismissing tone. She gave a slight laugh, amazed at what she was doing. "Pitt is prone to make something out of—" She couldn't finish—couldn't make it sound as if her brother were a prevaricator. She frowned and faced the marshal, his features obscured by shadows.

"Marshal Stamford, what do you want me to say, that I knew about Riding Boy's death? Do you think I had something to do with his murder, or that of Mr. Stone?"

"I think you know more than you're telling."

Ellen stalked to the barn entrance. As she stepped into the yard, the quick steps of little feet were accompanied by Reba's shout, "Olive! Get back here!"

Ellen watched the girl race toward her own family at the water trough. "Pitt! Tell me what happened. Tell *me!*" Olive insisted. Reba hustled behind the girl, her skirt held in one hand and George clasped under her other arm.

"Olive Rebecca Clayton! Get home!" Reba shouted.

Ellen stopped as Olive froze from the call. Chills skittered through Ellen's arms, down her back, and she drew a quick breath, shocked by the memory Reba's words brought to mind. Ellen's mother-in-law had told a story—had recited names...

"Mrs. Hargrove?" The marshal stepped to her while Olive slumped back toward Reba.

Ellen felt like a leaf caught in an eddy, not knowing which way to turn. To her mother, standing near the well pump? But no, Ellen thought. She won't really listen, won't hear me. She shrugged off Stamford's reach for her arm and started a brisk walk to the well-worn path that led toward the Mercys. A pinch of anger joined her other concerns; anger that Stamford already knew what she was just realizing. *That's why he thinks I know more than I'm telling.*

"What's happened?" Stamford asked loudly. That got her parents' attention.

Pulling her grimy skirt to her hands, Ellen began to jog, her chest tightening with dismay. "Ellen!" came her father's call as she hurried across the still-mushy greenery of the yard. She picked up her pace and stared hard at Lutecia's cabin, hoping her friend was home. Lutecia opened the door, her expression alarmed, as Ellen rushed into the yard.

"Ellen, what—?"

"Ellen!" Her father had caught up with her. "What's wrong?"

"I just want to talk to Lutecia." Her father frowned at her.

"Please, Pop!" A tear slipped down her cheek. Lutecia's arms closed protectively around her. Please, she thought, willing her father away.

Soon she was in the dimly lit cabin that smelled of herbs and a fragrant stew that simmered in the hearth kettle. Lutecia's arms still held her and the warmth helped ease Ellen's emotional chill.

"All right. All right. What? Tell me. Your papa's likely to break down the door soon, he's so worried. What?"

Ellen gulped air. "Riding Boy's dead," she said, trying to defer her real misery. "We found his body."

"Oh, dear. But, I know you didn't run back here in a state because of that," Lutecia said, pushing Ellen into a chair by the table. Her friend waved her hands in a shooing motion toward the window, and with a side glance, Ellen was relieved to see her father backing away. Lutecia produced a large square of clean cloth so Ellen could mop her face.

"Mother Hargrove," Ellen said after a moment. "We were getting along fairly well, you know. When we'd work together at canning or needlework—" Lutecia pulled a chair up close beside her and sat down.

Ellen drew a shaky breath. "Reba called Olive. Called her by all her names, you know how people do when they want to get a child's attention. She told me a story once, Mother Hargrove did, about when she was a girl. How she did something wrong and her mother yelled at her—just like Reba yelled at Olive. Nettie Jo Hendricks!, she said her mother yelled. I didn't remember until I heard Reba. I didn't know. It must be."

Ellen, appalled by her nescience, looked at Lutecia, waiting for a response. Her friend frowned, wanting more. "You know, Johnny always called his uncle *Uncle Vee*. I know, I'm right. Dear Lord! What have I brought on my family? Now I don't even feel sure about Johnny, about what happened. Oh, Lu!" Tears flowed and she slumped over so her head rested on the table.

"Ellen," Lutecia began quietly. "Is this something you've seen. You've had another dream? I'm not understanding."

"Oh, no, no, no. This is real, Lu!" She straightened and looked plaintively at her friend. "Mother Hargrove was a Hendricks—her maiden name. And Uncle Vee—" She gripped Lutecia's hands in hers. "That's why they were so upset when Johnny said he was going with his Uncle Vee. He's an outlaw, Lutecia. Vee for Voss. Voss Hendricks!"

Frustrated, Ellen withdrew into a trickle of tears. Lutecia patted her back. Soon steaming tea wafted fragrantly to her. She sipped and murmured muddled comments of remorse. "I know absolutely nothing about anything—especially not about my own life. For all I know, Johnny was an outlaw, too!"

"No he wasn't. Here. It's in the Fort Smith paper about the Hendricks gang." Lutecia smoothed a newspaper on the table. "They've identified the members and have their names listed here. Not one is named Hargrove—not even a John or Johnny."

"Where did you get this?"

"From a Cherokee bunch that came through this morning."

Ellen held up the paper and read the article about the twenty-year sentencing of Voss Hendricks and members of his gang. "They think two members are still missing," she said morosely.

"I'm sure they're just supposing. Nobody knew for sure how many made up the gang, and the ones caught haven't mentioned any other names."

Ellen let the paper flop to the table. "How can I see things like Mr. Stone dead, and not know my own husband was from a family of outlaws?"

"Ellen, this is crazy talk," Lutecia said, her exasperation showing. "Johnny wasn't an outlaw, and not either were his parents. Taking on some sort of guilt for this uncle is like if I went around apologizing all the time 'cause my mama's daddy was a white planter, or if I held it against Charles 'cause his parents weren't slaves." Lutecia leaned on the table, took Ellen's arm in her hand and jiggled it to get her full attention. "You and Johnny loved each other in a most strong way. That's what counts. It don't make no difference what his uncle did."

Ellen gave a wistful smile, thinking of that "most strong way" of hers and Johnny's love. Nothing had changed that. "You're so sensible." She covered Lutecia's hand with her own.

"You are, too, Ellen. You've just let your emotions get in the way a bit. A bad day, today. Um um um."

"Yes. A bad day."

The afternoon had cooled and turned cloudy by the time Ellen left her friend's comfort. She walked back to the well yard that was silent of human input. Birds chirped in the tree branches; there a chipmunk dashed across the damp lawn. Her concern was for Phineas, whom she had left unattended when she was struck with her dismal revelation. On reaching the paddocks, she saw the big draft loafing in the pasture with the other horses.

Of course, no one would have left him standing, she thought. Her father would have cared for him, or even the marshal. She winced on thinking of that law officer and the critical way he had been treating her. Yes, she was certain he knew of her family connections.

From a distance she heard occasional strains of music from a mouth harp. Wandering to the edge of the barn, she looked toward the sound. From the army tents, she decided, and thought she could make out Pitt up there. Now he'll probably want to join the cavalry, she thought, shaking her head.

Grateful none of her family was around to question her, she went back to the family cabin and her quiet bedroom. Inside, steamy air greeted her. The big number three tub set near her bed, filled with hot water. She closed her eyes for a moment, new tears threatening to spill from them, but this time tears of gratitude. "Thank you, Ma," she whispered, knowing Belinda's effort to get at least eight pails of hot water into this tub. "Thank you."

12

The music sounds so nice, and a piano now. Where did the piano come from? *No one is singing, but she knows the words. "De Camptown ladies sing dis song. Do daah. Do daah. De Camptown race track—" The piano music bounces along.* Why, this is a saloon! What am I doing in a saloon? Yet there I am, in a frilly blue dress. And there's Reed Carter. Look how handsome, that black suit. *"Reed. I knew I'd find you here!"* He's going to kiss my hand. *Reed bends, his fingers gently holding hers. She feels his lips on her palm ...*

"It's Pitt!" her mother exclaims. Why is he running so hard? What's happened? *Tall grass sparkles and trembles around him as Pitt runs, going no where and waving something. He runs toward them, waving something, runs toward them. ... "It's Pitt!" her mother exclaims. Tall grass sparkles. Pitt runs toward her, but doesn't get any closer ...*

Snow whirls around her. She turns in it, feeling lost. Then it is spring.

This is truly strange. What is when and where is now? But here I am, riding Phineas through the trees. *Green leaves.* We have to be careful. It's marshy. We have to be careful. *But she keeps Phineas to a fast clip, his big hooves thudding the ground.* We are careful, but he will not be. *Thlud, thud, thud, the hooves; branches scrape at her, leaves shade everything. Thlud, thud, thud...*

She squints and shields her eyes. A wagon jiggles onto the horizon, wavering for a moment before it becomes distinct. The big freight wagon. JARVIS is written on the side. "Mama, Pop, what's going on?" *Staring silently into the blue-line horizon, they ride away.* And there I am on the back of the wagon next to Pitt. *She waves to herself who waves back then changes to George Clayton waving:* "Bye, Aunt Ellen. Bye-ee!"

Spencer sits a brown and white horse and trots beside them. No! He's lying on the ground; he pulls a shiny revolver ...

"De Camptown racetrack five miles long. O, do dah dey."

Changes had taken place. Ellen realized it immediately upon awakening. Except for a brief dream she could scarcely remember, she had slept well, and morning had found her with a new resolve. Lutecia had been right, Johnny wasn't an outlaw nor were his parents; her marriage had neither compromised her own family nor made her a lesser person. At breakfast, she apologized to her family for making such a spectacle the previous afternoon—an apology they accepted without comment.

"The reason I was upset. Well. It came to me yesterday that—that Johnny's Uncle V he often talked about, is probably Voss Hendricks."

"The outlaw?" Pitt said, his eyes wide. Ellen nodded.

"Do you really think so?" Belinda asked, pouring more coffee. She seemed amused. "I hardly ever think of outlaws as having family," she muttered.

"Wait till I tell Hestor!" Pitt declared, lurching up from the table.

"You'll tell him nothing, young man," Matthew said sternly. Pitt's expression drooped. "This is a family matter that will not be spoken of to anyone—unless Ellen chooses to, of course."

"Yes, sir," Pitt said, slouching back into his chair. Ellen knew Pitt would comply. A "family matter" had always been a pact of privacy with them. Pitt respected that.

"The conversation yesterday, about the outlaws, must have prompted your thoughts," Matthew suggested to Ellen.

Ellen nodded and stirred her coffee. While she explained how Reba's words had put everything in place, a flare of anger toward Marshal Stamford developed. Would she have reacted as ridiculously if he hadn't been making stern comments and staring at her so oddly? She didn't think so.

Now, as she opened the front door of the store, she noticed other changes. The grassy site north of the Claytons' hotel held only one tent, where yesterday morning there had been three. Looking further north, she was surprised to see open, trampled grass where the cattle company tent had been.

Montgomery has gone! she thought with a mix of emotions. The arrival of the marshal must have scared him off.

She was glad to be rid of Montgomery's mystifying presence— one moment normal enough, and the next blurry and dark with portent. Yet if he were the killer, that meant he had gotten away unpunished. She stepped onto the porch to better peruse the area. Beyond Fall Creek, north in the woods on the west side of the wide trail, a patch of white seemed unnatural amidst the green foliage.

"He had a couple of fellas move the tent yesterday right after you all left," Reba said, coming across the road from the dugout. "Probably to get clear of the gambling and carousing."

Reba carried George with her and when they got into the store, the boy squirmed to get out of her arms. "I swear, this boy," Reba said, setting him on the floor.

"Would you like me to look after him today?" Ellen asked.

"After the day you had yesterday, you surely don't need to put up with him," Reba said, studying Ellen.

"I wouldn't mind." Having George to care for might divert her thoughts from talking to the marshal about Johnny and his uncle; finding Riding Boy's remains still bothered her as well as Beaver Laughing's comments about evil. She knew the Osage believed in the supernatural, and Ellen wondered if Beaver Laughing had seen a dark aura around James Montgomery as she had.

"Well, thank you for the offer, Ellen, but there ain't no real need. Got a lot of men in town, but none seem obliged to eat my cooking." Reba sighed. "Just as well. I got lots of other things to do. Hestor ripped out of another pair of britches."

"He's growing fast," Ellen said. "I noticed a change in some other tents, too."

"Yes, Lord. That Rose is gone, her and her cackle and skinny hips."

"Where did they go?"

"They? Not they. Just Rose. Tim got her buckboard fixed and she lit out."

George was making awkward hops across the floor. "Owah, wah, wah, wah," he cried.

"Hush, George." Reba said.

"What about Nancy?" Ellen asked, a tight, worried feeling settling in her stomach.

"Nancy. Uh! Tryin' to make herself respectable with Mr. Montgomery. I can't for the life of me figure what he sees in her."

Ellen bit her lip. Oh, Nancy, she thought, Don't get tied up with him.

"You doin' all right, Ellen? You look a little distracted."

"Just tired still, I guess."

"And I guess you ought to be. Goodness! I heard about finding Riding Boy and all. That Marshal Stamford said his body had been butchered. Cut up on purpose. Imagine!"

Ellen hid her shock. No one had told her that.

"And then the Osages and the buffalo," Reba went on. "Did you know all that was going to happen before you went out there?"

"No, Reba." The snap to her voice made Reba frown.

George crashed into Ellen's legs, hugging her through her dark skirt. She held his arms, his little hands quickly grabbing her fingers as he leaned back.

"Well, I need some thread, I reckon, for all this mendin'. Brown thread will do. Everything turns out brown no matter how it starts."

Ellen picked up George and took a box from a shelf near the hallway. "I do it!" George declared. Ellen let him help set the box on the counter.

"I've been thinking that we ought to move out of here. The millet field is already swamped and the corn looks poorly. Your ma was talking about Camp Wichitaw. There's gonna be a town up there." Reba fingered through the spools of thread. "Do you think we should move to Wichitaw?" She set a twist of thread on the counter, looking hopefully at Ellen.

Ellen put George down, feeling flushed—knowing what Reba was asking. "I have no idea, Reba." Reba, brown eyes intent, stared at her, waiting. Ellen shrugged. "I'm sure Luke has it all thought out."

Reba's disappointment was obvious and she pushed a half dime across the counter. "You know, Ellen, you got a real talent. Why do you turn away from it?"

A small fury churned in Ellen. "You think I can just look at a situation and know all the answers?" she said between clenched teeth. "Well I can't! And what I don't know is so formidable, I can barely stand it."

Reba gave Ellen a shocked look. "Well, you don't have to get huffy about it!" she said, pulling back from the counter and grabbing up George. "I just asked a question is all."

Her back was rigid and hands fisted as Reba went out the door. Ellen quelled the urge to apologize and scraped the coin from the counter. While putting it in the cash drawer and withdrawing her ledger she heard a horse out front, then Reba's greeting and the deep-voiced answer. Slowly, Ellen pulled in a long breath as she prepared to face Burton Stamford.

He strode in smiling that secretive half smile he had—like he knew something she wished she knew. She gritted her teeth. I *do* know, now, she thought.

"Good morning, Widow Hargrove. I'm glad to see you recovered from yesterday's malady."

"Marshal Stamford." Her tone could have frosted July. "You need something?" she asked. He was freshly shaven and his auburn hair held a sheen. Even his fringed leather shirt seemed clean over his dark brown trousers.

"Some pleasant conversation, milady."

"Pleasant conversation? Or are you going to look for another way to tie me to all the misfortune in Sumner County." His baffled look stalled her for only a second. "I am Mrs. Johnny Hargrove, and Johnny's uncle is Voss Hendricks, but that no way connects me or any of my family to these murders."

He spread his arms and leaned his hands on the counter across from her. "Madam," he began imperiously, "I think you forget that I am investigating a crime. I can not ignore a single possible suspect, no matter how attractive and charming the person may be." Ellen's face warmed as the marshal continued. "You seemed to feign lack of knowledge about your husband's family."

"Not his family," she blurted. "His uncle, who lived no where near the Hargroves and who never came to visit." She stood a bit straighter to keep her strength—she disliked confrontations. "And I didn't even realize the connection until yesterday—after your various questions and curious comments focused my thoughts."

"I see. Is that what got you so upset last evening?" Ellen nodded. "And the nervousness you exhibited when I arrived? Pacing, not meeting my eyes when you answered questions— that was from what? My immediate response was that you were trying to steer me from some important facts with your list of information and all."

"I was trying to be helpful!" Ellen exclaimed. Through the window, she noticed Luke standing in the middle of the road staring north.

"And that you were. No one else had thought to ask Blankenship any questions—about Mr. Stone's activities, his horse and such."

"I can't imagine it amounted to much."

"Possibly. Possibly," he said, sounding mysterious. He angled himself along the counter, leaning on one forearm which brought his face closer to her. "But I really stopped in here for answers to a puzzlement I've run into."

Two horses loped up to the store. Tim and Sergeant Malone dismounted. Luke shuffled over to join them.

"Yesterday, you said—" The marshal turned when the three men entered the store.

"Guess what," Tim said, limping across to the counter. "Mr. Stone ain't dead!" He grinned at the dumbfounded shock his statement brought to Ellen and the marshal.

It was a different Mr. Stone. Ellen overcame her astonishment as Sergeant Malone told about the courier who had ridden in with a dispatch from Fort Harker command. "We thought the man killed here was Mr. Charley Stone, but we've now found out he's doing just fine at his office in Topeka."

"He's not a relation of Mr. Francis Stone?" Ellen asked.

"Ah. Francis was the man here, huh?" Sergeant Malone scratched his jaw. "Well, no mention was made in the dispatch of any alarm or remorse when Mr. Charley was confronted with the mistaken identity."

"The way you're speaking sounds as if it makes a difference to your assignment," Stamford accused.

"Well—"

"The scouts have been recalled," Tim said. "I was up there when the courier arrived."

"I knew it! I could tell they were packing their gear!" Luke said. "You're gonna leave here when the Osage could attack at any minute!"

"Get on, Clayton. There ain't gonna be no attack," Tim said.

"This seems quite irresponsible," the marshal said to the sergeant.

"I have my orders," Sergeant Malone said. "It seems General Phil Sheridan, hisself, is coming out from Washington to inspect the Western posts. Major Forsythe wants us there. Oh, and this came for you." He handed Stamford an envelope. "We'll be moving out within the hour, Stamford."

Stamford studied the envelope briefly before slipping it inside his shirt. "I'm not bound by your orders," he said. His stiff retort surprised Ellen.

"Well, now. We were assigned as your escorts."

"But only when it seemed some influential person was killed, is that it?"

"If we chased around the brush over every corpse found on the plains, we'd be no good to anyone," Malone stated.

"I'm sworn by the U.S. courts to uphold the laws of Kansas and the federal government," Stamford said. "To me, a murder is a murder. I intend to find the perpetrator of this crime."

He sounded pompous, but Ellen knew he took his position seriously. "And it's more than one murder," she said. "Riding Boy—"

"Now, Miz Ellen, you know nobody's gonna investigate some dumb Injun gettin' killed," Tim said, a look of scorn on his face.

"Whoever killed Francis Stone, killed Riding Boy," she continued. She rubbed her fingers on the counter, uncomfortable with the sudden attention the men gave her. "Riding Boy probably saw Mr. Stone get murdered and was hunted down—dragged back to Sycamore Spring to make it seem like he did it." As she spoke, she could almost see James Montgomery hauling Riding Boy back to the scene, could imagine that man's shock when he found Stone's body already gone. That's why he asked me if I had seen any Indians, she realized, recalling his visits to the store.

"It could have been," Malone said. "By the Osage account, that buck of theirs was caught in a wash over a mile from the spring."

"And what about this rustling and the boy killed? It seems you could at least reconnoiter that area before you leave," Stamford persisted.

"We've got to be back before General Sheridan arrives," Sergeant Malone said.

Stamford huffed an irritated sigh. "I'll just do it alone."

"You can't leave, too!" Luke blustered to the marshal. "Them Osage are gonna come here in force, I tell you!"

"Luke, after what Matthew told me, them Osage think Big Horse and his family has got powers of grace," Tim said. "Miz Ellen and all them was protected by the black humps; the buffalo stopped Knocks-on-the-wagon from killing them and that's enough to convince most Injun folks I know to change their opinions. They ain't comin' here!"

The marshal leaned on the counter and spoke so only Ellen could hear him. "You did say we were safe, didn't you." His study of her made her nervous. "Are you a scholar in habits of the savages, or did you know by some other means? What mysterious talents do you have, my pretty?"

"Your familiarities are quite out of place, Marshal Stamford," Ellen said, unable to stanch her flush.

"My pardon, Widow Hargrove."

Aggravated, she moved along the counter to the other three men. "Excuse me Sergeant, Mr. Fykes if you're not wanting to buy, I'm closing the store for a while," she said.

They nodded and went to the door, with Luke still arguing with Sergeant Malone, Tim arguing at Luke. Stamford backed toward the door, a slight smile on his face. "I still have my puzzle, but I'll go now. Make certain the soldiers don't pack my gear in with theirs." He tipped his hat and walked outside.

Ellen stood behind the counter until Malone, Tim and the marshal rode away from the front of the store and Luke stalked angrily toward the dugout.

The marshal still suspects me of something, she thought as she secured the front door bar and went out the back, locking the store behind her. She felt jittery from their conversation, and even more in anticipation of his "puzzle." It has to do with my foreknowledge, she thought. My knowing the tools were still at Sycamore Spring, knowing about protection from the buffalo. Maybe even Reba or Tim has mentioned other things. ("You know, Ellen, you got a real talent. Why do you turn away from it?" Reba said.)

"Limited, stupid insight that makes me think I know more than

I do," Ellen muttered, striding to the house. *But it's there. I should be able to do something with what I know. Something!*

Mid morning, it rained. Nothing prolonged or ominous. Raindrops pounded into the earth; a drenching for the garden. The sun returned. Ellen sat on the bench in the well yard, sunlight filtering through the tree leaves, her hair loose to the light breeze. She put aside the mending she had just finished—sewing a new four-inch mud hem on the bottom of her maroon dress—and closed her eyes, enjoying the natural warmth that relaxed her more than her full night's sleep. In her mind the sunlight danced across a broad bleached plain of summer grass. A buffalo, dark in the distance, grew magically closer, swinging its head. ("Ellen and all them was protected by the black humps," Tim said.) One keen eye peered at her. Grass wavered. Trotting horses sounded, hoof beats gentle. *What is when and where is now?* The horses slowed. She heard one whiffle from its nostrils; metal findings clinked.

This is now! She snapped open her eyes. Reed Carter sat his horse four strides away, his harness horse with him at the end of a rope.

"I'm sorry if I bothered you," he said with a gentle smile. Dark pants, white shirt. His suspenders were pale yellow. "Were you sleeping?"

"No." She straightened on the bench. "Just enjoying the quiet. How's your mare?"

"She's healed up. I've been taking her out when I go places. I ride her under saddle sometimes, too."

"That's good."

Reed dismounted. "I hear you had quite an adventure yesterday. Indians and buffalo." He took off a dusty felt hat and moved into the shade of the tree. "That was awful news about that Osage body you found."

"Riding Boy," Ellen said. She had heard that Indians didn't like to speak the name of the dead, but she wanted him to be more than just *that Osage body*. "We knew his family—stayed for their ceremony."

"And then got chased."

"Yes. But I'm still glad we were there to show Pretty Willow and Waits-no-more that we cared." *And Beaver Laughing, too.*

Reed shook his head, as if he didn't understand. "I've been out helping Charles," he said. "Catching the little ones and feeding them some concoction Mrs. Mercy created." He laughed self-consciously. "That's hard work!"

"I imagine so," she said, not sure of his visit.

He leaned against the trunk and fiddled with the reins in his hand. His horses plucked grass. "Did you know? Rose Schaffner has moved out," Reed said. "She's gone up to Wichitaw."

"Reba told me," Ellen said. *Why do I feel so awkward with him? It's something he's going to say. He's leaving.*

A breeze caught her hair and flared it along her shoulders. She flushed as his gaze took that in. "You should have seen it when Rose left," he said. "She wouldn't let that Winslow fellow get in the wagon. Kept hitting him with her parasol and finally the driving whip."

"She stranded him here?" Ellen asked, hoping the odd weightless feeling would leave her.

"Looks like it. He doesn't even own a horse. Everything belonged to Rose. I don't think he has much money either—at least not to meet Tim's price for a horse. I saw them talking yesterday right after Rose left."

"That's funny, but it's sort of tragic, too. Him way out here with nothing."

"True," Reed said.

"The cavalry has gone back to Fort Harker," she said.

"Rob rode out and told us. Funny thing, that."

"Marshal Stamford stayed, though. He's ridden north to find where the Baxter herd was rustled." *Where Tommy Atherton was shot.* "He's also pursuing some outlaw named Kyle Montrose and thinks he might be in this area. Have you ever heard of him?" Ellen asked.

"Montrose." Reed's tone was flat. "Yes. I've heard of him. What did Stamford tell you about Montrose?"

"Not much, actually."

"You know, I've got family in Tennessee," he said suddenly. "I haven't seen them since I joined the army." Stern jaw, rigid line to his mouth. "Decisions. Like I mentioned a few days ago. Things you do even though you know the difficulties they cause. Now I've got to face those difficulties."

From Tennessee, Ellen thought. A Rebel state, yet he was in the Union Army. "Have you written to them? Let them know you survived?" she asked.

"A telegram in '65. October. Many places in Tennessee held Union sympathies, but Clarksville wasn't one of them. My parent's were furious with my decision, and my fiancée—"

"You're engaged?"

"Not any more," he said with a wry chuckle. "She was outraged—took it personally. Her older brother challenged me to a duel!"

Ellen's mouth dropped open in astonishment. "You—you killed him?" she asked, incredulous.

"Goodness, no," He looked alarmed. "I left the area immediately. Crossed the river, joined my regiment." He sighed. "Still, I think I should have handled it differently. I worry about it a lot—similar to how you hold concerns about your ability."

"That! Not nearly as emotional. I mean, I'm not estranged from my family." *Except for the Hargroves.* "Will her brother be waiting when you get back? I don't know the protocol in duels."

"He was killed in the Battle of Franklin," Reed said. "So you see, I have no excuse."

Yes, he's leaving, she thought. An unexpected sorrow assailed her and she wondered what prompted it. Perhaps only that he was a part of their community; perhaps his warm smile and quiet ways. Inside she tightened, relaxed, and tightened again. The brief sensual wash stunned her. *My Johnny's been gone less than a year,* she rebuked herself. *I shouldn't feel like this.*

"Anyway, I wanted to tell you—let you know why I'm so interested in your talent and how you deal with it—beyond my general interest. In the metaphysics, I mean." He flushed.

"Yes, metaphysics," Ellen said with a smile.

The steady breeze wafted through the trees, making a shushing sound. There, a bird and the high laughter of one of the Clayton children.

"Have you told Stamford about James Montgomery?" Reed asked.

"No. I don't quite know how to go about it. I need some hard proof against the man, not just this dream image," Ellen said, frowning. "Like where he was when Mr. Stone was killed."

"He told me he was in Camp Wichitaw," Reed said. "Yet when he arrived here, it seems I recall him coming in from the west."

"There's just nothing to prove anything awful about him," Ellen lamented. Reed seemed preoccupied—staring into the distance.

"It must be past noon," she ventured, standing. "Ma and Pop will be in from the field pretty soon." She gathered her sewing. "Would you take dinner with us?"

"What? Oh, thank you, but I ate with the Mercys before I left their camp." He pulled his horse around, a frown darkening his features. "Well, good day to you," he said, mounting his horse. He tipped his hat.

Ellen stepped back, feeling an abruptness in his departure. She watched him ride away, wondering what had caused the change in him, and reproached her emotions that throbbed for a gentle touch, to be held, her skin that wanted to be caressed. Johnny. It was Johnny she loved. Always! She had to; she didn't save him. She had seen what was coming and not gone to him. *But I didn't know what I was seeing.*

Yes, I did. And I didn't go.

To quell her frustration, she began industrious work toward a meal, stoking the stove, mixing corn, flour, and milk for pan bread; slicing smoked venison, stewing greens. The kitchen was steamy and hot, but she barely noticed. When her family came in from the field she had prepared enough for ten people, but no one made comment.

More clouds blew in, gusting rain. The creeks swelled from rains further west. Fall Creek banks, lower than those of the Bluff, sloshed over at the ford, displacing huge globs of dirt. The glut of water churned a big cut all the way beyond Tim's and flooded the Mercy's cornfield which, like the Jarvises, was already sodden.

Evening progressed. Pitt stayed out with the Clayton children, playing in the showers that staggered across the settlement. Ellen felt trapped and sat in the dogtrot with a newspaper, not wanting confinement by walls as well as the weather. She could hear her mother pacing in the kitchen.

"It's all changing," Belinda said. "I don't know, Matthew. I think all the good energy is out of this place."

Ellen looked up from the large advertisement she was perusing about the great benefits of McPherson County, Kansas.

"What makes you think so?" her father asked.

Ellen wondered if she should ease away—let this be a private conversation, but she didn't, caught mostly by her mother's words about good energy. The only time Belinda talked about *energy* was before the family made a change.

"The weather mostly. And then some little things."

She heard her mother pace more and waited, expectant, as she assumed her father was.

"Like Reba, the way she's gotten," Belinda went on. "She was so snippy with Rose and Nancy, and she's rude to Reed Carter. That's not right. And Tim and Luke seem to be at each other more. It's beginning to sound like real arguing!"

"Tim's restless," Matthew said. "Waiting for the boys to get back with horses."

"They should have been here by now, don't you think?"

Ellen's pulse thumped in her head. She closed her eyes. *Please, let Spencer be unharmed. Spencer and Hubert. Please, Lord.*

"It's not been three weeks since they left," Matthew reassured. "Who knows how far West they had to go. They're fine."

"And then these murders," Belinda said. Ellen heard her mother's sigh, even through the closed door. "I don't know," Belinda lamented.

Ellen could track her mother's progress across the kitchen and to the bedroom her parents shared. She looked back at the newspaper, but the dingy twilight discouraged reading. Quietly, she went to her own room, recalling her mother's words—The good energy is gone. For Ellen it had been gone since last autumn. Good energy. Johnny. Both gone.

Ellen wasn't sure what awakened her. She rolled over in her bed and studied the light that came through the window. Still dark, but graying to early morning. She listened carefully. No rain. Someone was up. She heard her mother's voice, and then:

"I can help, too!" Pitt was pleading from the open door.

Wrapping herself in a blanket, Ellen pushed aside the curtain and padded barefooted to the dogtrot. Her mother was carrying blankets from the loft.

"What's going on?" Ellen asked.

"There's a trail drive about three miles down in The Nations," Belinda said to her. "The point man rode in and woke up Luke. They were hit by rustlers and have injured men; half the herd's been scattered."

"And I'm gonna help round 'em up," Pitt declared.

"First you're to ride up and get Tim Fykes and Reed Carter."

"What about Mr. Montgomery?" Pitt asked.

"Have Tim talk to him. I don't want you across the creek," Belinda said. After Pitt bolted out to get his pony, Belinda said to Ellen. "With Nancy living over there now, I don't want Pitt barging in on anything."

Ellen shivered in the damp predawn, concerned for Nancy's involvement Montgomery.

Her mother put on her big hat. "I'm going down there with Lutecia, see what we can do for the injured."

"Should I come?" Ellen asked.

"No. We'll bring them up here, I'm sure. Cook up some coffee. Oh, and set out the rest of that food you prepared for dinner. They'll all need a hot meal."

Ellen nodded and stood in the door as her mother hurried out. Another rustling, she thought. More men hurt. Lutecia drove the Jarvis farm wagon, and stopped it near the house, her carpetbag of medicines propped on the seat beside her. "Be careful," Ellen called. In the dim light of near dawn, Ellen made out her father on a Kiowa pony riding beside Charles toward the Bluff. Luke wasn't with them. *No surprise there.* Within a few minutes, Pitt and two other men joined the group. They all started off, fading into the tree line of the Bluff River ford. Low clouds swept the sky. The air smelled damp. Far away to her right, thunder growled.

After dressing, Ellen prepared the food. A light rain fell steadily on the settlement, but further north a big storm swept through. She felt the growl and bump of thunder more than heard it. By the time morning sunlight brightened the clouds to a dirty white, Ellen had set the coffee, laid out meats, and put the bread in a vented tin on the stove warmer.

We'll need extra water for the wounded, she thought.

Rain spattered on her through the warm air as she carried a bucket across the misty yard to the well. When she reached the alders, he heard Phineas snort like he did when alarmed. She looked toward the barn. A huge hand clamped around her face— across her mouth—and swept her backward so quickly that the bucket flew out of her hand. Her scream gurgled in her chest, and she jabbed her elbows at her assailant while she twisted to get away. Quickly, her arms were pinned to her with a mighty grip that pulled her tightly against a man's body. She could smell his sweat as he dragged her to the far side of the cistern. She kicked, hoping to connect with a shin, but met nothing.

Montgomery! He knows that I know what he's done. He's going to kill me!

"No scream," whispered a heavy voice—English spoken with the precision of a nonuser.

Ellen's eyes widened. Her mind raced. *An Indian! I'm being attacked by an Indian!* She sorted through who was in the settlement to help her? Luke Clayton? Dillard Winslow?

"I not hurt you." The hand across her face relaxed. She gathered air to her lungs to scream, tears burgeoning on her eye rims. "I know you saw the Bad Dark," the voice went on.

The Bad Dark? This is Beaver Laughing! Relief nearly made her wilt.

"I come to kill him." He had totally released her now.

Ellen whirled to face him and let out a small yelp on seeing the red and yellow mask-like face with paint streaked from lower jaw to hairline; but she quickly recognized Beaver Laughing behind the paint. Indignation surged as she swiped at her face where his gritty hand had held her. "Why did you sneak up on me like that? Like some sort of murdering savage!"

Beaver Laughing, in long fringed leggings and a colorfully woven breechcloth, bare from the waist up, glared at her. "One day your quick words will give you harm!"

"I didn't say *you* were a savage. You aren't! That's the whole point." She straightened her apron with an angry jerk.

"Where is Bad Dark?" Beaver Laughing asked

Ellen folded her arms, suddenly struck with a different nervousness. This man was looking for Montgomery—wanted to kill him. It was all she could do to keep from pointing to the large tent across Fall Creek. There! she could say. He lives there! Go! Kill him! But that didn't quite seem right. Keeping her voice calm, she said, "This is white man's concern, Beaver Laughing. Our law will take care of him."

"He killed my brother."

Ellen licked her lips, unable to forget the dismembered body of Riding Boy. Purposefully butchered. But she spoke carefully, "He has killed white men. More than one. And—and he committed crimes all during the white man's war." *James Montgomery is Kyle Montrose*, she thought with certainty. She could imagine the atrocities he probably committed, maybe even riding with Quantrill—burning and killing her neighbors in Lawrence. "He must answer to white man law," she said strongly.

"You know him. I saw that."

"I'm sorry for how I talked to you," Ellen said quickly.

"You speak truth real good, daughter of Big Horse. Speak it now. This evil one is here? Or maybe with missionaries."

"No!" She wanted no trouble there.

"Then here!"

Ellen swallowed hard, frightened to say yes—to condemn Montgomery to Beaver Laughing's revenge.

Beaver Laughing grabbed her arm and jerked her toward him, his eyes seeming ferocious behind the war paint. "I fight him man to man," he growled. "I count coup on his body many times before I kill him. I am not afraid!"

Ellen closed her eyes against the pain his pincer grip caused in her arm. He released her with a shove and she staggered against the cistern. When she opened her eyes, he was gone.

She rubbed her arm, knowing it would bruise. Her heart thumped, and her mind raced through what had just happened. What could have happened. Beaver Laughing could have been out for more revenge than against James Montgomery, she realized. He could have ravished her as punishment for her accusing him of cowardice. He could have scalped her ("That's a purty head of hair you got there. Bet the Injuns eye it a lot," Tommy Atherton had teased.)

And he could yet!

Charged with new worry, she bolted for the house, hurrying through the dogtrot, into the kitchen. By the time her shaky hands had loaded the side-lock shotgun, she was thinking more rationally, realizing that she would already be dead and scalped if that were Beaver Laughing's intention. It was Montgomery who had to worry. And he didn't even know it. Didn't know at all.

13

*B*y late morning, the Jarvis kitchen had turned into a restaurant, with Ellen keeping coffee in cups, bread and meat on plates. Her brothers' side of the bedroom across the dogtrot had become an infirmary, with Lutecia and Belinda examining and cleaning the wounds of two drovers who had been shot. Another broke an arm when he was thrown from his horse; one man hit his head on something and had been unconscious for nearly an hour; three others had been sick before the rustling took place. Of the five drovers in the kitchen, three were hardly men, Ellen noted. Old boys, she could better term them—like Tommy Atherton had been. Fifteen, sixteen.

And Montgomery is responsible for Tommy's death.

"We been gathering these cows since January," one of the boys lamented. "And what do we got now?"

"If we can get that twenty-five dollars a head on the ones left—"

"Got my mama and two younguns still living in a wagon, waitin' for the money—waitin'. Gonna have a good ranch, if'n we can get the money. One Pa woulda been proud of."

"But that cattlemen says McCoy Brothers ain't offerin' but fifteen a head up in Abilene," said another.

Ellen busied herself over the skillet where she heated more smoked meat.

"Hell, we coulda sold 'em for fifteen in New Orleans—not of had so much travel."

"Got tariffs going that way," said the older man with thick sideburns.

"Well, them Indians—Choctaws and such—are talkin' about having a real tax on the herds come next year—not just askin' for a cow in passing."

"Uh. A cow to hedge against bad luck," another man grumbled.

"They're stingy with their land, is all. Want to raise cotton and corn on the prairie," the older man said.

"I heard something about an evil connected with cattle—superstition of some kind," said the youngest.

"An evil?" Ellen said. They stared at her as if seeing her for the first time. "Sorry," she said, turning away. And she thought, a Bad Dark...Evil, Beaver Laughing had said. James Montgomery. *He has killed Mr. Stone and Riding Boy, stole cattle, had men shot.* Her jaw clenched. She had to determine some proof to show the marshal.

"Anyway, there's other buyers," another man said.

"But it's McCoy what got the railroad to Abilene in the fust place. Seems he'd be offerin' a fair price," someone else grumbled.

"Fifteen. Ain't worth it.

"This Montgomery said he'd take 'em off our hands for twelve."

"Twelve dollars a head?" Ellen blurted out. "I can't believe that's fair! Last week's Topeka newspaper reported an average of twenty-five dollars a head all across the country, and another cattleman through here expected no less than twenty a head."

"But it may not be so," one tired man said. "Lady, if we have as much trouble in the next hundret and fifty miles as we done had already—" He shook his head.

"I say we take Montgomery's money and our injured, and head on back to Texas. It didn't cost us nothin' to round 'em up. Twelve dollars on what we got left will be some profit."

A man cried out from across the dogtrot.

"Must be settin' Jackson's arm," someone muttered.

"We're lucky we ain't got more dead," said another.

"Someone was killed?" Ellen couldn't keep from asking.

"Jackson's brother, Caleb—our trail boss, and Lewis, we figure."

"I saw Caleb go down," one boy said. "Right in the thick of the cattle when they were running hard."

The men sat in silence; Ellen put a hand to her mouth as the grisly circumstance flitted through her mind. Ellen poured more coffee all around, rethinking the comments—troubled by something more than the disaster described. After a moment it came to her.

"I'm sorry to bother you more, but—" She stepped to the table. The men looked up at her, their tired expressions withdrawn and gloomy. "This Lewis? Was he also caught in the stampede?" she asked.

"Probably so. No sign of him otherwise," the youngest said.

"Had he been with you since Texas?"

"No. Just the past five days. Said he knew the route and needed some cash. We had a few boys sick and had lost two at the Red."

Ellen's heart thumped so hard she was certain her apron bib must be shaking. "Was his first name Judd?"

"Yes'm, it was. I hope you didn't know him, ma'am. It's been enough grief—"

"I—No, I didn't know him." Ellen turned away to tend the skillet, doubting that Judd Lewis was dead.

"What did he look like?" she asked as she offered another round of meat. "This Judd Lewis," she continued when they looked at her in puzzlement.

The older man shrugged. "Tallish. Good set to him. Hard eyes like he'd been around a lot. Caleb—the boss, he wasn't to sure about takin' him on at first."

"Hair?" she asked.

"Brown. Dark brown and sorta long."

"And a mustache?" she asked.

"Yeah. Long, down around his mouth."

Ellen was unaware of their stares as her thoughts created the picture. *It could be the face over my Sycamore Spring dream,* she thought. She set the skillet off the burner and went outside, suddenly needing fresh air. Sunlight struggled to break through heavy gray clouds. *It could be the man Burton Stamford described as Kyle*

Montrose. The air was heavy and moist. From a distance, she could hear the remnants of the Texans' herd from where they had been settled in the meadow north of Fall Creek.

Her head began to ache. *Maybe all my ill thoughts about James Montgomery are false.* She was relieved she hadn't directed Beaver Laughing to James Montgomery. *He might have killed the wrong man.*

By mid-afternoon, the injured Texans had settled in the Clayton hotel, and Reba took over cooking (and selling) food. After the men left the Jarvis cabin, Belinda went directly her bedroom; Ellen knew by her mother's expression that she wasn't to be disturbed. Ellen saw Pitt and her father hard at work with shovels and rakes in the field when she took a basket of food to Lutecia's cabin.

"You must be exhausted," Ellen said when Lutecia came to the open doorway. "Here's some food. It should see you and Mr. Mercy through the rest of the day."

Lutecia, dressed in a fresh blouse and apron over her worn skirt, gave a tired smile. "Ellen, you're a godsend," she said. "Come on in."

The cabin smelled sweet from burning sage that still smoldered in the bowl of a large geode on the table. The front window by the door was open, and a needed breeze wafted green-gingham curtains.

"I was about to go out to the cow camp, and I couldn't even think straight about what to take with me." She set the geode on the mantle of the hearth. "Sit down. I just need a minute of quiet."

"I don't want to be in the way," Ellen said, placing the basket on the table.

"You? Of course not!" Lutecia gave a long sigh.

"At least there weren't any serious injuries," Ellen said.

"True. Even the boy that got knocked on the head has come around and looks to be fine."

"They were lucky you were here."

"I suppose." Lutecia shook her head. "You know, the rustlers got half of those poor boys' cows, and one man killed by the cattle rush. His brother's not taking that too well. Charles was plenty worried that we'd get back here and find our cattle gone."

"Everything's okay, isn't it?"

"Well, he hasn't come back here with bad news."

Ellen studied her hands, hoping some disaster hadn't struck the Mercys and the next person Lutecia had to tend was her own husband. "I was thinking the other day that this whole community is being set up. These rustlers could run their stolen cattle through here and also rob the store and Reba; even Reed has a lot of money from the gambling."

"And that cattle company for sure," Lutecia put in. "That thought crossed my mind, too. Maybe we all ought to pack up and go to Wichitaw, especially now that the cavalry and Marshal Stamford have left."

"The marshal. I forgot about him. He hasn't really left. He's looking for information about the rustling of Baxter's herd. He'll get back here today, I imagine."

"He's got his work cut out for him."

Ellen frowned, thinking of the information she had learned during the morning. She decided not to mention Beaver Laughing, but asked, "Does Judd Lewis seem a common name to you? A name you'd hear often?"

"Not particularly. Why?"

"That name has been mentioned with both rustlings."

"Really? How so?" Lutecia said, sitting straighter.

"Tommy Atherton hinted that Lewis—Judd Lewis—was one of the rustlers; and now this group claims Judd Lewis is missing from their ranks. They think he got killed. He'd been with the herd for less than a week."

"And it's been seven days since the Atherton boy was found by the Pierces." Lutecia slumped back in her chair. "Oh, my. That's important, Ellen. You need to tell the marshal."

"I know," Ellen said. The prospects of talking to that man unsettled her. He still had questions—his puzzle, as he put it. And what would he think of her having this new information? Would he believe her? Would he again think she was involved in the all the problems that had arisen?

"Well, I've got to get back—be at the store in case the men need something," she said.

"You should probably take the shotgun up there with you," Lutecia suggested. "Like you said. This place is prime to be robbed."

Ellen's heart beat quickened.

"I'm gonna get this food out to Charles," Lutecia said. "Thank you, Ellen."

"It's nothing, really." At the door, the two women hugged.

"Be careful," Lutecia said to her.

"You too."

Dingy afternoon light had squeezed through the heavy clouds onto the store when the sound of boots on the store steps caused Ellen to look up from her work. Her hand went briefly to the shotgun on the counter, as if to be certain it was there. The man who darkened the doorway wore faded twill pants, a plaid shirt and a battered straw hat. He took that off as he came in and Ellen laughed her surprise.

"Marshal Stamford! I barely recognized you." He had shaved off his beard.

"Hum. That's the point," he said, glancing around the store.

From a distance the charade would work, but his authoritarian manner and the piercing look from his green eyes were unmistakable. Ellen looked away from them as he strode to the service counter.

"I've just talked to the Texans at Claytons' place and they tell me you knew one of their drovers."

"What?" Ellen resented his accusatory tone.

"Lewis. A fellow killed during the rustling."

"Lewis!" Ellen sighed and leaned on the counter. This was not the way she intended to give the information to the marshal. "Judd Lewis is no one I know, and I seriously doubt he was killed."

The marshal looked angry the whole time she explained about the name and her conclusion. She was pleased that his gaze didn't make her stammer. "By their description, he could even be your Kyle Montrose," she finished.

"Hum." Stamford leaned his forearms on the counter in front of her and studied the wood grain as if it held answers. Finally he straightened. "Well, he isn't Montrose. Montrose would never stoop to herding cattle. Too common for him. He prefers leadership roles."

"Perhaps he's taken a disguise—as you have," Ellen countered.

He smiled, his eyes now lively rather than harsh. "He's always in disguise, Mrs. Hargrove. That's why we know so little about him. But some characteristics remain the same: he likes his creature comforts, he dresses almost stylishly for whatever his position," (Ellen thought of the marshal's tailor-made fringed leather shirt.) "and he usually has a woman at his side." (James Montgomery and Nancy came to her mind.) "All of those are hard to achieve on a cattle drive."

James Montgomery, she thought. It turns back to him. *If only I knew. If only I had proof!*

"Mrs. Hargrove?" Stamford leaned into her view, peering at her.

"I'm sorry. What?"

"I was saying that it was very astute of you to pick up on this Lewis fellow. It could be helpful."

"Only if we had a better idea of what he looked like. The description the Texans gave me is vague. I guess it could fit nearly anyone. Even you."

"True. And if he suspects anything, a mustache can be shaved off."

"Yes." Ellen thought of Reed's clean-shaven appearance, a style she much preferred to sideburns and mustaches. Johnny had realized that early on, and he sometimes shaved before he came to their bed—came to her smooth-skinned and smelling of soap and bay. Johnny, always striving to please her. ("I have to get this right," he once said. "I don't want to lose you.")

And I'm the one who lost, came the bitter thought.

"You seem quite distracted today. Mrs. Hargrove?"

"Oh, I'm sorry, Marshal." Ellen took a deep breath.

"And that brings me to another concern." He leaned again on the counter. "About Mrs. Hargrove."

Ellen, nervous and curious, gave him her full attention.

"Is there a chance, any chance at all, that you would call me Burton? And I could call you—Ellen?"

How odd that he would ask this right when I'm having sweet thoughts of Johnny, she thought. "Marshal, we met only three days ago."

"Four," he corrected, smiling broadly. Straight teeth, twinkly eyes.

"I really don't know you, sir, except as a law enforcer."

"Then you prefer Widow Hargrove," he said, his face theatrically downcast.

"I prefer *Mrs.* Hargrove, thank you."

"Not forever, I hope." He feigned shock.

"What might happen tomorrow is much beyond—my—knowledge." Her voice faltered.

"Hum."

"And now *I* have a question," Ellen said, hoping to turn the conversation. "Why is it you returned here in disguise?"

"Oh, this." He looked amused. "I'd been to the north—looking for the rustling site—the first rustling, and a few hours ago I came back through the area where Charles Mercy keeps his cows. He told me about the new rustling and was quite nervous.

"Anyway, it seemed that everyone assumed I had left with the cavalry. I decided to keep it that way for a bit and borrowed some old clothing from Charles." He tweaked the collar of the shirt, pleased with himself. "In retrospect, I'm quite glad you didn't mention my plans to anyone."

"Actually, I did. To Reed, but only in passing."

"Reed. That would be Mr. Carter?"

Ellen flushed, realizing she had used Reed's first name. Then she wanted to laugh, noting the apparent displeasure her words had caused the marshal.

The back door of the store opened, breaking the moment, and Belinda came up the steps into the main room, wearing work clothes and boots.

"Oh, Ellen, there you are. Marshal. How—" She frowned at him. "—odd you look," she ended. "Don't explain." She went toward the end of the room with the hearth. "Ellen, help me move things around here. We're going to have a meeting this evening. This is the best place." She started pulling aside one of the display tables. Marshal Stamford rushed to help her.

"A meeting?" Ellen asked.

"Yes. The Mercys, Tim Fykes, the Claytons, and our family. We have to decide our future."

Our future, the words rung in Ellen's ears; her mother's tone sounded ominous.

Ellen lay still in her bed, barely conscious of the room's quiet as she stared at the wooden beams under the roof. For the first time ever, she wanted to have a vision—preferably her old dream. She wanted to see again the Sycamore Spring scene with its ominous face hovering. If she could focus on that face and not the body, she might be able to identify that person.

Or maybe a new vision, she thought as she shifted to a more comfortable position. One that would clearly show the murderer in action and not just as a nebulous suggestion. Or one that would tell her what was in her future. How did they happen, these visions?

Moments passed while she attempted to reconstruct her previous premonitions. The common thread, she decided, was that they seemed to come from a void. Most when she slept, like Quantrill's raid, the prairie fire, Johnny's and Francis Stone's deaths. Her image of the marshal falling from his horse had occurred when she was numb from field work and heat, and that seemed to be a false alarm. Although her father recalled other incidents of Ellen's premonitions, Ellen only knew about them when they were told her.

Coming from a void, she thought, closing her eyes. She tried to *not think*—let an oblivion consume her—but memories of the evening started popping into her mind; that unanimous decision that the settlement should be abandoned. "The crops here are near ruin," Luke complained. Charles Mercy: "I'm gonna lose cattle to the trail herds, I just know it."

No. Don't think. Could she force a spontaneous occurrence?

The meeting: "And we're sitting ducks for the outlaws in the area," Lutecia said.

"Outlaws!" Luke blurted out.

Banter about that and about money available to be stolen started Reba grousing that having a gambler in their midst had caused it all. Ellen had been mute, marveling on how much of a community they had become. The discussion proceeded as if all four families had come here together—had a bond beyond Sumner County and the wooded banks of the Bluff River. She had also worried about Reed Carter. He hadn't given early-morning help to the trail drive. The two men she had seen with Pitt had been Tim— and James Montgomery.

"We can go up to Camp Wichitaw; see what it's like," Rob had suggested.

"And we all leave together," her father said. "Safety in numbers."

"We can't leave 'till the boys get back," Tim argued.

"Of course," Matthew agreed.

"But the weather." That had been the first Belinda said since the families gathered in the store.

The weather.

Lying in bed, Ellen knew this was her mother's knack. Belinda could read the environment, sense things beyond the normal clues of turned alder leaves, the thickness of wooly worm stripes, or mist across the moon. Ellen wanted to talk about that, to ask her mother how it was done. Belinda seemed so sure of things, while Ellen's uncanny thoughts were so illusory. She wondered if her mother's knowledge came from a void.

She drew a long breath. *Void. That's what I'm trying to achieve.*

Pitt coughed from the other side of the canvas wall. The rustle of his bedclothes seemed loud as he squirmed around. He coughed again, then silence except for the night chorus of crickets and tree frogs coming through the open window. The patter of light rain danced on the roof and blended in the susurration of a brisk breeze through the trees. Ellen fell asleep.

Early morning light didn't affect the western windows of the store, so Ellen worked with just a small candle for light, not wanting to heat the room with a lantern. To an outsider, it could seem she was just conscientiously cleaning the shelves of the display case, but she was really packing store goods. All of the families were working quietly toward departure—to be ready whenever Hubert Fykes and Spencer returned, or if, as her mother said, the weather turned.

She lifted out four buck knives and placed them in an empty cigar box. Beside the box were three hunting knives Tim had fashioned. Ellen best liked the one with fox design. The carved animal seemed to dash head first toward the hilt, its wide tail curving around the handle.

Looking through the north window, Ellen frowned at the empty quiet around Reed's wagon. No horses, no fire, no awning unfurled to attract customers. James Montgomery rode his horse toward the store, but seeing him didn't upset her as it had several days ago. She was certain of his guilt, but when she thought that, a strange calm beset her, replacing the jumpiness that had previously tended her thoughts about the murders.

At the Clayton tent hotel, the Texas men readied packs and horses. When they left, the area would be less populated and more vulnerable to assault by outlaws. Perhaps Beaver Laughing waited for these men to leave, too, so there would be fewer white men to pursue him after he killed the Bad Dark. If it weren't for her bruised arm, Ellen would have thought she dreamed his visit—a plain, regular, scary dream with no portent. She wondered where Beaver

Laughing might be. Perhaps he had to perform some rite to get up his courage. It had been quite obvious he was afraid. Maybe he went for help from Knocks-on-the-wagon. She shivered, not sure if Montgomery's death would be enough for the father who so hated whites.

Montgomery and three Texans headed toward the store. Ellen clenched her hands for a moment, and then smoothed them along her apron before resuming her work.

"We saw the door open and the light," the older man announced as they strode in.

"Come in," Ellen replied, facing them with a smile.

Normal conversation ensued about the sultry weather, about their trip home. They remarked on how lucky they had been to come into a generous community. Ellen responded as necessary, but was mostly aware of James Montgomery staying near the door. He had done that yesterday, stepping forward only to pay for purchase. His generosity deflected suspicion, as he paid for their supplies, for their hotel stay, gave them twelve dollars a head for their cattle when he had the rest of their herd somewhere out on the prairie free of charge. Men killed and injured, families devastated because of James Montgomery. These thoughts smoldered within her while she maintained a pleasant façade.

Montgomery came to the counter and paid for the purchases. Ellen merely laid the coin aside, not wanting to open the cash drawer with him here.

"I guess I'm gonna have to pass on this knife," one man was saying. He had studied Tim's workmanship yesterday, coming into the store several times. "Sure is a beauty, though," he said, tracing his finger along the fox handle.

"It ain't the same, but it makes me think of that bone stuff they sell down south near the coast," the youngest said. "Real neat designs cut out real small."

"I think they call the work scrimshaw," Ellen said.

She didn't miss the way Montgomery's hand strayed toward his waist, naked of the big knife, and then quickly away.

"Well, thanks again, ma'am," the oldest man said.

"Have a safe trip."

"Hope to. We'll stick together and keep an eye to our back side, that's for sure."

"And if you see Judd Lewis, ride in the other direction," Ellen said. The words seemed to float from some deep thought. She hadn't intended to say any more at all. Montgomery, already started for the door, stopped and turned a bit toward her.

"Oh, he's coyote food, by now," one man said.

"Don't be too sure," Ellen continued—baiting. "Around here, his name has been linked with a few strange occurrences involving cattle." Montgomery became a column of darkness. Even the silver ornaments on his hat disappeared in a blur. Her heart pounded. This was the first time in several days she had seen Montgomery that way.

"Be careful," Ellen stressed. The blur moved out the door.

"Yes'm. We will." They tipped their hats to her and left Ellen wondering if she had made a rash decision. The marshal would be quite upset by her comments, she was sure.

And where was the marshal, anyway? she wondered. Gone, with his smooth chin and borrowed clothes, to some other part of his investigation.

She put the coins in the cash drawer as the Texans mounted up and started riding toward the river. Montgomery headed back toward Fall Creek, never once glancing at the store.

14

The families congregated at the arbor near the Clayton dugout that evening, and Ellen realized it was the first evening in several that it hadn't rained. The ground under the trees was still firm, and they ate leftovers from Reba's restaurant cooking, supplemented with Belinda's pan bread and stewed greens from Lutecia.

"…right there in the muddy ground," Reba was saying after the meal. "Had mud in his hair and everything, and sound asleep." Reba tossed dishwater at the base of a sapling. The breeze through the elm cooled the air. Bobolinks called to each other across the fields while the setting sun transformed the cloudy sky from gray, to mauve and crimson.

"That George can surely sleep, all right," Lutecia said as she gathered up her dishes.

"Hestor fell right over him when they finished weeding the field," Reba went on. "I tell you, when he starts sleepin' like that, I know he's in for a growin' spurt. Never fails." The boy was asleep right then, lying on a blanket behind a chair.

"Are you certain he's not getting a fever," Belinda asked, closing the top of a basket. "Pitt's been runny-eyed the last day or two. I almost didn't let him go with Tim and Rob this morning."

Tim, Rob and Pitt had spent the day at the Mercy cow camp, making wooden crates for the Clayton livestock. By doing it there, Ellen hoped it didn't raise suspicion with Montgomery or the three men who had appeared the day the cavalry left. They stayed north of Montgomery's tent with the Texas herd, never once venturing south of Fall Creek. Ellen wanted to see these men, to measure her reaction to them. One could be Judd Lewis, she thought with alarm.

"It's this weather. Wet, cool, then hot," Lutecia said.

Luke, Matthew and Tim returned from examining the Clayton Conestoga. Matthew called Pitt from where he, Hestor and Olive skipped stones on the river.

"This was a good meal. Thank you, Reba," Ellen said.

"It's the way to do things, that's for sure. All of us sharing."

Ellen walked with Lutecia across the road. Her parents and Pitt just a few strides ahead of them. A half moon hung above the trees to the east, giving pale light.

"Now doesn't that Mr. Winslow look pathetic," Belinda commented.

Up the hill, by a forlorn tent, sprawled Dillard Winslow, a whiskey bottle in one hand. Empty bottles he had thrown in the grass, glinted orange in the evening light.

"I asked him to join us," Matthew said. "But he just stared at me all red eyed."

"He should be eating some real food," Lutecia put in.

"I've noticed him up at Montgomery's tent a few times," Belinda said. "Perhaps Nancy's feeding him."

As they rounded the store into the well yard, Ellen wondered if Nancy knew how to cook. She also wondered if Nancy knew anything that could help convict James Montgomery. Or could Nancy be part of his gang?

Stop thinking on it, she ordered herself.

"You must be worried about Charles, staying out at the camp alone," Ellen said to Lutecia as they neared the house.

"A bit. But he knows how to watch out for himself. And he knows I have to stay here to get things ready for the move." Lutecia sighed. "It's amazing how much we've accumulated in two years. Thanks for the loan of your buggy, Ellen. That will help."

"It holds quite a bit, and I know what I have will fit in my parents' wagons."

"Lutecia," Belinda called over her shoulder. "You and Charles don't know where Reed is, do you? I haven't seen him—"

A scream from the north made them all stop and stare toward the creek. Two rapid rifle shots sounded. Horses at Tim's whinnied and were restless.

Beaver Laughing. Montgomery's killed him.

Lutecia produced her pistol from the pocket of her apron.

"Indians! Indians!" came a call.

"That was Mr. Winslow," Belinda said.

"Get inside," Matthew instructed. He started back toward the road.

"Whad'ya think's happening?" Pitt asked with a hoarse voice.

"Shhh," was Lutecia's response as they hurried to the dogtrot.

"I'm a-tellin' you, we're gonna be attacked, and your store's the only fortified place around!" came Luke Clayton's argumentative voice moments later. The man hustled, half crouched, behind Matthew toward the house.

"Go home, Luke. If there's an attack, you ought to be with your family, don't you think?"

Luke jerked to a stop and looked suspiciously around before trotting back the way he had come.

"What happened?" Belinda asked. She held the shotgun.

Matthew shrugged. "Tim's ridden up to see."

When Tim came back after fifteen minutes or so, Ellen couldn't remember having breathed since the shots. Her father stepped out to meet him, with everyone crowded behind.

"People scared of nothing," Tim said from horseback. "That Kincaid woman thought she saw someone in the woods. Montgomery took a shot in that direction."

Ellen released a shaky breath. She hoped Beaver Laughing hadn't been hurt.

"Dillard Winslow was yelling about Indians," Belinda said, loosening her hold on the shotgun.

Tim shrugged. "I looked around with the lantern. Too dark to make out much. Montgomery and me will scout the area in the morning."

"We ought to sleep wary. Just in case," Matthew said.

"Do you want to stay the night here, Lutecia?" Belinda asked.

"Thank you, but I got a lot to pack yet," Lutecia replied. "I'll be fine."

"I'll walk you home," Ellen offered, an idea springing to mind. "I've got some cloths you might want to use for your herbs," she added, dashing into her bedroom to get the bags she had saved from the store. "I'll be right back," Ellen said to her mother when she came out.

They were three strides from Mercy cabin when Lutecia finally asked, "So what's up?"

"I need your help. Your support, actually. I want to talk to Nancy tomorrow."

"Really, now." They went into the cabin, Lutecia finding the lantern and lighting it. "What brought this on?"

"Well, Nancy's showed so much concern for me at times, I just thought—"

"Come on, Ellen, if you want my support. Tell me!"

"All right." Ellen swallowed hard. "I feel certain Montgomery is behind these rustlings."

"Another dream?" Lutecia asked, putting away the dishes she had carried home.

"No. Not exactly. Well, Montgomery's face is the one I saw over the Sycamore Spring scene, but—"

Lutecia stopped mid-motion, "Oh, my!" She hung a pan from a nail on the wall. "I take it you haven't told anyone else." She and Ellen sat on chairs by the table.

"I mentioned it to Reed, oddly," Ellen confessed. "He was—supportive." The family worries he had confided to her flitted through her mind. She shook her head. "You don't know where he is, do you?" she asked, another worry surfacing.

"No. I've been wondering, myself. He wasn't even around to ride with us when the Texans were hurt."

"Do you think he would go home without saying goodbye?" Ellen felt a sudden loss, thinking of Reed gone.

"His wagon's still at the site. He'll be back."

Unless he's injured—been shot by horse thieves and robbed.
She rubbed her hands along her arms *(This cannot be true!)*, then
returned her attention to her primary concern.

"So I want to talk to Nancy. I thought if you'd rode over with
me—"

"You really think she'd tell you anything?"

"I'm not sure, but I have to try. Mr. Fykes said Montgomery
was riding with him in the morning to scout the area. It will be the
perfect time to learn what we can."

"Sounds reasonable," Lutecia said.

"Early. Real early," Ellen stressed as she stood up. "I'll watch
to see when they leave and then you can meet me at the well."

"I'll take my medicinals. She could be in a state if she thinks
she saw Indians."

"Thanks." She gave Lutecia a hug.

"Oh, here. Take these back with you and leave them in the
barn." Lutecia took up a stack of neatly folded clothes. The hat on
top belonged to the marshal, and Ellen recognized his leather shirt.
"He's still wearing Charles's clothes, but wanted these where he
could get to them. I meant to bring them when I came for dinner."

"I wonder what he's up to," Ellen said, taking the clothes in
the crook of her arm. She flopped the hat onto her head. "How do
I look? Do you think I could be a marshal?" She laughed.

Lutecia shoved the hat down on her head. "I think you could
be a marshal's girl, if you took a hankerin' to."

"Lutecia! That's ridiculous!"

"Just an observation," her friend said smiling. "He's asked
Charles and me a lot of questions about you."

"That's because he doesn't trust me," Ellen said. "He thought
I had something to do with the murder and rustlings!"

"Hum," Lutecia said, mimicking the marshal as she stroked her
chin.

"Anyway, he's much too pompous for my tastes."

"He is that," Lutecia agreed.

They restated their plans for the morning and said good night.
Ellen walked back to the house in the dim light, the clothes grasped

across her chest, hat in one hand. The marshal and his questions, she thought. But she also remembered the flirtatious phrases and looks he had tossed her way. She had assumed he was trying to needle her—to flush out her nefarious ways (those would be his words), but maybe not. She wondered if he were capable of real conversation, a genial rapport about likes and dislikes, hopes and dreams. She fingered the wedding ring on her neck chain. Perhaps Widow Hargrove is too much of a prude, she thought. Feeling subdued, she went quietly into the dogtrot and to her bedroom.

As she had planned, Ellen was the first person in the Jarvis household to be up. She dressed quickly and went outside, carrying the marshal's clothes with her. She wanted to get them to the barn before she had to explain to anyone why she had them. She wrinkled her nose to the acrid smell of skunk that lingered in the air. She had heard Olive's dog bark not long ago, and now she knew why. As she neared the paddocks, she noticed Tim on horseback, his figure dimmed by the early mist rising from Fall Creek, headed for Montgomery's tent and the planned reconnaissance. Against pink-laced clouds, a formation of white-bellied birds scrolled an S.

Daybreak light increased, giving everything a yellowish cast. Phineas nickered to her as she took a rope from the paddock rail. Tossing it across the big horse's neck, she led him to the barn and along side the tool chest where she usually stood to saddle him. She set the marshal's clothes on a grain bin and went for Phineas's bridle.

"Well, well. Aren't we the early riser."

Ellen gasped and jerked to where the voice came from above her. Stamford peered down at her from the hay loft. "Marshal! What are you doing here?"

"I was just arising after a good night's sleep." He smiled. "And you?"

She continued bridling Phineas, knowing she wasn't going to

tell him her plans. He'd want to tag along—or take over the meeting with Nancy. Ellen doubted Nancy would say anything important with him around.

"Taking a morning ride?" he asked.

She glanced to where he was propped on his elbows. His muscular shoulders nicely filled out the top of his Union suit, and Ellen recalled Lutecia's teasing from the previous night. Heat of her blush started along her neck and she looked away.

"Would you like some company, Madam?"

"No, thank you. I wouldn't want to be accused of taking you from your duties." *Unless he thinks I am his duty—keep an eye on suspects.* "I thought you had perhaps gone into The Nations to look for the stolen cattle." She placed the pad and saddle on Phineas's back.

"No. That would be a fool's errand. Once the rustlers get a large enough herd, they'll push them north to the railhead. Probably go right up this trail. Besides, it's quite pleasant to be around families, for a change."

"Yes, I suppose you don't get home very often, New York being so far."

"I beg your pardon?" Stamford frowned, leaning down toward her.

"I'm sorry to have awakened you." She tugged Phineas out of the barn, checked the cinches and climbed into the sidesaddle. From the corner of her eye, she saw Stamford come to the barn door, watching her as he adjusted suspenders over his shirt and put on his hat.

"Hup, boy," Ellen said, giving Phineas a nudge toward the Mercys. The horse moved out.

The sun burned like a white disk through thick gray clouds when Ellen and Lutecia reached Montgomery's tent. The large canvas structure no longer sat on the ground, but was raised onto a log base nearly a foot high.

"Goodness, he's put in a raised floor and everything," Ellen murmured to Lutecia.

"That's why all those tree stumps back there at the creek."

A step went to the front flap that had been framed out, door fashion.

While sitting their horses, Ellen called to Nancy. After a few moments, the entrance was pulled open.

"Nancy, how are you?" Ellen asked. "After last evening, we were concerned."

"Well, I declare," Nancy said with a quick smile. The blue cotton robe she wore had several inches of tatting along the collar, which she pulled up to her ear on her left side. "You was worried about me? That's mighty nice." She stepped onto the step and fiddled with her hair. "The place is a mess. I— Well, I still need to learn about housekeeping."

Ellen and Lutecia still sat their horses, not having been invited to step down. Nancy's nervousness made Ellen wondered if coming here had been a mistake.

Nancy glanced toward the woods, alert and worried. Ellen frowned. *Was that a bruise on her jaw?* "Lutecia makes some fine remedies, if you need," she said. Nancy seemed to flinch—pulled again at the collar of her robe.

"Well, I—I don't really need anything. It was a quick scare, but with James here, I didn't worry none."

There's the opening! But Ellen's tongue seemed like lead.

"He here a lot, is he? Even with his cow business to run?" Lutecia asked.

"Oh, sure! He's got men working for him that do the hard stuff." Pride brightened the woman's tone.

"I had noticed a few men up here," Ellen picked up, her motivation returning.

"Uh huh. They're out with the herd James bought," Nancy replied.

"Is one of them Judd Lewis?" Ellen asked.

Nancy darted another glance toward the woods.

"That's real fine, having help," Lutecia put in. "How many men work for him, anyway?"

"Four. Five, maybe. I'm not sure. Seems they come and go."

"Maybe it was one of them comin' and goin' you saw last night," Lutecia suggested.

"Oh, no! I saw an Indian. That's for sure. Face all painted—"

They all three jerked toward twigs snapping and thudding hooves. James Montgomery crashed his horse through the underbrush and into the yard. "What's going on?" the man growled, pulling his horse to a quick stop. In his usual black, slim-cut trousers, he wore a short vest over a striped shirt. A flat brimmed hat with silver ornaments encircling the low crown shadowed his eyes. Mexican style, Ellen realized. She recalled Rose saying that, too—Mexican britches, and Kyle Montrose was thought to have lived in Mexico. Her awareness took in the hand gun that rested in a holster along his right leg and the coil of rope attached to his saddle near his right knee. "What are you doing over here?"

"Just concerned for Miss Nancy," Lutecia said. "After last night."

"Uh. Going to give her some of your geechie medicines?"

Lutecia's usually calm face showed surprise.

"She's fine," Montgomery declared. "Aren't you darlin'?"

"Yes, James. That's what I was just tellin' them." Nancy had backed inside so that only the tips of her toes were on the threshold.

Montgomery stared at Ellen, eyes squinted. A slight twitch started at the corner of his mouth before he dissolved to a blur. Ellen's heartbeat thudded and she barely breathed as his menacing voice bore into her. "Who are you, anyway? Always following me around. I thought I was done with you!"

Sunlight broke through the cloud cover. A thick shaft lanced into the yard, and widened as the clouds shifted. Ellen, wide-eyed, clenched her hands in Phineas's mane. *Who am I? What did that mean?*

"Well, we're burning daylight," Lutecia said, turning her horse. "Charles will be wondering for his breakfast."

Ellen forced her gaze to the tent "I'm glad you're all right, Nancy," Ellen said, hoping she sounded sincere. The sudden distortion that surrounded Montgomery had shaken her confidence.

"Thank you, Miz Ellen." Nancy backed out of sight.

From the darkness on a chestnut horse, Ellen heard a harsh voice: "Don't come around here anymore! Don't keep chasing me!"

"Good morning!" Tim said, riding into the clearing. "You tell 'em what we found?" he asked Montgomery. "Sign of jest one horse out west. Could be Indian, but not certain."

Ellen swung Phineas away and followed Lutecia from the yard. She glanced back to where Tim spoke with Montgomery, stricken by shock and fear. She barely heard Lutecia when her friend murmured, "So what did you make of that? Four or five men working for him."

"He was darkness again," she said in a tight whisper. "He blurred right when he started yelling at me. And those questions he asked." She shook her head.

"He said some pretty interesting things," Lutecia said, frowning at her. "He seemed frightened by something."

"Frightened?" Ellen continued to sort through the confrontation with Montgomery. "Maybe so. Maybe Beaver Laughing scared him."

Tim loped his horse to join them. "What the devil was that all about?" Tim asked. "You all were pulled taut as a bow sighted on a bull elk."

"I wonder what Luke will think of your finding tracks of only one person?" Lutecia asked, attempting to divert Tim's curiosity.

"Oh, he'll make it into a scouting party and go around scared all day—shoot a cow if it moves too fast," Tim said as they approached the Fall Creek crossing.

Lutecia pulled up. "I'm gonna cut east here. Go on to the cow camp," she said. "Not that I'm tryin' to avoid Luke's to-do."

"Thanks, Lu," Ellen said as the woman started along the trail parallel to the creek. "Don't forget to bring back a mule for the buggy."

"I will, thanks." She let her horse pick along tree stumps and mud of the north bank.

Phineas and Tim's horse sloshed across the ford and high-stepped logs strewn on the south bank. Ellen frowned at the downed wood. Several were dead trees blown over in the last storm, their rotting cores crumbling, and a few were just hulls of bark. Dark inside. Musty. Damp.

As they came to Tim's barn, Ellen saw Luke standing further south beside the dugout's stone fence, rifle cocked over his arm, staring at them. Tim spit a stream of tobacco juice into the road. "I better get down there," he said. "Luke's gettin' itchy for news and I swear, sometimes I think he really wants it to be bad. Ain't that sorry?" Tim shook his head and started his horse at a quick walk to the dugout.

"Come to the house when you're done. My parents will want to hear your report," Ellen called heading toward the well yard. She wasn't certain the morning effort had been a benefit. She still had no proof on Montgomery, and the more she harbored information about Beaver Laughing's intentions, the worse she felt. She stripped Phineas of his saddle, loosed him in the paddock and walked to the house, suddenly aware of another problem. The marshal. His horse was tied to the house hitching rail. Through the window, she could see him sitting with her parents at the table.

Tim joined them soon after Ellen had finished her first cup of coffee. He told the marshal and her parents the insignificant information.

I can't hold this back any longer, Ellen thought as the others discussed what the tracks of one Indian could mean. She gripped her coffee cup and gathered her courage. "I have a confession." Belinda paused in pouring the brew for Tim. Everyone looked at Ellen. "Beaver Laughing has come to kill Montgomery. That's who Nancy saw last night."

"Beaver Laughing? That Indian who did all the talking out at Sycamore Spring?" Stamford asked.

"Why would he want to kill Montgomery?" her mother asked as Ellen nodded.

"Montgomery killed Mr. Stone, and he killed Riding Boy, too, because he saw him kill Mr. Stone. That's why Beaver Laughing is here."

"You seem quite sure of this," her father said.

"He—Beaver Laughing told me."

"He's been here?" Belinda's eyes widened.

"The morning the cattle herd was rustled and everyone else was gone."

"He came here to the house to talk to you? Why?" Stamford asked, frowning.

"Actually, he accosted me at the well," Ellen rubbed at her bruised arm. "He told me he was going to kill the Bad Dark."

"Oh! The bad dark," Stamford said. "That doesn't mean Montgomery."

"But it does! I know Montgomery is the bad dark Beaver Laughing told about." Ellen drew a resolute breath. "I saw him. His face. When I dreamed Mr. Stone dead, Montgomery's face appeared over the scene."

"Good heavens," Matthew said, slumping back. He took Belinda's hand. Her mother's eyes were closed, fingers of her other hand massaging between her eyebrows. She sat down beside Matthew.

"Don't that beat all," Tim said, grinning.

"You dreamed—" Stamford's intense green eyes showed fascination. "Haw, haw, haw! That's droll, Mrs. Hargrove." Ellen's shocked expression did nothing to lessen his amusement. "You merely imposed Montgomery's face over some dream because you don't like him."

"I never even met James Montgomery until two days after Mr. Stone's death," she said, bristling at his skepticism.

Stamford leaned back, still chuckling. "Yet you think you saw the same face?"

"I know I did!" Ellen stated.

"Hum." Stamford rubbed his chin. Ellen stared at her hands. No one had ever questioned the validity of her visions before.

"Now, Marshal. Miz Ellen's had some right true predictions," Tim said. "What *are* the chances that Montgomery is involved in this?"

"Well, the poor fellow's been up to his ears trying to run a business he didn't start," Matthew stated.

"He was a partner in that cattle company. This ain't been

dumped on him," Tim reminded.

"Montgomery uses a rope, too," Ellen said. "Just like the man Beaver Laughing said killed Riding Boy."

"That's very circumstantial, Mrs. Hargrove," Stamford said ruefully.

"He looks like the man Beaver Laughing described."

"Because he has a mustache? That's a popular style these days."

"Well, where was Montgomery the day Mr. Stone was killed?" Ellen retorted.

"He told me he was in Medicine Lodge," the marshal stated. "Hiring on men for the operation here."

"Medicine Lodge! He told Reed he was at Camp Wichitaw!" Ellen said.

"Reed," Stamford said, glancing askance at the ceiling. "I'm checking his story."

"Beaver Laughing is here to kill the Bad Dark," Ellen said, aggravated. "He *saw* the man. He knows who he's after; and when he gets him, it will be Montgomery. Dead."

"If you'll excuse me," Belinda said. "I'm going to check on Pitt. He doesn't usually stay abed this late."

Ellen looked after her mother, finding her lack of interest in the mystery quite curious. Belinda loved riddles and intrigue—anything that took wit to fathom. But Belinda didn't like mention of Ellen's dreams. How would it be if it came out that Belinda made predictions, too?

"You are a puzzle, Mrs. Hargrove. You accuse the man of murder, but seem worried that this Osage buck might kill him. Are you trying to save Montgomery, or what?"

"I want him to get proper justice!" Ellen poured more coffee for her father and Tim. "Why he's probably that Kyle Montrose you're looking for."

"That's what you said about Judd Lewis," Stamford said. "You really are good at jumping to conclusions, Widow Hargrove."

Ellen gritted her teeth.

"Now now now," Tim said, squinting toward the far wall. "This makes a bit of sense. Montgomery's been pretty standoffish, you know. And where was he when Baxter's herd was rustled?"

"That was during that terrible storm," Matthew said, staring at Tim with disbelief. "He was up at your place with Miss Kincaid and the others."

"He didn't stay out the storm there, like the others did," Tim said. "He showed up that morning *after* the storm."

Belinda came in from the dogtrot, her brow furrowed. "Has anyone seen Lutecia this morning?"

"She's gone to their cow camp," Ellen said.

"What's wrong?" Matthew was on his feet.

"Pitt. He has a really bad fever."

Tim stood up. "I'll fetch Mrs. Mercy for you." He hurried out to his horse.

"What can I do?" Ellen asked, subdued from her fervor to condemn Montgomery.

"Make some tea, I guess. I'll get the poultice cloths."

Matthew had already gone to the well with the water bucket.

"I hope it's not serious," Stamford said, standing.

"It doesn't take much out here," Belinda said, pulling a storage sack from the loft over the dogtrot. Ellen took wood chips from a burlap bag and shoved them into the stove, then moved the coffee pot aside so it wouldn't boil over.

Matthew returned with the water, helped clear the table. Ellen dampened a cloth and went to the bedroom where morning light cast long shadows on Pitt.

"Not feeling too well, I hear." She wiped his face with the cloth. He didn't answer, made raspy breathing, his eyes fluttering slightly. She took his hot, dry hand in hers, trying not to squeeze too tightly, and wondered where were her powers of future sight now, when she'd like to know what would happen. He's got to be all right, she thought. He's got to!

15

*L*utecia approved of the trembling tea of poplar bark Ellen had prepared, and white-mustard poultice Belinda had laid over Pitt's chest and throat. "Looks like he's got touch of quinsy again," Lutecia said. Ellen sighed, a bit relieved. Pitt had throat problems every spring and fall. Lutecia boiled black-elder leaves with some other herbs and a tan liquid she had brought in a jar. "This will be a gargle for him when it cools," she said to Belinda. Belinda nodded, although the look of worry didn't leave her face as she started back to Pitt's room with a fresh poultice.

The day had brightened and grown hot. Ellen heard the store bell and stepped out of the kitchen just as Hestor ran into the dogtrot. "Cattle comin'!" he announced, grinning. He had a rope looped over his shoulder. "And the trail boss is up at the store wantin' to buy something. Is Pitt here?"

"He's not feeling too well, Hestor." Ellen tied on her bonnet. "He'll be staying in today."

"He's gonna miss the cows!" Rob rode by to the east on the family's only horse. "Hey! Where ya goin'?"

Rob just set the horse to a lope, heading out the trail toward the Mercy cow camp.

"Luke has sent him to get Charles. In case there's trouble here," Stamford said, stepping up from where he and Tim had been talking by the hitching rail.

Trouble, Ellen thought. They had to be suspicious of any strangers who now came through the settlement.

"I'll walk with you," Stamford said, leading his horse. "I need to talk to this trail boss."

"Do you think it might be the rustled cattle?"

"That's a possibility."

At the store, she had difficulty concentrating on the order from the blond-bearded man. He read it out to her, since the penciled handwriting was awkward and smeared on the dirty creased paper he had produced, and she rewrote it on a piece of wrapping paper. Her worries about Pitt wove through the morning confrontation with Montgomery. ("I thought I was done with you!") *What had he been talking about?* She took the man the whetstone he wanted.

"If you ain't a cattle inspector, my business ain't yours, Mister!" the man stormed as he tossed payment on the counter.

"I'm a U.S. Marshal." Stamford pulled a six-pointed bright metal star from his shirt pocket.

"Uh. Like the Rangers down in Texas. Kin ride anywhere, demand anything?" The man remained sullen.

"I'm investigating various rustlings and two murders."

"Three. Don't forget Riding Boy," Ellen put in, giving the man his change.

"Murders!" He swiped the whetstone off the counter with a grimy hand.

"And rustling. Now, if I could see your papers and the registry of your trail brand," Stamford said again.

The glowering man produced papers from the inside of his worn leather vest. "These murders had to do with the rustlin's?"

"That they did. One north of here, one to the west."

"Two to the west," Ellen put in.

Stamford frowned at her interruption. "I'm expecting the stolen herd to get driven through here pretty soon."

"Well, this herd ain't stolen. You kin count the cattle—they'll tally to this number minus fourteen we done paid the Indians. And the brands ain't been tampered." He shaved pieces of tobacco from a block with his pocket knife. "Murders," he muttered, shaking his head.

"Four of them," Ellen said, impressed by the man's shocked abhorrence.

"What?" Stamford gaped at her, eyes bright.

Ellen's breath seemed to leave her. Heat flooded her face. "I mean, three." She grabbed up the order she had written and turned away, her hand pressed on her chest. The last time she had inflated the number of murders they had found Riding Boy's remains, proving her right. She shook her head. *I'm still including Mr. Baxter.* Her hands trembled as she skewered the order over a nail. *Or the Texan killed; or— Reed.*

"You jest ride down there now! Get this checked out," the man insisted to the marshal.

"I intend to," Stamford said, starting for the door.

"We'll pick up them items after we bring the herd through," the man was saying.

"Of course," she managed. "It will be ready." She followed him to the door.

Ellen clenched her hands around the porch rail as the man and Stamford mounted their horses. If these really were the outlaws, she thought, perhaps this man has stopped here to scout the store for robbery. Then she thought of Stamford going into The Nations to check brands—riding his sorrel horse into a possible bushwhack situation. Stamford trotting along, smiling, falling ...

She turned away from the road and the image, hurrying inside. She had work to do, an order to fill. She hadn't even dusted the store yet this morning.

Two hours later, the marshal returned, his arrival announced by Hestor's loud call. Ellen went onto the porch as the boy sprinted toward the well yard to tell the news to her parents. Charles and Ellen's father had trotted their horses to the store several times, Charles wearing a side arm and carrying a rifle, her father with the shotgun propped across his lap, concerned that the marshal had ridden into The Nations alone. But what else to do, Ellen thought. Even if every man in the settlement had gone with the marshal, chances were good that bushwhacking rustlers would have outnumbered them, or at least outgunned them. Not to mention their desperate determination not to be caught!

Dust hung against the southern sky, white and fog-like, signaling the approaching herd, but she focused on Stamford who forged his horse through the high waters of the Bluff and then walked it up the road. He seemed in no distress, and she gave a relieved sigh wishing she hadn't stayed here, worrying, when all he was going to do was come in and question her more.

"I take it the trail brand was legitimate," she said when the marshal reined his horse up at the hitching rail.

"That it was." He dismounted, his trouser cuffs wet and dark from the river crossing. "They'll be through here in twenty minutes or so."

He leaned against the hitching rail and took a pencil and paper from his pocket and begin writing. Ellen went to the one shutter that worked and closed it over the window, relieved that Stamford didn't start questioning her. Hestor jogged back into view, did cartwheels across the road, and was immediately called by his mother.

Ellen frowned at the sharpness of Reba's voice, and turned to see the woman shaking Hestor's shoulders; Olive stood by, clutching her dog. One of the puppies waddled around her feet. Trouble, Ellen thought. No mysterious discerning told her that. It was obvious. Rob ran toward the hotel, calling Luke. Ellen went down to the road.

"What's this, now?" Stamford muttered, stepping to her side.

"Georgie!" Reba called, hands on her hips. The woman turned to Ellen's and the marshal's approach. "I swear. That George. I got no idea where he is."

"Well, he can't be too far. Not to worry."

"This is the time of day he takes his nap. If he's asleep, he won't hear a thing! I've told these younguns to keep an eye on him."

"He ain't up there with Pa," Rob said, coming down the slope.

"Well, go check the cornfield again. And Olive, did you look in the clothes bin? Under your-all's cot?"

"He ain't in the house, Ma," Olive said.

"Where did you see him he last?" Ellen asked Hestor.

Hestor pointed to the top of the dugout. "Watchin' for cattle. Then I run to tell that the marshal was a-comin'." He shrugged. "I'm gonna check the wood pile."

Reba went back to readying the dugout against the cattle drive, placing inside anything she didn't want filled with dust.

"Does the boy do this often?" Stamford asked.

"When he's ready to take his nap, he doesn't care where he is," Ellen said.

"I hope he didn't fall in the river," Stamford murmured to Ellen, eyeing the swift waters.

"Geor-gie!" Olive's little voice wailed. "One of the puppies is gone, too," Olive said, tying up her dog. "I hope it don't get tromped by the cattle."

Reba stood up straight, tense, staring at Olive. Ellen's eyes went to the steady plume of dust. The first steer had topped the rise in The Nations. *And when they cross—* Ellen swallowed hard. *George could be sound asleep in their path.*

"Good Heavens!" Stamford said, obviously having the same thought. "Rob! Go get Mr. Fykes and everyone. We've got to get a search party for George." He headed to his horse.

Ellen looked under the store porch, by the big alder tree and work shed. Olive ran along the Bluff where the banks had been eroded by the high waters. Gnarled cottonwood roots made niches on both sides of the ford before the three foot drop into high water. "Ain't no place over there for him to crawl to," she reported. Tim rode along the sopped cornfield and past the hog and chicken pens. Luke checked in the tent hotel and rousted Dillard Winslow from his laziness.

"Your Pa is giving the barn a thorough check, in case he followed Hestor back there," Charles told Ellen when he joined the search.

"He didn't fall in the creek!" Hestor insisted to Rob's questioning. "I know he didn't. He didn't!"

"How do you know, when you don't even know where he was!" the older boy growled.

"I'll go tell them herders," Tim said. "Get them to hold up those beeves till we find him."

He headed his horse to the river, but already the swing riders were urging the cattle toward water. Ellen could make out the point rider's blue bandanna and red shirt; she could see the lead steers' heads bounce lazily in their heavy trot. The thud of hooves filled the air. Too late to stop them now. Ellen looked around, feeling desperate. She could see Luke calling George's name, but couldn't hear him over the noise of the approaching herd.

"Oh, dear Lord." Tears clung on Reba's eye rims; Rob's face was taut with fright.

"Here! I found his shoe!" Charles called, riding to where Ellen comforted Reba. He held up a small brogan, dusty and with a hole in one toe. George's hand-me-down from Hestor—from Rob before that.

"Where was it?" Stamford asked.

"By the road over there." He pointed north near the hotel. "We must have gone by it all this time." He handed the shoe to Ellen.

Dark musty smell. "Oh!" She blinked.

"What?"

She stared at the shoe, took it in both hands.

Again she was surrounded by darkness and the smell of rotting wood. She closed her eyes and could hear water lapping softly and the whimper of a puppy. *Could it be? Where? Where!* The image expanded with the dark taking definition, like a tunnel. Small. Damp. *A hollow log!*

With her breathing shallow, Ellen's eyes were now wide open, and she scanned for what she had perceived. "It was so clear. It has to be. Has to be," she muttered.

And she remembered, along the Fall Creek ford, old logs had been washed up.

The first of the cattle plunged into the Bluff, and Ellen ran north up the road, George's shoe gripped to her. "This way!" she called. "At Fall Creek."

"Here. Give me your hand." Stamford leaned from the saddle. Ellen pulled up behind him. Following them came Rob, and behind him, cattle—wet and dripping from the Bluff River—were urged by the press of oncoming animals up the half-mile trail toward the next ford. Some stopped to drink, but most staggered to the road.

"There. I remember from this morning. The logs." She slid from the marshal's horse and hurried to the littered area. Six, seven logs had jammed one place, and others were scattered along the ford. The log Ellen went to had one end bobbing in the high creek water, the other slanting onto the trampled wet earth of the trodden path. A little human footprint was clear in the mud.

Don't let him be drowned, she prayed as she got on her knees to reach into the long rotten piece. The two-foot wide hollow core was dark and musty. "George!" she called, lying flat to reach in. She heard the puppy and saw George's legs.

"Do you see him?" Stamford asked, bending over her.

"Yes! But I can't reach."

"Grab the end!" Stamford called to Rob. He jumped into the water which was up to mid-thigh and flowing along the very lip of the creek bank.

Ellen pushed to her feet, her dress stained, bonnet askew, her hair streaked with mud. Charles handed her the reins of his horse as he got off. The men wrestled with the water-soaked log and Ellen glanced back, shocked to see the cattle jogging past Tim's barn, their wavy horns, like deadly open arms. She could feel their thudding through the ground as they came fifteen—eighteen abreast. Another thirty yards and the beasts would be on them. "Hurry!" she whispered, knowing the men were doing all they could. She grabbed the reins of the other two horses and tugged them into the trees. Rob and the two men groaned in unison as they lifted the log over the muddy lip of the bank and to the grass of the second flood level. They shoved and bullied the water-sodden wood, and from the end that had been in the water, the puppy squirmed out.

"Where's George!" Rob's desperate cry was lost in the rumble and bawling of cattle.

Ellen scooped up the wet puppy. The cattle stomped over the place she had recently knelt peering into the hollow log. The cattle leaped some logs, but other wood was kicked, trampled, dislodged into the water as the beasts bellowed and jostled to get through the narrows. Rob started tearing at the rotted wood with his hands and Stamford joined him while Charles kept the log from rocking. Finally, a little bare foot was visible and Stamford carefully pulled the boy out.

"George? Georgie. Wake up!" Rob pleaded, frozen as was Ellen, with fear that the boy was hurt.

George fretted and fisted his eyes. Rob gave a loud sigh and took him from Stamford. George pouted and then looked at Ellen. "Woofer!" he declared, reaching for the puppy. Rob allowed him take the puppy, but wouldn't let go of his brother.

Cattle surged steadily across the ford, water rippling from their shoulders and splashing around thin legs. By the time Ellen and the others clambered along the marshy tree line to solid ground, the intensity of the actual rescue was wearing off, and Ellen remembered how it had come about—how she had located George.

Rob, now astride his horse, gave Ellen a wide-eyed look. "Thank you." Then he grinned at George. "Let's get you to Ma." He urged the horse across the flat toward Tim's. George, with one bare foot kicking the air, grinned as the puppy licked his face.

Ellen put her hand in her apron pocket, fingering the shoe, and watched Rob trot the horse down the hill. She could see Luke and Reba on the store porch. Cattle mooed and careened, plunged into the Bluff, streamed wet up the road, jostled and filled the entire distance to Fall Creek and beyond.

"I know they're relieved to see him safe," Charles said, catching up his horse.

"He certainly wouldn't have been safe if it weren't for Mrs. Hargrove," Stamford said.

"How'd you know where to look, Ellen?" Charles asked.

She walked briskly out of the trees and to the back of Tim's, searching for the answer and wanting to deny that she had sensed

George's location when she held his shoe. Preposterous, yet she knew it was true.

"Mrs. Hargrove?" Stamford asked, as he kept stride beside her, leading his horse.

"I—" She frowned. Mud clung to her shoes and a stone rubbed her heel. "Lutecia and I were up here this morning," she said to Charles. "I remembered the logs." *Be satisfied with that. Please!*

Charles seemed to be, but Stamford's obvious interest didn't wane nor dilute the feeling Ellen had that he knew exactly how she had found George—how she had kenned his whereabouts. That was the term Mr. Baxter had used: that she had a ken for the weather—an unnatural knowledge of what was to be.

She was grateful to see her father loping his horse toward them when they passed behind Tim's barn. Matthew swung down.

"Are you all right?" he asked, peering at her with worry.

For a quick moment, Ellen let herself to the comfort of her father's embrace, then straightened and drew a deep breath as she continued toward the yard, remembering how she had held the shoe, sensed the musty darkness and George asleep. The incredible play of circumstance washed her with light-headedness as she approached the dogtrot and the open door of the kitchen.

"She's a witch!" Winslow declared backing out of the crowded room.

"Now, see here!" Stamford jerked the man's shoulder.

"It's all right, Burton," Matthew said.

Winslow extricated himself from the marshal's grip and slunk into the yard.

Ellen tried to smile at the marshal's attempted defense of her, but agreed with her father. Let it be. The marshal moved protectively beside her as they stood in the doorway. George played blithely on the dirt floor, oblivious to the situation while he accepted the attention of Olive and Hestor, Tim and Lutecia. Rob was in the midst of telling how Charles found the shoe and handed it to Ellen and she had immediately known where to find George. Ellen edged along the wall to the far end of the table and managed to ask her mother about Pitt.

"Feeling a bit better," Belinda said, studying Ellen with a scared look as Ellen sat beside her.

"It was a miracle!" Reba exclaimed. Then spying Ellen, she hurried to her. "Oh, Ellen, bless you." Reba's callused palms pressed Ellen's cheeks and the woman kissed her forehead with dry lips.

Reba finally herded her brood out the door, their chatter lingering across the yard and quickly blending into the steady drone of cattle moving along the road. Tim said goodbye and left. The room quieted. On the roof came the patter of light rain. "That surely blew in fast," Lutecia commented, looking out of the window.

Belinda shook her head and slumped into a chair. Thunder rumbled far away. Matthew stood behind Belinda's chair and began rubbing her shoulder. Ellen poured herself a cup of cool mint tea and sat down.

And I am alone, Ellen thought.

"What are we going to do?" Belinda whispered.

"What's to do?" the marshal said, sitting across the table from Ellen. "Your daughter has some unique attributes and I find them fascinating." The quiet intensity of his voice touched more than Ellen.

Charles stepped forward. "There's a bothersome way you say that, Marshal."

"She had crossed that ford this morning—just remembered the log, that's all," Matthew said with Belinda-style logic.

"Don't fool yourself. It's something else. She probably has a skill—"

"You're saying she has some special knacks?" Charles asked.

Stamford nodded, thin lips forming a bemused smile.

"What happened to the skeptic?" Matthew asked harshly. "You were laughing at her over coffee this morning."

Ellen flushed, resenting the way they spoke of her as if she weren't even there. *Alone.* Lutecia patted her shoulder.

"I'm a man who deals with evidence and proof. I'm willing to admit when I've been wrong. What she did was a marvel, but not an accident. It's a gift."

"Well, I once saw that kind of stuff advertised with a sideshow in Kansas City," Charles said, frowning. "But that was a parlor trick."

"Someone holding an object and telling about its owner? No trick," Stamford said. "I've even been the subject. It's mystifying.

"And what happened here isn't any hocus-pocus, either. It's Ellen's brain," Stamford went on. "They're looking into the brain as a science of its own, you know. In Austria—a Dr. Fechner has discovered there is more to why we do what we do than we've suspected."

Ellen sipped her tea. The others continued discussing about parlor tricks and the new science of psychology which Stamford insisted on. Ellen wished she could stop them and give a logical explanation for how she had found George, but she couldn't. She *had* noticed the rotting logs that morning, just as she told Charles and her father. But holding the shoe had prompted another reaction. ("Rather like stubbing my toe," she had told Pitt. "I walk along fine and then...") Her pulse fluttered. She swallowed more tea.

"Don't you see the potential?" Stamford's green eyes flashed excitement. "She holds an object in her hands and knows all about the owner!"

"You make it sound like I could do this anytime—all the time!" Ellen blurted. "I've never had a sensing from touching things. That's never happened before!" She shivered, wondering if her declaration were true.

"Don't make it more than it is," Lutecia offered. "It probably takes a powerful circumstance—like today—or some calling of your thoughts and interest before you'd sense anything."

Like washing and folding Johnny's clothes, she realized. Wearing his work gloves, holding his hat. *I loved him so.*

"That's encouraging," Stamford leaned back in his chair grinning at Ellen. "I'll assume it was a powerful interest in me that allowed you to know my background."

"What?"

"This morning. You were telling me about my family living in New York."

Ellen hands went cold.

"You had carried my clothes to the barn, as I remember."

Ellen cut her eyes to Lutecia, recalling wearing the marshal's hat the previous evening. She opened her mouth and drew air into her tight chest.

"Excuse me." Belinda got up and started toward the dogtrot.

"Belinda Jarvis, this ain't the time to be leavin' your girl," Lutecia said, acting more her mother's peer than Ellen's.

"I—I have to check on Pitt."

"Belinda, wait," Matthew said. "I think Lutecia's right. It's time to tell Ellen what's she's inherited."

"Oh, Matthew." Belinda put a hand to her mouth.

"This is a family trait?" Stamford nearly squeaked with surprise. Everyone's scrutiny was on Belinda and she gave a timid nod.

Belinda began reciting the family history in a soft voice which no one intruded on with even a cough. Ellen sat in a mix of relief and anger. Relieved to know that she wasn't alone with this odd attribute; angry that her mother had withheld the information, even when she could see the distress Ellen was in. *I'm from a family of seers.* She suddenly wished she could know them, especially her uncle Geoffrey, Belinda's older brother. His unique abilities had plagued him—had driven him to wander and seek reckless adventure with which to override his visions. *If I were a man, I'd do exactly that.* Geoffrey's visions persisted, however, often forewarning danger and giving him such insight into others that he acquired few friends. He was currently working in Europe—in Amsterdam, Holland—at a zoological park. The exotic sound of it made Ellen smile a bit. She thought of her own rapport with animals—the silent way she communicated with Phineas, the attention she received even from the pig. Her mother had that talent, too.

"A few cousins and my grandmother possess small bits of these abilities," Belinda murmured.

"Clairvoyance," Stamford said, getting up.

"I assumed you would grow out of it, Ellen. I thought—"

"What is when and where is now," Ellen muttered.

"What?" Belinda peered at her.

"That's how I feel sometime. Like I can't tell what is when…"

"And where is now," her mother joined in. "Geoffrey often said that." Belinda sighed. "Well, it's a relief to finally have it out." Belinda templed her fingers over her nose, half hiding her face.

"You should have told me," Ellen said quietly. "Especially last year. I was so miserable." *But she doesn't know about my other dream—about Johnny.*

Stamford began pacing in front of the open dogtrot doorway, hands clasped behind his back gripping his hat.

"Well, it's an amazing thing," Charles said, shaking his head.

Matthew comforted Belinda with his embrace. Ellen wished for some comfort, for a strong arm, a reassuring grip. She wondered what Johnny would think of all this. Johnny, who she didn't save. *I'm sorry.*

Outside the sun flashed through the thickening clouds. The rain had stopped. Ellen sipped her tea. The marshal's pacing chafed at her, and she suddenly missed Reed Carter's reassuring presence. Ellen wondered if she were to touch something of Reed's she would know where he was. Her thoughts raced along an unbidden course and she thought of his broad-shouldered build, dark hair, smooth jaw—just like the man Burton Stamford hoped to arrest. His neat clothes, blooded horses— He had no mustache, but that would have been easy to change. Had Reed left to avoid the marshal?

No! She clenched her teeth. *Reed is a gambler, perhaps, but basically a good person. And he fought for the Union.* Or so he said. What *did* she know about him? Kyle Montrose, her thoughts harassed. And he's run away. She had never been in contact with a single item belonging to Reed, although she had touched him (or he her) the times he helped her onto her horse or down from the wagon. Of course, the marshal had done that much, too, but it wasn't until she held his hat that she— *No. James Montgomery is the villain. The darkness around him surely means something! He's Beaver Laughing's Bad Dark. He has to be!*

"Mrs. Hargrove. You've got to come with me to Fort Riley," Stamford declared.

Ellen and the others looked at him blankly, pulled from their own thoughts by his sudden words.

"All you'll have to do is hold this watch, you see. I'd know right where he was, and—"

"Burton, what are you talking about?" Matthew asked.

"Montrose. Kyle Montrose." Stamford grinned mischievously at Ellen. "You're going to find him for me. You've already foreshadowed incredible things. And finding George was no fluke!"

"She's known Georgie since before he could walk," Belinda said. "You're talking about fathoming a stranger—a person who well may not exist at all! I think the weather's more of a threat than some nebulous outlaw."

"Montrose's pocket watch is at Fort Riley! Complete with initials and birth date," Stamford continued, undaunted.

"How'd they come by that?" Charles asked, sitting at the table. Stamford sat down. Lutecia walked to the front wall where she peered out of the window, hands on her hips. Ellen put down her cup, curious as to what Lutecia saw.

"...found it in the grasp of a dead man—one of his gang members, it's believed. He was—" Stamford turned to Ellen, a look of wonder on his face and drawing her attention from Lutecia's exasperated pose. "The man had been knifed."

"This is preposterous!" Matthew declared, raking his hand through his graying hair. "And what about the rustlers? We're trying to move out of here!"

"Oh, I've that well in hand. Government scouts are up at Camp Wichitaw. We'll go through there on our way north and tell them to get down here and help you out."

"I just want to prove James Montgomery killed Mr. Stone and Riding Boy, like my dream implies," Ellen declared.

"Ah, yes. That dream! Come with me to Fort Riley, and you could see if your suspicions are right. Maybe Montgomery really is Montrose. And then I promise I'll return here and help you prove he killed Mr. Stone," Stamford said.

"You expect me to travel with you to Fort Riley?" Ellen asked, her tone accusing him of lecherous treachery.

"Oh! I didn't mean we'd travel just the two of us!" Stamford flushed, and Ellen felt a moment's pleasure at his discomfort. "Certainly not unchaperoned. Why, you would come, Mrs. Jarvis." He beamed at Belinda, back to his usual brash style. "In fact, between the two of you, learning Montrose's whereabouts should be a cinch!" He spread his arms dramatically.

16

They left at dawn. Not Ellen and Belinda, but Ellen and Lutecia riding with Burton Stamford. Belinda refused to leave Pitt, although his fever had eased during the night. Ellen knew her mother hoped her resolution not to go would deter Ellen's sudden compulsion to see—to hold this watch. Ellen had asked for Lutecia's company and the woman had readily agreed.

Both Ellen and Lutecia had spent the evening and into the night with their packing, an insistence of Belinda's, in case the families decided to move in the six days they would be gone. Her father had Phineas saddled and waiting before dawn, resigned to her plans, although not approving. "Ellen, I won't let you go," Matthew had said in the kitchen the previous afternoon. "It's three days to Fort Riley, unless you ride at night."

"It's not your decision, Pop," she gently replied. "I have to go."

Have to go ... have to go ... She was haunted by a need to do this—to have her ability be more of an impact—make a difference as it had in finding George.

"I don't think we'll be seen going this way," Stamford said in a quiet voice as he and Ellen rode to Lutecia's. They would go east and swing around north of the woods and the cattle to get to the main trail.

"Good morning Mrs. Mercy. Ready for a trip?" the marshal asked as Lutecia came from her cabin with her carpetbag and mounted her gelding.

"Most definitely. Anxious to find out what we can about whoever," she replied lightly. "How are you Ellen?"

"Fine, Lu. I'm glad you agreed to come."

The marshal looked over his shoulder toward the livery, the north Fall Creek ford, and the distant tent that held James Montgomery. Ellen looked that way, too.

"Isn't that Reed's wagon at Mr. Fykes's paddock?" she asked, seeing the green vehicle. "Is he back?" Her heart fluttered, and she wanted to ride over there, find him, tell him what was happening.

"Tim moved the wagon there after the cattle went through. Said he saw someone poking around," Stamford said.

"From the cattle drive?" Lutecia asked as they set on the trail that crossed Fall Creek at the back fields. Water ran high and the flood had turned the planned potato field to mud.

"He didn't say, but the door showed where someone had tried to pry the lock."

"Probably that Dillard Winslow," Lutecia said with disgust. "You know, he was slinking around your family's place after the others left yesterday," she told Ellen.

"Is that what you were looking at!" Ellen said, recalling Lutecia glowering out of the window.

"Yep. I wonder if he overheard our plans?"

"Hum," Stamford said.

They splashed across the ford and Ellen looked back toward the settlement. Predawn mist made it appear like a fuzzy painting, the colors pale and lines without definition.

Now that they were on their way, it seemed there was little to talk about. Ellen told Lutecia about Beaver Laughing's plot. Stamford explained how he learned of the pocket watch in the letter he received when the cavalry was recalled. "It seemed useless information, until now," he told them.

"It will be interesting if this works," Lutecia said from where she rode between them. She was wearing her Pettingill revolver in a makeshift holster belted over her dress. "You said you felt you had to do something with what you knew, Ellen. This is surely your chance."

"Yes. Yes it is."

Once the sun was up, heat pressed around them, although their shadows were still long to their left side. Behind them, Ellen heard distant thunder and the slate gray sky broiled with clouds. By the time they reconnected with the main trail to Camp Wichitaw, a mile or so north of where the cattle were bedded, they had been rained on several times. Thrashers and brown headed cowbirds strutted along the muddy trail, gleaning the waste from the last herd to pass. White clouds dissipated in the bluing sky and Ellen was grateful she had worn her wide-brimmed hat. The midday would be extremely hot as they followed this odorous wake north. An eastern trail might have taken off a bit of time, but the marshal wanted to go through Camp Wichitaw and alert the government scouts to the possible danger to the settlement.

"I didn't realize Camp Wichitaw had government men. We could have sent Rob there rather than Fort Harker," Ellen said.

"Likely they wouldn't have done anything with out authorization," Stamford replied.

"But you have the authority?" Ellen asked.

"Yes. I do," he said with a cocky smile. Ellen looked at Lutecia and rolled her eyes. *His ego is nearly as big as the state,* she thought.

Finches and tricolored blackbirds cried from short grass. Phineas flicked his ears to the various sounds. Rabbits and other rodents had already retired from the heat to their burrows.

"Look at that. Aren't they glorious?" Stamford pointed at two doe and their fawns high-stepping west through the woods ahead. A buck leaped and zigzagged the opposite direction. Lutecia drew her bay aside to examine a cherry tree.

Ellen noticed the cutoff to Pierces and her hands tightened on the reins. *The cutoff...* Disquiet filled her. It seemed she would be ill, her stomach rolling, fingertips chilled. And the vision returned: *The man smiles at her. Fringe. Dark. Falling.*

"Marshal," she said, her voice tight. "Marshal Stamford!" She jerked Phineas to a stop.

Stamford turned, smiling as he reined up his horse. *Cra-ack!*

His lips formed a grimace, green eyes wide with surprise as he jolted forward, still in the saddle, but he held his right shoulder and clutched his horse's neck, struggling for balance. His horse tossed its head and pranced. Ellen spurred Phineas forward, vaguely hearing Lutecia's exhortation to take cover. She grabbed the sorrel's headstall. *Craack*, came another shot. Phineas snorted. Ellen urged Stamford's horse toward the tall serviceberry bushes beside the trail. Two shots came from Lutecia's Pettingill.

"Get down!" Stamford growled at her. "It's you he's after!" The dark stain on his jacket spread as he took control of his horse and slid to the ground. With his left hand, he pulled his rifle from the scabbard.

Craack! Phineas jerked. Red blossomed across the big draft's left ear and the horse whinnied a protest and bolted into the thickets.

"Run, Ellen! We'll hold him down!" Lutecia called.

She was running, but it was Phineas's idea, not hers. By the time she regained control, they were in the black elder grove moving along a deer trail.

He didn't fall. Marshal Stamford didn't die. This was one thought, jumbled with the marshal's orders to get away, and recall of Lutecia at the cherry tree aiming into the distance—one brown hand tight on the revolver, the other grasping her horse's reins. Details so clear, although they had been only a flash to Ellen's vision.

She slowed Phineas to a trot, studying the clean groove in his ear, already darkened with congealed blood. A few more shots sounded behind her, then nothing. Her pulse raced. What did it mean? Phineas's hooves made a heavy sound on the damp ground. *I should go back.* Fump, fump, fump, fump: Phineas trotting. Branches crackled to her left. The horse's ears cocked, swiveled. The whump of a bullet in a nearby tree trunk was too close. ("It's you he's after," Stamford had said.)

Phineas needed no urging to move faster, and Ellen steered the horse into the trees, hunching low over his broad neck. *Run, Phineas.* She could hear a pursuing horse and glanced back, seeing a big man on a bay. Plaid shirt, slouch hat, mustache. He raised a rifle.

Ellen veered Phineas left. The bullet whipped tree leaves. *Run, Phineas.* But speed wasn't the draft's strong point; she already knew that.

If she could hide; if she could get down— No. She didn't want to be off Phineas—be stuck on foot. The horse veered right. A branch whisked off her hat. Thorns from the haw bushes snagged her dress. The ground was wet and a glimmer of hope came to her. *The cutoff to the Pierces!* She knew how to slow her pursuer.

Ellen reined right to stay in the thickets, even though her hands were scratched, dress torn. The horse behind her was closer. She could hear its footfall, the snap of branches. The ground became soggy.

*What is when and where is now? But there I am, riding
Phineas through the trees.* Green leaves. *We have to
be careful. It's marshy. We have to be careful.*

Phineas seemed to know what to do, too, and clomped along at a heavy lope.

We are careful, but he will not be—

Thlud, thud, thud, the hooves; branches scraped at her, leaves shaded everything. Thlud, thud, thud. ...

She had lost her pursuer. She circled left, heading north, skirting the thickets. She had heard the man's curse and his horse snort with fright when the wet sand trapped its legs. She imagined the horse floundering, wild-eyed, sinking deeper with each move until it stopped, chest deep and quivering. And if the man jumped off, he too would be trapped in the clinging pit. It could take hours for him to work loose.

But his arms might be free, still holding the rifle. That thought kept Ellen from going back to take a good look—to discover just who that man was. Her concerns were focused on Lutecia and the marshal, anyway. Phineas pounded on.

Ellen readied Marshal Stamford's Henry rifle she carried and walked Phineas forward, wary of every move. Perspiration rolled down her back in the oppressive heat. An occasional squeaky trill of the blackbirds sounded. No breeze. Ellen couldn't make out sign that anyone had preceded them down this trail. But in this area where trail herds had passed, the ground was pitted and hoof-scarred, making it hard to tell. Behind her, Lutecia helped Stamford drink water as he sat on his horse. He looked awful, his system wracked from a bullet that passed through his right shoulder. Lutecia had fashioned a sling for his arm with his leather shirt, and under his blue cotton shirt she had packed against both holes a poultice of minced alder bark and mud. He still bled, but not as much as he could have.

Ellen looked ahead to where the trail shimmered in the heat. Her hat was lost. Sun burned relentlessly on her skull. Not much further to home, and then Lutecia could give better care to the marshal's wound.

The bullet was for me, Ellen thought with anger.

The anger was twofold: first, that someone would want to—dare to!—try killing her; second, that her advanced knowledge of Marshal Stamford falling from his horse hadn't let her foresee why he was falling. The total situation hadn't come to her, and her reaction to the only part she knew had actually caused the vision to be true. If she hadn't hesitated, hadn't called out to him so he slowed his horse and turned—

I'd probably be dead. The thought stopped her breathing for a moment and a fresh burst of perspiration beaded her forehead.

Lutecia and the marshal rode up beside her. They continued their careful journey. The heavy air made their progress seem slower than it was, as if they were wading home. Stamford's gallant effort to appear undaunted weakened with each mile.

"Maybe we should have taken him to the Pierces," Ellen said to Lutecia as Stamford leaned awkwardly on the saddle's pommel.

"We must get you to protection, Mrs. Hargrove," Stamford managed to say. "That's the most—" He winced. "Most important. Whoever did this is very likely to try again."

"He's right, Ellen. We wouldn't want to bring any trouble on to those unsuspecting folks, anyway," Lutecia said. "And I want to get to my medicinals. I've got a tonic that'll perk him up in no time."

"I'm sure you do, Madam." Stamford attempted a chuckle that croaked a bit. "I'm sure—"

"Hush. We ain't there yet."

Ellen's head ached. Heat and worry drummed at her temples. So much worry. A noise beside the trail made them all tense. A muskrat scrambled into thicker underbrush. From her right came the lowing of cattle; those were Montgomery's cattle. *Montgomery-Montrose. He had to be the one, but how did he know?* Soon the back of the large tent was in sight through the trees and Ellen peered at the paddock, hoping to see James Montgomery's horse gone or still slick wet from being in a sand trap. Five horses were there, calm and clean. At the tent, Nancy stood in the doorway. She didn't wave.

Ellen put aside her curiosity, concentrating on the ford where Fall Creek's silty water swirled over the steep banks. Phineas snorted and hesitated before plunging into the break. Water sloshed around the big horse's chest, fast moving and dark, totally covering the second flood plain. When they reached the other side, Ellen was sopped to her calves. Behind her, Lutecia had hung her carpetbag on her shoulder and held the headstall on Stamford's horse, guiding it along. Ellen faced Phineas to the stream, ready to help, but they got across without incident. Stamford was now quite pale as his horse jerked and lunged to solid ground.

"Is it my imagination, or is the water higher than it was yesterday?" he gasped.

"It's higher, all right," Lutecia said with worry.

Ellen's gaze followed the water east where a wide rivulet furrowed a path through the worn slope in Tim's paddock. Then she noticed Tim, moving toward them from the door of his barn. She braced herself for the barrage of questions he and the others would have. Luke and Rob turned from where they worked on their old Conestoga, its wooden frame showing faded blue paint.

"The freight wagon has been moved to the house," Ellen said. Shock touched her. She knew they were going to be moving, but so soon?

"It appears your ma's decided it's time to go," Lutecia said. "No wonder she told us to finish packing last night."

Belinda, her pale hair wisping from beneath her bonnet, looked up from the well as they started through the yard. "Great heavens!"

"What happened?" Matthew came from the barn, a hammer in his hand. Charles followed, holding a slat of wood.

Ellen hated retelling, but the facts were crucial. Certainty that a murderer lived among them galled her thoughts like radish juice on a sore throat. And the murderer had tried to kill her.

"Hold on a bit longer, Marshal. We'll bed you back at my house, and I'll tend that shoulder proper," Lutecia said.

"No." Stamford pulled his horse up. Perspiration formed in big droplets on his brow. "Have to stay here. Safety in numbers."

Pitt came to the entrance of the dogtrot, hair tousled and wide-eyed. "What happened?"

Stamford wavered in the saddle and gripped the saddle horn. "Charles!" Lutecia called, bracing Stamford with an arm under his left shoulder. Charles kept the marshal from falling.

"Put him in our room," Belinda said, hurrying into the Jarvis house.

All the Claytons had arrived, along with Tim. Since Lutecia and the marshal moved inside, only Ellen remained to tell what happened. She went into the kitchen, the others pushing close behind. The telling sounded more strange than ominous since neither the Claytons nor Tim knew why Ellen, Lutecia and Marshal Stamford had been traveling north on the Chisholm Trail. "Gollee!" Pitt kept saying, impressed by the danger. Charles hurried from her parent's room and out the door as Matthew began explaining the trip to Fort Riley. Belinda came in to get a pan and cloths from the crates along the wall.

"You mean for Ellen to do like when she found George?" Reba asked, eyes wide. Rob was retelling the whole thing to Olive and Hestor who looked confused.

Luke kept chanting, "Are you sure it wasn't Indians?"

"All right. You've got to go," Belinda said before any answer could be given. "We've a wounded man in there who doesn't need to hear all this racket."

Ellen was grateful for her mother's words, yet felt helpless—foreign in this nearly-dismantled room that seemed all the more empty as Matthew ushered the others to the door.

Pitt came to her. "You were in the middle of it all! What an adventure!"

"It wasn't fun, Pitt," Ellen said, aware that Pitt's ailment seemed to be gone.

"Had you dreamed it before?"

"No!" Not exactly, she thought, anger again surfacing. She turned to her mother. "How's the marshal doing?"

"He's passed out, but they needn't know it," Belinda said low.

"One thing," Tim said as he straddled the door jamb. "Montgomery was here all morning. Chopping wood, settin' with his Nancy." He looked solemnly from Matthew to Ellen and sighed. "Only person who hasn't been around recently is Reed Carter."

"Oh, come now," Matthew began. Tim shrugged.

Had you dreamed it before? Pitt's question. Dreams. Ellen clenched her fists. It all started with that dream of Sycamore Spring. How long ago? Four, five weeks? *About the time Reed Carter got to town.*

No!

"I'll keep my eyes on your front door," Tim said. "In case whoever tries again." He gimped to his horse, taking up the reins and surveying the area before mounting.

"So what if Montgomery never left town," Lutecia said a half hour later. Using herbs Charles brought from their cabin, she had stanched the marshal's bleeding, rebandaged the shoulder and roused him enough to make him drink a wild-endive tonic. Now he slept while the rest of them sat in the kitchen, Pitt squeezed onto the chair with Matthew. "He's got people working for him. There were two men involved in this."

"You didn't mention that, Ellen," Matthew said.

"She may not have realized it. But the marshal and I was being fired on when we heard a rifle shot behind us. Then our attacker just slipped way."

"But the three of you traveling north shouldn't have seemed a threat." Belinda folded bedding and packed it in a crate. "How would anyone but us know where you were going and why?"

"I guess Winslow overheard the plans," Ellen said.

Lutecia told how she had seen him in the yard the previous afternoon.

"But why would he tell Montgomery?" Belinda asked.

"He probably tried to sell the information," Charles said. "I've seen his type before."

"I'm going to talk to him," Matthew said, getting up. "We've got to know what he heard and who he told." Matthew checked the load on the shotgun.

"I got a revolver," Charles said, joining Matthew. "Leave that shotgun with the womenfolk—just in case."

Ellen licked her lips. *In case the culprit tries again. Here? In the settlement? But who could know the workings of a desperate man?*

Winslow was missing, Matthew reported when he and Charles returned. "The fire ashes at the man's camp were cold."

"He's connected to this some way," Charles declared. "Where could he go without a horse?"

"Maybe that's what he got for his information—a horse so he could leave here," Lutecia suggested.

"Montgomery rode over to find out what had happened," Matthew told them. "Acted real concerned."

"It could be he isn't involved," Charles said.

"Who else here could be Kyle Montrose?" Pitt said. "And Ellen saw—"

"I'm beginning not to trust what I see," Ellen said. "Not totally, at least."

"He knows how to throw a rope real good," Pitt muttered.

Matthew nodded, his eyes narrowing. He pounded his fist on the table. "I'd like to get someone as dangerous as Montrose identified and locked up where he belongs!"

"Catching outlaws is the least of our worries," Belinda said.

"But he killed Riding Boy and tried to kill Ellen!" Pitt declared.

"And all our talk isn't going to change that. Whoever it was has shot a U.S. Marshal and has probably left the area. Our biggest concern now is to get packed and moved to high ground. Start at the Mercys," Belinda ordered. "The water's already coming through their floor."

"Just since we left?" Ellen asked, shocked. Charles nodded. Matthew sighed, his worry creasing age lines along his mouth and forehead.

"Can I help?" Pitt scrambled up and glanced at Belinda.

"You stay here. Your fever's been down only since dawn."

"Aw, Ma! I miss out on everything!"

The men left. From the bedroom, Ellen could hear a slight mumble from the marshal as Lutecia urged more liquid down him.

"Don't think on it too much," her mother said, hugging her. "No one knows all the answers."

Ellen repressed tears of frustration and returned her mother's hug, taking comfort in Belinda's lingering embrace. *Can't know all the answers, and what I do know is distorted.* She thought of Sycamore Spring, the marshal falling; what else?

In the room she shared with her brothers, she did her final packing, closing her sewing box, and taking the maroon calico dress and a night frock from the wall pegs. No point in changing into anything else. Her brown skirt was already torn from this morning's rough riding, the skirt hem bedraggled from crossing the creeks. She folded the items and placed them in the chest next to her bed. The beaded purse she had traded to Pretty Willow for a mirror was there (Riding Boy, dead). She moved it and nestled the sewing box among her two pair of woolen stockings, an extra bonnet and apron. The fine cotton chemise her mother had sewn for her wedding was there, too. The linen dress with taffeta bodice inset and lace trim in which she had been married, lay folded beneath all that. From the edge of the chest showed the top of a wooden horse Spencer had carved for her Christmas two years ago. Spencer. Ellen took up the little statue, concentrating. Spencer.

He rides a pinto horse, his golden hair gleaming. He draws a shiny revolver.

Ellen dropped the figurine in the chest and closed the lid, her breathing rough. What did that mean! What was going to happen? But holding the carving wouldn't really tell her anything, she was convinced. And besides, she didn't want to know what it meant— she didn't want to see anymore trouble or anguish or confusion; not any more at all!

17

*C*attle comin'!"

That cry surprised Ellen, having so much on her mind. Rob Clayton, leading the ox-drawn, two-wheeled cart stacked with tools and two crates of chickens, had called the news to Ellen and Belinda when he rode by the house. The smell of the chickens lingered even as Rob kept on east toward the ruined cornfield and swamped bottom land behind the Mercys. The rest of the Claytons' belongings already set there in the mud. Ellen's father, Luke and Charles were lashing timbers to make a raft since the place where the Fall arced before its confluence with the Bluff, normally a casual meandering, was now a-swirl with eddies and drops where soil had washed away.

"Cattle. Uh!" Belinda muttered. She and Ellen secured a slicker around baled bedding. Belinda's wall mirror was protected in the middle of the soft bundle. They wrestled the bulky package into the wagon next to the dismantled cook stove. Sacks of flour and dried goods had been pushed into the stove pipes to keep them from rattling and to protect the foods from inclemency.

"They're coming down the slope already," Ellen said, looking across the Bluff. Grunts and loud moos became a counterpoint to the loud shushing of whirling water. Birds darted away from the creek. "I don't remember a point rider coming by." *Are they the rustlers? Could we fight them off if they attacked?*

"Maybe the Claytons saw him when they were packing," Belinda said, but she eased to the dogtrot and took up the shotgun.

Pitt came out of the house. "Cattle!" he exclaimed, eyes

brightening as he handed Ellen the broom and rug beater. She wedged the handles between the wagon wall and the trunk that held clothes and dishes.

"Pitt, go warn your father," Belinda said.

Pitt sprinted toward to the barn and Ellen soon saw her father, Charles and even Luke standing in the yard with their weapons ready. The grumble and pound of cattle increased, punctuated with the cracks of bullwhips.

"They can't move cattle and attack at the same time," Ellen said.

"That's true," Belinda agreed, propping the shotgun against the cabin wall. "But if they notice, they'll see that we're ready for them."

Ellen's heart thumped as she returned to the house for more items. She wondered how many men worked for Montgomery. Enough to hold cattle north of Fall Creek; enough to hold an even larger herd in The Nations. Ten, twelve, fifteen men? She cringed, wishing they had already moved. But would they be safe on the trail, strung out along the prairie grass with no where to hide? *Stop thinking like this!*

Back outside, Tim's raspy voice made Ellen jump as she rounded the wagon. He rode a horse in makeshift traces attached to the green wagon she knew belonged to Reed.

"They're really pushing it, to ford now," Tim said, frowning.

Splash! Bellows of fear. The noise increased.

"Better than tomorrow," Belinda said.

Ellen stepped forward, intrigued by Reed Carter's wagon. She wondered if she were to touch it, what she would learn.

"Looks like Lutecia and the Claytons are ready to go," Belinda called over the racket made by the cows.

"I'll get on back there. Give a hand." Tim urged the horse on.

Ellen's right hand reached out to where the wagon had been. *If I had touched it ...*

"What's the matter with you?" came Pitt's voice.

Ellen flinched, drew back her hand. He's not Montrose; he's not! insisted her thoughts.

"Ellen?" Pitt's eyes widened, his face drawing to a smile. "Are you having another dream? What? What's going to happen?"

"Don't ask me that any more! I don't know. Even when I know, I don't know!"

Now her mother was staring at her, and Ellen hurried through the dogtrot, into the kitchen, and into the room where Butron Stamford, his auburn hair tousled, jaw relaxed, lay in sedated slumber. She wanted the marshal awake; she wanted to know more about Kyle Montrose and if the marshal knew why Reed Carter was gone. Anytime Reed had been mentioned, Stamford had that gloating look he got when he knew something. What did he know?

Cattle. Continuous sound. *Mooo-aw!* Clack, clack long horns. The earth shook. Cattle.

"The dugout is completely run into the ground," Belinda was saying. "I'm just glad Reba didn't see that. And the hitching rails, Tim's corral fencing."

Cattle rumbled through Ellen's brain, stomping just above her eyes. She leaned against the wall, staring around the barren kitchen. The only things not packed were tin cups and plates, a food sack and the bed in which the marshal slept. The walls looked ugly with all the twisted-grass chinking and troweled-in mud exposed—the blackened hole from the stove pipe.

"That herd was bigger than Mr. Baxter's," Pitt declared.

"Those drovers didn't make a single effort to contain those cows. I hope Mr. Fykes won't have any trouble retrieving his stock that got loose," Belinda said. "I can't believe he's actually going to ride in there and ask for them!"

Tim planned to retrieve his stock and then cut through the woods to join the others who were already northeast of Fall Creek.

"I have a feeling he's going to employ some Kiowa tactics," Ellen said. "Steal them back without their even knowing." She smoothed back the sweat-dampened hair at her temples.

"Wow! You think so?" Pitt exclaimed. After being cooped in the house for two days, his exuberance seemed greater than usual.

"I wish I could've gone with him."

"Pitt—" Belinda didn't say anymore, just shook her head.

Ellen thought they should have sent Pitt to the remote camp with the Claytons and Mercys. Being with the other children could have settled him down, but Ellen knew her mother wanted to keep the family together—as much of the family that was here. She rubbed her temples, the cattle sound storming through her head. Or was that thunder? She looked out of the window, barely making out her father as he walked through the humid evening from the barn.

He scraped mud from his brogans and stomped his feet in the dogtrot before coming in. "I've tacked up instructions for Spencer. But I think it's too late to raft across to the Mercy camp. It would be dark before we got our belongings aboard. We couldn't see what was coming in the current."

Belinda began pacing, her brow furrowed. "What about the stock?"

"The cow and pigs went over with the Claytons' stock. The ponies were tied to their Conestoga. We've only got the Burgundians."

"At least that." Belinda smoothed her short hair. "First thing in the morning. We need to be at the creek at dawn."

"Is that an angel I hear, or just the sweet voice of Mrs. Jarvis?"

Stamford's call took them by surprise. They heard him moving around and Ellen had to hold back laughter when he appeared at the door wrapped in a blanket and looking much like drawings Ellen had seen of ancient Romans.

"Well, you're on the mend," Matthew said with a chuckle.

"Indeed. Lutecia Mercy has a physician's touch. But what is this?" He looked around. "Have I slept a moon span? You're moving!"

"It's either that or float away with the currents," Matthew said. "Don't worry, we wouldn't have left you. Strapped you to the raft while you slept, if necessary."

"Raft! That bad, is it?"

"We had a big cattle herd come through!" Pitt told him. "Ripped up everything! The dugout, the livery fence."

"Hmm." The marshal frowned, leaned on the wall and rubbed his chin with his left hand.

"They didn't send a point rider through or stop to say anything to anyone," Matthew added.

"Ya think they were the rustlers pushing their herd north?" Pitt asked excitedly. "I'll bet Mr. Baxter's beeves were in there, and the cows from that herd rustled in The Nations, too."

"Moving them before the water gets too high to push them north—or they get found out," Matthew said in agreement.

"Possibly. But we really have no proof those beeves are stolen," Stamford said.

"You could check the brands," Pitt said eagerly. "I know what Baxter's trail brand looked like, 'cause Mr. Mercy bought some of his cows!"

"That's the simplest answer, son," Matthew said. "But the hardest to do. If they've stolen the beef, they're surely not going to let us examine the herd brands."

"They've probably covered the old brands, anyway," Stamford said, then he frowned toward Ellen. "And you, Mistress Hargrove. I take it there have been no unruly attempts against you?"

"No, Marshal." All the questions she had wanted to ask him stuck in her throat.

"I imagine the culprit is far from here by now," Belinda said.

"James Montgomery has left?" Stamford asked.

"No, but—"

"Then the danger still abides."

"Reed Carter's still gone," Pitt put in. Ellen wished Pitt would stop reporting everything.

"Yes. That is a worry," Stamford said.

"And Mr. Winslow, too," Pitt went on. "Mrs. Clayton thinks they were in cahoots!" Ellen let out a long breath and noticed her father shaking his head. Because he had suspicions about Reed?

"Pitt. Don't repeat gossip," Belinda said.

The marshal didn't seem concerned with the talk. He pushed awkwardly from the wall. "Tarnation! Mrs. Mercy has trussed me so firmly, I can barely negotiate."

"She wanted to be certain the bleeding didn't start again," Ellen said, going to the jar of dark liquid that set near the food sack.

"All well and good, but it will be difficult to be your right arm when I effectively have none."

"Oh, Marshal," Belinda laughed.

Ellen poured some of the liquid into a cup, knowing he wasn't joking. She, too, felt continued dangers shrouding them. "Here. A restorative you're to take."

"And then into the floods?" He peered suspiciously into the cup and took a tentative sip.

"No. We'll wait until morning. Claytons and Mercys have already gone over with the livestock," Matthew said.

"Hmm." The marshal moved to the window and peered into the early evening before closing the wooden shutters with his elbow. "Latch that," he ordered. He drained the cup and grimaced before striding into the bedroom. "What armaments do we have?" he called to Matthew.

"Come now, Marshal. You can't believe we'll be attacked this evening!" Belinda spread an oilcloth square on the floor. Ellen bent to help her.

"Someone considers your daughter a threat, Mrs. Jarvis." His voice was strained, as if wrestling with something. "Damn this shirt!" he muttered.

While Matthew went into the bedroom to help the marshal, Ellen checked the load on the shotgun, her tension increasing. Belinda set out cornbread and smoked venison, her face drawn. The two men returned and sat cross legged on the floor at the edge of the cloth: the marshal with his revolver near this left hand, her father with the marshal's Henry.

"Eat. All of you," Belinda said. "That's something we can do now. Give us energy for whatever else."

"You're right, Mrs. Jarvis. We must be practical," Stamford said.

While Belinda passed around plates, thudding raindrops started on the roof. "Oh, Lord," Belinda murmured, looking up as if the rain were coming through. And then a call from out front.

"Ma? Pop? You in there?"

"It's Spencer and Hubert," Belinda breathed, a smile coming to her face.

Ellen followed her father into the dogtrot, Pitt and Belinda crowding behind, and grinned at the tall figure in wet buckskin at the entrance.

"Everything looks awful!" Spencer exclaimed. "The dugout ruined—corral fences down."

Another man was with him, but Ellen realized it wasn't Hubert Fykes. Tall, dark hair, white shirt showing beneath a plain jacket and open slicker. "Reed!" Ellen exclaimed.

"Everyone's all right, aren't they?" Spencer's alarm held in his voice.

"Yes. Especially now that you're home safe," Belinda said, hugging her son.

"Where have you been?" Ellen asked Reed while the others ushered Spencer into the kitchen.

"The marshal didn't tell you? I was on a legal mission. Met Spencer in Medicine Lodge." He stared down at her, his expression lost in the dark hall, but she felt the intensity of his gaze. They entered the kitchen.

"What did you find out?" Stamford strode over. Pitt, Matthew and Belinda surrounded Spencer whose face was haggard. Ellen studied her brother, chilled by the wide belt he wore with holster—gun handle riding along his thigh in easy reach.

"What happened to you?" Reed asked, pointing to the marshal's bandaged arm.

"Mrs. Hargrove and I were on our way to Fort Riley and were attacked."

Reed scowled at Ellen, as if it were her fault. "You two were on your way to Fort Riley?"

"It's a long story," Ellen said wearily.

"And an exciting one," the marshal said, mystery in his voice. Reed's frown deepened.

Ellen hugged her arms. "Why didn't you tell me you had sent Mr. Carter to Medicine Lodge?" she scolded the marshal.

"My dear, I can't announce my procedures to the general public—have everyone knowing in advance what I'm looking for."

"But—"

"Actually, I had gone to Camp Wichitaw to see if Montgomery had been there as he said—to follow up your suspicions," Reed explained. "On my return, I ran across the marshal, and he asked me to go to Medicine Lodge for the same purpose."

"Enough of this," the marshal said with irritation. "Tell me, Carter. What did you find out?"

"Montgomery was in Medicine Lodge, all right. But not when he says he was there. It was maybe two or three weeks before Stone's death. He came in from the east and set up with a hard-bitten lot that trailed in from the southwest. They stayed a few days, then Montgomery came this direction, the others—" Reed shrugged.

"I can do it!" Pitt's excitement squawked through the room. "I'll go tell Mr. Fykes about Hubert stayin' west, and let the Mercys know Mr. Carter's back and everything!"

"It's too late, Pitt. Too dark out," Belinda said.

"No it ain't. You were tellin' Spencer he oughtta go and he's tired. I can do it!" Anger edged Pitt's voice.

"Tim should be told that Hubert's all right," Matthew was saying. "That he wants him to come West and join the Kiowas."

"Morning is plenty of time. He doesn't even know Spencer's returned," Belinda said, shaking her head.

"You-all don't think I'm good for anything," Pitt pouted.

"It's a comfort having two more defenders here," Stamford put in. "Who knows what Montgomery will do next. Mr. Carter tells me that man wasn't in Medicine Lodge when Mr. Stone was killed."

"Is *that* where you were," Belinda declared. "I must admit, Mr. Carter, after the attempt on my daughter's life, I was—"

"Attempt on Ellen!"

"Mother!" Ellen was appalled that Belinda nearly admitted those awful suspicions about Reed that she herself had harbored.

Belinda smiled and patted Reed's shoulder. "Glad you're back," she said.

"Where's Pitt?" Matthew suddenly asked.

Amid the rain falling on the roof, Ellen heard the clop of horse hooves in the mud. Her father ran outside, calling Pitt's name. She soon heard another horse as her father rode after Pitt. Conversation was minimal while Matthew was gone. Spencer, sprawled on his back on the floor, fell asleep. He looked much like the boy he was, for all his lanky form and strapped-on gun.

When Matthew returned, he was alone. "I couldn't get him before he crossed Fall Creek," Matthew said. "But he's all right. I saw him safe on the other shore."

Belinda released a long sigh and Ellen felt like she was breathing again for the first time in ages.

They slept on the floors in the cabin—except for the marshal who was persuaded to return to the bed. Reed Carter with a blanket also retired to that room, and as Ellen settled beside her mother, she could vaguely hear the two men talking. Perhaps continuing conversation about what they had started after Matthew returned: Ellen's saving George, the trip to Fort Riley, Kyle Montrose, Dillard Winslow.

The rain stopped, but the sound of wind in the trees was nearly as loud as the high dashing waters in the Bluff. It seemed Matthew fell asleep as quickly as had Spencer, his deep breathing putting a certain calm to the warm room, but Ellen knew she wouldn't sleep; listening to the creek, the wind; worry about murderers, hearing the fast waters, the wind ...

"Ellen, up. Quickly! We have to get out of here."

Her mother's anxious voice roused her and she blinked with surprise. Lanterns were lit and Matthew carried one into the bedroom. Spencer pulled into his calf-high moccasins and smoothed back his long hair. It gleamed honey golden in the lamp light.

"Get up!" Belinda ordered again.

No rain. The room was muggy warm. The creek didn't seem

as loud. Ellen, still groggy from sleep, frowned at her mother. Spencer pulled open the door to go out and that was when Ellen heard the thunder. Far off, the growl of it faded quickly then thumped ... thumped.

Marshal Stamford came into the room. "When you said early, Mrs. Jarvis, I never realized—"

Belinda cut him off. "If your gear is packed, put it on the farm wagon. Mr. Carter, go help Spencer hitch the teams. Ellen, get that bedding packed. We'll have to leave the bed."

Ellen was awake now, hearing an urgency to her mother's words that belied the systematic way Belinda moved. Here, then, was Belinda's prescience. The deepness of her voice, the surety of actions and words were things Ellen and the boys—even Matthew—always heeded. Do it!, she'd say. Yes, Ma. And the reason would make itself evident before they expected. Belinda was always ready. "Ride way out to the plains today. I want eight bags of cow chips," Belinda had ordered that last September in Cloud County. Ellen and Spencer had worked until sunset, having heard the imperative. By dawn, the soddy was buried in an early winter blizzard. They had stayed warm.

Again, that ominous sound. Thunder? Or a huge monster moving in on them from the southwest? Perhaps one of those fire-breathing dragons like were drawn in magazine articles about the Asian immigrants. Steady, grumbling, rumbling, ground shaking whump, bump bumpbump the whole time they packed the wagon and tied over the canvases. When they started the trip to the Fall Creek east ford where the raft was tied, Belinda didn't even look back at the barn and store or house they had lived in so comfortably for three years.

Mama, wait! Ellen wanted to cry. Her chest hurt. If ever she felt forced toward a different life, this was the time. Leaving so many memories here! This is where she and Johnny were married. This is where she learned about her "gifts." She swallowed hard.

With dawn, came a warm breeze, and as the men lashed the two Jarvis wagons onto the sodden raft, rain started—heavy—chased by the thunder from the low clouds. Logs raced from lost moorings further upstream and jammed on exposed roots of a downed cottonwood. The changing terrain astounded Ellen. The creek and river were moving to new positions—powering their way together—displacing the land with flood. Ellen was struck by a terror more devastating than any of her nightmares or visions. She balked at the edge of the lurching raft. In the stormy dawn, the water looked black. Upstream by several hundred yards Spencer, riding Phineas, and Reed herded three draft horses, Reed's extra horse and six half-wild mustangs Spencer had brought back with him. Ellen choked down a scream as they forced their mounts into the careening waters, leading the others on long ropes. Reed angled his horse upstream. It scrambled/swam across. Swirling waters. *Johnny was up to his chest*— No. Spencer on Phineas. The big horse struggled, being swept downstream. They finally made the other side, four hundred feet from where they started, right before the creek and river converged.

"Marshal. Go!" Belinda ordered him onto the raft. The loud water, the rain and wind made it hard to hear or speak. "Get on the raft!" Belinda yelled, tugging at Ellen's sleeve. The sky darkened as if time had reversed and it were night again. Rain pounded around them.

"Mrs. Hargrove. Get aboard!" Marshal Stamford held out his healthy arm to her. She gripped it and stepped onto the raft which felt soggy—water logged. Heart racing, she squatted behind her mother by a wagon wheel.

Something like a thrown pebble struck her cheek and then her back and head. Icy. Cherry-sized hail bounced on the raft and the wagon canvases. The raft jerked and then they were in the current. Behind them, manning the guide rope from Bob's back, sat her father, wind blowing his slicker around the horse's neck. Spencer and Reed tugged on ropes from their side. So much wind! Hail peppered them a few moments more before rain fell as if poured from a celestial bucket. Ellen's stomach lurched with fear as something whacked the raft and caused it to hove right. Water soaked her legs and dress, and she gripped the wagon wheel—felt her mother's hand clenched on her shoulder. Rain. Wind. The hairs on her wet arms tingled. Brightness flooded around and the cracking of lightning made her head ring.

Then both rain and wind ceased. In the improved vision, Ellen could see the edge of the huge eddy that marked the confluence of creek and river. She gripped her mother's shoulder and gagged on a scream, certain they would be sucked into it, but the raft slowly began moving back upstream. Her brother's voice urged Phineas to pull. They retreated more. Behind the charcoal-gray clouds, the sun had come up. Everyone's skin looked pale green.

Steadily the draft horses pulled them to the flooded east bank, and when the raft touched shore, Ellen hurried behind her mother to the slippery ground. Following Belinda's lead, she grabbed ropes on the raft. The marshal stepped off and they all tugged the raft and its burden out of the creek. It was easier than Ellen expected, because the creek waters ran higher now, slopped over her feet. Matthew swam Bob across to their side.

"Mother of God," Stamford muttered.

Looking up, Ellen saw it. Blacker than night, the gigantic funnel materialized from the heavy clouds south of the Bluff River a mile away. It grew larger, came closer. The tail of the twister lashed down. Timber billowed like match sticks, swirled and vanished. The air growled around them and the cyclone seemed to bounce down the slope from The Nations and across the river. It swooped, jerked, sucked in all air and roared like fabled banshees enraged.

Stamford pushed Ellen to the ground. She lay flat in the mud, his good arm across her shoulders. But she craned her neck to look back. Dread riveted her gaze to the cyclone as it sucked up the smokehouse and work shed, zigzagged along the road, scattered the cabin, hung over the store for interminable seconds while it gorged itself—wood flying, careening, vanishing. The barn was next before the destruction plowed north. It hopped over Tim's barn and hovered, as if making a decision, then lifted straight, grew skinny; the tail pulled into itself above the trees and it blended into the moil of clouds.

Ellen's skin tingled. Lightning streaked the gray dawn. A tree flared briefly before rain doused the flames.

"Everyone's all right?"

Ellen's eyes welled with tears of relief on hearing her father's voice. She pushed to her feet, rain washing her face and plastering her muddy dress to her body. Spencer and Reed, pale from what they had witnessed, stood behind Matthew.

"You saved us, Mrs. Jarvis," Stamford said to Belinda. Water streamed from everyone's hair, pulling it to dark stripes along their faces. "You're as remarkable as your daughter. I'm forever indebted— and awed!"

Belinda didn't seem to hear as she stared, trembling, across to the rubble of their home. One side of the cistern had crumbled under a fallen alder. Nothing else was standing. Matthew stepped behind Belinda and closed his arms around her. The rain hid their tears.

Ellen drew a shaky breath, understanding her mother's sudden despair. *She had saved them, as I saved George.* And Ellen could remember that odd wash of shock—that horrified worry: What if I hadn't known?

Water sloshed around her ankles, filling her shoes. Startled, Ellen looked down. "We've got to get these wagons hitched and moved!" she said. "Or we'll get swept clear down to the Chikaskia!"

"She's right! Hurry!" Reed said. He had Grams and Clio in tow, but he stopped a moment, gave Ellen a long look and admiring smile.

I was scared, Reed, she wanted to tell him. More scared than I've ever been in my life. She went to help hitch the teams.

Water roared behind them, loud even through the renewed sound of rain and wind. Matthew and Reed took control of the wagon teams, while Belinda and Ellen blundered along in the gusting wind with the loaded farm wagon. Stamford slogged beside the freight wagon. Spencer, now riding a sorrel pinto, had the loose stock in control and was already ahead of the wagons, his tall figure looking blurry through the steady down pour.

"Hiahh, Grams! Hup Clio!" Reed yelled.

The draft animals strained to pull their burdens through the sopped land where mud rode four inches on the spokes—coated the tires. Each time Ellen glanced back (and she couldn't seem to help herself) the land looked different. Water churned and careened in new places: trees were displaced; the Mercys' animal shed had vanished along with corral posts and sodden cornfield. The water was like a growing lake. It swelled over everything and the surface was lashed in huge waves by the wind.

"Don't look back!" her mother said, leaning close and gripping Ellen's hand. "We're on to something new. Something new!"

Ellen bit her lip, amazed at her mother's fortitude. She forced herself to stare ahead.

18

*T*he rain dwindled to a slow patter as they moved from the creek bank. The footing improved for the horses. Quarter mile. Half mile. Morning sunlight suffused the clouds, illuminating wet foliage and shrouding their surroundings in an eerie patina. Ellen, seated beside her father on the spring bench of the freight wagon, squinted through the ground fog that rose steadily into the cooling air and swirled in the forceful gusts of wind that shoved and butted around them. Ahead, she could make out Spencer on his handsome pinto (where had she seen that horse before?) leading his own string and other horses not in harness. Then something else—hazy at first. Spencer waved his arm.

"Someone's coming," Ellen said.

"It's—Lutecia!" Belinda said from the seat of the farm wagon.

"And Tim Fykes," Matthew identified.

The two riders stopped beside Spencer, then Spencer was galloping toward them. Tim gathered up ropes for the loose horses her brother had left behind, and Lutecia jogged her horse toward the farm wagon. Ellen's gaze stayed on Spencer; she could feel his tension, knew his worried expression before he was close enough to make out his features.

"Pitt!" Spencer choked out to Matthew when he reined beside the freight wagon. "He's not there. He never got to the camp!"

Pitt is all right, Ellen kept thinking. She had studied the thought as her father, Spencer, Tim and Reed prepared to search the flooded creek for Pitt. The thought didn't feel like a desperate reassurance pronounced to keep panic at bay, but she didn't say anything—still distrustful of what her senses told her. Yet the though persisted: *Pitt is all right!*

Now she drove the farm wagon, Marshal Stamford —his arm in a sling—sat beside her on the bench seat. Her mother managed the reins of the freighter, and Lutecia had taken over the string of horses. The rain showers stopped and sunlight burned through the cloud layers, as intense as the distress of those with the wagons. Ellen wished she could see to the front wagon—hoped her mother had lost that drained, pinched look.

From ahead, Ellen could hear Olive's dog yapping and soon Reba and the children appeared at on the edge of the camp. One figure began running across the wet meadow toward them.

"It's Pitt! He's here!" Belinda exclaimed.

Pitt held his hat in place with his right hand and clutched something in his left as he ran headlong to them.

I've seen this before.

Hestor ran behind him. The last distance they came seemed incredibly long.

"Ma! Mama!" Pitt called. Belinda had stopped the freighter. "Oh, Ma! I was so scared! I saw that cyclone—" Pitt cried in Belinda's arms as Ellen stopped the farm wagon. "The house, everything. I saw it go. Oh, Ma!" His arms clutched Belinda's neck.

"We're all right, Pitt. We were across Fall Creek before it hit. It's all right," Belinda said soothingly.

"Everybody? But where're Pop and Spencer?" He pulled back, sniffing.

"They're off looking for you."

In an eye blink, Ellen saw her mother's relieved consolation change to maternal anger.

"Get up there on that wagon seat," Belinda ordered. "And tell me why you didn't come to this camp last night. Where have you been? You put a worry into everyone! What were you doing?"

"Gollee! You're all right!" Hestor said, panting as he joined the group. "We was plenty scared for you-all. My Pa and Rob are out helping Mr. Mercy with his cows, or they would've come. Gollee! Did Pitt tell you what he done?"

Pitt's face lit to a big smile and he ran to the farm wagon, ignoring Ellen and going straight to the marshal. "I got it! I got the proof on the rustlers and Mr. Montgomery, too!" He flailed the object he was carrying.

Ellen squinted, trying to make it out. A foot-square piece of hide, red-brown hair still intact. She took it from Pitt and held it for the marshal to see, easily making out the Diamond Bar O brand burned into hair—the Stone Cattle Company brand.

"Turn it over," Pitt insisted.

Lutecia and Belinda had come to see. Ellen turned over the damp cow skin that had been scraped of flesh and fat. Imprinted there, was an earlier brand—the Cross Bar 6.

"That's Mr. Baxter's! Same as on the cows Mr. Mercy bought!" Hestor said, beaming at Pitt. "And Pitt done it last night. Got that cow skin and everything!" Hestor pounded Pitt's back.

Stamford took the skin, turned it one side to the other. "A neat rebrand, too. Looks like it was invented just to cover Baxter's mark."

"Some of those men who rode in with that last herd had been with Mr. Baxter's. Mr. Fykes told us he recognized them," Lutecia said.

"Montgomery's had this whole thing well-planned," Stamford said.

"I wonder if Mr. Stone knew," Ellen mused.

"Three or four thousand cows. That would be a lot of money, when he only had to drive them from here to Abilene. Hardly any expense involved," Lutecia put in.

"Ain't Pitt something? You oughtta make him a deputy, Marshal Stamford!" Hestor declared.

"How did you managed this, Pitt?" Stamford asked before Pitt started away.

"I had a rope and my knife." Pitt kept on toward the freight wagon.

"Wait a minute. You mean you roped the cow and killed it yourself?" Belinda asked.

"Well, yeah. I had to hide a while first. Took longer than I expected." Pitt turned to face them, a sudden flush to his cheeks.

"And he said the night riders was comin' all around and it got real dark!" Hestor was telling.

Ellen watched Pitt fidget under their scrutiny. Hisi expression wrinkled to discomfort as Hestor recited incredible details of Pitt's accomplishment.

"Be quiet a minute, Hestor," Ellen said, frowning at Pitt. "You tell it, Pitt."

Pitt swallowed hard. "I—I wanted to do it all myself," he started. "That's what I set off to do when I left the house. I got right up to Montgomery's herd."

"And?" Belinda asked.

Again Pitt glanced at Hestor. The younger boy had sobered. "Beaver Laughing," Pitt said.

"That Osage buck?" Stamford said.

"He—I—"

"You said you done it all yourself!" Hestor declared.

"It was my idea. I was over there and everything!"

"If my Pa finds out there's an Injun sneakin' around here—"

"Hush, Hestor," Belinda said. "Where's Beaver Laughing now?"

Pitt hunched his shoulders. "Someplace. He had a cold camp over near Montgomery's. I stayed there last night and this morning we watched the cyclone—" Pitt looked from Belinda to Ellen and then to Stamford. "Last night, he saw me sneaking to Montgomery's and came to help. 'Twas him that killed the cow," he added sadly. "But I skinned the hip! I knew what to look for."

"And you did an admirable thing, too, Pitt," Ellen said quickly. She glanced around, wondering where Beaver Laughing might be and if other Osage were with him.

"I hope the men don't run into any of those rustlers," Belinda said, stalking through the wet grass to the freighter. "I wish they'd get back here."

"Had to get help from a Injun," Hestor said disparagingly.

"Ride up here with us, Pitt," Stamford offered, scooting closer to Ellen. "Tell me more about it."

Ellen eased to the far edge of the seat, took up the reins, and said a silent prayer for everyone's safety.

"Beaver Laughing told me you wouldn't be hurt by the cyclone," Pitt was telling Ellen as they reached the camp. "But when I saw it coming—" Pitt drew a sharp breath. "He said our family was blessed by the black humps—just like Mr. Fykes told us. It was awful, though. The chimney blown apart. I could see part of the barn fence right up there in the air! Montgomery's cattle stampeded off northwest and Beaver Laughing helped me get over here. I wanted to go right home! But he said you'd be here."

Ellen listened to Pitt's discourse with only half an ear, worried more about their situation. If the rustlers found that dead cow with part of its hip hide missing, what would they do? Of course, now they'd be busy getting the cattle herd together. But after that? She pulled the team to a halt. Olive's dog barked from where it was tied to the wheel of the Claytons' Conestoga.

"I don't think nobody else was with Beaver Laughing. He said he'd tried to kill the Bad Dark—Montgomery—but couldn't get close enough or nothin'."

Ellen climbed down. Belinda had already been accosted by Reba, and Hestor was running up to Olive while Lutecia tied the horses along a picket line. Pitt helped the marshal off the wagon, still talking. "He didn't say what he was gonna do now."

"You were a brave lad to even think of going over there," Stamford complimented.

A weak smile came to Pitt's face and he hurried to Belinda.

"I think Pitt got quite a scare, last night," Ellen said, loosening the traces on the team.

"I suspect it was this morning," Stamford said. "Seeing his home, and possibly his family, getting blown away while only in the company of an Indian."

"I'm glad Beaver Laughing was with him. It would have been much worse if Pitt had been alone."

"Yes. That's true." The marshal's forehead was deeply creased with a frown. "Now if the others would just get back." He strode to where Reba was pouring coffee for everyone and talking excitedly about how relieved she was to see them. Olive and George ran to Ellen and gave her a hug. Stamford said, "Ladies. I hate to impose more tribulation." He took an offered cup of coffee. "But we need to plan a defense for this camp. What armaments do we have?"

"Defend the camp?" Reba's eyes widened.

"We're afraid the rustlers already might know that we're onto them," Ellen said. Olive's face went somber. "They could come here."

"Not to mention Montgomery's desire to kill Mrs. Hargrove." Stamford studied the environs and Ellen wondered if they were already being watched—stalked—had become targets for the outlaw gang.

George leaned against her leg and she stroked his hair, trying to drive away her fears.

"Reba, you pack up your children and drive out to where Luke and Rob are with the cattle," Belinda ordered.

"But Belinda—"

"Say no, Ma. We'll miss all the fun!" Hestor complained.

"You good people have no place in what may happen here," Belinda insisted.

"She's right, Mrs. Clayton. And it would be an extra worry having the children around," the marshal said.

Olive started picking up the few items that were off the wagon. Reba grabbed up George while Hestor sulked.

"Lutecia. You should go, too," Belinda said. "It's the Jarvises these people have picked a fight with, not you."

"Really?" Lutecia mused, checking the load on her Pettingill. "That's why I was being shot at yesterday morning, I guess." She went to her wagon. "We've got another shotgun in here. An old fowling piece, but it fires true."

Belinda glowered, but Ellen knew there would be no persuading Lutecia to leave. Pitt helped Reba hitch their ox team to the wagon.

"We can get the wagons like a vee against that stand of trees over there," Stamford said. "Take our cover in the middle."

Ellen finished her coffee and started for the farm wagon. Her wet clothes felt cold, with one warm patch where George had held to her leg. Blue sky showed in ever-increasing patches behind the high racing clouds.

The dog barked, staring west toward the wooded trail.

"Halloo the camp," came a call.

"It's Mr. Fykes." Relief showed in Belinda's voice. Lutecia, however, kept close to her wagon, her revolver in hand until Tim was visible along the trail.

"Hey, Mr. Fykes!" Hestor called. "We might get attacked by rustlers!"

"Hush, Hestor!"

"Where are the others?" Belinda asked.

"Spencer's still riding west along the Fall. Reed and Matthew went east. I come back 'cause Spencer and me was worried about your slim manpow—" Tim squinted toward the Clayton wagon. "Pitt's already here!" he exclaimed.

"Got here not long after you left," Hestor said. "He done cut up a cow and everything!"

"He brought proof against Montgomery," Stamford said.

"Yes. And now he's riding out of here with the Claytons," Belinda said sternly.

"Yes'm," Pitt said, his eyes downcast. Ellen wondered how many days this quiet obedience would last.

"Matthew oughtta wale the daylights out of him, the scare we all got," Tim said. "I'll ride out for him and Reed."

"It would be better if you stayed here," the marshal said.

Ellen lifted George onto the wagon seat as the marshal explained what Pitt had discovered. Pitt and Beaver Laughing, Ellen thought. The Osage warrior puzzled her. He had seemed so vehement, she had expected some irrational act from him: blood curdling screams as he threw himself on Montgomery in the midst of everyone. *Yet he's been watching Montgomery—stalking him, actually.* She wondered if Montgomery knew this—if Beaver Laughing had embarked on a war of nerves to gain an advantage. Whatever, she was thankful the Osage man had been with Pitt. Recall of the cyclone churned through her thoughts—especially the sturdy trading post crumbled and sucked away as if made of paper. She shivered.

"Bye, Aunt Ellen. Bye-ee!" George waved vigorously as Reba cracked a whip over the lead oxen's ears. The puppies wriggled under the seat bench and whined.

"We'll see you soon," Ellen said, waving back. Olive clutched her dog, eyes wide. She didn't smile. Hestor rode behind Pitt on Pitt's pony.

"Maybe nothin' will happen," Pitt said when he passed Ellen. He looked very solemn—much older, too—as he reined his horse beside the wagon.

While Ellen, Belinda and Lutecia moved wagons to form a small fortress, Tim and the marshal stood guard. Having Tim present helped the marshal relax, and at Lutecia's encouragement, and after the defense of their little camp was decided, he dozed. Shadows from the stand of scrubby trees nearby were still long toward the west and birds noisily chirruped morning songs from the branches. Ellen felt like it should be midday, so much had occurred.

She had just finished combing her damp hair when Tim stepped over and spoke quietly, "Rouse the marshal. We got company coming from the south."

Apprehension gripped her. She took up the marshal's Henry and sighted it over the front wheel of the freight wagon, her body protected by the wagon box of the Mercy wagon. Her mother woke the marshal. Tim had already slipped into the thickets to her right. Birds flushed up from along the south trail, and her mother and Lutecia readied their weapons. The clicking of percussion hammers sounded loud to Ellen's ears.

Then Belinda held the gun aside and smiled. "It's your father," she said with relief.

Tim stood up at the trail's edge at that moment, waving his rifle. The big draft, Bob, and a darker horse came into view, carrying Matthew and Reed respectively. Ellen could hear Tim's voice, but not his words, but knew he was telling that Pitt was all right— probably how Reba and the children were out where the cattle grazed. She expected overwhelming relief to color her father's face, but when he and Reed jogged their horses to them, Matthew still seemed tense. Reed glowered and perused their surroundings.

"At least Pitt's safe," Matthew said, dismounting and embracing Belinda.

"And he produced evidence against Montgomery, too," Marshal Stamford said. He awkwardly gave each man a left-handed shake. "Glad you two are back."

"With news, I'm afraid, of yet another murder."

The words pulled Ellen taut. She dared a glance at the marshal who had turned toward her.

"Number four," he said quietly. "I should have known."

"A stranger?" Lutecia asked.

"Dillard Winslow. His body's tangled in a snag right before the Chikaskia. Been hung up for a while," Reed said.

"Reed managed to get about eight feet from him. The water was too rough to get him loose."

"Maybe he just drowned," Belinda suggested.

"No. He—" Matthew sighed heavily.

"I could see where his throat had been cut," Reed said. "He was murdered."

They were silent for a moment, with Ellen contemplating that she had obviously foreseen this murder—having said there were four well in advance of the body being found.

"As soon as Spencer gets back, I think we should start to Camp Wichitaw," Matthew said.

"Montgomery's men could pick us off on that open trail too easily," Reed said.

"And it would get the Claytons involved. There must be something else we can do," Belinda said.

A shrill two note whistle came from the west.

"All right. Now we can make some decisions," Matthew said. "That's Spencer."

Ellen faced west, sunlight hot on her back and a mental itch of anticipation building in her. That was supplanted by surprise as Spencer loped his horse into the camp. With him on the saddle, held firmly by his left arm, rode Nancy Kincaid.

"Oh, Miz Ellen, thank the Lord everyone's all right! That cyclone—" She shook her head. Spencer let her down and dismounted while Ellen and the others stood fairly dumbfounded by Nancy's presence. Nancy fiddled with the draw string of her embroidered purse, then curtsied. "Mrs. Jarvis. Sorry to barge in on you this way." She ducked her head, but Ellen saw the dark blue bruise on her jaw.

"Caught her running through the thickets over near the Fall Creek north ford," Spencer said. "When she said she was hiding from the man in the tent, I just brought her along." He grinned.

His words seemed to unlock everyone from their silence.

"I thought he was an Indian when he grabbed me," Nancy said, laughing a little. "Those moccasins and all."

"Where's Montgomery, Miss Kincaid?" Marshal Stamford asked.

"No tellin', now. I— He—" Fear came to her face. "I'm sorry to say, Miz Ellen, but he wants you dead in the worst way."

A swell of outrage caused Ellen's fists to clench. "Do you know why?"

"Well, it has somethin' to do with those knacks you got. Bein' able to see things and all. He hated for me to even mention it, and after you saved little George Clayton— I was standing on the stoop—saw the whole thing! That was wonderful! But James got really crazy when he heard about how you done it. He's not at all like I thought he was gonna be. Not at all." Nancy started crying.

"He's beat you, hasn't he," Belinda declared indignantly, stepping toward Nancy.

"I'm all right," Nancy said. She put her hand to the bruise— another showed along her arm where her sleeve fell back—but pulled herself straight. "I knew it was all wrong when Dillard came around talking about needing money for information."

"Just as we suspected. Did Montgomery ride off the next morning?"

"No. *He* didn't, but he had a long talk with two of his men that same day Winslow came by. One of them—I heard James call him Lewis. Ain't that the name you asked me about, Miz Ellen?"

"Judd Lewis," the marshal said, voice hard and cold.

"The next day, I saw you comin' back," Nancy continued. "With the marshal hurt like he is." She drew a deep breath. "Later on, James pitched into Lewis somethin' bad for—for letting you get away. He did it 'cause he was scared, Miz Ellen. You scare him plenty, with your magic ways."

"It's not magic, Nancy."

"He calls it hoo doo stuff."

"This man ever tell you where he was from?" Lutecia cut in.

"He's been lots of places, but when he got crazy talkin'—after anytime he'd see Miz Ellen—once he said he seen a lot of her ways down where he come from. I asked where, tryin' to soothe him some." She rubbed at her arms and grew tight. "He said something like Dooplineer."

"Aha! Duplanier!" Lutecia said. "I should have known. He's from down in bayou country. That's why he's so sure Ellen is a threat to him. He said something about geechie ways the other morning. Remember, Ellen? I should have realized then."

"A Southerner," Marshal Stamford said bitterly. "Did he ever mention the name Montrose? Kyle Montrose?"

Nancy's eyes widened. "*He* didn't, but Dillard said that name when he came by two days ago. James hustled him out of the tent real fast, so I don't know much about that." Nancy smoothed her purse straps, stared at the ground.

"Well, that cinches it. He's probably organizing his men right now to attack us," Matthew said.

"Mr. Fykes has already gone off to keep watch," Spencer said.

"How are we going to work this?" Reed asked. "He must have nearly twenty men."

"No he don't. Not no more," Nancy said. "They all left. He had a big argument with one man this morning after they found a cow dead and cut on."

Pitt's proof, Ellen thought.

"James wanted to stampede the herd through here—kill everyone. That's when I knew I had to get away from him. Them other men said no. They figured you all was tore up in that cyclone and said if you wasn't they weren't havin' no part in killin' so many women and children; shootin' the marshal had been enough as it was. They said that they were taking the cattle north to get their money before the law found them out. He fussed long with them. That's when I slipped out and hid. I watched them ride off. James cursing them something horrible, and sayin' how once he got rid of you, Miz Ellen, everything would be fine. I was so scared! But I was determined to find you and warn you. Then your brother, here, grabbed me. I thought I was done for! James has probably forgot about me by now."

"So what can he do alone?" Belinda asked, frowning toward the underbrush.

"He could be out there right now, taking bead—" Reed steered Ellen to the protection of the wagons. She let herself be propelled to safety, feeling listless from all the revelations—the confirmation of what she had always known to be true. Montgomery killed Mr. Stone and Riding Boy; he wanted to kill her, and Montgomery was Montrose.

"I'm going to scout to the north," Reed said, going to his horse.

"I'll go along the west trail to make sure you weren't followed, Spencer," Matthew said.

"I don't like this. Not a bit," Stamford said as Matthew and Reed were obscured by high brush and prairie grass.

"If only we knew where he was!" Belinda lamented.

Nancy's stilted attitude drew Ellen's attention. The woman stepped hesitantly toward the wagons. Could she be duping us? Ellen wondered with shock. "What is it, Nancy?" she asked.

Nancy squeezed the top of her purse.

"Do you know where he is?" Lutecia demanded.

"No. But Miz Ellen could tell you. I brought some stuff."

Nancy came to the wagon seat and opened her purse. "I got a snip of his extra undershirt. Cut it this morning while he was arguin' with those men. And here's some hairs from when he shaved." She placed a twist of paper next to the swatch of woolen cloth. "And I got these. He really likes pretty things—glittery things." She pulled out a gold link chain, ten inches long and a man's diamond ring.

"A watch fob," Stamford said. "Probably to hold that watch they have at Fort Riley!"

Lutecia took the ring; Ellen didn't want to look at any of it. She put her hands behind her and backed away.

"I thought with these you might could witch up some warding against him," Nancy went on.

Ellen shook her head, repulsed by how Nancy thought of her.

"I had a hard time gettin' some of this. He was real careful whenever he cut his hair or shaved. Got mad at me a plenty when I tried to clean up for him. He never did like it 'cause I was friendly to you and he said you could hex him good if you had anything personal."

"I don't hex anyone, Nancy!"

Nancy pursed her lips and looked away from Ellen, obviously not convinced.

"Marshal, look at this. This ring's got initials etched inside," Lutecia said. "F S."

"F S—Francis Stone?" Belinda queried.

Stamford took the ring. Ellen cringed, remembering the mutilated fingers on the corpse—hacked to get that ring.

"The dead man?" Nancy seemed disconcerted. "I thought it was James's." She looked chagrined. "Well, this other— He fiddled with that chain a lot when he'd get upset. Bet you could hold it like you did that little boy's shoe—tell right where he is."

Ellen drew a long breath.

"You could do it, you know. It's why we were going to Fort Riley," Stamford said. "For you to hold the watch and find him. With this watch fob— Mrs. Hargrove—"

"He's probably dead by now," Ellen said. "With his guard gone, Beaver Laughing has most certainly killed him."

"But he may not be," Belinda said. "We really should know where he is, Ellen. The marshal's right."

"For pity sake, Ellen, hold the watch fob and find out!" Spencer said with irritation. "Stop making such a big deal out of it. You've been doing this kind of stuff ever since I can remember."

Ellen looked wide-eyed at Spencer. He grinned. "When we lived in Douglas County, I used to invite boys over—have them leave their hats inside and bet them Ellen could tell whose was whose when I called her to bring them out. She was always right. I won a jackknife, a bag of marbles once—"

"Spencer!" Belinda rebuked. Lutecia and Stamford held back their amusement.

"Come on, Sis. Let's get this over with." He picked up the gold chain and handed it out to her.

She wanted to know. Montgomery had seemed a compulsion, even if he weren't Montrose. The Sycamore Spring dream with his face hovered above the murder scene, the dark aura she often saw around him all led to her relentless belief that he was "evil"—a Bad Dark. Now she would touch something of his—a possession, a favored ornament. If what Spencer had said was true and if what had occurred when she envisioned George's whereabouts was part of her *gift*, than she should be able to hold this item and decipher his character, perhaps identify some of his past as she had with the marshal, and hopefully discover this murderer's whereabouts.

It may not even work, she realized. She had consciously tried to discern Spencer's whereabouts several days ago and learned nothing. Everything else had been spontaneous; perhaps nothing would come of this at all. She felt a moment's relief, overlaid by disappointment. *If I'm going to have this mental talent, as the marshal calls it, I'd at least like to have some control over it!*

With determination, she took the gold fob. The yellow metal felt cool in her hand; the end of the chain drooped over her fingers.

Fighting. Guns. He's running. A boy clambering along endless rows of black earth. There is a watch at the end of the chain, round and gold: something jerks at it. Ellen feels a protest. His protest. People surround and incite a battle; he is in it. ... A shack with one chair on the porch. A rag doll bobs by the door, its head tied off tightly by a miniature noose. He protests something with his young face contorted. Hands reach for the doll, but the end of a cane smashes down; welts puff; the cane, fists. He grips the watch.

Ellen, tense, tried to determine what was when, where was now in the murky broil of emotions. Behind her conscious thoughts, battles raged, a melee of Montgomery's anger and fighting—his life in turbulence.

Montrose/Montgomery: the face wavers over the dark, slatted shack, the swaying doll bobbing—mocking; the cane strikes. ... He is running. Montrose. People surround and incite battle and he scuffles—fights back; an old man's face appears and blossoms into red and yellow gore before the gloom darkens.

The rampant visions increased, the intensity tightening Ellen's muscles as she tried to determine a current reality within it. *What is when—*

Cross sabers on his shoulder as he rides, fights, slashes out. His pistol arm extends, soundless explosions burst from the end of the gun, shattering the dark with brightness again and again, dissolving into a cloth figure noosed. He chases it, running like a rabbit crazy with fear. Montgomery. He is running; he is riding after a stage, and it bounds down expansive rows of black earth toward bleak sky before it vanishes into a ramshackle hut. ... Boy fights, is beaten. ... Gun arm extends, sabers slash. ... There! A brown arm descending— holding a hatchet—and bright colors mark pain in this gloomy montage. Running. ... Scrubby trees, anger. Pain. He's running, turning, fighting, intense with rage at a red and yellow-streaked face. The knife, ivory handle. Blade glints in the sunlight as he glares at the Indian.

"That's now!" Ellen jerked around, staring to the northeast at the dense barrier of hackberry and black walnut that bristled green leaves.

"What? Ellen, what did you learn?" her mother asked.

"Beaver Laughing. He'll be killed!" she muttered. Without thinking, she bolted from the cover of wagons, pulling up her skirt as she ran. Four—five strides.

"Ellen!" Her mother's voice.

Footsteps came behind her. She was almost there. *Not another murder. Please! No more deaths.*

"What are you doing?" Spencer pulled on her arm, slowing her.

A horse broke from the trees, charging toward her. Someone screamed. She looked up and halted as if running into a wall. Then panic hit. *(He reaches for a shiny revolver.)*

"Spencer, don't!" she cried, knowing his actions. She whirled and shoved her brother as a rifle sounded. A pistol shot came from behind her. The rifle spat again.

Spencer lay on the ground, his hand easing away from an empty holster, the pistol he had drawn near his feet. He was unharmed, but a trough gouged the earth next to his chest.

The rifle action clicked. Loud, it seemed to be the only sound for miles. Birds had taken flight; furry creatures froze in their tracks to hide themselves. Ellen was aware of her mother, Lutecia and the marshal ten strides behind her, their weapons poised and unable to use them for fear of shooting her. Nancy cowered behind a wagon wheel. Ellen turned, feeling the hot breath of the horse on her arm. She looked up at the black-barreled Henry rifle three feet from her face, and then at the man on horseback behind it. James Montgomery was sweating, flushed, eyes glinting with fever caused by mental anguish, she was certain, not any physical distress.

And in the trees behind Montgomery—

Ellen saw this, didn't dare move her eyes to really look, but she knew someone was there. Her heart pounded as she hoped it wasn't Pitt come back, or Mr. Mercy concerned about Lutecia.

Beaver Laughing! She drew a startled breath.

Montgomery was talking. Talking at her. The words sounded like whips slapping around her, harsh and ugly. His hatred jumbled out and was caught in abject fear. ". . .hoo doo..." she heard.

"You're Kyle Montrose," Ellen cut in, feeling a compulsion to face him down.

"Ellen, don't," Spencer whispered.

"Only you could know that! Sent here by those devil dolls. Following me for years," he said.

"No one sent me. It's this. I learned here." She held up the watch fob.

Montgomery jerked his horse closer, eyes bright with rage. "Nancy gave you that. I thought I could trust her!" He leveled the rifle toward the wagons. "Nancy! You thief! You traitor!"

"Get down!" Belinda cried.

Rifle shot.

A brown body charged from the trees.

"Now this will end it!" Montgomery levered the rifle, swung the bore toward Ellen. "End—" A panther yell pierced the air. Montgomery's horse neighed and reared, causing the man a moment of imbalance. His rifle wavered from its bead on Ellen's face and Beaver Laughing moved like a charging bull. So fast! Montgomery didn't look back as he steadied his horse and brought the rifle to bear at Ellen. He fingered the trigger. She stepped back. *Is this where it ends? My life, shattered by a bullet? The day is too beautiful!* The Osage growled and leaped, striking Montgomery's shoulder. The shot went into the air as both men fell across the horse and to the ground. The animal pitched and snorted. Ellen scrambled away from the powerful legs. Spencer, on his feet, grabbed her arm and pulled her toward the wagons.

Tim arrived. More horses. Her father and Reed rush into camp, their weapons ready. But the tangle of arms and legs offered no shot for them as Beaver Laughing and James Montgomery fought.

"This is not the way I saw it. I had it wrong again," Ellen murmured, her hands clenched.

The huge knife was in Montgomery's right hand, and the two men wrestled, rolled, growled in their struggle. Knife to Beaver Laughing's chest. A cry of pain. The combatants rolled, twisted, contorted away from and against each other on the earth. The knife fell loose in the grass. Beaver Laughing loomed over Montgomery, his knee in the man's groin, his right fist around the handle of a hatchet. Montgomery's left fist smashed Beaver Laughing's jaw.

The Indian took the blow, and brought down the hatchet as Montgomery twisted to find the knife.

"Ahhhgh," Montgomery cried as the blade sank into his left shoulder. Beaver Laughing jerked it out, raised it again.

"Stop!" Ellen had run to them. "Beaver Laughing, stop!"

She stooped quickly and tossed away the knife Montgomery reached for. "If you kill him, *you'll* be a murderer. Beaver Laughing. Think!"

The other men moved in quickly, their weapons trained on the two. Blood spilled from Montgomery's wound while a bright diagonal line oozed red across Beaver Laughing's chest.

"Get away. Not you! Leave me," Montgomery rasped, turning his head from where Ellen stood.

Ellen's pulse drummed in her neck, her temples throbbed. "You know white man law, Beaver Laughing," she managed to get out.

"I am not bound by white law."

"But we are. And we want him to face it. We don't want to hold you for murder."

"He killed Osage."

"He has killed even more of us."

"He has too much evil."

"Yes. And you counted coup on him bravely, you have struck him down!" Ellen insisted, recalling the warrior's thirst for honor.

Beaver Laughing still held his tense stance over Montgomery.

"White man's law will make him die by the rope," Tim said.

"This is true?" Beaver Laughing asked. That seemed to offer a measure of satisfaction to the Osage.

"Yes," Stamford said quickly.

"Kill me!" Montgomery anguished. "Don't let her win me again!"

Beaver Laughing looked at Montgomery with surprise, and then at Ellen. And his next movement was so swift, all Ellen could do was gasp. The hatchet up, then down. Only a whimper from Montgomery as the blade whisked through the man's right wrist. Nausea wrenched at Ellen.

"For Knocks-on-the-wagon. My promise." Beaver Laughing took up the bloody hand. Spencer turned away, shocked.

"Mrs. Mercy!" Reed called. Blood pulsed from Montgomery's limb.

"Great heavens!" Stamford stepped between Ellen and the grisly scene. "Have you never heard of assault, you?" He grabbed Beaver Laughing's arm. The warrior glared at him.

"Leave him be," Tim said, pulling Stamford away.

"He's mutilated the man!"

"We'll pretend we found him this way," Tim argued.

"I didn't see it happen," Reed said as he tightened a belt around Montgomery's arm.

Lutecia hurried over with her bag and knelt at Montgomery's side.

"Arresting Beaver Laughing will only infuriate his people," Matthew put in.

Ellen wanted to move away, but felt as dazed as Stamford looked. She agreed with her father; couldn't help but remember Riding Boy's strewn limbs in the glen. "Beaver Laughing could have done worse," she stated. "Much worse."

"Here, Beaver Laughing." Matthew loosed cinches and pulled the saddle from Montgomery's horse. He handed the Osage the reins.

"My God! You're rewarding him for attacking a white man!" Stamford exclaimed.

"Beaver Laughing saved Ellen's life!" Spencer declared.

Beaver Laughing grabbed the lines and swung onto the horse. "I will not forget," he said. He put heel to the horse. Hoof beats drummed the ground and grew distant.

Montgomery stirred. "No. Get her away," was his weak mumble.

"She's tending your wound," Matthew said, stooping down beside Lutecia.

But Ellen knew Montgomery didn't mean Lutecia.

19

*E*llen adjusted her right glove, pulling the leather closer to the edge of her sleeve—a protection against the steady sunlight. She relaxed her grip on the reins of the three horses that pulled the farm wagon. Phineas marked the lead, with two of the Kiowa steeds on the wheels. They were pulling well. Ellen tried not to look too far ahead, hoping to keep anticipation at bay. They were six days out of Camp Wichitaw traveling northwest across the rich Kansas prairie that ran between the Arkansas and the Little Arkansas rivers. Blue stem and gamma grasses wafted high along the wagon wheels while sharp-shinned hawks cruised the blue sky. On her left, Lutecia drove four mules which pulled the Mercys' covered wagon. On her right, Ellen's mother sat on the high spring bench of the Jarvis freight wagon (Ellen's well-packed buggy hitched to the back) while beyond that large conveyance, Ellen could make out her father, Charles Mercy and Pitt riding herd on the thirty-five Mercy cattle. Spencer led his string of horses from his elegant pinto.

Ellen had half expected Spencer or Pitt to volunteer to be a deputy—help the marshal get James Montgomery to Fort Riley, but neither of her brothers even mentioned it. She was grateful that none of her family had to testify at his trial. The items found in Montgomery's possession were more than enough for a conviction. His saddle bags had held three money sacks from a robbed bank, and there were stolen papers, including a deed of trust that named Ralph Butler—not Montgomery—secondary owner of Stone Cattle

Company. The paper, stained with blood, had been folded around the silver head of Doyle Blankenship's cane. *Five murders. I only had foreknowledge of four of them.* Ellen wasn't sure if that were bad or good.

Then there were the rustlers. Nine of them had been captured the day before Ellen and the wagons arrived in Camp Wichitaw. Mr. Baxter rode with the government scouts the marshal had instructed to be on alert, and when the outlaws drove the herd across the Arkansas, Baxter and the scouts were waiting. No shooting confrontation or anything, the handful of settlers had reported; and some of the captured men were eager to implicate Montgomery and Judd Lewis.

Ellen sighed. It all seemed so simple. Few people would know the tense intrigue that fostered all this bringing to justice. She adjusted her new straw hat with the wide brim that kept even her lap shaded; the light blue blouse she wore, one from her teaching days, was a bit too big, but that made it more comfortable in the afternoon warmth.

Of the people who had lived along the Bluff River, only the Mercys and Ellen's family remained together. Tim had left them before they crossed the north part of the Chikaskia in Sumner County, headed west to join Hubert and his Kiowa in-laws on the plains of Colorado Territory. The rest of them—Montgomery with a fever—had camped the night at the Pierces, who had seen the tornado and were glad to know everyone was safe. When rain besieged them again, they took shelter in the Pierces' ample barn. Goodbye to that family two days later, and when they crossed Slate Creek, Ellen imagined that the Pierces were the only white settlers left in Sumner County.

At Camp Wichitaw, Nancy had been dismayed to learn that Rose Schaffner wasn't around. A freight wagon was headed to Topeka, however, and Nancy eagerly hitched a ride. "I can't bear to be around him a moment longer!" she had said, cutting her eyes to the travois that held James Montgomery. She gathered her valise from the back of the Jarvis wagon.

"What are you going to do?" Ellen had asked, not wanting to

think about the woman's occupation.

"I'm taking a stage back to Cincinnati." She gave a resolute nod. "My sister and two brothers live there. After that—" Nancy shrugged and then embraced Ellen. "Thank you, Ellen, for being such a friend." Those words made Ellen uncomfortable, not feeling she deserved them.

The Claytons' anticipation to settle in the new town of Wichita dulled quickly when they saw the motley assortment of people there. The saloon was the most productive business, and the town plat hadn't been completed by the surveyor Mr. Munger brought down from Topeka. After disappointed grousing and a suggestion from Matthew, the Claytons decided to go to Eldorado. If that didn't work, they would head back to Arkansas, where, Reba assured Luke, no one would care what he did in the war. Ellen hoped that was true. Olive had hugged her and cried. George, oblivious to the emotions of the moment, gave her wet kisses and then scrambled into the wagon after the puppy.

So hard to say goodbye, Ellen thought. So often it was final, unless it was to family. Even then doubt and worry lingered behind departing words.

Pitt trotted up, holding his arm high and showing the body of a plump turkey dangling by its claws from his hand. "Dinner," he said. A large russet dog ran behind his horse, its tongue lolling.

"Well, isn't that fine!" Belinda said as Pitt deftly clambered from his horse onto the freight wagon seat where he tied the bounty to a ring on the side of the wagon wall.

He remounted his horse and, trotting away, called, "Come on, Sampson." The dog barked and dashed off.

"It seems Pitt has grown two inches in the ten days since we left Sumner County," Ellen said.

"I noticed that, myself," Lutecia put in, speaking loudly so both Ellen and Belinda could hear.

"One turkey might not be enough, with the appetites Pitt and Spencer have," Belinda said.

"Maybe we'll come across a buffalo Pop can take down with his Hawken," Ellen suggested. She didn't examine that sudden statement for any sign of pre-knowledge. *What will be, will be.*

"Not anytime soon, I hope," Belinda said. "We've barely got enough room for all we're carrying."

"I surely wouldn't want to leave any buffalo meat out here to rot," Lutecia added.

"Ellen, look!" her mother called. Ellen's gaze followed her mother's outstretched arm to where more than twenty antelope stalked along a nearby rise, keeping their distance, but curious about this procession.

"There's so much game out here," Lutecia said. "Deer, antelope, turkey, buffalo."

"It seems a goodly place, all right," Belinda agreed. "Good energy."

"And the weather has been calm," Ellen added. "Not even a breeze."

"After what we've been through, I find that rather refreshing," Lutecia said with a chuckle.

"I wonder if they get cyclones in Clara Barton County?" Belinda added. Since the decision to move, her mother always proudly said the full name of whom the county honored.

Ellen's excitement about this move surged through her. *Her* move, is how she thought of it. At Camp Wichitaw, her father had been approached by a businessman who had learned of their loss on the Bluff. He asked Matthew to set up a store in the central part of the state: "Barton County—just formed last year. Between Fort Harker and Fort Lyon," the man said. "Going to be a thriving area in a few years."

"Thank you, sir, but I think I'll call in my markers with the government and find a plot of land I can farm," Matthew replied. "My sons are of an age they need some permanence—a homestead."

"Well, the land there is quite productive. Excellent choice of black or sandy loam, depending on where you settle."

"But about this store," Ellen said, stepping forward to the businessman.

Her offer to open the establishment for him left the man blustering, even after Matthew chimed in. "A good idea! Ellen has really been in charge of our mercantile concerns since she was seventeen, except for the year she was away teaching. I must say, that year was the low point of the business."

Her father's admission surprised Ellen, and she knew that she wanted this chance more than anything.

"It's still quite wild there," the man demurred. "Indians and buffalo and all."

"Well, now," said her father, chuckling. "Know anything about that, Ellen?" They exchanged smiles.

With fervor, Ellen had procured a map of central Kansas, noting the Santa Fe Trail cutting southwest through the new county, the proposed railway in Ellsworth, the lay of the land and streams. When later in the day the Mercys produced a similar map and confided thoughts about moving either to Ellsworth or Barton County, her parents had agreed to join the move. "Clara Barton County!" Belinda said merrily.

"Well, if your parents are there, too," the businessman said when Ellen approached him again.

"General mercantile, correct?" she broached. "You would pay costs for building and stocking the establishment; we'll work out equitable percentages; the stock we already have on hand is property of my parents to be sold at their discretion; and I propose a two-year buy out contract." His eyes had widened as she continued her shrewd outline of terms.

Papers were drawn up, signed and notarized, although the man insisted her father be listed as her partner.

The three families from the Bluff River settlement had celebrated their decisions that evening with a big meal at their campsite. It was the night before the Claytons left for Eldorado, and Luke pulled out his fiddle; Pitt joined in with the mouth harp. Reed had been there.

Ellen gave a wistful smile as the wagon jounced along the rudimentary trail. Reed was now a deputy, assisting Burton Stamford in getting

Montgomery to Fort Riley. Helping Stamford, a man it turns out Reed had met last year in Manhattan—when Stamford accused Reed of being Kyle Montrose. "I'm only doing this since the marshal's injured," Reed had said during the evening party.

"And after that?" Ellen asked. What had she wanted him to say? She still wasn't sure.

"I'm going to Tennessee—to see my family," he replied in a studious tone. "I have to know exactly how—where—I stand; tie up loose ends."

Ellen had been unable to respond, even though she understood his need—even agreed with the logic.

"Then I'll come back west," he continued. "To Kansas." Firelight playing on his face made his features hard to read—her features hard to read.

"We'll miss you," she had said, touching the back of his hand with her fingertips. He covered that hand with his other and gave a firm squeeze.

Luke started fiddling a new song; Reba and the children began singing "Hey hoo, Skip to my Lou. Hey hoo, Skip to my Lou..."

"Mrs. Hargrove!" Burton Stamford strode to them. "Would you honor me with this dance?" he asked, bowing.

"Dance? But Marshal, I'm—"

I'm in mourning. Over my friend Reed's departure, over the loss of our community, over loss of my husband dear.

But she had danced with him, (her right hand on his bandaged shoulder, his left hand gingerly at her waist) not wanting to bring somber thoughts to the others. That was when the marshal promised to be one of the first visitors to her new life. "I plan to deliver that reward money in person!" he had declared.

Reward money, for the capture of the desperado Kyle Montrose. Yes, she thought. I'll have no problem buying the store in two years.

Now, as she rode toward that new life, her quiet thought wanted Johnny to be with her, although she knew the circumstances would be different if he were. No parents and brothers by her side, no store that she intended to own. Maybe even Lutecia and Charles would have taken another route. But other positive, warm benefits would have attended them. Her and Johnny. She would be part of The Hargroves, building their life together; she would not be The Widow Hargrove.

Ellen laid the reins in her lap and pulled a long tin box from the satchel stashed under the seat. The letters J H were neatly etched on top. After smoothing her hand across it, she lifted the lid. Inside she had placed the blue wool scarf Johnny had given her, along with the dried flowers from her wedding bouquet. Shifting those items, she withdrew the folded letter that lay atop hers and Johnny's marriage certificate. The letter was from Nettie Hargrove, her handwriting a careful, sharp-edged script.

> *My Dearest Ellen,*
> *And you are dear to me, even though I have taken*
> *so long to answer your letters. I treasure those, just as*
> *my son treasured you.*

Dated in February, the package had languished in the Emporia post office until last month when it was forwarded to Eldorado. Her father had retrieved it when he went with Luke Clayton to peruse the town.

> *We wanted to protect you. That's why we rushed*
> *you home. I reckon we had much less faith in our dear*
> *son than you did, and believed he got hisself mixed up*
> *in trouble. You see, his uncle—my brother—is Voss*
> *Hendricks.*

Ellen knew how hard it must have been for Mother Hargrove to write that—to admit that. Even now, she wanted to be at the woman's side—embrace her.

> *I'd worked hard to bring my Johnny up right, and*
> *when it seemed he had took up with Voss— We didn't*
> *want that bad light to cast on you, dear child. Especially*
> *when you had brought so much joy to our homestead.*
> *So we sent you away. And we left, feeling certain Voss*
> *and his men would try to use our place as a hideaway.*
> *He'd done that before. But Johnny hadn't been stealing*
> *cattle with the Hendricks gang. Voss wan't on the run*

*that day. Was arrested much later for nothing to do
with cattle.*

*I am not so good with words as you, my dear, but I
tell you now, on oath from my misguided brother, that
our beloved son—your husband—was not ever involved
with any of Voss's lawbreaking. Although Voss had made
the arrangements, the cattle drive Johnny went on was
for a legitimate stock owner who had promised him
over a dozen head in exchange for the work. The man
paid us some money—the value of Johnny's cows, he
said. I am forwarding it to you along with the tin box of
his savings and papers…*

Ellen smoothed the pages, not reading again the details of the
Hargroves' departure, the subsequent resettling in Missouri, the
winter illness of Mr. Hargrove. Four pages of tight script in Nettie
Hargrove's effort to show Ellen that they considered her part of
their lives. Ellen had already responded to the letter, thanking them
for their caring. That had been before the Barton County plans.
She would write them again once she knew more detail about her
new life.

"The last creek comin' up!" Pitt called as he galloped his
pony to the wagons. "Mr. Mercy says we'll be there in less than an
hour!"

Ahead, the thick stand of trees ran a northwestern angle,
dense in summer foliage. The hot afternoon air intensified the smell
of honeysuckle and pipestem. Bees droned. Several animals
lumbered out of the shadows as the wagons drew closer to the
creek line, and Ellen wasn't surprised when her father loped toward
the wagons.

"Belinda!" Matthew called. "Ready my Hawken. There are
buffalo down there!"

Author's Notes

As an historian, I focus on the Old West—a time when daily life was a monumental struggle and even the smallest accomplishment was considered triumph. I identify this period as anytime prior to 1870.

In the 1860s, southern Kansas was virtually uninhabited by non-Indian peoples. Only a few traders and military details frequented the area, moving north and south from Kansas and into Beautiful Indian Territory (BIT). Jesse Chisholm, was one of the traders. In 1864, he travelled north from his trading post in Indian Territory with Wichita Indians who fled to Union territory at the beginning of the Civil War. He continued to go back and forth between his old post and the small settlement at Camp Wichitaw. The path his and other wagons took became a natural route for cattle drives to reach the railhead in Abilene. Jesse Chisholm died in BIT, March, 1868.

In this Old West setting, the large cattle drives so often associated with Westerns were just beginning. As yet there were no six guns nor cowboy boots (or hats) and the term *cowboy* was just coming into use as a Western term—used disparagingly, actually, to denote the lowly status of the drovers; a machine to make barbed wire wasn't developed until 1874, and cash registers came along in 1879. Mysticism and the occult, however, were greatly accepted. In fact, psychical phenomena, spiritualistic séances, hypnotic trance states and mental healing were considered commonplace to most educated Americans; while rural communities and a variety of religious sects continually touted mental or divination abilities of various individuals—for good or for evil. A person with "knacks" was greeted with much less skepticism than they are today.

General Phil Sheridan did inspect western forts in 1868, including Fort Harker; and the Medicine Lodge Treaty of 1868 opened the southern regions of Kansas to white settlement. Even with that, Sumner and Barton counties remained sparsely populated. In 1870, Charley Stone of Topeka, traveled to Sumner County and erected a store on the north bank of Fall Creek. This area is now Caldwell, Kansas, and it was one of the last cattle boom towns of the 1880s. As for Barton County, its few settlers were routed by Indian attacks in the fall of 1868, and until 1870 farming was nearly impossible because of the abundant buffalo. I intend that Ellen and her community (her character has no connection with the Barton County town of Ellinwood) were unscathed by all this since they had positive interaction with the Kiowa and Osage through Tim Fykes and Beaver Laughing, respectively—and they were protected by the black humps.

Final notes:

1. The spellings of Camp Wichitaw and Eldorado are taken from journals and references of the day that I read while in libraries in Wellington County and Caldwell, Kansas. I am indebted to all the valuable information obtained while there.

2. Clara Barton founded the American Red Cross in 1881; Kansas was a forerunner in acknowledging this great woman's medical and relief efforts during the War Between the States.

Kae Cheatham is a writer and freelance editor who lives and works in Helena, Montana. She has published eleven books of fiction, two of nonfiction, and numerous poems and articles. She is also a professional photographer. Visit her Web site at www.kaios.com

Made in the USA
Charleston, SC
21 February 2016